Praise for the *Perspective* Series

"Give Amanda Giasson and Julie B. Campbell a chance and they'll draw you into a world of intrigue…It's a place where beauty and horror live side by side."
- Susan Doolan
Special Arts & Life Reporter to the Barrie Examiner

"Amanda Giasson and Julie B. Campbell have crafted the perfect combination of strength and vulnerability in Megan Wynters and Irys Godeleva, the female dynamic duo that resides within the fantastical world of Qarradune. We are whisked away with our delightful female protagonists where there are twists and turns and nothing is as it seems in this mesmerizing tale of chivalry, bravery, and honor."
- John Darryl Winston
Author of the IA Series (www.johndarrylwinston.com)

"I instantly fell in love with the writing and the characters in Love at First Plight. Right from the start, the plot draws you in and I appreciated the great deal of care that went into writing this novel - the expertly crafted sentences and subtle details made for a very satisfying reading experience."
- Kat Stiles
Author of *Connected* (www.katstiles.com)

"Julie B. Campbell and Amanda Giasson easily bring you into the world of Megan and Irys, and once you are in their world you never want to leave. From the first page, to that last moment you are left wanting more."
- Diane Hodgson
Elementary Teacher

"J.Campbell and A. Giasson do a brilliant job of weaving their two writing styles together to create well developed characters and a captivating storyline that had my daughter and I struggling to share the book! We are eagerly awaiting the next novel in the the series!"
- J.Tauskela
Avid Reader

"Diving into a debut book proved exciting and extremely rewarding – especially when the book ends up blowing away my expectations and surprisingly, it left me hanging."
- Sandy Pestill
Nautica Book Club coordinator

Second Wind

Book 2 of the Perspective Series

Amanda Giasson
&
Julie B. Campbell

Qarradune Books
Ontario, Canada

Copyediting by John Campbell and Cathryn E. Campbell.

ISBN-13: 9781790140121

First Printing: 2016

www.PerspectiveBookSeries.com

Love the Perspective book series?

Check out the official website at
http://www.PerspectiveBookSeries.com

Follow us on social media:

Facebook (@PerspectiveBooks)
http://facebook.com/perspectivebooks

Instagram (@PerspectiveBooks)
https://www.instagram.com/perspectivebooks/

Twitter (@QarraduneBooks)
https://twitter.com/QarraduneBooks

YouTube (Perspective Books)
https://www.youtube.com/channel/UC9Sx6EXyP_oQ5pVQFxdk_Dg

Acknowledgements

What an amazing year! The launch of *Love at First Plight* was a dream come true, but it was nothing compared to the year that followed and that led up to *Second Wind*. If you ever want to know who is truly there to support you, we highly recommend publishing that book you've always wanted to see in print. Amazing!

In that light, we'd like to give special thanks to some of the people who went well above and beyond to help us make sure we'd survive both the trials and the victories of the first year after publishing a first novel in a series. They've helped to keep us motivated to continue sharing Megan and Irys' stories.

Our team of "beta readers", who once again put up with our typo-ridden first draft so that we could create a polished, final novel that actually made sense, included: Jason Giasson, Laura Campbell, Patrick Giasson, John Campbell, Linda Evans, Donna Campbell, Greta Giasson, Bill Evans, Cathryn Campbell, Samantha Hartlen, and Sean Evans. We can, without a doubt, say that *Second Wind* couldn't have happened without this generous, insightful team.

After the beta reading comments were in, we moved on to the massive editing process. We'd like to give special thanks to John Campbell and Cathryn Campbell, who both shared their time and linguistic prowess, despite their busy schedules and our short deadlines. If there's anything we can say about editing, it's that another set of eyes goes a long way. Their help made this process much easier for both of us, and we learned a great deal about the process we will use for the next book in the series.

Finally, thank you (thank you, thank you) to the readers who took a chance on *Love at First Plight* after we'd been talking about it for fifteen years. Thank you for sticking with us to pick up this copy of *Second Wind* to continue following Megan and Irys as the Perspective series continues. You're the reason we've done this. You mean more to us than you'll ever know

Chapter 1

Irys

The party was over. The masks were off and the ugly truth was exposed. Megan was gone.

Despite the presence of the Knights of Freyss; despite the Imperial Guardsmen who had come and gone with Emperor Gevalen, despite the fact that only an elite list of guests were meant to be in attendance, the Warriors had infested our enchanting evening and had abducted the most important part of it.

They took Megan Wynters and they stole the last of my belief that any one thing could be genuinely and thoroughly good. Everything, no matter how delightful, had a dark side. It took eighteen cycles of my life for me to come to this discovery. Now that I had made it, I hated it.

Great Goddess, why, among all the lessons that you have taught me, did you have to teach me this one, tonight? Why did Megan need to be taken from me in order for me to learn it? Had I not been good enough? Had I not tried to do what you had taught me to do? Why have you punished her because of my ignorance?

The gowns and glitter that had so entranced me during the Masque had now been replaced with uniforms of green, brown, and grey, as Knights, Apprentices of the Knights of Freyss, and soldiers had assembled to plan the rescue of Megan and the salvage of the honour of the Godeleva name and of Syliza as a whole.

Lord Imery and the Knights would have made a priority of the rescue of Megan, regardless of the situation, but the Warriors had snatched her from among the nobility at one of the most important social events of the cycle. The Knights had been there. Even the emperor had been present. The humiliation was as much a motivation for this rescue as anything else could ever have been.

I didn't care. It didn't matter why Syliza would seek to rescue Megan as long as I could be certain it would happen.

I found myself standing in the middle of the rooms that I had carefully designed for her. I couldn't stay in my own suite and the bloody scene it contained. The body of Lasilla, my maid, and the trail of blood that traced the path of her murder still stained the floor of my sitting room, not to mention the crimson evidence from when Galnar, Captain of the Warriors, had carved his dagger into my body.

The wound ran straight up the inside of my forearm but was not deep enough that permanent damage would result from it. It bled profusely, but the doctor had insisted that it would not need to be stitched and that by allowing it to heal naturally, there would be less of a scar. I could feel the throb beneath the long bandage; an ever-present reminder of my spinelessness and of everything I had lost, only hours ago.

Desda was busily cleaning Megan's rooms, regardless of the fact that they didn't require any cleaning. She'd lost Megan, too. I hadn't any idea how close they might have been. Certainly, not as close as I had been with my own sweet maid and confidant, Lasilla, but I could understand that she would be deeply distraught. She was keeping busy in order to stop herself from thinking about the events of that evening. I didn't have the heart to disturb her and bring her back to reality.

I wished that I could grieve for Lasilla now, but my mind would not let me. I yearned to fall to the floor and sob until my tears ran dry, but there were no tears within me. I had shattered inside. Instead of kneeling to pray, I was pacing the rooms like an animal in a cage.

Indeed, I knew that I would weep for many hours when the situation had settled. I would let myself realize that I would never see Lasilla's warm smile again and that she would never bring me precisely what I needed, even before I knew I wanted it. All these things would flood my emotions with a violent torrent, once I allowed them. But not yet. I could not permit it.

I was focused on Megan. How long would it be before the Knights would bring her back to this room where she was safe? What would the Warriors do to her, this time? My mind roiled as I used my surge of thoughts to keep my emotions at bay.

This was all my fault. I'd known that they had infiltrated the Masque. I had spoken with one – had danced with one – and had been instructed not to tell a soul. Acksilivcs told me to hide and that's exactly what I had done. I'd known that they would do something. Something awful. They weren't attending the Masque just to dance and dress in costume. Regardless, I'd been a coward and had walked right through the ballroom and tried to hide myself in my suite.

My actions allowed the Warriors to complete their mission. My actions handed Megan over to them without a single obstacle. If I had alerted someone, Megan may have been able to hide as well. Certainly, there were enough Knights in attendance that something could have been done. It was too late for that, now.

There could be no more waiting and no more hiding. Not for them and not for me. I couldn't stay here. I couldn't continue to pace in my cage while everyone else tried to fix the damage that was my doing. One more moment, trapped here with my thoughts and with my memories, might kill me.

I knew what I had to do. The solution was powerful enough that it affected me to the very physical part of my being. It was pounding with my heart and pulsing through my veins. It pushed away my desperate thoughts and replaced them with a chance to redeem myself before my Goddess, before the friend whom I had betrayed, and before my own reflection.

I would join the men who were assembling for the mission to rescue Megan and the dignity of our country. I would board one of the ships that they would send, and I would take part in Megan's return. It was madness, certainly. There was even the chance that I could die, but anything was better than this. Anything was better than the confines of this beauty and luxury.

This thought gave me the strength I needed to stop my pacing. I sank to my knees and crossed my hands over my heart, raising my gaze upward as though I could have looked the Great Goddess directly in the eye.

I have heard your message, Great Goddess. I will not fail your test. Please, let me prove to you that I have grown. I am not the naïve girl who could have died in that Kavylak prison. I am the woman you rescued through your gift: Megan. I am the woman who will save her again. I am the Clever One.

I rose from my prayers. Megan was out there, and she needed me. I could not simply sit back, this time, and wait for the Knights to bring her home. I needed to be a part of it. I had to be.

Since Galnar's attack, I had been washed and redressed in a comfortable gown that was quite plain and simple when compared to my costume from the Masque; my gorgeous winged Eransian costume that had, like me, started the evening pure and white but that had ended it covered in blood, fear, and shame.

Still, my current dress would not be what I needed if I were truly planning to join the men who would be departing on the ships. I would require something that would allow me to move even more freely than this simple gown would allow. I needed the unrestrained movements afforded by a young man's clothing as well as the image that came with such attire. If I were seen as a young man, I would be able to travel and move about, unimpeded.

I stepped up to Megan's wardrobe and rifled through the gowns that it contained until I came upon what I needed: a riding habit. Stripping away my gown, I pulled on the dark grey breeches. I continued my search until I found a blouse to wear under the waistcoat and jacket that matched the breeches. I took extra care to tuck my necklace – a silver ring with a purple stone that was my only possession from before my life with the Godelevas – under the front of the blouse. Surely, a young man working on a ship would not be adorned with such a piece.

In a moment of daring, I left the skirt behind, pulling a black cloak over my shoulders. I hoped this would be enough to allow me to blend in with the young men aboard the rescue ship.

Wishing I could have found a boy's hat to wear, I settled for a simple braiding of my hair and would draw my hood up over my head when the time came to conceal myself.

Much to the dismay of Desda, I left the room. Not a word was exchanged between us. Just as I had known that she needed to keep herself distracted by cleaning, she clearly knew that I would not be convinced to remain there. With nothing more than a glance in her direction, I stepped out into the hall.

How easy it was to move in these clothes! I strode confidently as I descended the staircase to the Great Hall and walked to the drawing room off the ballroom where there were several Knights assembled with Lord Imery Godeleva. I could already hear them from the foot of the stairs and had no doubt as to where I would find them.

As soon as I could make out the words of the men, I paused. For a brief moment, it was as though the wind had been knocked out of me. Doubt rushed through me, and I was nearly convinced that I would be sick. I clutched onto the wall and repeated my earlier prayer to myself. I listened to my breath as it entered my body and left it again. From there, I was able to listen to the men's voices, once more.

Straining to take in every syllable, I heard that three ships – including one of the navy's fastest – would soon be leaving for Fort Picogeal, a port where a number of other naval ships were docked. They were already preparing and would sail by dawn.

A Skydasher bird had been sent ahead to warn the fort of the approach of at least one Kavylak vessel as well as of the impending arrival of three of our own. The razor-taloned bird of prey would arrive well before of any of the ships. It would provide the Knights and soldiers in Fort Picogeal with enough time to take part in the plan that was being laid out in the drawing room ahead of me.

It was out of the question that I would remain here. My feet would be on the deck of one of those ships before it left Lorammel's harbour.

Without a hint of hesitation, I entered the room. A number of Knights, including their Commander, Thayn Varda, were still dressed in their masquerade costumes, though their masks had long been abandoned. Lord Imery, himself, still sported the stunning black jacket that was the backdrop for his embodiment of a night sky.

As soon as I had stepped beyond the threshold, Sir Varda's head raised and his eyes rested upon me. He paused what he had been saying and nodded to Lord Imery, assuming that I needed to speak with my family.

That wasn't it, at all. I was there to join the war.

Chapter 2

Megan

Stupid! Stupid! Stupid! How could I have believed anything that came out of that monster's mouth? How could I have let him kiss me and, even worse, why did I kiss him back?

I was a stupid fool.

Galnar never had any intention of helping me find my way home. He wasn't sorry about anything. No, he was a sick and twisted psycho, and I believed his lies because I wanted to imagine he wasn't the villain that I always knew he was. Yet as much as shame burned deeply inside me and as much as I hated myself for being duped by that no-heart freak, it wasn't his kiss that haunted my thoughts; I couldn't get the image of his blood-stained dagger out of my mind.

Galnar wanted me to believe that the blood on his dagger belonged to Irys. He wanted me to think that he had hurt her, or worse. It wasn't hard to imagine him doing something violent. I had seen him hurt Irys before, and I knew that he couldn't have cared less if she died. It was for that very reason that I had taken her place as his slave. But why would he go out of his way to track Irys down and kill her at a Masquerade ball? Would he really go so far as to kill a person in cold blood?

No. He didn't kill her, Megan.

I realized that I was jumping to conclusions and was once again making assumptions about a man I clearly knew very little about. I felt a bit of my tension ease. I had no reason to believe that Galnar was a murderer. It was one thing for him to be violent, it was entirely another for him be a cold-blooded killer.

I had to stick to the facts that I knew about Galnar and not assume the worst. The one fact that I knew for certain about him was that he was a liar. The blood on the dagger could have belonged to anyone. Heck, it might not even have been blood.

However, as much as I wanted to entertain that thought, I knew it was only wishful thinking. Galnar didn't get stab-happy with a bottle of cherry juice. The blood was real. Keavren's shocked face had confirmed that much when Galnar revealed the nasty weapon.

I glanced at Keavren. I couldn't quite read his expression as he steadily rowed our boat. The light from the lantern that he had lit and placed on the boat's floor was not bright enough for me to make out any clear details. He was more than a shadow, but he could have been making a funny face at me or smiling, and I wouldn't have known the difference.

I looked away from him and out over the water. I was still mad at him. He hadn't answered any of my questions about Irys' whereabouts, about what had happened to her, or about Galnar. He had only picked me up from the carriage and carried me directly to the rowboat that was waiting for us at the shore, proving again to me that he was not the friend I had once hoped him to be.

Under other circumstances, I would have kicked and screamed and done my best to attract attention or try to get away, but I was more than outmatched, and I was terrified. Keavren's superior strength aside, "Miss Kiss," the woman whom I had met at the Masque, but whom I now knew had to be the female Warrior, Stargrace, was there. I didn't want her to put the same "enchantment spell" on me that she had used to get me to leave the grounds of the Godeleva estate without a fuss.

She and another male Warrior, whose name I didn't know and whom I had never seen before, were in the boat with Keavren and me. As much as I didn't like sharing a boat with the three of them, at least they weren't Galnar. Thankfully, he had taken a different boat with the Warrior, Acksil, and they had gone on ahead.

Stargrace and the other Warrior-guy were curled up together in the boat and were silent. Based on what I could see, when I was brave enough to steal a glance at them out of the corner of my eye, I guessed that they had to be more than friends. Stargrace was curled up in his arms in an intimate way that I definitely wouldn't consider platonic. Don't get me wrong, my best friend back home was a guy, but Cole and I were never *that* cuddly when we were sitting together; which had definitely been a good thing. Otherwise, his girlfriend likely would have given me a well-deserved black eye!

I tried to let my thoughts of the people whom I loved back home on Earth fill my head, to stop me from thinking about Qarradune, the Warriors, and Irys. I tilted up my head to look at the night sky. It was overcast, but I could see a bright half moon, peeking out from behind the clouds. I focused all my attention on the moon, which didn't look any different from the one I remembered and let myself imagine I was home.

My serenity was short-lived. The soft rocking of the boat and the smell of the salt water invaded my senses and wouldn't let me escape my new reality or the insanity within it. Even though everything and everyone around me seemed ridiculously calm, I felt like I had been swallowed up by chaos. My pounding heart grew steadily louder in my ears.

Finally, my fear won out over my anger. I just couldn't stand it anymore. I had to break the silence.

"Please, Keavren," I implored, turning my gaze back to him, "Where's Irys? Is she alright?"

Keavren looked at me for a moment and said in a low voice, "We didn't take her. I really don't know."

I frowned, my fear swelling, not because I thought he was lying but because I felt he was telling the truth.

"What about the blood on the dagger? Was that hers? What did that madman do to her?" I was desperate for him to tell me something.

He shook his head. "I don't know. I was watching you, Megan."

Okay, maybe he was watching me at the Masque, but someone else had *to be watching Irys.*

I turned to the love birds in the boat. "Do either of you know what happened to her?"

They both turned their heads toward me and the weight of their combined attention made me instantly regret addressing them.

The man gave an innocent shrug of his shoulders, causing me to focus my attention solely on him. In spite of being unable to see his eyes in detail, I felt the intensity of his gaze on me, and I liked it.

My heart beat faster and my face flushed. I wished I could see him more clearly but the dim glow of the lantern gave me only a teasing preview. I wanted more. I wanted to run my fingers through the fine strands of his dark hair that were fluttering carelessly in the breeze and caressing his forehead. I wanted to touch the delicious curve of his jaw and kiss his…

"I couldn't stop looking at you, Baby."

I started at the sound of Stargrace's flirtatious voice. I looked at her and realized that without meaning to, I was leaning in toward the captivating male Warrior. I quickly drew back, very unnerved from having been so easily sucked in by that guy. There was something extremely wrong with my level of attraction to him and to Stargrace, for that matter. Yes, they were undeniably hot but the attraction I felt toward them was unnatural.

I turned my head away from them, amazed, frustrated, and thoroughly freaked at how difficult it was to look away. In a desperate attempt to distract my mind from them, I made a fist with my hand until it hurt. Thankfully, it worked.

In an attempt to calm myself, I focused my gaze on the small waves Keavren was creating with the oars that dipped in and out of the inky-black night time water.

"Are we going back to the big ship?" I asked no one in particular when I felt brave enough to speak.

"We're going back to a smaller one that will bring us to the big one."

I looked at Keavren when he answered and was surprised when I saw him receive a subtle kick in the leg from Stargrace.

Hmm…interesting. Was I not supposed to know that? Okay, mental note-to-self: direct all future questions to Keavren.

"What about me?" I queried, deciding to see what else I might be able to learn. "Am I no longer a slave or was that a big lie like everything else I've been told?" I did my best to sound as haughty as possible. I wasn't interested in playing the role of the sweetheart victim for these jerks, no matter how scared I was.

"You're not a slave anymore, Baby. I'm not sure what you are, but you're not a slave," Stargrace said. "We wouldn't have been dispatched to chase a slave," she added with a teasing smile as if I were being silly.

I certainly didn't feel like I could trust everything she said, but I could believe that I wasn't a slave anymore. That was the one thing that made sense. The alternative was too ridiculous. There was no way that these Warriors would have been sent to infiltrate a fancy party just to reclaim a slave. From what I understood, in their eyes, a slave was less than a person. A slave had no rights and little value. In essence, I had been Galnar's property.

In his eyes, I was on par with his furniture. Going out of their way to reclaim a slave would be the equivalent to wasting a lot of time and effort as well as putting the lives of elite soldiers at risk, to reclaim a nice chair.

Don't get me wrong, you may like a chair enough that if you lost it you might consider snatching it back if a convenient opportunity presented itself. Otherwise, you'd have to accept the fact that you no longer had your chair and you'd get a shiny new one because, dude, it's a chair! Even if I happened to be Galnar's favourite possession, he could have easily replaced me in a snap. Honest to goodness, the guy clearly had a few screws loose and seemed like the tenacious sort, but I didn't clean his room *that* well.

I was drawn out of my thoughts when I suddenly spotted a light in the distance, several feet away from us. The light appeared to be blinking off and on in a specific pattern as if someone was sending a coded message. Seconds later, a soft yellow light illuminated the darkness, cutting across the water just out of reach of our rowboat. Keavren altered our course and began to row toward it.

The light came from the top of what appeared to be a large ship that was just slightly bigger than the sailing ship on which I had first met Thayn. That said, the major difference was that Keavren wasn't rowing us toward a sailing ship. I didn't know what they called this kind of vessel on Qarradune but to me, it looked like a battleship.

I saw the first rowboat, which had been responsible for the initial light signal, approach the side of the ship. I watched Galnar stand up from where he had been seated on his boat and heard him call up to the people above. Seconds later, a rope ladder was dropped down toward him. I secretly kept my fingers crossed that the falling ladder would clobber Galnar in the head but no such luck. Instead, he caught it with ease and deftly climbed up the rungs to the top.

Lucky jerk makes it look so easy. I'd like to see him try that stunt in a giant ball gown!

I looked down at my massive Knights of Freyss-inspired green and gold masquerade dress. It was beautiful but about as impractical as you could get for climbing up the side of a battleship.

They don't actually expect me to climb that dinky ladder in this parachute, do they?

I remembered, then, that I wasn't the only one who was wearing a ball gown. Stargrace was also wearing a dress that equaled the size of my own. I guessed I'd just have to take my cue from her and follow whatever she did. Maybe they'd just raise our boat up the side of the ship while we sat on the floor as the sailors of Thayn's ship had done when I was rescued by the Knights.

Keavren rowed our boat into position and it bobbed uncomfortably in the water against the side of the ship. Stargrace and the other Warrior stood up as if the boat wasn't even rocking. I looked up at her with anticipation. She winked at me, turned toward the ladder, took a firm hold of it, and began to steadily climb it at an impressive rate, considering her attire. The other Warrior followed swiftly behind her.

I blinked in both astonishment and horror. I was astonished because I didn't think anyone could make that look easy and it was freaking weird to see a chick in a ball gown scale the side of a metal ship. On the other hand, I was horrified because I now knew I was expected to do the same.

It was official: these people were certifiably insane.

"Do you think you can get up the ladder in your dress?" Keavren asked, sounding nearly apologetic. "I can carry you," he added in a slightly raised voice so that he could be heard over the sloshing sounds of seawater.

Well, at least I'm not the only one who has zero confidence in my ability to pull this off.

I looked down at my dress, looked up the ladder, and then looked at Keavren. To be honest, the idea of him tossing me over his shoulder to carry me up the ladder seemed even more disconcerting to me than going solo.

"I'll manage," I told him.

"I'll be right behind you. I won't let you fall," he said.

I nodded to him. His words were comforting but the rocking rowboat was not. Taking a deep breath, I stood quickly, making sure my boots wouldn't get caught in the several layers of dress that surrounded them. Immediately, I reached for the ladder to steady myself.

I was grateful that I was still wearing my gloves when I touched the thick, coarse rope. I slowly began my climb, hoping that my feet would continue to make purchase with the rope rungs during my ascent.

Once I reached the fourth rung, I felt the ladder pull more taut and knew that Keavren had joined me. I wasn't concerned that he was below me. In another circumstance, I might have felt uneasy knowing the guy below me could see directly up my skirt, but Keavren would have to have been a superhero with X-ray vision to see through all the layers I was wearing. All he would see was mounds of cloth and my boots.

Oh well, at least if I fell, he'd have a lot to grab on to...then again, if I actually hit the water in this dress I'd likely only float.

Maybe I should test that theory and drop into the water, grab an oar, and start paddling back to Syliza.

I shook the silly thought from my head and kept climbing. I climbed for what felt like hours. With each step, my heart rose higher into my throat, and my hatred for the ball gown grew.

I kept my focus upward and, finally, when I was nearing the top, I saw Stargrace appear at the rail. She smiled at me like I was a friend she was welcoming home. When I was close enough, she leaned a little over the rail and held her hand out for me to take.

The last thing I wanted to do was to take help from a woman who pretty much hypnotized me but this was the time for thinking about the bigger picture and not the grudge I was harbouring. I took hold of her offered hand.

Her grip was firm and solid. She pulled me up and forward with strength I never would have guessed she had, just by looking at her. With her support, I awkwardly climbed over the metal rail. I felt better as soon as I was free of the rope and my feet were, once again, planted on a solid surface.

I let go of Stargrace's hand as soon as I could but was unable to bring myself to thank her for her help. I wanted to keep my distance.

She didn't try to stop me, nor did she seem offended. Instead, she slipped her arms around the Warrior with whom she'd been cozy in the rowboat, and he held her in return. Standing there together, smiling at me, they looked like they were made for one another; like the only pieces of a puzzle, precisely designed to fit each other to create the perfect image of seamless beauty.

Now, in the light of the ship, I got my first real look at Stargrace's "other half." Just like her, he had supermodel-good looks. He was a few inches taller than her and had short, silky jet-black hair, porcelain skin, and electric-blue eyes. Like her, his eyes were his most intoxicating feature.

I didn't want to stop looking into the paradise of his eyes. His eyes that were gazing into my own. His eyes that I was sure could see the secrets of my heart that could...

"I'll take you to your room."

I jumped when Keavren spoke. I blinked rapidly and tore my gaze away from the Warrior, whom I'd suddenly realized had once again sucked me into some sort of heart-eyed hypnosis.

I turned my attention to Keavren and saw him standing next to me, but he wasn't looking at me. His focus was on Stargrace and "Other Stargrace" and, I couldn't be certain, but it almost looked liked Keavren was giving them a warning glare.

Neither one looked perturbed. Stargrace simply blew a kiss at me before she and the other Warrior turned and walked away from us. I watched them briefly before turning back to Keavren. He gave me a nod, and I nodded back to silently confirm that, yeah, I was happy to go with him to get away from his freaky "brothers."

Chapter 3

Irys

Lord Imery excused himself from the room full of Knights and approached me, speaking in a hushed voice. "Irys, what's the matter?"

"I have decided that I want to join the mission to save Megan Wynters. I want to leave on one of the ships with the Knights," I said with determination. I couldn't falter. I couldn't lose my nerve. The last time I failed to act, Megan was abducted from my own home.

He was understandably shocked and remained silent for a painful moment. I'd never seen him react in such a way. Lord Imery was usually the type of man who always had an immediate reply to any statement or situation. Finally, he spoke.

"You know that will not be permitted by the Knights. Nor would I allow it, if they did."

"I must go. I must find a way, Lord Imery. It's my fault that Miss Wynters was taken, and I am convinced that this is the only thing to do. She risked her life when she freed me from Kavylak. Now, it is my turn. I have prayed all evening, and I know that this is my path."

Despite the frustratingly shrill sound to my quieted voice, I felt proud of my words and allowed my hope to climb a little as Lord Imery listened without interrupting. Slowly, that hope began to fade as he gathered his reply.

"Clever One," he began with a soothing voice, "you have already saved her, once. I won't allow you to place yourself in any more danger. You must trust that the Knights will return her to safety, just as they have done before."

"I am very grateful to the Knights for everything they did when they rescued Megan the last time, Lord Imery," I said as calmly as I could. "I am also grateful to you for the part that you played in ensuring that I would be taken seriously. But I need to do this. I have never felt more certain of anything in my life. I feel as though the

Goddess has sent me a message. She wants me to prove that I did not fail to learn from what has happened to me."

"I understand that this is important to you, and I understand that Miss Wynters is important to you. But going with the Knights to try to find her could not be what the Goddess wants from you. She does not require young ladies to risk their lives on missions that were clearly meant for soldiers."

"Her message was very plain to me, Lord Imery. I don't feel as though I have a choice. I want to do it, as does She. I cannot simply remain here and wait this time. I must find a way to take part. If you force me to stay, I will be miserable."

Lord Imery's face was sympathetic, but I could tell that he had not been swayed. Resting a hand on my shoulder, he said, "I don't want you to be miserable, Clever One, but I cannot let you go."

"Then don't let me go but please do not despise me for going anyway," I replied sadly. "The last thing I want to do is disobey you, but I don't feel that I have a choice. Both my heart and my soul require this of me."

His expression was supportive but melancholy and as much as I could tell that he wanted to ease my suffering, I also knew that he did not believe I would go without his permission.

"You will feel better about all this in the morning, Irys. You have been under a lot of stress and it speaks to your character that you would go to such lengths on behalf of Miss Wynters, despite what has already happened. However, I think that the best thing that can be done for you both is to leave the rescue mission to the Knights while you have Desda keep you company. With any luck, by the time you wake up in the morning, Miss Wynters will already be on her way home again."

What else was he supposed to say? Of course this sounded like madness to him. At the same time, it did not diminish my resolve.

"I will let you return to your discussions, Lord Imery," I said, sounding deflated. I curtsied to him.

"I will be up to check on you soon," he replied. "We are almost finished here."

I turned to walk across the Great Hall and by the time I had reached the stairs, he had already rejoined the men in the drawing room. I could hear his voice among them.

Climbing quickly up the curved staircase, I virtually flew into my bedroom. If not for the stale smell of metal that still hung in the air, I could nearly pretend that there wasn't a tableau of horror in the adjacent sitting room. I couldn't allow myself to think on that.

I needed a bag. Looking around my room, my eyes fell to the carpet bag that I used to hold my needlework, hoops, patterns, and other such items. Upending it into a drawer, I then filled it with all the things that I thought I would need on the mission to rescue Megan.

Looking at the items spilling out of the bag and onto the surface of my bed, I lost my breath again. How could I do this? How could I pack a bag and run off on the only family I'd ever known?

I'm not running away, Great Goddess. I'm running toward something. Toward someone. I'm running after Megan, and I will find her and bring her back here, where we both belong.

I had selected far too much for the little bag to handle, so I spread the items out on my bed to try to decide which among them were the most vital. I brought a skirt and clean blouse, under-things, and a few personal items. What was most difficult was in choosing only one book to bring along with me. The three that I had originally selected were clearly too many.

With no space at all left in the bag, I slipped out of my room and tiptoed down the hall to the room that we had nicknamed the *laboratory*. It wasn't that any experiments were conducted there, but it was the room in which Lord Imery kept all his new finds and discoveries, from ancient vases to rare texts and everything in between. The items were safely stored there while he wished to examine them until he knew what he would do with them.

It wasn't the ancient artifacts that interested me here. It was the herbs and powders stored in the little apothecary jars and glass vials. I wanted to be prepared for anything. This included the circumstances that I did not wish to imagine – trauma, injury, or deep emotional pain. I tapped a few of the substances into small envelopes and slipped them into my bag. Small envelopes were likely the only thing that my poor needlepoint bag would have accepted at that point.

Though my first instinct was to descend the stairs into the Great Hall, the sight of an apprentice who was making his way across the pale marble floor, reminded me that I needed to improve my stealth quite a bit if I did not wish to be caught. I chose instead to take the servants' stairs.

I'd always detested those stairs. As a child, they terrified me. Unlike the grand, curved staircases that the family and our guests typically used, the back stairs were encased in a tight vertical space in which they spiralled steeply without a railing. The lighting cast shadows that brought to mind all manner of dark images that would haunt me at night and leave me praying in fear.

The rise of each step was greater than those of the main staircase, giving the impression that one was climbing a mountain when going upward, or teetering on the edge of a sharp cliff when headed downward. This was only worsened with the short run of each pie-shaped step. The closer one came to the inner curve, the less stair there was to hold one's foot. I always clung to the outer wall and dreaded the moment when a servant would travel in the other direction, forcing a step to be shared, if only for a moment.

This was the first time that I had entered the back staircase in cycles, and I didn't need a reminder as to why that was. My descent was the first major obstacle of my journey, and my safe exit from it felt like quite an accomplishment. Only the kitchen lay between me and the back door. I would need to pass through it before I could step into the rear gardens of the estate.

Though I'd expected the kitchen to be empty as the Masque was now long over, I was surprised to discover that it was still abuzz with activity. There were mountains of food being stored and every sink and tub was filled for washing and scrubbing everything from pots to silver, china, and crystal. Yet, beyond all that activity, there were still footmen rushing about to bring tea and food to the men upstairs.

Drawing my hood over my head, I waited until the path appeared to be clear, and I dashed quickly through the kitchen and directly out the door, turning only once to shut the door and latch it.

Again, I was surprised to find that there were far more people about than I had expected. There were men dressed as guards who were walking the gardens and standing at the gates. I jumped when I discovered that they were also posted at the doors to the estate, and that I had been standing directly next to one when I stepped out the kitchen door.

Nodding to him, I walked briskly through the gardens, trying to appear as though I was supposed to be there. Unfortunately, my exit from the Godeleva property was not nearly as smooth as that from the kitchen. A guard at the gate spoke to me as I passed, and I knew that it would not be wise to continue onward and ignore him.

"Are you where you should be?" he asked in a way that made it clear that he wasn't suspicious but that he hadn't recognized me and didn't intend to let me pass without his permission.

"Yes," I replied, taking down my hood. "I have been sent to stay with the Fhirells while everything is in disarray, here," I lied. As Sir Varda, the Commander of the Knights, was already inside, I chose the home of his second-in-command, Sir Dynan Fhirell, as the next safest place to be.

"Oh, Miss Godeleva. I'm sorry, I didn't recognize you with your hood up," he said, easing his tone a little. "Does Lord Godeleva know that you are out here all on your own?"

"It's only a short walk," I answered, attempting to dodge his question so that I would lie to him as little as possible.

"Still, Miss Godeleva, there are the wrong sorts about, tonight. Let me call someone to bring you."

I wanted to refuse him but at the same time, I was afraid that if I seemed too determined to walk on my own, I might draw unwanted attention to myself, and Lord Imery might be called.

"Be quick about it, then," I said, unwilling to allow this hurdle to cause me to miss the ship.

The guard nodded and flagged down one of his colleagues, who approached and bowed to me.

"Bring Miss Godeleva to the Fhirells' and return as soon as you know she is safe," instructed the first guard.

The second guard nodded, and I wished the first one a pleasant evening before walking on. If the guard who was assigned to me had any intention of completing his assigned task, then he would have to keep up.

By the time we arrived at the gates framing the base of the drive to the Fhirell home, the muscles in my legs were burning. Determination had continued to propel me forward despite the outcry of my legs and the throbbing of my injured arm.

Turning to the guard I said, "I can find my way from here. Go back to the Godeleva Estate to find out where you are needed." I turned my back to him and walked toward the manor in order to show that my words were not up for dispute.

"Yes Miss Godeleva," the guard replied, though I barely heard him.

I continued up the path toward the substantial brownstone house, until I was certain that the guard was well out of sight. Keeping to the shadows as much as I could, I slipped back onto the sidewalk and walked as swiftly as I was able toward the docks.

I had never taken this route before, particularly not at night. It was striking that a distance that could be travelled in a handful of minutes in a carriage, felt as though it was taking a lifetime on foot. The urgency in my heart made each pace seem painfully slow but, at the same time, it gave me the courage I needed to continue forward. I was well aware of how little it would take to deflate my confidence and lead me to doubt my cause. I couldn't let that happen.

My feet began to ache as each stride became heavier. I could feel the jagged curve of each cobblestone under my feet. Where the ground usually felt smooth and easy at my typical stroll, every stone now seemed to be at an odd angle, and my toes were determined to slip into each crack and crevice, turning my ankles this way and that. The handle from my bag cut into my fingers, but I was unable to relieve some of the pressure by switching hands as my bandaged forearm cried out whenever I tried.

Had I been required to go much farther, I may not have made it but the moment my resolve had started to falter, I could suddenly hear the shouts of the sailors as they readied the ships to depart.

Tucked out of sight I watched them, trying to determine which ship would be the one that would leave first. It wasn't long before I noticed that the sailors and other workers appeared to be placing the greatest amount of focus on one ship over the others.

Keeping the hood of my cloak pulled down and squaring my shoulders, I strode with large steps toward the ship, trying to look as though I knew where I was going and that I was meant to be there. As I walked, I looked for something to carry, so that it might seem like I could be one of many men who were making a rapid attempt to stock the ship.

A man called out to me and I whirled to face him, only to have a large, heavy sack tossed in my direction. I brought my arms up in time to catch it and was nearly taken backward off my feet. Despite the fact that the breath was whisked from my body and my bandaged arm roared in pain from the sudden impact and weight, I turned abruptly toward the ship without dropping either the sack or my bag.

Please, Great Goddess, don't let them see me. Let them focus on their tasks and ignore anything that I am doing incorrectly. I am trying to do what is right, Great Goddess, but I need your help. I can't do this alone, but you are the only one who can help me.

By the time my prayer was over, I had climbed the gangplank and was standing on the deck of a large sailing ship. It rocked gently, but I kept my footing under the heavy sack and my own bag. I just kept walking. The moment I spotted the ladder to below deck, I tossed the sack down and descended after it, awkwardly clutching my bag.

Continuing below again, down a second ladder, I reached the hold for barrels, crates, and other large sacks like the one I was currently dragging by one of its corners. Wondering where I should hide, I decided that the sack was probably a sign. I could conceal myself there among the rest of the soft-sided, misshapen lumps in the darkness.

"Where do ya think yer goin' with that?" asked one of the men who were coming and going from the space.

Clearly, I'd paused for too long in deciding where to hide. Instead of speaking, I simply nodded my head toward the pile of similar sacks, to which he grunted and climbed the ladder.

Thank you, Great Goddess.

I would need to be more alert; more quick-thinking. Someone who belonged here would not hesitate and look around the hold. He would walk directly up to the pile of sacks and heave the next one on top of it.

That's precisely what I did next. It was much more difficult for me than it appeared to be for the men who had done so ahead of me but the fact that I was still able to lift the bag in the first place, made me feel rather proud.

As soon as I was certain that everyone had turned away, I climbed up and over the sacks, wedging myself and my carpet bag in behind. I slipped into a gap that had formed between the sacks and a number of barrels that were strapped down.

I would have thought that the discovery of this tidy little hiding space would have calmed me – particularly when I made my way into it, undetected. The problem was that I was now faced with nothing to do except to remain quiet and pray that nobody would find me.

I did pray.

Silently, I begged and pleaded that the Goddess would keep me hidden and that I would soon become a vital part of the rescue mission for Megan. I also prayed that the rats would keep to themselves.

*   *   *   *   *

There was no way for me to know how much time had passed. Men came and went with more goods to be stored; food, ship supplies, and arms, I suspected. After a while, they weren't coming to the hold anymore, but I could hear their boots on the planks of the decks above me.

The last man to leave brought the lantern with him, so I was left seated in my little nook, hugging my knees and watching the darkness in front of me.

The swaying of the ship that had been a series of slow, tired yawns, eventually groaned and heaved until it seem to burst into bright, graceful leaps. We had drifted our way from the docks and were headed out of the harbour. Soon, we would be in open water.

Megan, we're coming.

At first, the new pattern of the ship's rocking caused my stomach to rise and fall along with it. I wondered if I would need to try to find some of the herbs I'd brought with me to soothe the growing feeling of nausea. I wondered how I would manage to properly dispense them in the dark. Instead, though, I focused on Megan and on keeping as calm as I could.

I thought about the amusement on her face when she'd discovered that I was dressing her as a Knight for the Masque. Shutting my eyes, I pictured the beauty of the swirling gowns in the ballroom and how lovely I felt among them.

From the start of the evening, both Megan and I had been striking successes. We'd each danced with Knights and other noblemen. I'd danced with the emperor, himself...but then I'd danced with Warriors. Two, in fact, but one in particular: Acksilivcs.

He'd found me at my little escape by my favourite fountain in the gardens. He'd pretended to be shy and awkward with women, despite his obvious charisma. He'd made me feel confident as I guided him through a dance he'd pretended to be too nervous to attempt in the ballroom, where everyone would be watching. He'd stolen a kiss. My first kiss. How tender it had seemed. How I'd thought I would cherish that perfect little secret.

Now that I was aware that it was all merely a scheme to keep me busy while other Warriors moved in and captured Megan, I knew that I should not look back on that kiss with any degree of delight. Yet, in a tiny hidden place in my heart, I did still treasure it. The memory of that gentle moment, only just before the truth was revealed to me, was soothing enough to soften the movements of the ship as it eased up and down like the swaying of branches in a warm breeze.

Without even knowing that I was starting to feel tired, I fell asleep. The only reason I knew that I had drifted off at all, was that when I opened my eyes, I could see light travelling through seams around the door in the ceiling above the ladder to the next deck.

If there was that much light, we had to have been on the water for at least a couple of hours. It was long enough that they would not turn back, even if they had discovered they had a stowaway: me.

Rising from my little hiding spot was much more challenging than I had expected it to be. My legs had gone to sleep and my knees felt as though they had seized and were locked in place. I managed to pull myself onto the pile of sacks, using my arms, and I slowly moved my legs until I regained feeling in them and control over them, once again.

When I felt strong enough, I picked up my bag, gritting my teeth against the pulsing of my heartbeat in my arm, and climbed the ladder to the trapdoor and its border of bright sunlight. I had expected to be able to push it open but this was not the case. Checking it for latches of some kind, I found none. The dull thud of a boot heel solved the mystery. Someone was standing on the door. As I listened, I could make out hints of a conversation that he was having with another man.

Summoning all my courage, I balanced myself carefully on the ladder and rapped on the door above me. The talking paused, so I took my opportunity and knocked again, saying, "Good morning?"

There was a change in the silence, which was punctuated by a curse that I could hardly have imagined would be appropriate upon hearing the voice of a lady. I had barely a moment to consider that, though, before the trap door was thrown open and I was faced by a stern-looking crewman.

"What's this? A stowaway?" he demanded.

I raised my bandaged arm to shield my eyes from the sudden flood of white light and before I could reply, the other sailor took hold of my upper arms and pulled me onto the next deck. I squeaked in surprise as I was set onto my feet. By only the grace of the Goddess did I manage not to let go of my bag handle.

"It's a woman," said the second sailor. "A pretty one."

The men looked at each other and then at me as though debating what they should do with me.

"Good morning," I said nervously, hoping that they would find me pleasant enough not to become too upset. "Are we well on our way to catching the Warriors?" I then asked. Perhaps if I sounded as though I knew about the mission, they might believe that I was somehow permitted to be aboard.

"Sure thing, dumpling," he replied with sarcasm as he glanced at the other sailor. "We should tell Sir Fhirell."

"Oh lovely, this *is* Sir Fhirell's ship," I said, continuing to try to appear as though everything was proceeding as I had hoped. It was true, in a way. "I was hoping to make it onto the first ship."

The men exchanged a glance. "She's trouble," said the first one.

"Gentlemen, there is no need to discuss me in the third person. Please bring me to Sir Fhirell." My voice had come to life. It was virtually a command. "I wish to speak with him without delay."

The first man looked unimpressed. "Keep your skirt on, dumpling."

"She's bad luck. We should get her off the ship," said the second one.

"This is no way to treat a young lady," I scolded. "Enough of this. I will speak to another Knight, if you won't bring me to Sir Fhirell." I prayed that they had not heard my voice tremble as my body had begun to shake.

The first sailor took hold of my upper arm and pulled me toward the ladder to the next deck.

"Stop pulling me," I objected forcefully. "I can walk for myself."

"Then walk," huffed the sailor who promptly released me.

I nearly lost my footing when he let go but I quickly recovered. I climbed the ladder with one sailor ahead of me and the other behind me and stepped up onto the top deck of the ship. Men moved about with purpose, each of them clearly having their own duties and tasks to accomplish. However, I was not given the chance to observe them for long. I was escorted directly to the captain's cabin and I did not want to fall behind and risk having one of the sailors feel that they needed to start pulling me again.

Holding my bag in front of me with both hands, I watched one of the sailors knock on the door.

"Enter," responded a voice from within.

The sailor opened the door and stepped inside, giving a brief bow. "Sir Fhirell, we have a stowaway. A woman."

Inside the room, I could see the edge of a desk, behind which Sir Dynan Fhirell had been seated. Deciding that I would not allow the soldiers to cut into my confidence, I stepped into the room. It was only then that I realized that another Knight was also present. Clearly, my discovery had interrupted a discussion that they had been having. Both of the Knights were looking at me with surprised expressions on their faces that they made no effort to disguise.

Sir Fhirell rose to his feet and I curtsied respectfully, feeling proud that I had managed to do so without losing my balance. He was dressed in the full Knight's uniform, aside from his hat, which sat on the surface of the desk in front of him. His deep blue eyes were fixed on me in a combination of confusion, concern and gravity.

"Please excuse my intrusion, Sir Fhirell," I apologized.

"Miss Godeleva?" he replied in what was certainly disbelief.

"Yes," I confirmed.

Before I could add to the statement, Sir Fhirell turned his attention to the crewmen. "Thank you. Dismissed." The crewmen nodded and gave me a final glance before returning to their duties. "Sir Vorel, please excuse me, but it seems that we will need to continue our discussion in a moment," he added.

To that, the other Knight, Sir Vorel, gave a deep nod to Sir Fhirell and a bow to me, before he left the room entirely. I responded with a brief curtsy but I wasn't feeling quite as steady as I had been with the first one, so I chose not to press my luck by attempting anything fancy. My expression, however, was apologetic.

When the door closed behind Sir Vorel, I returned my attention to Sir Fhirell. "Again, I do apologize. This is not at all how I had hoped to take part in this mission."

Instead of a response to my statement, Sir Fhirell fixed an appraising gaze on me for an extended moment.

"Are you alone, Miss Godeleva?" he asked, when he finally spoke.

"I am," I replied. I *was* all alone. Suddenly, the weight of my decision to board this ship and attempt to help in Megan's rescue seemed to strike me for the first time. Until this moment, I had been forcing myself to maintain a certain degree of denial so that I would not lose my confidence. Now, all that was washed away and I found myself face-to-face with reality. I wasn't entirely certain that I liked what I saw.

"Does anyone know you're here?" he continued with his interrogation.

It was as though I were a criminal! Indeed, I was being treated far better than a common stowaway but it was clear by Sir Fhirell's tone that my presence was not welcome. Why had I expected that it would be anything but this? Had I truly been foolish enough to believe that Sir Fhirell would be happy to see me, once I revealed my presence?

"I imagine that Lord Godeleva will guess that this is where I have gone. I told him that I wished to be aboard one of the vessels that were to be sent in pursuit of Megan Wynters. He forbade it."

"I think we are both aware that you should not be here. At the same time, it is too late to return you to Lorammel. I think we are both aware of that as well," he said factually. His tone was serious and carried only the slightest hint of disapproval. Otherwise, he gave no indication of his opinion about what I had done.

"I was counting on that. I chose not to reveal myself until we had travelled too far to turn back," I replied.

To that, I received a nod of comprehension, nothing more. "Please, have a seat," he said after a moment had passed. "Would you like some water?"

"Yes, please. That would be lovely, thank you."

Sir Fhirell poured a cup of water and set it down on the desk ahead of me, before returning to his seat. After a thoughtful moment, he spoke. "I am aware that you were recently attacked by Captain Galnar and that your friend, Miss Wynters, was taken from your family home but I must ask you, Miss Godeleva: Why are you here? What has compelled you to take such a risk and to sneak aboard this ship?"

I sipped the water as I listened to his questions. Composing myself, I attempted to select my words in a way that might encourage Sir Fhirell to understand my point of view in a way that I was not able to express to Lord Imery.

"Sir Fhirell, I know that my actions appear to be quite rash and unreasonable but please understand that Miss Wynters once saved my life at what could have been the cost of her own. Then, when I had the chance to return the favour at the Masque, I did not take it. I chose to save myself. Now, in order to save my friend and my soul, I must be a part of the effort to bring her home again."

To Sir Fhirell's credit, while he must have thought that I was touched with madness, he listened to me with his full attention.

"What do you mean when you say that you chose to save yourself? From what I understand, you were attacked."

"I was. However, before that happened, I had been the only one to know that the Warriors had infiltrated the Masque. A Warrior spoke to me in the gardens and warned me that if I told a single person about their presence, the safety of the guests could not be assured. He instructed me to hide myself and remain quiet and that if I did, everyone would be fine." I took a breath to calm myself as I felt my anxiety rising. "I should have found a way to tell someone. Lord Godeleva, himself, stopped me as I made my way through the ballroom. I could have said something then but I didn't. I knew I had that one chance to try to spot Miss Wynters and alert her but I barely tried. This is my chance to redeem myself."

"I see," was all he said.

"Do you, Sir Fhirell?" I asked softly. I was certain that Lord Imery thought he understood me but he clearly did not. I took care not to sound impertinent but I needed to know that he had truly grasped what was driving me to go to such extremes.

"You must firmly believe that this is what you must do, to be willing to take such a risk," he responded.

His words relaxed some of the tension that I had been holding in my shoulders. It was only then that I was reminded of what a handsome man Sir Fhirell truly was.

His eyes were as blue as the sea on which we sailed. His rich brown hair was tied at the nape of his neck allowing it to follow the line of his spine until the base of his shoulder blades. The style was such that it would appear just slightly roguish if it were not for its neatness. His typically clean-shaven face was now shadowed with a hint of stubble and his calm expression was slightly tired.

"I made a promise to the Goddess," I explained to him, intending to illustrate precisely how important it was that I be a part of this rescue effort.

"Is your hope merely to be present during this mission or do you believe that you will be able to provide us with some form of assistance?" he inquired.

Goddess, why don't I know the answer?

"I would like to help, if I can. I'm not entirely sure what sort of assistance I can offer but I do know that the only way that I will be able to take part is to be here."

"I do not know how you will be able to help, Miss Godeleva. We are well provisioned and have crafted a rescue strategy that does not involve or require your presence. At the moment, I think the only recommendation I can make is to ensure that you keep yourself safe and that you don't impede the efforts of my men. Should that change, I will be certain to inform you."

"Thank you, Sir Fhirell. You are a very understanding man," I said genuinely, realizing for the first time that I had not taken any real opportunity to think my decision through. I had placed such a focus on being present that it had not occurred to me that I would actually need to complete some type of task in order to be useful. What sort of purpose could I possibly serve here?

"Thank you, Miss Godeleva," he smiled. It was a warm expression that soothed me, even in my rattled state. "I find that one must be at least a little bit understanding in order to make the best of a situation."

"I hope only that I can make my presence worthwhile. I have every intention of making up for any inconvenience I have caused."

"May I trust that you will do as you are asked in order to ensure your safety and that of those aboard my ship?"

"In anything other than returning home without Miss Wynters."

"Our mission is to rescue her, Miss Godeleva. I am not in the habit of failing in my missions."

Again, comfort embraced me. "Then it seems that we are entirely on the same side, Sir Fhirell," I responded with a smile.

Returning my encouraging expression, he added, "While you remain on this ship, you may stay in the captain's cabin."

"Won't you need it?"

"From time to time. But this is where you will sleep."

"Thank you." The words had barely escaped my lips when my stomach growled. "What time is breakfast served?"

At his chuckle, I realized that this was not the typical request of a person aboard a ship such as this one.

"Pull the rope later this morning, and someone will come to check on you," he said, indicating the rope that hung near the door.

"Lovely. Is there anything that I can do to be of assistance, at the moment?" I inquired, attempting to regain some of my dignity. If I had been able to imagine a task that I could accomplish, I would have made my offer more specific. However, I simply could not imagine myself hoisting a sail or swabbing a deck. Clearly, I required more precise instructions.

"For the time being, it would be best if you simply stayed out of the way as the men complete their own duties. There are a few books here that you are welcome to read and there are a few sheets of paper and some ink that I can spare if you would like to write. I will see what I can do about a bit of tea for you," he said and rose to his feet. "Please make yourself comfortable. I will return shortly."

I nodded my appreciation. "I will stay here," I assured him. Perhaps with some tea and some time for thought and prayer, I would be able to imagine a way to help in Megan's rescue. I was confident that I would be quite useful once she was brought aboard. What I needed more presently was to discover what I could do until that time.

Sir Fhirell stepped out of the cabin and I found myself seated alone, obliged to face my thoughts and my situation.

Great Goddess, what am I doing here? What have I done? I know why I have done it but what is my next step? I have taken a great leap to show my trust in you and to prove myself to you but where is it that you hope I will land?

I was proud of myself for having withheld the tears for this long. Now, they streamed hotly down my cheeks.

Chapter 4

Megan

I followed Keavren across the deck and down two fights of very narrow metal stairs. We walked along a tight hall with low ceilings and close walls, both littered with pipes. It was so tight, in fact, that the ample skirt of my costume hugged the wall on either side, making me feel like I should be wearing a "wide load" sign on the back of my dress. This ship was very disconcerting and a claustrophobe's worst nightmare. It was definitely nowhere near the size of the massive vessel from which I had previously escaped and it lacked its sophistication.

The other difference I noted was that this ship rocked slightly and produced the occasional groan, whereas its superior "big brother" had been virtually silent and still.

Differences aside, the lights that dotted the walls were the same. I didn't know how they were powered but whatever Kavylak used to illuminate its ships wasn't the same type of gas lighting that was used in Syliza. Even in the individual rooms of the Kavylak ship, the lights were switched on and off. Maybe they had some sort of generator setup. I wondered why they would have different and – what seemed to me – more advanced technology compared to Syliza's.

Weird.

It was exceptionally odd following Keavren because he was still in his costume, too. Although he had dumped his mask and his hat back in the carriage, where my own hat had been left, he was wearing a long black dress jacket that made him look like the perfect high-born Sylizan gentleman. Without his black leather Warrior's uniform, he looked just as out of place on this ship as I did.

Keavren stopped at a door. He pulled down its lever and pushed it open. Light spilled into the hallway, brightening the dimly lit area. He stepped aside and waited for me to enter first. I did, looking around the new space I would call "home" for who knows how long this time.

The room was small but not unbearably so. In truth, the most unpleasant thing about it was that it had no window and the four grey walls were smooth and bare, giving it an overall jail-cell feeling, which I suppose was fitting considering my new prisoner status.

Meh, on the plus side, at least I wasn't put in the brig.

"There are clothes coming for you," Keavren said, drawing me out of my thoughts. "I made sure you had a good pillow."

I gave him a short nod to convey my dutiful "thanks" and glanced at the pillow on the cot-style bed. I couldn't stop my frown. Good pillow or not, this sleeping setup paled so far in comparison to the dream-princess canopy bed in which I'd had the privilege of sleeping at the Godeleva Estate, that I was finding it hard to care that he had gone to the effort. I didn't care about the stupid pillow. I didn't want to sleep on that stupid cot and I certainly didn't want to be trapped in that stupid room. I wanted to go back to Irys. I wanted to go back home.

I'm not supposed to be here.

Taking a deep breath, in an effort to beat down my rising tantrum, I focused on Keavren. I had to be calm. I had to be polite. I wanted answers.

"What's going on, Keavren?" I purposely made my voice soft and quiet. Even if I couldn't trust him, I could at least pretend to be nice, to see what I could find out.

"I don't actually know, yet. I'm just following orders," he confessed. "I never thought I'd see you again. I'm glad that you're here...but still, I'm not, really."

I nodded to him. He sounded so genuine. I wanted to believe him but I had wanted to believe Galnar, too and because of that, I had played right into Galnar's game and had kissed him. I couldn't afford to trust any of them – not even Keavren.

"Did you want me to bring you something to eat?" Keavren asked in a way that made it seem that he was desperate to do something for me.

"No, thank you. All I want is to know if Irys is okay. If you can find that out for me, Keavren, I would greatly appreciate that."

He tensed instantly when I mentioned Irys' name, suddenly looking like he was more desperate to get away from me than to help me as he had only moments ago. I was losing him.

"I'll see what I can find out. I don't know if any of us saw her, though, Megan."

My pretend confidence wavered at his words. My throat tightened as my worry over Irys' safety swelled anew.

"Thank you for trying," I said in a barely audible voice as I turned away from him to face the cot. I didn't want him to see my lip quiver. My courage was crumpling. Tears pricked my eyes.

"I understand why you don't think of me as a friend," he said. "It's alright. I don't expect you to but I still hope you'll be o-kay."

I believed him to be sincere. Even if we'd never be friends, he'd always been decent to me.

I turned back around to face him and said, "Thanks. For what it's worth, I know that you've done all that you can for me." I hoped my words sounded more genuine to him than they did in my ears.

He listened to me and watched me with an unreadable expression for a long moment, until finally he walked toward the door he had left open. I had expected him to leave but to my surprise he only shut the door and walked back to me. He looked intense.

"I can't help you escape again," he whispered. "I nearly got caught the last time."

I stared at him in shock, barely able to process his words.

"You...helped me escape?"

It was Keavren's turn to look surprised. It was evident from his expression and prolonged silence that he'd thought I had known he'd helped me get off the ship and away from Galnar.

"They didn't say anything to you?"

I shook my head. "No, and I never thought to ask. I honestly didn't care at the time. I was just glad to be rescued."

He nodded. "I caught them when they'd boarded. I sent one back but the other one had been looking for you in the brig."

"And you let him take me away?" I couldn't believe what I was hearing.

He paused before answering. "I was scared that you might not make it," he confessed.

I looked at him for a moment and let the memory of the night of my escape with Sir Obithran surface in my mind. Suddenly, what I had never cared to question before, began to make sense. Of course! Someone on the inside had to have been involved in my rescue. How else would the Knight have found me? Why else would the halls that were normally guarded by soldiers have been empty to allow us safe passage without being seen? Keavren must have been the one to help. No one else aside from him, Galnar, and Xandon ever interacted with me.

The revelation caused a flood of emotion to wash over me. Closing the distance between us, I flung my arms around Keavren's neck, hugged him tightly, and cried on his shoulder. To my utter relief, he hugged me right back. He wrapped his big burly arms around me, giving me the secure bear hug I had wanted and needed since waking up on Qarradune.

I let myself cry for a few minutes, getting the worst of it out, until I felt I could regain some composure. Keavren never once shushed me or told me to stop. He only held me and rubbed my back in a soothing gesture. It did bring me comfort.

In that moment, I forgave Keavren for everything I had blamed him for. He'd helped me a lot more than I had realized. He took a big risk for my safety, helping his enemy to rescue me because he cared about me enough to want to save my life.

I felt a sting of guilt and shame, remembering all the bad thoughts I'd had of him. Now, I didn't know what to think of him. We weren't friends but we weren't enemies, either. We were simply two people on two opposing sides, who didn't want bad things to happen to the other one. I had no idea what you'd call that unexpected relationship.

I guess that made Keavren my "sort-of friend".

"Sorry," I whispered, when the worst of my crying was over. I sniffled and wished I'd had a box of tissue, in the worst way.

"You needed it," Keavren said, taking a neatly folded beige handkerchief out of his pocket and tucking it into my hand. "Bravery will carry you for only so long."

I nodded to him, sniffling, and used the handkerchief to mop up my face. Something about his words made me believe that he was speaking from experience. For the first time, I found myself wondering if Keavren had some kind of dreadful past.

"Thank you, Keavren. I won't forget what you did for me and I won't ever tell anyone," I promised.

He nodded seriously and said, "It's actually better if you do forget it. It's safer for us both. I only told you what happened because I figured that they would have told you. I just hope that nothing like that will be needed this time. I can't imagine it will," he added with certainty, "Why would we go all that way to have you wash floors?"

"I honestly don't understand why I've been taken," I shrugged. "But I can't even begin to understand Galnar and I definitely don't understand Xandon." Nothing about this made sense. I couldn't figure out why I was no longer a slave and apparently Keavren didn't know, either.

What does this mean?

Keavren looked at me to show he was listening but he didn't express an opinion.

"I know that Xandon's your leader," I stated flatly, hoping that would elicit a reaction.

Although he continued to keep his silence, he gave a small nod of confirmation, which I appreciated because I had just forgiven him and I didn't want to get mad at him for insulting my intelligence. For both our sakes, I decided to drop the big "X" topic for now. Besides, I had more important things to worry about, like my safety aboard this ship.

"I know you can't tell me a lot, Keavren but am I in danger here? I mean, can people hurt me if they want to? Can I still be punished for no reason?"

"You're not working for Captain Galnar as his slave anymore. I think you're just a regular prisoner at the moment. Well, better than a regular one since you have a room."

Woo! Better-than-regular prisoner status!

I almost had to resist the urge to fist-pump at his words. I felt relieved to know that I was indeed a prisoner as Stargrace had said earlier, and not a slave.

"So, I just stay locked in here?"

"I honestly don't know what the plan is, right now," Keavren continued, "but I'm a Fighter. It's Intelligence that comes up with those strategies."

Um, Intelligence? Okay, I'm going to assume he means a faction or something and he didn't just call himself dumb.

"Intelligence? As in, there are Warriors who are part of an Intelligence faction and Warriors who are part of a Fighter faction?"

"Yes."

"And you're part of the Fighter group?"

"Yes."

Finally, things were starting to make more sense.

Yeah, right. Who am I kidding? Nothing about this makes sense! Ah well, at least I now understand why he keeps referring to himself as a "Fighter."

"Um, so are you split up into different groups based on your skills or something like that?"

"Mostly."

I knew he wasn't going out of his way to be cryptic but he was doing a good job of it, regardless.

"Okay, so you're a Fighter," I pressed. "What does that mean, exactly? I'm guessing that all the Warriors can fight, to some degree, so what makes you an expert in this group over someone who would be in Intelligence?"

Keavren tilted his head slightly to the side as he considered how to answer my question.

"I can get big really fast. I mean, I'm normally fit, but for missions, I don't need long to build up a lot of strength. It lets me do a lot and I can fight with my bare hands."

I listened to him and tried to process what he was saying.

"So, what you're saying is that you can build up a lot of muscle faster than a normal person?"

He nodded. "I looked like the other guys before leaving for this mission. I've been working out only since we've been on the ships."

The skeptic in me couldn't resist testing his words. Without thinking, I moved forward, reached out with my hand and touched his bicep, giving it a bit of a squeeze as I had done before, when I first discovered he was super-fit.

He smiled at me in amusement and flexed his muscles.

I gasped. Even though there was a shirt and jacket between my hand and his arm, I could feel that this dude definitely had raging muscles going on! To be honest, I couldn't say for certain that he was a lot bigger than he was before, because it's not like I had previously spent a lot of time squeezing Keavren's muscles, but right now, he was definitely built like Hercules.

"Wow, you're super muscle-y. That's..." words failed me.

"Crisp?" he subbed with a growing smile.

I drew my hand back and looked at him confused. "Crisp?"

"Yes, 'crisp'. It's like 'impressive' and 'good' and..." he paused to think. "I don't know. It's slang for 'very good'."

"Oh! It's like the word 'cool'." I told him with understanding. That "crisp" word was slang I could get on board with.

"Cool?" he queried looking interested.

"Yeah, it means the same thing as 'crisp'."

He looked pleased. He flexed his arm and grinned at me. "Pretty cool, right?"

I had to laugh. The way he did that was far too funny to resist. "Yes," I said.

He smiled warmly at me and brought his arm back down. The tension between us was now gone. We were both feeling more at ease with each other.

"If you're going to stay a while, do you mind if we sit?" I asked.

"Oh yeah, of course."

I was glad that he both agreed and that he was going to stay. I sat on the cot with my dress puffing up all around me. I did my best to shove it out of the way as Keavren took a seat beside me.

This gown, that I had once found so beautiful, had officially lost its charm. All I wanted to do was rip it off. Instead, I decided to distract myself by asking Keavren questions about the Warriors, to see what else I might learn.

"So, do you all have magic powers?"

Keavren looked amused by my question. "We call them skills," he clarified.

"Okay, so do you all have *skills*?"

"Yes."

I nodded. "What is Stargrace's skill? What did she do to me?"

"She's one of the Charmers."

"A Charmer? What's that?"

"She enchants you. It's like you'd do anything just so she'll want you."

Yikes! That's possibly the scariest thing I've heard in a long time.
What made it truly upsetting is that I knew he wasn't kidding. She'd done her charm thing on me and it had worked really well. Though I didn't feel that way toward her now, I would have done anything to make her happy and to stay near her when she had used her *skill* on me. I tried to swallow down the rising anxiety this revelation had caused and I failed.

"What about the man who was in the boat with us?"

"Atrix? Oh, he's the other Charmer."

I tensed at his words and broke out into a cold sweat at the idea of being charmed by that guy. I was glad that it explained why I had a wildly unnatural attraction to him every time I laid eyes on him but it freaked me out to imagine how I might react if he exercised the same control over me that Stargrace had used.

"Megan, are you o-kay?" Keavren asked, no doubt noticing my blanched face and alarmed expression.

"Um, yeah. Uh, Atrix isn't the visiting sort, is he?"

Keavren shook his head. "Probably not. He's busy with other stuff and Aésha's already interested in you. They don't tend to tread on each other's turf."

I nodded, feeling a bit better about that and then realized he'd used the name "Aésha." That had to be Stargrace's name.

"What about Galnar?" There's no way that guy was a Charmer.

"I'm not allowed to talk about Captain Galnar," he responded.

I sighed.

Yeah, I really should have seen that coming.

Keavren always clammed up as soon as I mentioned Galnar or Xandon. Oh well, it's not like it mattered, anyway. I was pretty sure I knew what Galnar's special skill was: colossal sized jerk with a touch of manipulative psychopath.

Better to move on, Megan. Hmm, who else could I ask about?

"Is there anything I can bring you other than the clothes that are coming later?"

Darn! Chance lost. Geeze! How does Galnar somehow manage to ruin everything? Must be another one of his skills...

"Um, maybe a book, again?" I tremendously appreciated the last one he had snuck me when I was confined to my room for hours with nothing to do, when I had been a slave.

He smiled and nodded. "I'll bring you the book you were reading."

"Thanks," I said, feeling a little touched that he had remembered what book he'd lent me and that he'd even brought it with him.

"I'll go get it," he added and stood up.

I'm pretty sure he was taking this opportunity to escape before I asked him something else he didn't want to talk about.

"Okay." I didn't try to stop him.

He opened the door without looking back and shut it behind him, after exiting the room. I heard a click and knew that I'd been locked in. Just to make sure, I got up from the cot, walked to the door, and tried the knob. It was definitely locked.

I decided to examine the small space while I waited for Keavren to return. There was another door, which I assumed lead to a bathroom. I made my way over to it, opened it and, sure enough, there was a small bathroom inside. It consisted of a good-sized sink and a toilet. Beyond being functional, the bathroom was as grey, plain, boring, and stark as the rest of the room. I did notice as I shut the door, that there was a rise in the floor. I'd have to remember that for when I did actually go in there. Otherwise, I'd end up tripping over the ledge to get into the bathroom.

I returned to my cot and took off my gold gloves. My hands had become unbearably sweaty. I dropped the gloves on the cot and was about to take a seat beside them, when I heard the un-clicking of my room door lock. This was followed by a knock.

"It's open," I said jokingly to Keavren.

The door opened and I was surprised to see that it wasn't Keavren standing on the other side. Smiling at me, in all her drop-dead gorgeous glory, was Aésha Stargrace.

This woman wasn't the "Miss Kiss" I had met at the Masque. This was the Warrior. She had changed out of her dark pink gown and was now clad in what I guessed was her Warrior uniform...or, at least her unique version of it.

Similar to the other Warrior uniforms I had seen, she wore black leather. The major difference was that her outfit was a full-body jumpsuit; a one-piece that hugged her form perfectly as if she had been born wearing it. Although it looked like it could be fastened all the way up to her neck, Stargrace opted for a V-neckline that was deep enough to show off a tease of cleavage.

The supple fabric of her suit had a slight sheen in the light. It moved smoothly with her, barely making a sound as she entered the room and shut the door behind her.

The fitted boots she wore weren't of the typical military-style that I had seen, so far, on Qarradune, either. Though polished to perfection and nearly the same shade as her suit, they were lace-less and tall, stopping a couple of inches below her knee. They made it seem like her legs went on forever.

While, at first glance, they looked like clubbing boots, the well-defined treads of their thick rubber soles and their two-to-three inch block heels gave the boots a sturdy and practical edge.

Based on the confident way that she walked in the boots, I had no trouble believing that Stargrace could do just about anything in them; from sprinting across a field to kicking someone's butt.

I stared at her in envy. She appeared both strong and feminine. She was fit, lithe, and elegant. I suddenly understood why her last name was Stargrace. She looked like a superstar and moved with feline grace.

I hate her.

She looked around and raised a brow as if she couldn't believe the disaster she'd walked into. Finally, she locked her gaze on mine. "I've come to rescue you," she purred playfully, her blue eyes glittering with mischief.

Yeah, right.

I arched a brow at her. "Really? From this room, this boat, or this dress?"

"Yes," she responded, smiling like she was the solution to all my problems.

She breezed over to my cot as if she'd done it a hundred times before. She took a medium-sized, black tube-shaped bag – which I hadn't even noticed she'd been carrying – off her shoulder and set it down on the floor. She untied the flap, loosened the drawstring, and began to pull out several items.

To my surprise, the first few items she withdrew from her bag weren't clothing. She extracted a hot-pink blanket that looked ultra-cozy and soft and covered the cot with it. I immediately wanted to wrap myself in it. Next, she took out a matching fuzzy hot-pink throw pillow. Both looked so bright and girly, in contrast to the room's bleak landscape, that I almost giggled.

Stargrace took out a small toiletries bag, also in hot-pink (I was starting to notice a theme) and set that down on the round little table that served as my nightstand.

Then, to my utter relief, she started taking clothing out of the bag and setting these items on the cot. Each one was very basic and everything was black. There were two wide-strapped tank tops, a t-shirt, a pair of pants, and two pairs of socks. Underwear had also been added to the mix, including a few of the boyshort-style panties and sports-bra-style underwear, just like the ones I'd been given to wear pre-Syliza.

Yippee! Bye-bye to the bloomers, shifts, corsets, and the other seventy-five hundred layers I'm wearing.

Black and hot-pink were rapidly becoming two of my new favourite colours.

Done with the bag, Stargrace kicked it out of the way and tossed the long tail of her pristine French braid over her shoulder. Even her chestnut-coloured tresses were flawless; not a hair poked out of place.

"Now, let me get you out of your dress," she grinned, rubbing her hands together.

I raised my brows in surprise. That was the last thing I thought she would say.

"Um, alright. I guess I could use the help and I assume you've had experience with getting in and out of these dresses before." She had been wearing one after all.

She laughed. "Oh, yes," she said confidently and stepped up to me, looking at me like she was going to eat me alive. "Goddess, you're gorgeous, Baby."

I stared at her, dumbfounded. Her words left me feeling both flattered and in a state of shock. She sounded so genuine.

She's not being genuine, Megan, I reminded myself. *Remember what Keavren told you. She's a Charmer. She's just screwing with you.*

She walked around behind me with the intention of undressing me. For a moment, I debated my decision to accept her assistance. Not being able to have my eyes on this woman at all times unnerved me. However, my desire to get out of this increasingly uncomfortable gown won out and I chose not to stop her from helping to rid me of it.

She worked surprisingly quickly, unfastening the dress and methodically dismantling all the layers until I was wearing nothing but my bloomers and shift. I sighed, feeling blessedly free of all the weight.

"We should have done this in a bigger room," Stargrace muttered.

I turned my head to the side and saw that the floor of the room was swimming in layers of my costume. I couldn't help but snort a small laugh at her comment and was even more amused as I watched her kick at the dress until she successfully crammed all the fabric under the cot.

Once she was done, she took a seat on the cot, picked up the fuzzy throw pillow, held it in a loose hug, and looked at me expectantly as if she was waiting for me to put on some strip show.

Um...

"These are for me?" I clarified, indicating the clothes she had brought.

"I'm not showing off my wardrobe," she said. "These are the only pieces of my clothing that would fit you...unless you like eveningwear." Her grin was entirely wicked.

"Thanks," I responded, not taking the bait. I knew that if I tried to get smart or sarcastic with this woman, I'd end up regretting it, likely more than I could imagine. She definitely wasn't Keavren. That said, my mind began to wonder what her closet looked like.

I grabbed the underwear, tank, t-shirt, pants, and a pair of socks and headed into the bathroom to change. I quickly took off my boots, stockings, shift, and bloomers and changed into the new clothes.

Even though Stargrace and I weren't exactly the same size – as she was a couple of inches taller than me, was definitely in better shape than me, and her chest was easily twice the size of mine – her clothes fit pretty well overall.

Once I was dressed, I realized that she never gave me shoes, so I put my boots back on and pulled the pants down over them. I decided to leave my hair in the updo that Desda had created for my costume. It kept my hair out of my face and reminded me of the short time I'd been happy on Qarradune.

I looked down at myself and wondered what Thayn would think if he could see me now. If he got a little squirrely over the idea of seeing my boots at the Masque, he'd probably have a heart attack if he saw me in this getup.

I smiled when I thought of Thayn. I hoped I meant enough to him that he would come for me. I hoped he didn't think that I had run off willingly. He had to know how much I liked him. I felt like it was written all over my face every time we were in the same room.

Of course, he knows, Megan, I assured myself.

I had to believe that he at least cared for me as a friend. I had to stay strong. I needed to get back to the people who I knew weren't liars; the real people, who would help me find a way home.

I shut my eyes and made a promise to myself: somehow, I would find a way back to Thayn and a way back to Irys.

I took a calming breath before opening my eyes and leaving the bathroom. I was hoping that Stargrace would be gone but I knew I wouldn't be that lucky. I was right.

Stargrace was stretched out on the cot, on her side, hugging the pink pillow. I couldn't stop my eyes from travelling up her form.

Oh my gosh! I think I just checked out a chick. What's going on with me? I don't have the hots for Stargrace. I don't even like girls that way!

I shook my head to clear my thoughts and to calm my inner freak-out. I just needed to be cool and keep reminding myself that nothing about that woman, or the way I felt toward, her was real.

I looked away from her and saw that she had folded the rest of the clothing she had brought and had placed it on my nightstand. My gold gloves and the toiletries bag were resting on top of the pile.

"Is the bag for me too?" I asked.

She nodded and I walked over to it, picked it up, and unbuttoned the flap to check out the contents inside. I discovered a toothbrush, toothpaste, soap, a hairbrush, and a jar with a translucent jelly in it.

Fishing out the jar, I held it up to her.

"Is this for my hands?"

"Anything dry," she responded. "It makes your lips more kissable, too," she added, looking at me as if she were daring me to test her theory.

Wow! Okay. This is so not the same sweet experience I had with Thayn when he kindly gave me moisturizer to treat my messed-up hands. Imagine if he had said what she had just said to me...yeah, on second thought, let's not.

"Thanks...Stargrace, right?"

"Aésha."

I nodded. "So, what's the deal, Aésha? Are you being nice to me because you're following orders?" I kept the snark out of my voice. I really did want to know.

"I'm being nice to you because I'm bored and you're hot."

"Um, okay," I said awkwardly, not really knowing what else to say to that response.

There was a knock at the door. At this point, I didn't care who was on the other side, I was just glad that I wouldn't be alone with her anymore.

"Expecting guests?" Aésha grinned at me.

I shrugged. "I guess you're not the only one who is bored."

She laughed and said, "You should have been assigned a bigger room."

I shook my head at Aésha's comment and secretly hoped the knocker wasn't the other Charmer.

"Megan?" Keavren queried from the other side of the door.

Oh, thank goodness!

"You can come in Keavren," I answered, hearing the relief in my voice.

Keavren opened the door and froze when he saw Aésha.

"You're still here?" He didn't mask his surprise.

"No. I left. You're fantasizing again," Aésha teased with a grin.

I couldn't help but crack a smile at her comeback.

Keavren's ears went red but he took her comment like a trooper and simply shook his head in a way that made me believe he was used to her teasing.

"Go play with Atrix. You shouldn't be here so long," he said good-naturedly.

Aésha looked like she was debating staying but then got up and set the pillow down. She looked at me and smiled deeply.

"Goodnight, Baby. I'll be back soon."

I stared back and gave a small nod. I wished she were kidding but I believed her.

"Thank you, for all the stuff, Aésha." I meant that. I was grateful for everything she had brought me.

She blew a kiss at me, licked her lips at Keavren, and exited the room. I watched her leave and didn't turn to look at Keavren until the door was shut. I was happy to see that he looked just as stunned as I did. Aésha was a whirlwind.

He stepped over to me and held out the book that he had gone to retrieve. I took it from him, noticing that he, too, had taken the time to change and was wearing his Warrior uniform. He'd also freshly smoothed out and tied back his previously windblown plummy-brown hair. He was the all-military Keavren I remembered.

"Thanks."

"You're welcome. I'll bring you something good for breakfast tomorrow, unless Aésha gets to it first."

I nodded, really hoping that he'd beat her to it.

"She's, uh, interesting."

Seriously, how do you describe a sexy tornado?

"She's a good brother."

"Not as good as you," I said to him with a half smile.

He smiled back and said, "I'm going to ask Acksil if he knows what happened to your friend. Atrix would never tell me and Aésha was with me most of the time."

My smile broadened at his words.

"Thanks," I said, not needing to force the genuine appreciation into my voice, this time.

"She's probably just fine. We weren't there for her," he assured me.

I didn't know if that was true but I believed that he believed what he was telling me and that counted for something.

"I have to go soon. Will you be alright here all night? I can send Aésha to check on you if you don't want to be alone."

"I'll be alright. I'm all locked in and I feel safer on this side of the door, anyway." I forced myself to sound braver than I felt. I didn't want him to send her back here.

He nodded with understanding.

"I'll see you in the morning."

"See you in the morning, Keavren."

He reached out and gave my shoulder a couple of pats and then left the room, quietly locking the door behind him. I didn't watch him go. It was nice to have the freedom to make this choice without feeling the compulsion to watch his every move, unlike how it was with Aésha.

There's something seriously wrong with those...what did he call them? Oh, yeah: Charmers.

I was too tired to allow my brain to further entertain the thought that these Warriors could possibly have supernatural powers. I could barely swallow the fact that I was on another planet for frig sakes. In spite of everything that had happened in the past few hours, I was exhausted and I just wanted to shut everything out.

Picking up the toiletries bag, I set the book on the nightstand and headed into the bathroom to wash my face, brush my teeth, and apply some moisturizer to my hands. Leaving the bag behind, I went back to the cot, sat down, and took off my boots, before lying down.

I curled on my side and pulled the pink fuzzy blanket up over my body and my head, leaving a small opening near my nose to avoid under-blanket-claustrophobia. I'm not typically a blanket-over-the-head kind of sleeper but I didn't want to shut the light off and it had nothing to do with laziness. I felt like I was seven years old again, scared of what would go bump in the night.

I was afraid of the dark.

Chapter 5

Irys

By the time Sir Fhirell returned with tea, I had managed to recover from my wave of fear and grief and had dried my face with the handkerchief from my pocket.

He knocked before he entered and announced himself in a pleasant tone. "It's just me, Miss Godeleva. I have tea."

"Wonderful. Please join me."

Sir Fhirell entered the cabin and set a covered tray down on his desk, taking a seat across from me.

"I have sent my Skydasher bird ahead of us. She will alert the Knights in Fort Picogeal of our approach and that you will be disembarking there," he informed me. "I have discussed your presence and your wishes with Sir Vorel and we have agreed that you cannot be on this ship when we engage Kavylak. It would not be safe for you."

"I want to be a part of the rescue, Sir Fhirell," I replied sadly as my heart sank. "How am I to help if I am sent ashore while this ship continues onward for Miss Wynters?"

"I understand your struggle, Miss Godeleva. I do," he said, lifting the cover from the tray to reveal a teapot and two cups as well as some toast with some jam. "As much as I would like to ensure that you remain among us as we seek to find Miss Wynters, we cannot think of any way in which you would benefit the mission such that it would justify the increased risk that you would bring to yourself or even to Miss Wynters."

"Please do not send me away, Sir Fhirell. What if I were to remain in here or to hide below deck? I must be onboard to help in some way. I have come so far and I am so close..."

"You will be able to help Miss Wynters once she has been rescued. Hiding on the ship won't help her but it will put you both in danger if it is boarded by Kavylak soldiers, or worse: a Warrior. It won't help anyone if you are captured or injured."

It struck me to a profound degree that he was right and that I couldn't find an argument that would bring any credibility to my wishes.

"What if I dressed as a deck hand? Then they would not view me any differently than the rest of your crew." I suggested, weakly. It was a terrible suggestion. Unlike when I boarded the ship in the darkness, it would have been very difficult for me to try to pass for a member of the ship's crew during daylight hours.

"Miss Godeleva, you are far too pretty to pass for a young man," he replied with a smile as he sipped his tea.

Although a compliment such as that one would typically have caused me to blush, my upset was enough to keep the colour from my face.

"Is there no way at all for me to stay, Sir Fhirell?" I asked. I could hear the deflated tone in my own voice.

"No, Miss Godeleva. But I know that you will be the one to provide Miss Wynters with the comfort and security she will need once she has been safely rescued. Until then, it will be far better for both of you if you trust men and my me to do our jobs. We won't fail you."

It was as though my heart had stopped beating. "I have done it all for nothing," I said sadly. "I have left Lord Godeleva to worry about me. I have risked being a stowaway on this ship and I have delayed your mission, all in my own vain efforts to prove that I am worthy of having been saved by Miss Wynters, in the first place."

"You have not done this for nothing. On the contrary, I think you have made quite a clear point to Lord Godeleva and to the Knights, for that matter. You did what you believed to be good and right. You did the only thing you felt you could in your circumstance. You have shown that you feel a great deal of love in your friendship with Miss Wynters," he spoke genuinely, which I found to be immensely reassuring. "While you may not have chosen the ideal logical path, you selected the one that made the most sense to your heart. That counts for something."

I trusted his words. I couldn't be sure if they were said out of true belief or if they were spoken merely to ease my conscience but, whatever their source, I could feel their encouragement.

"Thank you, Sir Fhirell. You are a wise man."

"Thank you, Miss Godeleva. Soon, you will be met by a Knight from Fort Picogeal named Sir Rral Radone. He is a good and honourable man. I know him well and have every respect for him. He will keep you safe until it is time for you to return with Miss Wynters."

I had never heard the name or any name like it but now was not the time to ask about the Knight's lineage.

"Where will Sir Radone take me?"

"He will take you to the place where he believes you will be the most safe. In all likelihood, it will be the town's command centre for the Knights or to a local house that is secure and out of the way. We are hoping that any engagement we have with Kavylak will be brief and that you won't be required to stay for very long."

"Will you bring me back aboard once you have Miss Wynters?"

"Yes. I intend to personally look after your safety and ensure your return to Lorammel. Sir Varda will take you back on his ship if I am unable to do so or if his men recover Miss Wynters, first. I will be sending him a letter to inform him of your presence here as soon as Mikkhaw returns from Fort Picogeal."

"Will I be reprimanded for what I have done, Sir Fhirell?" I could hear the hesitation in my own question.

"Not by the Knights," he assured me. "I will see to it."

"Thank you, Sir Fhirell."

Sir Fhirell must have seen the sorrow that I was feeling as he seemed to want to continue to comfort me.

"I assure you that you will be very safe with Sir Radone. I'm not sure if you are familiar with the Paladins of Gbat Rher but he had been one of them and joined us shortly after the area became a province of Syliza. He is a very large man."

Although my disappointment over having to disembark had not eased, I felt a spark of interest light inside me when I heard the name of Sir Radone's home province.

"I know very little about the culture of the place but I have, only recently, learned of the incorporation of Gbat Rher into Syliza and of the details involved in changing those borders," I said as tactfully as I could manage.

Sir Fhirell's face became grave, suggesting that he had heard similar stories to the ones that had been shared with me, about the wars in the north.

"Then you know that there has been a bit of nasty business there, for a while," he said, breaking our momentary silence.

"Yes," I agreed, swallowing down the rush of emotion and the urge to begin a rant that would have been entirely unladylike and quite out of place in our current conversation. "Yes. Nasty, indeed," I finally concluded. I felt ashamed from having settled for such an understatement.

"Pardon my curiosity, but how is it that you came to learn about the circumstances in Gbat Rher? I didn't see a single article describing it in the newspapers in Lorammel."

"I had the privilege of speaking with a man from the province, when he visited the city. I have only just finished writing my own article about his story and Lord Godeleva will be submitting it to some of the better newspapers and magazines, upon our return," I explained with a touch of pride in my voice. "Lord Godeleva spoke with the emperor about the treatment that the people are receiving in Gbat Rher and we have been assured that there has been some kind of mistake. Those people are to be treated as proper Sylizans."

I had captured his attention with the topic and it thrilled me. It boded well for the reception that my article about Kolfi Ingmardr would receive. Still, his next statement took me by surprise.

"Soon after our return, I will be leading an expedition to Gbat Rher to provide assistance to the people there," he said, quite seriously.

My heart raced. "That is wonderful news," I said, barely able to cap the sound of my own excitement. Perhaps I had not let Kolfi down. Finally, I had managed to keep my word and follow through when it mattered most to someone. "Is it that the emperor has become genuinely concerned with what Lord Godeleva has told him? Has he sent the Knights to put things right?"

There was a flash of thought before Sir Fhirell's reply. "The emperor faces a great many concerns. I'm certain that the plight of the people of Gbat Rher is one of them. However, my mission is not one that is the result of his orders and our request to travel there was approved only for a limited amount of time."

My brow furrowed upon hearing this. "Whose order was it?"

"After speaking with Sir Radone, I personally looked into the matter and discussed it with Sir Varda," he explained. "Together, we agreed that the Knights should send special assistance. We have managed to accumulate some helpful resources and will be joined by several others who believe in the cause."

"May I ask how it is that Sir Radone became a Knight? Gbat Rher has been a province for only a few cycles. Did he enter into an apprenticeship the moment he received his citizenship?"

"He came to Lorammel nearly two cycles ago to seek both answers and a new purpose. Sir Radone's entire family was lost in the battles that took place in Gbat Rher. He was insulted when he was offered livestock as reparations for his dead family members. I imagine that the man with whom you spoke had a rather similar story as well," he said and I nodded in agreement. Indeed, Kolfi's experience was strikingly similar in its sorrowful details. "When the Paladins were disbanded and when he did not receive the response that he wanted, he made the very honourable choice to complete an apprenticeship that would allow him to make a positive difference in a situation that he found to be deplorable. Under my mentorship, it did not take him long at all to prove himself to the Knights and to be welcomed among us."

Swallowing the lump in my throat, I found myself looking forward to meeting Sir Radone. If I had to step aside from taking part in the effort to rescue Megan, at least I would be spending my time with a man who might be able to further enlighten me with regards to the situation in Gbat Rher. I wished that there was some way to tell Kolfi of Sir Radone's story. Perhaps he, too, would want to wear the green and gold and make a difference for his home province as Sir Ingmardr.

"Were the Paladins a type of knighthood in Gbat Rher?" I asked, realizing that I'd heard the word more than once but I did not know to what it referred.

"They are the men from the province who are now often simply called the "giants", though that does not do justice to what they truly are. Indeed, these are very large men but they are raised from birth to base their entire purpose on upholding a strict system of honour and of protecting the land and its people. It is not merely a title. It is a way of existence for them."

This was fascinating. I took in every word as though Sir Fhirell were reading from one of the more enthralling texts that Lord Imery would have asked me to study as a part of our research.

"It was very good of you to see the potential in Sir Radone," I said softly, still partially lost in the wonder of all that I was learning. "I am certain that I will be safe with a Knight whom you had apprenticed."

"You will be," he agreed. "He will meet you where you will be brought ashore and then he will take you into Fort Picogeal. I believe it will be safer for you to go ashore this way than to try to do so at the town, itself, where Kavylak may already be watching and where there will already be battle preparations underway."

"Will it be soon?"

As he nodded, there was a knock at the door. "Enter," he said to the knocker.

Sir Vorel stepped in with a gorgeous Skydasher bird perched proudly on his gloved hand.

"Mikkhaw has returned," he told Sir Fhirell, though I barely heard his words as I was fixated on Mikkhaw's gorgeous form.

I had never seen a Skydasher bird at such a close proximity. She was a large bird of prey with long, decorative tail feathers. Each of those slim plumes ended in a teardrop shape. Her head was the colour of storm clouds and as her feathering progressed down her body, it graduated into the sky blue shade of a warm, sunny day. Her hooked beak, her feet, and the curved talons at the end of each digit were all a cool slate grey. When her head turned, she looked at me with pale blue eyes that appeared to have been composed of skillfully polished crystal. It wasn't until she blinked that I could break away from my own fixation with her and shift my attention to the Knights, once more.

Sir Fhirell had slipped his hand into a thick glove and Mikkhaw was passed from one Knight to the other. Sir Fhirell gave the Skydasher's chest a gentle stroke with his free hand and he nodded to Sir Vorel.

"Thank you," he said as he extracted a note from a small capped tube attached to Mikkhaw's leg. Giving the note a quick glance, he added, "Miss Godeleva will be ready to leave within the hour."

"I will," I said, hoping to sound agreeable.

Sir Vorel nodded to me and then to Sir Fhirell, taking Mikkhaw onto his hand again before exiting the cabin.

I looked down at my toast. How unappealing it suddenly looked but at the same time I was afraid that there might not be another meal offered for a while. Quietly, I withdrew a clean handkerchief from my bag and wrapped the toast within it. Saved toast wouldn't taste very good but at least it would be something. Perhaps it would stop me from becoming even more of a burden to everyone who was now tasked with my safety. I tucked the toast in among my belongings in my bag.

"If there is anything you think you will need, please only tell Sir Radone. He will make sure that you are comfortable for as long as you must stay in his town," Sir Fhirell said, breaking the silence.

"I'm certain that I won't need anything, Sir Fhirell. I want only for this to be over. I've been a fool. I hope that the Warriors will relinquish Miss Wynters peacefully," I confessed.

"I hope for the same, Miss Godeleva. In the meantime, try not to be too hard on yourself. It has been my experience that self-deprecation does little to bring about positive outcomes. You're a strong woman. Use your strength to prepare yourself to support Miss Wynters upon your return home with her." He smiled to me with genuine warmth. "It took courage to do what you did. That courage has brought you this far and it will bring you home again, too."

"Thank you," I said, appreciating his kind words. "I will do my best. I will comfort myself with the thought that I will be able to soothe Miss Wynters on our way home, regardless of whether or not I should have been on this ship in the first place."

Sir Fhirell smiled handsomely and I felt a rush of heat prickling my cheeks. When had he become so fetching? Had I truly been sitting in front of him for this entire time without having noticed?

"I'm needed on deck now but when you are finished here, please do come out. That way, you won't need to be called when it is time for you to head ashore."

"I won't be long," I confirmed. There wasn't much that I would need to do before heading out. There was still a part of me that wanted to try to hide so that they could not send me away but I was afraid that this would only cause a greater delay to Megan's rescue. I had already harmed the mission enough.

Nodding to me, he swept his plumed hat off his desk and crossed the space to the door. As he exited, he set the hat upon his head in one swift motion.

Once he was no longer there, the room felt suddenly empty. Had I ever been so alone? Without anyone at all? I was heading away from everyone I knew and now I was no longer moving toward the one whose rescue was of the utmost importance to me. Had I lost everything?

I couldn't allow my mind to answer such questions. If I did, I was certain that the weight of them would risk sinking the ship. Rising from my chair, I used the tiny water closet and washed my hands and face to try to refresh my body in the hopes that my spirits might follow the example.

Great Goddess, please don't forget about me. Give me the strength and the wisdom to make the right choices. Please do not think that I am abandoning my promise to you. I am not giving up on finding Megan. I am trying to keep out of the way of her rescue.

Am I making the right choice, Great Goddess? I feel that I am. If I am taking the wrong path, please direct me. Send me a sign that I have strayed from your intentions for me. Tell me what you want from me, I beg of you.

Taking the handle of my bag into my fingers, I stepped out onto the top deck of the ship. The sun brought a bright yellow light onto the gleaming planks across which some sailors were quickly moving about while others appeared to be fixed in their places to complete their various tasks.

A glance upward showed me a webbing of ropes as intricate as if it had been made by a masterful spider. Only, in this case, there were many spiders as the riggers climbed. They looked as natural in their web as any other man looked while walking on solid ground.

Beyond the rail on the starboard side, I could see the land alongside which we were travelling. Ahead and in the distance, the port city was already becoming visible.

Fort Picogeal was a small city that sprawled neatly along a segment of the coastline and was surrounded by dense green forest on all sides that didn't meet the sea. On the side closest to the ship, a river carved its way between the trees and out into the ocean. This created a tidy border for the city and was likely the fort's main source of fresh water.

Even from here, I could see the orderly rows of roads that ran parallel and perpendicular to the coastline. It appeared that the area closest to the water was reserved for military and trade buildings, while the townhomes and blocks of houses spread out further inland.

I would need to leave quite promptly. At this realization, it became clear to me that all the motion I was seeing among the crew was in preparation for my disembarking.

Sir Vorel was the first familiar sight. He was calling out orders to various crewmembers, who scrambled about to complete their assigned tasks.

Glancing up and behind me at the helm, I spotted Sir Fhirell, who appeared to be chatting with the helmsman. He was holding Mikkhaw, stroking her chest in an absent way. Mikkhaw's attention moved directly to me and I felt nearly intimidated by her. I had an inclination to curtsy to her, which I promptly ignored.

Sir Fhirell seemed to recognize that his Skydasher bird had spotted something and he followed her gaze to me, giving me a deep nod and his handsome smile. I could feel the pink rushing into my cheeks again but I nodded in return, resting a hand on the rail to help keep my balance while staying out of the way.

"Are you ready, Miss Godeleva?" asked a voice from behind me, which caused me to jump. I hadn't realized how deeply I had been focused on Sir Fhirell.

"Yes, Sir Vorel," I said. The obedience had returned to my voice. It was as though the courage that had brought me onto the ship was slipping away into the smooth waters behind us. How would I ever live down this humiliation?

"Good," he said simply. "The boat will be ready, shortly. You will need to be lowered down to it. If you feel nervous, I recommend simply looking straight ahead and trying to distract your mind with poetry or prayer." His voice was calm but to-the-point.

"I will. Thank you for your advice, Sir Vorel," I said appreciatively, but I could feel the cold fingers of fear crawling across my skin at the thought of being lowered from the ship into a boat that was waiting below. I had believed that I would be lowered within a boat, not sent down to meet one that was already in the water.

"Once you are seated in the boat, Sir Radone will row you to the shore. You needn't do anything at all, after that point. Simply follow Sir Radone's instructions until we return for you." He paused before asking, "Do you have any questions before you leave?"

I shook my head. "I'd like to say only that I am very sorry. This was not how I had imagined this would happen."

"What's done is done," he said with a light nod. "We can only move forward."

"You're right," I agreed. "And I will be ready to move forward as soon as the boat arrives. Thank you, Sir Vorel."

He nodded again and gestured to a boat that was being rowed toward us by a giant of a man. Even from a distance, it was easy to see that he was much taller than a typical man and was far greater in bulk. If there was any bravery left in me, I would need it soon; not so that I could be courageous while I was lowered from the deck of the ship to the boat, but rather so that I could face Sir Radone who would be waiting below.

Peeking up at Sir Fhirell, I saw that he was looking directly back at me. I wished I could speak with him again before leaving. I hadn't realized that we wouldn't be talking again before I was to go. I raised my hand and gave him a small wave. It warmed me, somewhat, when he returned the gesture with an added smile.

By the time I had turned away from our shared moment, I had readied myself to be harnessed and roped to the ship so that I could be lowered by a winch.

Goddess, give me strength...

Chapter 6

Megan

Something brushed my face. I reached up a hand to swat it away.

"...what are you doing, Cole?" I muttered moodily. My sense of humour hadn't woken up yet and I didn't have the patience for his teasing.

He didn't respond, at first, and I felt confident he'd gotten the message until there was a small snuffling sound that was followed by sniffing at my face and cheek.

What the frig? Why is he acting like a dog?

I huffed and opened my eyes, not amused and ready to ream him out; but it wasn't Cole. A wolf was millimetres away from my face, staring at me.

I shrieked and scrambled up into a sitting position, in a lame attempt to try to put some distance between myself and the wolf.

I stared in wide-eyed fear at the animal, suddenly realizing where I was and how much trouble I was in. My heart drummed loudly in my ears and I held my breath waiting for the wolf to make its move and shred me to bits.

It didn't attack. It just stood next to the cot and looked back at me with its dark brown eyes.

I'd had barely any experience with dogs and I knew next to nothing about wolves but, even though I couldn't explain why, I didn't feel that the wolf had any sinister intentions toward me. In fact, based on its overall expression, I could have sworn that if it could talk, it would have cheerfully said, "Hi, Megan!"

Oh man, please don't tell me this is a werewolf Warrior.

I stared at it as if willing it to transform into a person. Nothing happened. The wolf didn't morph into a Warrior. It just continued to stare at me. It panted a few times but then shut its mouth. When it did, the end of its lip caught on its tooth, giving it an almost comical expression. It looked more like a big-old dopey family dog than the fierce creature you'd fear running into in the woods.

After a few moments, when I felt I could take my eyes off the animal, I quickly scanned the room to see if there was anyone else in there with us.

Nope. It was just me and the big bad wolf. The door wasn't even open.

Is this someone's idea of a practical joke or does fate have one twisted sense of humour? Great. Looks like I've gone from being Cinderella to Little Red Riding Hood. Just when I thought I'd found my Prince Charming, the big bad wolf shows up.

"Uh, hi," I said to the wolf. I felt desperate to break the awkward silence.

It looked at me, panted some more, then stepped forward. It climbed onto the cot and lay down right next to me, resting its head near my lap. I tensed, afraid to move a muscle. I was sure that if I blinked, it would eat me.

Holding my breath, I waited for the worst to happen. Nothing did. I slowly exhaled and observed the wolf, who looked pretty content lying beside me. Its fur was a blend of medium, light, and white grey. I was seized by a sudden desire to touch it.

Cautiously, I reached out my hand to tentatively pet the wolf but jumped and immediately withdrew my hand when someone knocked at the door. The animal, on the other hand, didn't seem to care.

"Miss Megan Wynters, may I come in?"

I didn't recognize the voice of the man who spoke but I figured if I told him to "go away," he wouldn't listen.

Might as well keep things civil. With any luck the wolf would protect me.

"Yes." I said.

The door opened and a man dressed in a Warrior uniform entered. He appeared to be a young man around the same age as Keavren and the rest of the Warriors I'd seen. However, what stood out to me about this particular Warrior, was that his long smooth black hair had a small braid woven into it on one side. It was fastened with a red and black feather. His skin was a rich tan colour and his eyes were dark brown. He reminded me of the First Nations: the various aboriginal peoples in Canada who are neither Inuit nor Métis.

He had a deep scar on his face. It ran diagonally from his forehead through his left eyebrow, over the bridge of his nose, and finally stopped on his opposite cheek.

Yikes! I don't want to know how he got that or who might have given it to him. He was lucky he still had his eye! Speaking of which, his eyes look oddly familiar to me. Have I seen him before? Maybe at the Masque?

"Good morning," he greeted me with a warm smile, drawing me out of my thoughts.

I nodded to him in response.

He shifted his gaze from me to the wolf lying beside me and looked at it, unimpressed.

"I see he did a wonderful job of waking you up and telling you to get ready." The Warrior shook his head in playful disgust at the creature.

I looked at the man in surprise. "This is your wolf?"

"One of them," he nodded.

"One of...you have more than one wolf?"

He nodded again and looked back over his shoulder. I looked where he was watching and saw two grey wolves that looked similar to the one lying next to me, tearing down the hall. My eyes widened in shock and my mouth dropped open when a moment later a third grey wolf chased after the first two.

What the...? How are there four wolves on this ship! Am I dreaming or have I officially gone nuts again?

As if to assure me I wasn't dreaming or losing my mind, the wolf beside me lifted his head and rested it in my lap. The weight of his head and the heat coming from him – through the blanket, my pants, and into my body – told me this was indeed real.

I worked up my nerve and stroked the wolf's head with my hand. He didn't seem to mind.

"What's his name?" I finally asked the Warrior, who had been decent enough not to laugh or mock me, although I had no doubt my shock had amused him.

"Amarogq," he said. "But I call him Two, since they're all called Amarogq," he chuckled.

Um, that's a cool name and all but either this guy lacks imagination or I'm guessing there's a logical reason for his choice.

"Why would you call them all Amarogq?"

"I guess I'm not a very creative guy," he laughed.

I had to smile. This guy definitely had a sense of humour.

"I didn't name them," he continued, "They did."

"Oh, I get it," I said, laughing at his silliness, "It's not you who isn't creative, it's that the wolves aren't very original when it comes to picking names." I looked down at Two and stroked his ear. The fur was thick and soft. He looked content with my attention.

The Warrior laughed at my response and said, "Well, Two here was supposed to tell you to get up and pack anything you want to keep. We're going ashore."

"Ashore? So soon? Are we in Kavylak, already?"

The Warrior shook his head. "We're passing a city that is supposed to have a number of vessels docked. There are a lot of them gone and there are a number of them readying to leave. Unless there is a new trend in night time fishing, someone's alerted them that we're on our way. We don't plan to be on the ship when they catch up to it."

My heart leapt a bit at his words but I was careful not to let any of the hope that I felt show on my face.

Thayn could be on his way to find me!

Two lifted his head from my lap and licked my cheek. I don't know what shocked me more: the fact that the wolf did that or the fact that he didn't leave any slobber behind. My cheek was totally dry.

Weird. Seriously, what's the deal with this guy and his dry pack of wolves?

I decided not to ask this guy what his "skill" was. I had a funny feeling I didn't want to know.

Instead, I said, "I'll get my stuff together."

I moved away from Two and got off the cot. He made a kind of "marrumph" noise before he, too, hopped off the cot and walked over to the Warrior, who was standing in the doorway.

"Do you need a minute?"

I shook my head and went into turbo-mode. Grabbing up the duffle-style bag that Aésha had left behind, I quickly filled it with the clothes she'd brought me and the toiletries bag. I also jammed the fuzzy pink blanket and pillow in it. There was no way I was leaving those behind! Keavren's book was the last thing I added to the bag before I closed it.

I flopped down on the cot and pulled my boots on. Standing up, I realized I didn't have a jacket or a sweater to put on but I wasn't going to let that bother me. I'd have to make do with my tank and t-shirt. I wasn't going to let my bed-head bother me, either. My captors would just have to deal with my braid, which was likely in a fine state of decomposition. I couldn't care less what they thought of my appearance. I slung the bag over my back and looked at the Warrior. "I'm ready."

He nodded but said, "You can leave your bag, someone will get it for you."

Wow. Five-star service. Who would have thought?

I didn't ask questions and slipped the bag off my shoulder, set it on the bed, and walked to the door to leave.

He turned his body slightly to the side to step out of the way and I noticed that he had an axe secured to his back.

"You don't need me to cuff you, do you? I hate doing that."

I looked at him like he was nuts and said flatly, "You're wearing an axe, you've got a pack of wolves for friends." I nodded to Two, who remained by his side, "and you've probably got some special 'skill'. I think that's all the handcuffs I need, thanks."

A crooked smile formed on his face and grew into a small grin at my words.

"Pretty crisp, huh?" he chuckled.

"Quite," I retorted.

He stepped out into the hall and waited, indicating that I was to walk ahead of him. Two, on the other hand, scampered off ahead.

I stepped out and started to walk forward down the narrow hall in the direction the Warrior wasn't blocking. I had no delusions of escaping. I wanted off this ship, so I wasn't about to do something stupid.

"What's your name?" I asked as we walked, realizing he'd never introduced himself and I'd never thought to ask until now.

"Amarogq."

I couldn't see his face but I imagined there was a big smile on it.

"You've got to be kidding."

"Nope. Amarogq Ioq'wa."

"Well, um, I see where your wolves got the inspiration for their names." Because, what else was I supposed to say there?

"They all want to be me," he teased.

I snorted at his response.

When I could see the steep steps that would take us to the top deck, I climbed them, grateful not to be wearing a gigantic dress.

Oh no! My dress!

I had forgotten all about it! It was still under the cot where Aésha had "graciously" shoved it. Oh, well. It's not like I could have packed it anyway and I had bigger things to worry about right now, than leaving a pretty gown behind. Maybe whoever brought my bag for me would find the dress.

When I reached the top deck, I discovered that the sun was close to rising but wasn't quite ready to make an appearance. Though the sky was getting lighter, promising that dawn would arrive soon, it was still dark enough that the ship had to be illuminated by other sources of light.

Soldiers were quickly moving about, performing various tasks. I found it hard to focus in the sea of strangers who were darting all around me. I didn't know where I was supposed to go.

Amarogq (the Warrior) stood beside me, gently took hold of my arm and walked forward. I went with him, letting him guide me to wherever we were supposed to go. I didn't see his wolves anywhere. Come to think of it, where had they gone? How did they climb up to the top deck?

We had reached the ship's rail and I was about to ask Amarogq about his wolves but my curiosity was momentarily smothered at the sight of Galnar. There was no mistaking his stark white hair. He was sitting in a boat that was being lowered from the ship. He wasn't alone. There were two other Warriors in the boat with him, whom I didn't recognize. I couldn't make out much about them, other than that they were both male. One had exceptionally long hair that appeared to be slate grey in colour and the other had what looked like dark blue hair. There wasn't enough light to really tell for certain.

I turned my attention to Amarogq when he released my arm. He nodded toward a waiting boat and offered his hand to help me in, indicating that I would be getting on board. The boat already contained other passengers who, were getting settled. I recognized every one of them: Keavren, his best friend, Acksil, and Aésha.

I took Amarogq's offered assistance and climbed in, feeling nervous and wondering where I should sit.

"Right here, Baby."

I looked at Aésha and saw her smiling at me and patting a space next to her in the belly of the boat. I didn't need to be told twice. Not wanting to be sucked into one of her spells, I did my best to ignore her and watched Amarogq join us in the boat. He remained standing.

"Hi Megan," Keavren greeted me with a smile.

"Hi," I replied. I looked at him but was unable to force a smile back. I was too tense.

I shifted my gaze to Acksil, who was sitting next to Keavren. Acksil had an arm casually draped over a drawn-up knee. He looked perfectly at ease and confident. He was the picture of cool.

I realized that I was truly observing him for the first time as our initial encounter was brief. I had been too busy at that time, worrying about how to free Irys, to care about what he looked like.

Like the others, he was young and attractive, probably the same age as Keavren. Acksil's bright hazel eyes were a striking contrast to his dark smooth skin. His hair was cleanly twisted in dreadlocks that hung loose, just past his shoulders.

I wonder what he can do?

When he met my gaze, he gave me a crooked smile that was somewhere between playful and friendly and then turned to Keavren and wiggled his brows. Keavren punched him in the arm and Acksil laughed.

Um? What's that about?

I didn't have time to ponder the thought. Amarogq Two (the wolf) jumped into the boat, startling me.

Where the heck did he come from?

"No," Aésha said to the wolf, possessively bringing her arm around me as if the wolf was going to come between us somehow.

Amarogq (the Warrior) sighed dramatically and the wolf disappeared.

"Whoa!" I exclaimed, jumping. "What the hell just happened? Where did the wolf go?" I blinked rapidly and looked all around the boat expecting to find the animal somewhere.

"He'll meet us on the land," Amarogq responded casually, "Aésha doesn't want to get spirit-fur on her clothing," he chuckled as if nothing out of the ordinary had just happened; as if a wolf hadn't just suddenly vanished right in front of our eyes!

I glared at Amarogq like he was totally insane. A wolf had disappeared into thin air and apparently nobody but me found that crazy. How could these people be so nonchalant about a disappearing wolf? And why had he referred to its fur as "spirit-fur?" Was the wolf a ghost?

Don't be ridiculous, Megan. Ghosts aren't real. The wolf isn't a ghost. You touched the wolf. You petted its fur. You felt the weight of its head in your lap. You felt the warmth of its body. Ghosts aren't corporeal, that wolf was! Yes, it may have vanished like a ghost but there has to be some sort of logical, scientific explanation or maybe Amarogq is just really good at magic tricks...yeah, that's got to be it. He's a magician.

It was either that or I was possibly going mad.

Keavren stood and he and Amarogq worked on lowering the boat toward the water. When the boat met with the sea, it lurched. Everyone adjusted how they were sitting and Keavren and Amarogq began to row the boat toward land.

I moved up to a bench with Aésha, who took the opportunity to snuggle closer to me.

Oh, goodie.

"We're going to find a place to hide until the action dies down," Aésha quietly told me. "Then we'll find ourselves some horses. Do you ride, Baby?"

I couldn't help but notice that it sounded like she got great enjoyment out of asking me that question.

"No," I said to her. I'd never ridden a horse in my life.

"You can ride with me. That way, you can hold onto me for hours. It'll make it a good day," she grinned at me.

Boy, was I suddenly sorry I hadn't taken riding lessons instead of those three years I spent failing piano class.

"Thanks," was my meek reply. I didn't know if she was kidding but I wasn't about to reject her offer at the moment. However, if the time came that I did have to ride with them, I promised myself I'd somehow find a way to ride with Keavren.

I looked away from Aésha, not trusting what would happen if I let my gaze linger on her for too long, and focused my attention on the approaching city. It was definitely alive, with ships moving out of the docks. I had to agree with Amarogq's earlier statement that either there was a new night time fishing trend or something was up. Personally, I believed the latter. I mean, come now, who in their right mind would choose to go fishing at this hour, when they could be sleeping?

Our boat was heading away from the activity at the docks to a quieter area. It wasn't long until we reached the shore. Keavren, Amarogq, and Acksil got out of the boat and pulled it onto the pebbly beach. Once it was secure on land, Aésha stood and stepped out of the boat and I followed her, noticing for the first time that a long sheathed sword, attached to a belt around her waist, hung from her hip.

Once we were out, the guys picked up the boat and hid it behind some bushes. I debated making a break for it and screaming for help at the top of my lungs but decided to hold off on that plan. It was dark, I had no idea where I was, and I was fairly certain the magician and his disappearing wolves, the Charmer, the bodybuilder, and whatever the heck Acksil was, would catch me before I took two steps.

I didn't want to risk being mind-tricked or controlled in some other way or being shredded by wolves. I wanted a clear head and to learn my surroundings so that when another opportunity to escape came my way, I'd have a greater chance of actually getting away.

Keavren stepped up to me and whispered, "We'll need to split up."

I nodded to Keavren and felt Aésha bring her arm around me, walking me forward. I went with them, looking around as much as I could, in the poor light, to try to get an idea of where I was.

Amarogq and Acksil walked ahead of us. Currently, we were all heading in the same direction but it was obvious that those two had their own agenda, so I guessed that's what Keavren had meant about splitting up.

I walked with Keavren and Aésha until we reached the first house. We stopped in front of it. No lights were on. If there was anyone inside, they were sleeping. Keavren checked it out. He looked in windows and crept around the building, returning shortly afterward and nodding to Aésha, who nodded back. I had no idea what that meant, but I had a feeling I was about to find out.

Chapter 7

Irys

Sir Rral Radone was every bit the giant that he had appeared to be upon his approach. Yet, as I watched the massive Knight as he propelled us toward the shore, I found myself feeling awestruck at the grace of his movements. Despite his size, he was very well proportioned and moved with deliberate care.

As he was seated, I was unable to tell exactly how tall Sir Radone must have been, but I would have guessed that he was easily half a head taller than even the tallest Knight I'd seen aboard the ship. That said, much of his large size was made up of the utter bulk of his muscular body, which was twice as broad as my own. His brown hair was long and shaggy, it was tied back for some semblance of neatness. His beard was neither long nor short and of a similar texture to his hair. It had the look of having been well kept and carefully combed as a beard with such a texture could easily have appeared unruly.

The oars cleaved powerfully through the water like a hot knife through fresh butter. The strength of the man, merely because of his sheer size, was certainly impressive. When we arrived upon the shore, he lifted me out of the boat with the ease of carrying a small child. It had been that way when I was lowered from the ship as well. He had simply braced his feet in the bottom of the boat, reached up, and easily plucked me from the rope-seat that was used to lower me to him.

He remained silent, though he did so in a way that made it clear that if I wished to speak, I could. As much as I tried to think of an appropriate topic of conversation, I could find none. It occurred to me that I might tell Sir Radone about my encounter with Kolfi

Ingmardr and about the article I had written but I couldn't find the words. While it would have been exciting to discuss Kolfi's culture with a man who was once a part of it, there remained the unavoidable topic of the takeover of Gbat Rher.

The last thing I wanted to do was to remind Sir Radone of the profound losses that he must have suffered, particularly when I was already causing him considerable inconvenience.

Great Goddess, thank you for sending me such a powerful Knight to take care of me while Megan is being rescued. Thank you for giving me the opportunity to speak with one of Kolfi's people. Please grant me the cleverness to know what to say to this man. I do not wish to lose this chance that you have given me.

As I was not keen to walk the distance to the city, I was pleased to see that two horses were tied and waiting for us nearby. When he helped me up into my saddle, I reached down and held his hand for a moment.

"Thank you, Sir Radone," I said to him, looking into his eyes. "You are a good man to help me."

Quietly, he nodded to me, before speaking in accented Sylizan. "It is my honour to help you, Miss Godeleva. You will be safe with me."

"I haven't any doubt," I replied, releasing his hand.

Nodding again, he stepped up to his own horse and mounted. We rode the rest of the way to the city in silence. Sometimes, the most meaningful messages are shared through the fewest words.

* * * * *

The city was alive in a way that only an impending threat could explain. Everyone moved with purpose and there was no effort made for greetings or pleasantries.

Civilians had brought in any personal items that had decorated their properties and their windows were heavily shuttered. I imagined that many doors were barred from the inside as well.

As we drew closer to the military buildings, the action was even heavier. Orders were being barked and few of those orders were carried out at a pace any slower than a run.

A stable boy barely spoke a word to me when he helped me down from my horse so that he could care for the animals. The expression on his face made it clear that we were an interruption from the tasks that he felt were more important.

"Remain close to me, Miss Godeleva," Sir Radone said, startling me out of my observations of the place. He had not spoken harshly but there was a great deal to see. "That way, you will not become lost in all the activity."

"I will," I agreed and stepped closer to him. "You are the second man from Gbat that I have met, recently. I have every respect for the culture that raised you, Sir Radone." I blurted out the words before I could think them through. As I heard them repeat in my mind, I knew they sounded foolish without any context or segue but I simply could not risk losing the opportunity to speak to him of his homeland.

He looked at me curiously and offered his arm to me. I took it and walked with him.

"I can't imagine the circumstances that brought you to meet another Gbat man, particularly as I am told that you are from Lorammel," he spoke in his deep bass voice. "Was he a Paladin?"

"No. He was a young man. Perhaps slightly younger than me. He was a large man but not in the way that you are."

"Perhaps he is not yet fully grown."

"Perhaps," I agreed. "Regardless, he was very kind to me and granted me the opportunity to speak to him of Gbat Rher and the experience of the region as it became a province. I have written an article about it that will soon be published in a newspaper or a magazine. It will give the nobility the chance to know what has truly happened."

Sir Radone nodded. "It sounds as though it was a good talk."

I smiled. "It was a very good talk."

"We have some time to spend together. It would be an honour if you would share your story with me."

"I'd like that. Thank you, Sir Radone. Perhaps, if you have anything to add, I might write a follow-up article, should the first one prove popular enough to warrant one. I have little doubt that it will."

He nodded and gave me a look of respect. It was something that was more important to me than I had realized. That single acknowledgement of his approval was enough to raise my spirits nearly as far as they had fallen when I was told that I would not be aboard the ship for Megan's rescue.

Thank you, Great Goddess. You always have a reason for everything. I understand this one, now. You are infinitely knowing.

We stepped up to a brick building and Sir Radone slid his key into the lock in the door.

"This is my home. I will make us some tea so that we can talk," he said as he swung the door open into the house.

To my absolute astonishment, I found myself face-to-face with Megan...and at least one Warrior.

"Megan!" I cried out, but before I could do or say anything else, Sir Radone had thrust me behind him and braced himself to fight.

Chapter 8

Megan

Aésha released me just as Keavren came to stand beside me, and she walked confidently up to the front door of the house.

Oh my gosh! Is she really going to knock on the door and charm the person who answers?

She didn't knock. Instead, she bent toward the door knob and, a few moments later, she opened it as if she had the key.

Okay, I was wrong. She's not going to knock, she's just going to pick the lock and break into someone's home.

Aésha entered the house, and I felt the slight pressure of Keavren's hand at the small of my back, encouraging me to walk forward. I did and entered the house with him.

All of this felt so wrong. Although I knew there wasn't really anything I could do about this situation, except put my safety at massive risk, I couldn't help but feel like a bit of a criminal for going along with them. I silently apologized to the homeowner for invading their private space. At the same time, for their sake, I desperately hoped that they weren't home.

Keavren and Aésha wasted no time and shut all the doors inside. When they were finished, Keavren stood near me. It was the first time I had noticed that he had a small bag on his back. He wore the strap of the bag diagonally across his body. I wondered what he had in there.

A small sound drew me out of my thoughts. Aésha was moving around in what I assumed was the kitchen. I couldn't believe it! She was snooping, and I saw her take a few things. I couldn't get over her audacity. I really didn't like her.

"How long do we have to stay here?" I whispered to Keavren, not hiding my unease.

"Until things seem to calm down. Probably when the sun is fully up. Once they think they have our ship surrounded, we'll be able to move about more freely," Keavren answered.

I nodded to him and secretly crossed my fingers behind my back, silently hoping that Thayn was already here, that he would find me, and that he would tell me that Irys was alright.

Keavren turned his attention away from me and looked out the windows that faced the side of the house. Aésha stood close to the front door and was busy organizing her new loot in her bag.

Unable to stand still any longer, I moved slowly throughout the home. I was careful not to walk too quickly. I didn't want them to think I was attempting to get away. That being said, I was definitely keeping my eyes open for some kind of window or back door that would offer me a potential chance for escape.

As luck would have it, there was a back door. Maybe if I moved fast enough I'd be able to make my escape through there. I glanced back to see what the Warriors were doing. Keavren was still looking out the window. Aésha, on the other hand, was strolling toward me and was smiling as if she knew exactly what I was up to.

I gave her a light smile back, feigning innocence. She grinned in response, walking past me to the back door, and stood in front of it.

Darn her! I should have…

I didn't have time to finish my self-scolding. The back door suddenly burst open, slamming hard into Aésha. The force of it knocked her forward, and she landed hard on the floor.

I stared, gaping at the man in the doorway, who had swung the door open. One glimpse at the dark green doublet he wore told me that he was a Knight of Freyss, but with his towering height and massive build he looked more like a giant than a man.

"Megan!" a familiar female voice shouted.

It was then that I noticed that the giant Knight wasn't alone. A young woman was with him.

It was Irys.

She was alive.

My heart leapt.

"Irys!" I cried, running toward her and the giant.

Before she could respond, the Knight quickly pulled her backward and behind him with a surprisingly gentle grace that I would never associate with a man of his appearance.

"Irys! No!" I screamed, when I could no longer see her.

The Knight reached out and took a firm hold of me, while at the same time turning his body to the side to shield me from something I didn't see. Immediately, I heard the sound of a dull thud and realized that the he had sheltered me from a blow he had just received. I winced. I had completely forgotten about Keavren.

The Knight pushed me forward and out of harm's way. I stumbled ahead but didn't fall. I turned my head frantically, looking from one side to the next, in a desperate search for Irys, but I didn't see her.

I caught sight of the Knight fighting Keavren. I'd never seen two people fight like that before. Though Keavren was much smaller in stature than his opponent, he fought expertly, delivering many fast blows and blocking more than he was receiving. The two men fought so skilfully that I half felt like I was watching a coordinated fight scene for a movie shoot.

The Knight managed to give Keavren a powerful shove with his foot, directly to Keavren's gut. Keavren grunted from the blow and stumbled backward, losing his footing.

Before he hit the ground, I had snapped back to my senses and was already running away from the home, instantly wishing I wasn't wearing boots with heels. I did my best to keep my eyes peeled for Irys as I passed house upon house, but my fear grew when I heard heavy footsteps behind me, gaining on me. I tried to run faster, but a large arm grabbed me around my waist, lifting me from the wooden sidewalk. It was the Knight.

"Come with me," he said in a deep Sylizan-accented voice.

He didn't wait for me to respond. He kept running, practically lifting me off the ground as he pulled me along with him.

"Miss Godeleva!" he called.

"Irys!" I shouted, glad that neither one of us had any intention of leaving Irys behind.

There was no response.

Where could she have gone?

"I-*whoa!*"

Without warning, the Knight fully swept me up into his arms like I was some damsel in distress, cutting off my second call to Irys. He took off like a shot, running full tilt.

I put my arms around his neck, holding on tightly. When I did, I looked over his shoulder and saw why he had bolted. Keavren was in pursuit.

The Knight ran from the line of homes and down several deserted streets. He cut through various empty alleyways and effectively managed to lose Keavren by clearly having the knowledge of a man who knew the lay of the land. He must have lived there.

We left the city and headed into the woods. He ran through the trees for a little while longer before he finally slowed to a walk, panting from exertion.

He stopped and gently set me down on the ground.

"Are you alright?" he whispered.

I released my choke-hold on his neck and nodded, even though it was a lie. I wasn't alright. I was terrified.

In a shaking voice I answered, "Yes. I'm alright but, please, we've got to go back for Irys. They could have her." My whispered plea came out like a panicked squeak.

"Yes," he agreed calmly, "Those were Warriors. They have cleared the streets and there is no one here to help us. We cannot go back for her alone."

I wanted to protest, but I knew he was right. We didn't stand a chance against the Warriors alone, especially not that many. I had arrived with four and three others, including Galnar, were also here somewhere. All Aésha had to do was bat her eyelashes at us, and we'd both be drooling. If we couldn't handle one Warrior, how would we ever deal with seven of them? I silently prayed for Irys' safety.

"You are a Knight of Freyss?"

"Yes. Sir Rral Radone. You are safe with me," he vowed, "I will protect you with all my honour."

I believed him. I saw his fists in action, and I didn't doubt he knew how to use the large sword that hung at his side.

"Thank you. Those Warriors are very dangerous people."

"Yes," he agreed.

Abruptly, he turned his head away from me, listening.

I'd heard it, too. The distant sound of something headed in our direction.

Without another word, he picked me up again and ran. We never left the woods, but I could tell we weren't deep into them, either. I could still see the city through the trees. He ran for a long time and was quiet, for a man of his size. He didn't stomp or tromp along as one would expect. His movements were fluid and smooth, and his footfalls made a dull thud on the forest floor.

He slowed once more, when he felt there was enough distance between us and our pursuers, and he set me down, catching his breath.

"Kavylak pigs," he muttered under his breath.

I nodded. "They are," I said.

I couldn't recall a time I'd thought of anyone like that but, at the moment, I couldn't have agreed with Sir Radone, more.

His head snapped toward me when I spoke, and he looked at me in shock.

Crap! I'm with a Sylizan! If they're weird about a woman's shoes, I guess they don't like her agreeing with crass statements like...

"You speak Gbat?"

I stared blankly back at him.

Oh, no. Not this again.

"If you can understand what I'm saying and it sounds like, uh, Gbat, then, yes. I guess I can."

He looked at me, very weirded-out by my response but, to his credit, the expression faded and he nodded, accepting my reply.

"Yes. It seems that you do."

That's when I noticed that his accented-Sylizan was gone and had been replaced by an entirely new accent that sounded somewhat, but not quite, Scandinavian.

"You're not from Syliza, then?" I asked.

He lightly shook his head. A few strands of his dark brown hair, that had slipped free from his low ponytail, fluttered with the movement. His hair had been neatly tied when I had first met him, but it had become dishevelled from all the running and fighting he'd done. Coupled with his thick beard, it made him look rugged and a little out of place in a Knight's uniform.

"Originally, I came from Gbat Rher. I moved there after my country was taken and became a province of Syliza."

My brow crinkled in confusion.

"Taken? You mean your country was taken over by Syliza?"

Wow. Not cool, Syliza. You're supposed to be the good guys. Maybe there's some kind of explanation. Maybe they saved Gbat Rher.

"We were invaded and taken over," he confirmed.

Nope. Really not cool, Syliza.

I had no idea what to say in response to that and chose to remain silent when I noticed he had gone perfectly still. I knew he was listening for something.

"We must run again," he said.

He scooped up my legs, I put my arms around his neck, and he ran.

He ran for a long time, moving between the trees, sidestepping bushes, leaping over roots that protruded from the ground, and over fallen branches. I was blown away by his stamina, but I knew that it wouldn't last. As impressive as this hulk of a man was to carry me and run for as long as he did, he was slowing down. His run was quickly turning into a jog.

I could hear something gaining on us. The distinct sound of something close and fast, moving among the forest foliage, erupted in my ears. I looked around and could see no one, even though the sun had risen and enough light pierced through the trees to provide me with a decent view of our surroundings.

Then I saw it. The mixture of green and brown leaves that blanketed the forest floor whooshed as though an invisible animal had quickly run by. I gasped, and my heart almost stopped at the sudden realization of what was chasing us.

Amarogq's wolves.

I felt sick.

"Sir Radone," I said urgently. "I think there may be wolves that we can't see chasing us. I know it sounds crazy but they belong to one of the Warriors." I didn't care how ridiculous that sounded. My fear told me I was right.

For a split second, he looked at me like I had grown a second head, but then he nodded seriously and ran directly up to a tree with a thick trunk and low branches.

"Reach up your arms," he instructed.

I did as he asked. He raised me up in his arms, which noticeably shook from the effort because they had been taxed with carrying me for such a long time. When I could reach the large branch, I pulled myself up onto it. I straddled it, placing my hands directly in front of me for balance.

"Hide," he whispered.

"What about you?" I whispered back. I was shocked that he wasn't going to be climbing up the tree with me. I figured we'd be hiding together.

"I will keep them from finding you. Go," he said and walked away from me before I could protest.

I didn't argue and I didn't tell him that I wasn't a natural tree climber, either. Forcing myself to think only about hiding, I reached up one hand above me to the next branch, which was low enough that I could touch it from where I sat. I added my second hand and hauled myself upward, bringing up one leg and then the other, planting my boots on the first branch where I had been sitting. Pulling myself up to the second branch, I straddled it as I had done with the first. I completed the process, one more time.

I didn't climb any higher and settled on the third branch. The tree's leaves provided enough shelter, now, that I felt confident that no one would see me, unless they stood directly under the tree and looked up. I held on tightly. The rough bark of the tree dug uncomfortably into my palms, but I didn't care. I was determined not to fall out of this tree.

The sharp sound of a blade being released from its sheath drew my attention. I looked in the direction from where the sound had come and, through the small gaps between the branches and leaves, I spotted Sir Radone. He was standing like a sentinel about twenty feet away from the tree where I was hiding, with his sword in one hand and a dagger in the other, braced for anything.

One of the wolves materialized out of thin air, mid-lunge, ramming into Sir Radone's back. He stumbled forward with the force and three more grey wolves appeared and charged at him. He quickly struck at them, swinging at the animals with his sword and dagger. The blades had no effect. They sliced through the wolves as if they were sweeping through air alone.

I bit my lip hard, to keep myself from shrieking or screaming for help. I shut my eyes wanting to block it all out, but I couldn't block it out. It felt wrong to do it. I forced myself to watch Sir Radone. If a chance came for me to flee, or even to help him, I had to take it. Trying to block out what was happening wasn't going to help anyone; least of all, me.

Another wolf managed to ram him, knocking him down to one knee. He quickly pushed himself back up, not surrendering the battle. He swiped at one wolf but was bitten on the back of the leg by another. I winced as he grunted in pain through clenched teeth. It was awful to watch and maddening at the same time.

No matter how many times Sir Radone slashed at a wolf, neither of his weapons connected with flesh. The wolves kept disappearing and reappearing, yet their attacks on him were causing him physical damage. How was that even possible?

Without warning, the wolves stopped attacking and backed off. The four predators circled him but didn't advance. It was like they were waiting for Sir Radone to make a move or waiting for a command. I held my breath.

"Where is she?" Amarogq asked calmly.

I nearly fell out of the tree when I heard his voice. He had been so quiet on his approach that I hadn't even realized he was there.

Sir Radone said nothing. He just stared at Amarogq, his weapons at the ready. The leg that had been bitten by one of the wolves was bleeding.

I felt hatred building inside me for the wolf-Warrior. If looks could kill, he would have dropped dead from the glare I was giving him.

Aésha stepped into sight as well, making it clear that Amarogq was not alone. I hated them both. I wanted nothing more than to help Sir Radone, but I knew if I were to reveal myself now, it wouldn't make the situation any better. If anything, it would probably make the Knight's situation much worse. This wasn't like when I sacrificed myself for Irys. I had nothing to bargain. Maybe if I remained quiet and hidden, they would leave him alone and continue looking for me elsewhere.

To prevent the building scream of terror, frustration, and helplessness from bursting from my mouth, I bit my lip hard, tasting blood.

Amarogq withdrew his axe and stepped toward Sir Radone, who was waiting for him. They took a few swings at one another. The sound of clanging steel sent shivers down my spine.

Aésha, who had only been staying out of the way until now, strolled around the two fighting men. She caught the eye of the Knight, and I saw him get sucked into her. He lowered the arm that was holding the dagger and Amarogq took advantage of Sir Radone's moment of distraction, slugging him in the face.

Sir Radone retaliated with a swing at Amarogq, but Amarogq ducked out of the way and delivered a punch to the Knight's gut. Aésha moved away from the fight, looking entirely unconcerned. She turned her attention toward the trees, obviously looking for me.

I felt sick watching the men fight, knowing that I was the cause of it. I couldn't stand it anymore. I couldn't remain hidden. It was foolish of me to ever think that the fighting would stop or that they would leave Sir Radone alone. If I didn't do something, the battle would continue, and he would lose. He was outnumbered by mean freaks who weren't interested in fighting fair.

"Stop it!" I hollered.

Chapter 9

Irys

I had barely a moment to know for certain that it was Megan. Before any hint of doubt could set in, I heard her voice calling out my name. Panic struck me as Sir Radone engaged one of the Warriors in combat, but I did not have the chance to act.

A blink had not passed before I was grabbed from behind, and a hand clamped itself over my mouth. An arm wrapped around my middle and held my own arms at my sides, dragging me backward with a surprising force.

I tried to scream. I tried to break free from my captor. I even tried to bite the hand that was covering my mouth as though I were a feral animal. None of my efforts helped. In fact, they did not even appear to slow the person down.

We didn't travel far before I was pulled into a nearby house where I was released in time for me to hear the sound of the bolt locking the door.

I turned quickly and then froze when I saw who was with me in the room.

"Mr. Acksilivcs..." I sputtered. Only then, did I notice that we were not alone. Another man, one that was vaguely familiar to me, was standing next to him. He had splendid, lush blue hair and was instantly the most attractive man that I had ever glimpsed in my life. A description that would do justice to the sheer exquisiteness of his face would defy every poet who had ever held a quill.

It took a moment before I realized that the companion of Mr. Acksilivcs had been one of the Warriors disguised at the Masque. His hair had been black then: Mr. Atrix.

I was drawn from the enchantment that his eyes appeared to have had on me as I heard Megan calling my name, outside. The sound ceased as quickly as it had arrived.

"Please let me go," I begged, hoping that Megan's silence meant that she was safely hidden or that she had been rescued by Sir Radone. I prayed that harm had not come to her.

"Relax, Doll," Mr. Acksilivcs replied in such a casual tone that I could feel my colour rise, just from the insult of it. "I didn't bring you here to capture you. I brought you here because I don't want you to be caught up in the battle out there. Once it's safe, I'll let you out."

Mr. Atrix merely watched us as he leaned against the door. The way that he stood somehow suggested that the door, the room, and everything in it belonged to him. I had the feeling that he might give the same impression regardless of where he was or what he happened to be doing. It was as though he were wearing the space as an extension of his clothing.

I blinked myself out of my distraction, once more, and fixated on Mr. Acksilivcs. "I have no doubt that it would be safer for me out there in the midst of battle than it is in here with you two. Let me go. I must help Miss Wynters."

"You can't help her, Doll. We both know that. You won't be taking her back with you. She, unlike you, will be coming with us."

"Why are you doing this to her? She is my friend and she hasn't done anything to you."

"She might be your friend, but she is our property," he replied. Had there been an answer that could have incensed me more, I would not have liked to imagine what it could have been.

"Not here, she isn't," I replied in a building rage.

"I'm not going to argue about it, Doll. You've got your opinions and I've got mine. If it brings you any comfort at all, then know that no harm will come to her. She will be safe."

"How can I trust what you say? The last time I saw you, you told me that if I went to hide, I would be safe. Captain Galnar was waiting in my room, and he nearly killed me." I could hear the frustration and hurt building in my voice as I spoke. By the end of my statement, I was nearly shouting. I likely would have continued if I had not seen the shock in his expression. He looked surprised, and my heart was telling me that it was genuine.

"I didn't know he was there," he said. "I would never have sent you there if I'd known he was waiting for you."

I believed him. My confidence was only bolstered when Mr. Atrix nodded his head in agreement with Mr. Acksilivcs. Still, I fought with my instincts. They didn't make any sense.

"Why wouldn't you have sent me there? Is Captain Galnar not your leader? Clearly the Warriors seem to enjoy harassing me and those whom I love."

"You weren't our target, that night. We – I – had no idea that Captain Galnar intended to go after you as he did."

I placed my hands on my hips, defiantly ignoring the sharp pain that throbbed through my bandaged wrist while clutching my bag handle in my other hand.

"If I was not your target and you were not sent to capture me or to herd me into Captain Galnar's trap, then why did you..." My words fell away as I glanced momentarily at Mr. Atrix, feeling my cheeks flushing as I realized that I could not bring myself to discuss that night's kiss in front of an audience. I tried again. "Why did you spend as much time with me as you did?"

"Because I wanted to. I like you, Doll," he replied with a smile that I could not deny was appealing as much as I wanted to.

"I don't believe you," I lied. "You once told me that you would kill me if you were ordered to. What's more, you went ahead and ruined my first kiss!" I accused. As soon as the words escaped my lips, I regretted them. Not only had I meant to keep that knowledge to myself but, upon hearing my own voice, I realized precisely how silly and girlish I sounded.

To further my humiliation, I heard Mr. Atrix snort a laugh as he gave Mr. Acksilivcs a mocking look. "Did you really tell her you'd kill her?" he asked in a voice filled with ridicule. At least he hadn't focused on the revelation that Mr. Acksilivcs had kissed me.

"Shut it, Arik. Why don't you go make yourself useful and go distract someone with how lovely you are?" Mr. Acksilivcs retorted sarcastically.

"Touch-y," Mr. Atrix teased smoothly in reply. "Alright. I'll leave you two alone. But if you're hoping to patch things up with her, you might not want to tell her that you're going to kill her, this time."

To that, Mr. Acksilivcs merely shook his head and Mr. Atrix left the room, wandering into another part of the house with a smug look on his face.

"Sorry about that. He can be difficult at the best of times," Mr. Acksilivcs said as he turned his attention back to me.

"Perhaps, but he was right," I took the opportunity to say in a haughty way.

"He was," he agreed. "But at the time, I felt that it was what you needed to hear. I didn't realize that I'd ever actually see you again."

"You can stop trying to guess at what you think I need to hear. You don't know me and I don't intend to see you again after today. When I walk out of this house, it will be the last time I ever think on you."

"I understand," he replied without emotion. "But for now, you need to stay here. It really isn't safe for you out there, Doll. In fact, it's more dangerous for you than I realized when I first brought you in here. If Captain Galnar went after you before, then he'll do it again. At the moment, no one knows you're here and I plan to keep it that way."

"Why should I believe that you would go against your own captain's wishes? Aren't you finished playing games with me, yet?"

"I'm doing it because, at the moment, I can get away with it without getting myself in trouble."

"Why won't you do the same thing for Miss Wynters? We want only to be left alone."

"In her case, I have orders that I have to follow. I can't go against them just because it's what you want. I don't know why Wynters needs to be returned to Kavylak. All I know is that my orders are to bring her there and I intend to follow them. Taking you with me isn't an order, so I don't need to be your enemy."

I crossed my arms. Suddenly, he didn't look as appealing to me as he had a few moments ago.

"As difficult as it may be for you to imagine, I'm not playing games with you," he continued. "I wasn't even playing games with you at the Masque. I lied about who I was but only because it was the only way to talk to you without having you leave or alert someone that I was there."

"You were playing games. You were pretending to be a shy man who was too nervous to dance. You weren't just pretending to be a Sylizan man with a name that I would not recognize."

He smiled his magnetic smile again, but I found it as frustrating and insulting as it was captivating.

"It was all for you. Oh, and while we're on the subject of names, allow me to clear things up. I'm Acksil," he said.

"You ruined the most important night of my life, Mr. Acksil," I spat this new name at him with disdain.

His smile faded until a frown had replaced it. "That wasn't my intention. It felt like we were having a good time while we were dancing. And you can drop the 'Mister,' Doll. It's just Acksil."

"I thought I was enjoying it but it wasn't real. I was having fun only because you were playing a character that appealed to me. The truth of the matter was that you were lying to me while your friends infiltrated my home and kidnapped my dear friend."

"That would have happened whether you danced with me or not, Doll."

"Why did you take it as far as you did?"

"I guess I did let myself get a little wrapped up in you. As much as I may have been playing a role, I was still being genuine in my actions and intentions."

"You humiliated me, and you terrified me. You stole a moment that was supposed to be one of the most special times of my life, and you made it filthy."

His expression was that of a man who had just been slapped. Somehow, my words came as a complete surprise to him. Regret strained his eyes.

"I'm genuinely sorry, Miss Godeleva," he said formally but without any hint of sarcasm. It was clear that this was his attempt to be respectful to me.

This confused me. I had nearly expected him to laugh at me; to make fun of the way that I clung so girlishly to my romantic dreams. At the same time, I could feel my guard rising in case I was being drawn into yet another lie. It was clear that this man knew exactly how to tell me just what I wanted to hear.

"Are you?" I asked more tentatively than I would have liked. It had been my intention to sound much more confident in my question. "I wish I could believe even a single word that you say, Acksil."

"I am sorry. I didn't realize it was your first kiss. I didn't know that I would be ruining anything for you that would hurt you on such a profound level. I was having fun and I thought you were, too. I felt that you wanted to kiss me and since I wanted to kiss you, too, I did." He spoke so plainly that I was inclined to be drawn in by his words.

I wanted to believe him. I wanted to think that my first kiss had been a special moment shared with a warm-hearted person and that there wasn't any deception at its core. At the same time, I wouldn't allow myself that comfort.

"How could you not have known how much it would mean to me? You created the perfect romantic moment and you allowed me to fall for every part of it, even though you knew that it was a fraud. You let me kiss you without knowing who you truly were, immediately before you revealed yourself to be a man who was a part of an invasion of my home, a threat to my loved ones, and the kidnapping of my friend. How could you possibly have thought that you would not hurt me?"

Acksil was silent for a moment, looking thoughtful. "You're right. I wasn't thinking about you. I was thinking about me and what I wanted. I won't do it again."

"You certainly won't," I said with renewed confidence. I turned away from him to face the nearest partly-boarded window. Although I would have expected that I would feel victorious after having forced the Warrior to admit his own thoughtlessness and selfishness, this was not the case. I felt deflated. Certainly, I had put Acksil in his place, but he had not responded in a way that could allow me to feel proud for having done it. It was a battle not to permit myself to feel sorry for him.

"Why are you here?" His question broke a considerable silence between us. "Why would the Knights be stupid enough to put you in this danger?"

"It wasn't their decision. This was the safer of two choices that I had left them," I replied stubbornly, glancing over my shoulder at him.

His eyebrows lifted a little, betraying his surprise and what I chose to interpret as amusement. "You came without their permission? What did you do? Stow away on a ship?"

It was more than evident that he thought the idea of my rebelliousness was ridiculous. I could feel the stab at my pride and I didn't like it.

"I had to," I said defensively. "Megan gave up her freedom for me and risked her own life. When I had the chance to repay her for saving me, I was too frightened by your threats, and I chose to run and hide. I left her to be recaptured by you. Joining the effort to rescue her was the only chance I had to show the Goddess that I had been worth saving. You can smirk all you'd like, but I have to help her. My soul now depends on it."

Though his brows lifted higher on his forehead at my explanation, the amused expression started to fade and was replaced by one that was far more serious.

"I understand why you'd feel strongly about helping her and why you'd do everything you can for her. But Doll, if we're involved, there's nothing you can do to help her. You're only putting yourself in danger."

"Then that is what I must do. Her life is worth it." It felt good to know how genuinely I meant this, but it didn't stop the tear from escaping and running a trail down my cheek.

"Your life is worth it too, Doll. Don't forget that she gave up her freedom for yours. Throwing that away won't make it any better. If I'd known how strongly you felt about this, I never would have danced with you."

"You can make it up to me through Miss Wynters. The Goddess is watching you just as She is watching me. She can see that you and the Warriors are stopping Miss Wynters from being where she ought to be. She will also see if you help to send Miss Wynters back to where she will be safe and happy." I knew that it was unlikely that a Warrior would ever change his ways in an effort to save his soul, but I hadn't any other way to convince him. I was determined to use what I had.

"I will do what I can to make sure she is safe and happy where she is. She has already made a good friend among us and..." His pause revealed an obvious debate within him. "She is no longer a slave. She is still a prisoner, but she is receiving decent treatment. She eats well and has her own quarters."

Speechless, I studied his hazel eyes, carefully searching for even the slightest hint of dishonesty. I could find none, and I granted myself the comfort of believing him.

"Will you make sure that her situation never turns for the worse?"

"I will do what I can. I can't make you any promises. That would be a lie."

I set my teeth. How I wished that I knew what to believe. "Will you do anything that is in your power, at least?"

"Yes," he said firmly. "That, I can promise."

I swallowed hard as a few more tears slid down my cheeks. It was a strange feeling. At the same time that I was ashamed of the tears, I was also proud of them. They were a genuine display of just how much Megan's safety meant to me.

"I believe you."

"Irys," he said, reaching into his jacket pocket, "I don't want anything bad to happen to you or your friend." Withdrawing a handkerchief, he held it out to me.

I took the plain white square of fabric from him and dabbed its soft fibers to my cheeks, folding it before I offered it back to him. He spoke again and my hand froze in the air, halfway to returning his handkerchief.

"When I took you back to your home, I had been ordered to kill you," he said in a tone that was purely confessional. "I danced with you at the Masque because I wanted to see you again and because I could. I didn't know that Captain Galnar had other plans for you that night. I am keeping you here now because your Knight guard was outnumbered by Warriors and there is no one in town who can save you from Captain Galnar if he should see you again."

"What are you going to do with me?"

"Nothing. As soon as I receive the signal that the Warriors will be leaving, I will leave this house. I can only recommend that you stay here for a few minutes after I am gone. Then, you should go out and find a Knight and let them take you back home where you will be safe. You can't save Megan Wynters now, Irys. None of you can."

At the same time that his words eased me, a pain cleaved its way into my heart. This was devastatingly difficult. The sheer suggestion that I would have to turn my back and go home without my dear friend, who meant so much to me, felt as though I was being asked to give up a vital part of myself.

"What is most important now, if you truly want to honour your friend, is to stay safe and stay alive. If you believe that this is the path that the Goddess has laid out for you, then you are going to need to be patient. Even if this is the last and hardest thing that you want to do, it's what I think will be best for you. I promise that I will do what I can to make sure that she is safe, within my limits. She has more people on her side than either of you realize."

As I attempted to speak, I discovered that my tears were now flowing freely and not just one or two at a time. I brought the handkerchief back to my face and dabbed at my eyes as I nodded. "Alright," I finally managed to say with a breaking voice.

"Thank you," he said as though I were doing him a favour.

"I wish that there were some way that I could bring her reassurance. Is there any way for you to let her know that I will never give up on her?"

"I will find a way. What is it that you would want to give her?"

I wished that I had brought more with me than the small bag of essentials. If only there were something that was uniquely mine and that she would recognize from our time together.

"I don't know. I can't think of anything. I have so little with me."

"Do you have your own handkerchief?"

I looked down at my hand, which was clutching his handkerchief, realizing that I did have one of my own in my pocket.

"Yes," I said simply, extracting the clean, carefully folded white fabric with the little purple 'I' that was neatly embroidered in its corner. "You will give this to her?" I asked, needing reassurance.

"I promise," he said with certainty.

As I offered my handkerchief to him, it was as though all my hopes for Megan's safety and for seeing her again were folded into the crisp linen. I looked up and into Acksil's eyes. Hesitating before I spoke, I finally said, "I forgive you, Acksil."

"Thanks, Doll. I know that wasn't easy for you," he said as he tucked my handkerchief away. "You've got a good heart. I hope it stays that way."

I would have replied, but the door suddenly opened, and Mr. Atrix stepped in.

"We're leaving," he said.

It was confusing that a man whose appearance was so welcome brought such a feeling of intrusion to the room. That sensation didn't last as he exited as swiftly as he had entered.

"Remember what I said, Doll," Acksil turned his attention from the door back to me again. "Wait here for a few minutes before finding a Knight as quickly as you can."

"I will," I agreed. "Before you go, will you please answer one question?"

"What's that?"

"Did you return the horse?"

I could see the confusion in his expression as he tried to understand what I was asking, but the look faded and was replaced by a smile when he made the connection.

"Actually, yes, I did," he said with amusement.

Knowing this brought a strange sense of relief. At least, in this one thing, I could feel a slight easing in the strain on my soul.

It had bothered me to know that he had stolen a horse from a town in order to rescue me. Indeed, he needed it in order to bring me into Lorammel after I'd been enslaved by Captain Galnar on his ship, but to steal from someone to get me there was wrong.

I had comforted myself in believing that he must have returned the animal when he had gone back. I had prayed that the theft of the horse would not be hanging over my soul. Now, I could be reassured in knowing that all was right again.

"Thank you," I replied, offering his own handkerchief back to him.

"Keep it." He closed my fingers over it and held his hand over mine for a moment. "You might need it. You just gave yours away. When you look at it, it will remind you of the reason you're not using your own. I'll keep my promise."

"Thank you again, Acksil," I said with a hiccup of tears.

"Be safe, Irys." He turned to leave, and I noticed for the first time that he had a large sword with a decorative handle strapped to his back with a sheath that ran diagonally up to his left shoulder blade.

I had only enough time in which to nod before he left the house, and I was alone, standing in the center of an empty room.

Chapter 10

Megan

Climbing down as quickly as I could from the tree, I dropped from the last branch but lost my footing and landed on my rear.

Ow!

"There you are, Baby," Aésha said.

She stepped up to me and held out her hand to help me up. I slapped her hand away and climbed to my feet.

"Stop fighting!" I raged at Amarogq.

Both men stopped fighting. Amarogq looked at me calmly, but Sir Radone looked at me with deep shame in his eyes. His expression knocked the anger right out of me and left regret in its wake.

What did I do wrong? Did he really think I could just stay hidden and watch him get torn apart by Warriors and wolves? Didn't he realize that this would be better? That the fight was over and that he could return to finding Irys?

"Come now," Aésha spoke. "It's time to go."

She brought an arm around my back and started to guide me in the direction she wanted me to follow.

I didn't resist her, but my attention was on Sir Radone. He was shaking his head.

"I tried. I'm sorry. I was not enough," he apologized. He spoke in his Gbat Rher accent.

I could hear the shame in his voice now as much as I could see it in his soft blue eyes. I didn't understand it.

"Find a way for yourself. Run if you can but stay safe and strong, first," he advised.

"I'm sorry, too," I said to him and nodded in response to his advice. "I will," I promised, and I made a vow to myself in that moment that I would take his words to heart. He would have fought to the death to keep me safe. I'd never forget that or him.

"You speak Giant?" Aésha asked, sounding surprised.

I didn't respond to her. I doubted she would have taken kindly to me telling her to drop dead.

That said, I did follow her to wherever she was leading me. We had walked a few steps before I realized that Amarogq wasn't following us.

"Why isn't Amarogq coming with us?" I demanded. "Why isn't he leaving him alone?"

"He will," she assured me. "He can't have the giant following us and trying to take you away again."

I pressed my lips together and nodded. What she said made sense, but I didn't believe her. All I was imagining was Amarogq and his wolves finishing off Sir Radone. I hadn't saved him at all, had I?

She stepped down onto a dirt path, and I followed, realizing now that we were headed toward the city.

"Come now, if I didn't know better, I'd think that you weren't looking forward to holding onto me on our horse, Baby," she teased.

"Stop calling me that!" I snapped. "If you haven't figured it out by now, I don't want to be anywhere near you people." My hate rolled off in my words.

She looked at me. She didn't look angry or offended, but she lost all signs of play from her expression.

"We all have to do things we don't like, at times. It doesn't mean that we need to make things worse for ourselves. I'm doing my job, but I like you. We don't need to be miserable," she said.

I so didn't care that she had a job to do, but if she did indeed like me, it would be far better for me not to make unnecessary enemies. I thought about what Sir Radone had said, nodded to Aésha and swallowed down my rage. I had a promise to keep.

We walked in silence. The quietness of the city was eerie. It took everything in me not to scream and run away from her, but I knew I wouldn't get very far if I tried to escape. Now that the sun was up, I tried my best to·take in my surroundings, in case the knowledge would help me later on.

Finally, we stepped up to a building. The door opened almost immediately upon our arrival, revealing Keavren. I followed Aésha inside, glancing at him as I went by.

"It won't be long now," she told me as she took a seat on one of several wooden chairs that lined a wall.

I nodded and sat as well, leaving a chair between us. I tucked my hands under my legs out of nervous habit. I felt like I was in the waiting room of a doctor's office.

"Want some?"

I looked over at Aésha and watched her uncork a dark, thick glass bottle. I guessed it was a liquor bottle.

Is she seriously offering me a drink?

I shook my head.

She nodded and took a small sip from the bottle and scrunched her nose at the taste.

"Good choice," she said, capping the bottle and putting it down on the floor, with the clear intention of abandoning it.

Um, did she just steal someone's booze, drink it, and then ditch it because she didn't like it? That was rude on, like, every level! Let it go, Megan, keep your eyes on the bigger picture.

"Where's Irys?" I asked them.

"Baby, I have no idea. I've been running after you and a giant all morning," Aésha said.

Fair enough; that could be true. I turned my gaze on Keavren, who was watching out the window. He hadn't been running after me, so what was his story?

He shook his head. "I don't know. I was finding a new place to hide and arranging for our horses."

I wanted to trust Keavren – but could I? We weren't exactly on the same side right now.

"Baby, if we had her, there wouldn't be any reason not to tell you," Aésha said, getting up and sitting in the chair directly next to me.

I swear, if she calls me that one more time...

I looked at her, pulling my hands out from underneath me and crossing my arms. I didn't know what to believe.

"There's the signal. We're leaving," Keavren announced.

I looked at him and then at Aésha when she stood. She offered her hand to help me up and I took it, standing.

Keavren opened the door. Outside, waiting for us on one horse and holding the reins of two others, was the devastatingly handsome Warrior, Arik Atrix: the other Charmer. I noticed that there was something different about him.

He flashed a smile at me, causing my heart to beat faster and turned his head to talk to Keavren, relinquishing the reins to him. Atrix' hair fluttered in the breeze with his motion, and I realized then what was different about him. His hair was a dark shade of royal blue. Last night, it had definitely been jet black.

Okie dokie. I guess he was struck with the urgent need to dye his hair blue. Whatever.

Aésha mounted one of the horses, and Keavren stepped up beside me. He crouched down and cupped his hands, interlacing his fingers to create a foothold for me. Aésha reached her hand down to me. I took it and used Keavren's hands as the extra boost I needed to get on the horse. Awkwardly swinging one leg over the side of the horse, I managed to settle myself behind Aésha, sitting astride. I locked my arms around her waist. It was all I could do without a horse-seatbelt.

I inner-sighed to myself as I remembered the last time I was on a horse. It was an entirely different experience from this one. How much I wished it was Thayn I was holding onto, at that moment.

Once Keavren was on his own horse, we started riding, heading into the town. We hadn't been riding for more than two minutes, when I saw the first signs of thick, dark smoke rising from buildings about two-hundred feet away from us. I didn't see the flames, but I knew it was a fire.

Screams erupted moments later, followed by a bone-chilling cackle. Just as I knew the smoke belonged to a fire I could not yet see, there was no mistaking that the laughter belonged to the monster who was nowhere in sight: Galnar.

Leave it to that freak to find it funny that buildings are on fire. He probably started it!

The once ghost-like town abruptly came to life. People who had been hiding behind the wooden walls of the compact townhouses now ran through the streets. Some were screaming, others were crying, and others were barking out orders to those running down the planks of the sidewalks with buckets.

I held more tightly to Aésha as we made our way further down the streets of the town, toward its centre. I tried to look across the road, through any non-shuttered building windows, or down alleyways for Knights and even Irys among the sea of people, but there was so much noise and activity, it was hard to focus.

Above us, the sky grew darker as the black smoke continued to stretch out its curling fingers, blanketing the blue, an indication that the fire must be spreading.

We turned sharply down a tight alley. When we reached the other side, I saw the flames for the first time. Three men, dressed in matching blue jackets, pants, and hats, were tossing water from buckets into a burning building, in an attempt to put out the fire. I guessed, based on the swords that hung from their belts, that they were Sylizan soldiers and not the town's local firefighters.

As we were riding by, one of the soldiers spotted us and moved quickly. He swung his bucket of water up toward Aésha, smashing her in the face. The force of the blow knocked her from the horse, and I screamed as I was dragged off with her.

I released my hold on her before we hit the ground, landing on my side. My left hip and shoulder took the brunt of the fall. It hurt, but I was grateful I hadn't hit my head.

Our horse took off in a panic. The soldiers who had been fighting the fire were heading toward us, swords drawn. I was about to call out to them to let them know that I wasn't their enemy, when I spotted Keavren riding up behind them.

Hearing the hooves, one of the soldiers turned, but he was too late to react. Keavren drove his fist down hard on top of the man's head. He reached out with his other hand to grab the man's sword before the soldier dropped to the ground like a stone. I gaped, stunned.

The two remaining soldiers placed their attention on Keavren, who moved his horse to block Aésha and me from them. Keavren raised the sword to attack, and the two men took off.

"Are you alright?" Aésha asked, looking directly at me.

"Yes," I answered, moving to sit up. "Are you?" Her right cheekbone was turning a dark red and had already begun to swell.

She nodded and stood, taking hold of my arm as I climbed to my feet. I was glad to discover that, aside from a few bumps and bruises, nothing was sprained or broken.

Keavren got down from his horse, holding the reins in one hand, his sword firmly gripped in the other.

"You two take my horse. I'll follow."

I looked at Keavren when he spoke, but before I could respond, I saw that the two soldiers who had taken off had returned and had brought backup with them.

Keavren whirled to face them, sword at the ready. Aésha withdrew her own sword from her belt, revealing a blade with a pink inlay. If this had been an entirely different circumstance, I likely would have marveled at the fact that she had a magenta sword but, circumstances as they were, I was working on not throwing up. I took a step back from them.

"Stay near me, Baby," Aésha told me.

I didn't listen. I had reached a now-or-never moment. I turned and ran as fast as my legs would carry me without looking back. I had to find another Knight or anyone who could help me.

I ran down an alley and stopped short. There was no help. There was only fire. The smoke and brightness from the blaze burned my eyes and made them water. It crawled into my lungs and made me cough. I quickly backed out of the alley seeking another direction, but Aésha grabbed my arm.

"You're going to get yourself killed!" she warned sharply. "We need to get out of here. The town is going to burn."

She made the declaration with such certainty that, not only did I believe her, but she left me with the impression that this wasn't her first experience with a burning town.

I nodded and didn't fight her when she ran, pulling me after her in the direction opposite the fire. Keavren joined us, leading the way to clear our path of any soldiers. Only a few tried to get in his way, but once he had quickly dispatched them, no more tried to stop us. The fire was taking priority.

Traces of smoke were everywhere now. I couldn't believe how rapidly the fire had spread in such a short time. I hadn't heard any big explosions, so it couldn't be the result of bombs. How was it spreading so fast?

As if in response to my question, Galnar's demonic cackle erupted close by. I couldn't see him, but his twisted laughter made me feel certain that he was behind the fire, somehow. How was he doing it? I didn't have a clue and right now it didn't even matter. I desperately wanted to get away from the city and breathe clean air.

The smell of the smoke, mixed with the sounds of people's screams and cries, and the sounds of fire devouring wood and smashing glass, made me feel sick as I ran.

We wound our way through countless streets and alleys but finally had to slow our pace when we hit a dark grey fog of smoke and ash. I choked on the thick air, feeling panicked as I coughed and gasped for breath. Suddenly, a cloth was placed over my mouth. Through my tear-blurred eyes, I saw that Keavren was holding a handkerchief over my mouth. I reached up my hand to grasp it, and he let go of it, coughing as he brought another handkerchief to his own mouth.

The handkerchief helped, but the environment was too brutal for us to stay for long. Aésha, who had also placed a handkerchief over her mouth, quickly pulled me along. Keavren put an arm around me, in a clear effort to get me to move with haste.

The smoke was unimaginably awful. My lungs burned. I coughed and wheezed, barely able to breathe. My eyes were watering like crazy and they were stinging so badly I could barely keep them open. If I hadn't been guided by Keavren and Aésha, I would have been lost.

We managed to make our way through the worst of it. When we were clear of the smog, we stopped for a moment, all of us coughing and sucking down air.

"Are you alright?" rasped Keavren.

"Yes," I coughed out.

"Can you keep going?"

I nodded to him. There was no way I was stopping. I was certain we'd burn with the city if we quit now.

"Put your arm around my shoulder," he coughed. "I'll keep you moving."

I nodded, put my arm around his shoulder and looked over at Aésha. She looked rough. The swollen side of her face was beginning to form an ugly bruise, and her tearing eyes had left several tracks down her smoky face. Yet, in spite of her rough appearance, she didn't complain and kept up with Keavren and me.

We walked and walked through the town for what felt like hours. My throat was burning from breathing in smoke and from continually coughing. All that kept me going was the knowledge that each step I took was putting more distance between myself and the fire.

Just when I felt like I wouldn't be able to walk another step, men on horseback approached us, and Keavren and Aésha stopped walking. I looked up to see Arik and Acksil slowing their horses as they drew near.

Upon seeing Aésha, Arik immediately rode directly up to her and reached out his arm, helping her onto his horse. She looked relieved when she saw him and didn't hesitate to take his help, straddling the horse behind him. She wrapped her arms tightly around him and rested her head against his back. She was holding onto him like she never wanted to let go. With one arm, Arik securely hugged the arms that encircled his chest, keeping the reins of the horse in his other hand. He kicked the horse into action, riding away from us. Neither one of them looked back.

Yeah, we're okay too, Arik. Thanks for asking!

Unlike me, neither Keavren nor Acksil seemed even slightly surprised that Arik took off with Aésha.

"Here. Take her on the horse. Sunetar will be by soon. I'll head back with him," Acksil said to Keavren as he got down from his horse.

Keavren nodded. "Thanks," he said, clapping Acksil on the back before getting up on the horse.

Keavren reached his hand down to me and I took it, hauling myself up with his help to sit astride, behind him. I was too exhausted to attempt an escape, and I had no idea as to where I'd run. At the moment, the only sensible option I had was to hold on to Keavren and hope for the best. That's precisely what I did.

With a single farewell nod to Acksil, Keavren rode us in the same direction as Arik and Aésha. We didn't talk as we traveled and it felt strange to hear only the sounds of nature and horse hooves beating against the ground. Not long ago, horror had filled our ears.

We left the town far behind us and journeyed for about two hours until finally we reached a shoreline. Keavren slowed our horse to a stop and dismounted, reaching up to help me off. I would have fallen, but he caught me, steadying me as I put my feet on the ground. My legs felt like noodles. The first few steps I took were wobbly, and every one after that was uncomfortable. My inner thighs ached, and I felt bruised all over from having fallen off a horse and then riding one for such a long period of time.

We abandoned the horse and walked down to the pebbly beach. To my annoyance, the heels of my boots sank into the soft ground as we made our way toward the shore where other Warriors were already climbing into rowboats.

Keavren took my hand and led me to the boat where Arik, Aésha, Acksil, and another Warrior I'd never seen before were already seated. The mystery-Warrior had light blond hair and wore a silver circlet with a blue gemstone on his forehead. I climbed in and sat on the only empty bench. Keavren sat beside me and continued to hold on to my hand. I didn't mind. It brought me some comfort.

Unlike the last time I got into a boat, Aésha didn't attempt to claim my attention. In fact, she didn't even look at me. She was curled against Arik. Her arms were around him, and she had her head resting on his shoulder, with her eyes closed. Arik was securely holding on to her. He looked as protective over Aésha as a mother bear protecting her cub.

My eyes drifted from them to the other Warriors who were getting into another boat. My free hand balled into a fist when I spotted Galnar sitting smugly. Unlike the rest of us, who looked as though we had taken a bath in ash, Galnar was perfectly clean. His gleaming white hair didn't have a fleck of soot on it.

As if he could sense my gaze burrowing into him, he turned to look at me. I was ready to give him the glaring of a lifetime, but my breath hitched when I saw his eyes; my own widened in shock. His eyes weren't the grey or the red I had seen; they were a wildly blazing red-orange. The glow of his irises appeared to flicker as if his eyes were actually aflame. I stared at him in disbelief, and two words popped into my brain: fire starter.

Amusement crawled into his features as he looked at me. He casually sat back. It was as if he could read my mind and my reaction had left him deeply satisfied. He turned away, and the boat he was in rowed out sea.

What had I just seen? Were my eyes playing tricks on me? Is Galnar's skill somehow related to fire? Is he pyrokinetic? Is that even possible?

The more I thought about it, the more my heart and head began to pound, and the less sense everything made around me. I felt like I was close to cracking up. I shivered, suddenly feeling cold all over.

Keavren released my hand and put his arm around my shoulder, drawing me in a little closer to him. I looked into his soot-stained face. His eyes were gentle and caring. I felt calmed by him and willingly accepted the comfort he gave me. Neither one of us spoke, not because we wouldn't know what to say, but because we didn't want to cough in each other's faces. I knew, without even having to try, that as soon as I opened my mouth to speak, the constant tickle in my throat would graduate into a cough. Instead of talking, I rested a hand on his knee and my head on his shoulder.

Acksil and the blond Warrior rowed in silence, following the path of the first rowboat. I lazily watched the sunlight glisten on the water, until it occurred to me that I couldn't see any large vessel in the distance. Experience told me that we wouldn't be in these boats for long, so where was the "mother ship?"

As we approached a cove, I noticed a haze over the water. I stared at it, wondering what it was, and realized once we got closer that it was a huge metal sea ship.

How is it that I can now see it in front of me, as plain as day? Had it been camouflaged, somehow? Weird!

The ship was much larger than the one we had previously left; at least twice the size. As we approached it, I was not looking forward to having to climb up the side of it, even though this time, I wasn't wearing a ball gown.

We continued to row toward the ship, but to my confusion, neither boat slowed down. At this rate, we were going to row right into the side of it!

I was about to ask Keavren what the plan was, but then I saw the side of the metal ship slide open, and the first boat rowed in through the opening. We followed.

I looked all around me as we entered. Once we were inside, the door slid shut with a resounding, yet dull, boom. I guessed we were in the ship's docking bay, or something, but from where I sat, it looked like we were hanging-out on boats in a large swimming pool that was mostly surrounded by a metal deck. This looked so bizarre to me that under other circumstances, I might have laughed.

Our boats were rowed to the edge of one side of the dock, and two soldiers waiting on deck secured them. Keavren released me and stood, climbing out of the boat and offering his hand to help me out. I took it and stepped up onto the metal surface.

"I'll bring you to your room," he whispered.

I nodded. I knew he wasn't being secretive. He was whispering because if he talked louder he'd likely cough.

Keeping hold of my hand, he wasted no time in leading me away from the area. We exited through an open door and walked down a hall to a flight of metal grated steps.

As we ascended the stairs, I couldn't help but feel defeat wash over me. The sound of our feet on the metal steps, the lingering scent of salt water, and the growing clamminess in the air, invaded my sense with an unwelcome familiarity. I was back on the ship where I had first woken up on Qarradune. Back in the place where I had found Irys, freed her, and been enslaved. I was back in my own personal hell.

Keavren lead me directly to the room I had once occupied. He opened the door, and we stepped in. Everything was as I remembered. The only difference was that my duffle bag was on the bed.

Thank goodness for small mercies.

"Get cleaned up," Keavren said before coughing. "I'll be back soon."

I nodded, not wanting to talk and cough. He gave my hand a squeeze. I squeezed back, and his expression softened. He released me and left the room, locking the door behind him.

Making a beeline for the bathroom, I picked up the metal cup sitting on the side of the sink and filled it with water. I was desperate to relieve the scratchy dryness in my throat and rid my mouth of the disgusting flavour of ash.

I tried to drink slowly, but I couldn't resist and drank too fast, swallowing the wrong way. I was struck by a coughing fit that was so violent, I dropped the mug into the sink and fell to my knees, trying to suck down air between coughs and heaves. When I was finally able to catch my breath, my face felt like it was on fire and tears streamed out of my burning eyes. Feeling lightheaded and dizzy, I leaned my head against the door frame and shut my eyes. My coughing had subsided, but my effort to hydrate hadn't done my throat any favors. It hurt even more now than it had before.

Brilliant, Megan.

When I felt I could move without my head spinning, I debated crawling into the shower then and there, but decided to get my duffel bag, first. If I were at home, I'd just shower and wander into my room in a towel, to get the clothes I wanted – but this wasn't home. There was no way I'd walk around in only a towel in a room that I couldn't lock from the inside.

Very slowly, I stood and walked to my duffel bag, grabbing it off the bed. I noticed that other clothing had been left for me, but I ignored it and returned to the bathroom, shutting the door behind me.

I dropped the bag on the floor, peeled out of my soot-stained clothes and boots, and stepped into the shower. The warm water felt good on my skin. I wanted to stay in there forever, but I couldn't risk dawdling. I quickly washed every inch of my skin and hair and got out.

I was glad to discover that I had been provided with towels. I dried off in a hurry and opened the duffel bag, pulling out the contents until I found the clothing and toiletry bag. I put on fresh underwear and socks but realized that the only other clean clothing I had was a tank top. Aésha had given me only one pair of pants and a t-shirt. I looked over at the soiled heap of clothing on the floor. My lip curled. There was no way I was putting that t-shirt back on, but I'd have to suffer the pants until I inspected the other clothing that had been left on the bed for me.

Pulling them on, I decided that if the worst thing that happened to me from this point on was wearing dirty pants, I'd consider myself lucky.

I brushed my teeth, brushed my damp hair, and moisturized my hands, feeling much better when I was finished. Refilling the mug with water, I took a small sip. My throat was still raw, but at least I didn't cough.

Abandoning everything but the mug in my hands, I left the bathroom and walked into the main room, stopping short when I realized I wasn't alone. A strange, greasy-looking man was standing there, watching me.

I gasped and coughed, nearly dropping the mug.

"Who are you?" I rasped. "Why are you here?"

The man's mouth twisted into a sleazy grin, revealing one nasty black tooth among several discolored and missing teeth, successfully giving me the creeps.

"Captain Galnar wants to make sure you have everything you need," he said, sounding as slippery as he looked.

Yuck! I need another shower.

"I'm fine...thank you."

Go away, Sleaze Ball!

He laughed. I had a feeling it was less at my response and more at the fact that he knew how uncomfortable he had made me feel.

"I'll be sure to tell him."

I just watched Sleaze Ball, doing my best to ready myself for anything. He briefly looked back at me, but then turned to leave. I forced myself not to sigh relief when he placed his hand on the doorknob, but my relief was short-lived when he turned his head back toward me as if he had just remembered something he'd forgotten to say.

"He wants to know if you'd like a friend."

My brow crinkled in confusion. "A friend?"

He nodded, his grin returning. "He caught one and thinks you might want it."

Yeah, right. As if I'd want anything that Galnar "caught".

"No. Thank you," I retorted stiffly.

His grin widened. I felt nauseated.

"He is sure you'll be interested in this friend," Sleaze Ball insisted, but then shrugged. "I guess not."

He turned back toward the door to exit, and it was then that my breath caught as understanding sparked my fear.

Oh, God! Is he talking about Irys?

"Wait! Who is it?" I coughed.

He paused and turned his damned grin on me again. I grimaced. It was either that or throw-up.

"A friend," he repeated.

Sleaze Ball obviously wasn't going to tell me who this "friend" was and, if it were Irys, I didn't want to waste any more time talking to him if there was a possibility that I could see her. It was a gamble I had to take.

"Alright. I accept his offer."

Sleaze Ball nodded, satisfied, and left the room, bolting the door behind him. I stared at the door wondering who would walk though it next.

What warped game is Galnar playing now?

Chapter 11

Irys

It was difficult to remember a moment in my life in which time felt as though it were passing more slowly. I remained exactly where I was until several minutes had expired and I started to hear people returning to the street outside.

I peeked out through the window and noticed that there were actually quite a few people quickly moving about. From my vantage point, I couldn't see anything aside from the movements of a growing crowd, so I made the decision to open the door and follow Acksil's instructions to find a Knight.

I stepped out of the short grey row house and onto the wooden sidewalk. I was careful to keep to the boards, despite the fact that people had filled the streets as I was afraid I might slip into the gutter. The crowd was not thick, but it was heavy enough that stopping wasn't an option.

I hurried along in the same direction as everyone else so that I would not collide with one of these rapidly moving people. The crowd continued to build, and just as we all seemed to turn toward a new direction, I caught the reason for the rush out of the corner of my eye. Part of the city was burning. I was not near the flames, but black smoke was lifting up from buildings somewhere out of sight as though it were making its own escape, just as we were making ours.

As we charged along, all I could see were the planks beneath me, the houses, and the rooftops. So much of the city was wooden. It would take a miracle to stop a blaze from travelling in this place.

A moment later, the throng from another street joined my own, and things became far more chaotic. Soldiers were attempting to direct the frantic civilians, and I tried desperately to follow their instructions. A woman screamed as she tore past me, causing the tension around me to tighten.

The wind shifted, bringing with it the unmistakable charred scent of the fire behind us. I felt my stomach knot as the smell of the smoke combined with the turmoil of the mob. We poured into a central square. I nearly shrieked when my arm was grabbed, and I whirled to find myself facing Sir Vorel.

"Miss Godeleva," he said urgently. "We have been searching the entire city for you. Come with me."

"Thank the Goddess," I breathed as I turned and walked as quickly as I could, only just keeping up with the Knight. That said, I couldn't have fallen behind even if I had tried. Sir Vorel maintained his firm hold on my arm the entire time. I supposed that I could not resent him for choosing not to be the perfect gentleman, at a moment like this.

Abruptly though, we came to a halt as a panicked woman stepped in his path. A crush of people rushed upon us.

"Help us!" she pleaded, looking directly at me, though Sir Vorel was immediately next to me and in full Knight's uniform.

"Come along then," I instructed, raising my voice as loudly as I could manage, in the hopes that they would hear me over the commotion.

"Follow us," Sir Vorel added, far more audibly.

Together, a growing group of us all-but ran in the direction chosen by Sir Vorel. I hoped it would take us away from the fire. I could see certain buildings ablaze, to the left of where we were. They were only a couple of streets away. The fire was spreading more quickly than I would ever have thought possible.

After a short distance, it was starting to feel as though our considerable flock was actually quite an organized one. We were all moving swiftly and wordlessly along, all according to Sir Vorel's directions. As more people joined us, they just seemed to work their way into the main group and kept going wherever we did.

We would have continued in this way, if another woman hadn't suddenly burst from an alleyway between two houses, grabbing hold of Sir Vorel's doublet.

"My child is trapped in the fire!" she both declared and pleaded to the Knight.

"Tell me where to take the crowd, Sir Vorel," I said, suddenly feeling as though these people were my responsibility, in Sir Vorel's absence. "We will be fine."

Sir Vorel's face was the picture of calm. "Follow this street until it takes you into the woods. Take the crowd away from the city until you reach the place where the river meets the sea. You will be safe there. I will return or send another Knight for you as soon as I can."

I listened carefully to the instructions and nodded with a confidence that I did not feel. "We will stay there until you come to find us," I assured him and then turned to the people behind us, unwilling to waste another second. "Follow me! Quickly, please!" I called.

A young man in civilian's clothing repeated my instructions back to the crowd, ensuring that more of them would hear my words. I quickly nodded my gratitude to him as I noticed that flecks of soot were falling through the air and darkening what would have been shoulder-length pewter hair.

Many of the people brought handkerchiefs to their faces to help to filter the ash from the air they were breathing. I refused to take Acksil's handkerchief out of its hiding place and decided that my sleeve would need to do. Fortunately, there were very few instances after that point in which I needed to say anything to anyone. The farther we were along the road, the cleaner the air seemed to be, which also made things somewhat easier.

In a crowd of this size, every bit of movement felt slow, despite the fact that we were all hurrying to the best of our abilities. Though I hadn't noticed it while I was walking with Sir Radone, my feet were still very sore from all the running I'd done across the cobblestones, the night before. While the wooden sidewalks were far softer to trod upon, they eventually ran out, and I was forced back onto the unrelenting stone surface. I could feel the soles of my feet bruising a little more with every step.

Along the tighter parts of the street, we were shoulder-to-shoulder, and I nearly dropped my bag on several occasions. At one point, I hugged it to my body instead of trying to keep hold of its handle.

Arriving at the woods, it was a relief to step onto the packed ground. It certainly wasn't soft, but it wasn't cobblestone. My legs were demanding that I stop as every joint gave its own form of torment in punishment for having overused it. I brought the crowd to a stop when we came upon a sizeable clearing from which I could hear the river and I could smell the sea. The water must have been just beyond a rise in the land past the clearing.

People were coughing and many were struggling to continue onward. It seemed more fair to stop here than to try to force them to climb that final hill, only to halt at the river beyond. As soon as I stopped walking and lowered my bag to one hand again, many people fell to their knees or embraced one another. My eyes watered, but I was unsure as to whether it was because of the relief from arriving here or because of the smoke that had stung them.

I had only just decided to try to see if I could find anyone who needed assistance, when a small hand slipped into my free one. A little boy of around six cycles in age looked up at me with his soot-stained face and wide eyes.

"What a sharp little boy you are to have come here with everyone," I told his bright expression, hoping to keep him calm. "Is your mother here, too?"

He shook his head, suddenly taken by shyness.

"What is your name?"

"Kielen," he answered very quietly.

"I am Miss Godeleva. I'm going to pick you up so that more people can see you, Kielen. That way, if someone knows you, they will find you," I told him.

Once he had nodded his agreement, I brushed some of the soot from his little suit and lifted him up.

Please, Great Goddess, let us find his mother. Don't take his family from him. Not at such a young age, before he is old enough to remember her well. Not this way. I beg of you.

"Hold onto me. I'm not very good at holding little boys yet, and I have my bag to carry," I explained to him as I shifted him until he seemed to be properly supported. I ignored the renewed pain this pressed into my forearm. I would have time to be sore and afraid later.

I walked slowly through the crowd, hoping that someone who knew the boy would look up and spot him.

"Is Kielen's mother here?" I occasionally called to the people I passed. My heart pounded as I looked over the dozens upon dozens of people who had made it to this little open spot in the woods. How many of these people would return to the city only to have lost everything? How many of these people were missing loved ones? I prayed that things were not nearly as bad as they seemed and that we were all here merely as a precaution.

I'm begging you, Great Goddess. Keep these people and their loved ones from harm. Allow them to go back to their homes, only to find that a miracle has saved them: your miracle.

At first, I was met only with shaking heads, in response to my question, but soon I could hear voices murmuring as they asked others whether they knew a boy named Kielen or had seen his mother. The message was being passed along. We were doing what we could.

I started to make my way to a place that was higher on the hill and, therefore, more visible. Looking back at all the people, my attention was captured by a very young woman who stepped toward me and said, "His mother's the one who went with the Knight."

"Does she know that Kielen is here?" I asked, hoping that she would know the answer. Unfortunately, all I received was a shrug as a response. "Someone must make sure that she knows her son is safe. I am going to leave Kielen here with you. You are to stay here with him until I return," I instructed her.

Before she could step forward to take the boy from me, he protested. "I want to go with you," he insisted, despite the fact that he had only just met me.

"You can't come with me, Kielen," I told him calmly and with confidence, "but I will return very quickly. You must stay with this young lady and behave yourself. Will you do that?"

"You should stay here, Miss," said a man's voice as he approached from behind me. I turned to see the young pewter-haired man from the smoky streets, who had called out my instructions so they would be better heard. "I will go back. You should remain here."

"Are you certain that you know where they are?" I asked, not wishing to send him through burning streets, unsure of where he was going.

"I know where they are, Miss. They live right across from the milliner," he replied confidently.

"Thank you. This is very courageous of you."

With a reassuring smile, the young man turned and jogged away. I sent a prayer with him, in the hopes that the Goddess would protect him against the smoke and the flames that he had chosen to brave on my behalf.

I turned my attention back toward the many people who were now gathered here in the clearing. I tried to stop myself from seeing the fear in their eyes; the tears that had cleaned paths through the smoke-stains on their cheeks. How they suffered as they waited, wondering what would be left of their lives. Regardless of how hard I tried, I could not turn away. I knew this was the Goddess' way of telling me that I must not shelter myself. My life had been far too sheltered until now. This had to change.

How wretched I am, Great Goddess. Thank you for showing me. Please give me the wisdom to change my childish and narrow ways. I want to be the person that you have given me the chance to become. Please don't allow me to fail you.

Setting Kielen down, I took a seat in a little grassy space that was unoccupied, not quite knowing what to do with myself. I set my bag down and opened it, withdrawing the toast I'd set aside from this morning and offering it to him. He took it and seemed to be content as he snacked upon it.

The young woman who had recognized him, earlier, sat down with us, picking Kielen up and resting him in her lap. He allowed her to do so without complaint, still eating his piece of toast.

"That's a pretty dress you're wearing," she said.

I looked down at my dress, which looked as though it had clouded over in ash. "Thank you. It is rather difficult to feel pretty at such a time."

"Yes," she agreed simply. "Are you new to town?"

"I am merely here for a brief visit. It appears as though this was not the best day to be passing through."

She looked as though she might say something else, but we were interrupted by the sound of heavy footfalls. They were the thudding of soldiers' boots.

The young woman and I stood. As I rose, I picked up a large stick, and the young woman stepped in front of Kielen, clearly prepared to defend him with her life. I edged myself in front of her and held my stick with both hands. I may not have been entirely sure as to what I planned to do with that stick, but when the time came, I would be ready.

As the men came into view, it became immediately obvious that the soldiers were ours, and they were led by two Knights, one of whom was Sir Fhirell. The stick fell from my hands as the sigh of relief passed from my lips.

I was taken aback not only by the presence of a familiar face, but by the fact that he looked as relieved as I likely did. Once he had made his way through the swarm of people, he removed his hat. I picked up my bag and looked up at him, speechless.

"Miss Godeleva, I am glad to see that you are safe," he said, speaking up over the dozens of discussions that were going on around us, and the instructions that were being barked by soldiers to the people of the city.

"Thank you, Sir Fhirell. I am grateful to see you as well." They were stiff words, but they started at a gush until I was able to collect myself and remember what I urgently felt he should know. "Sir Vorel is still in the town. He was helping a woman to find a child who was missing. Sir Radone is gone. I don't know where. We were still together when we suddenly came upon Miss Wynters, but the Warriors were there, too." I explained, whispering the word "Warriors" as I shared my rushed and confused story. I didn't want to upset the people around us.

Sir Fhirell nodded with a serious but calm expression on his face. "Yes. *They* were spotted. They have moved beyond the wall of fire, which blocked our path to them on land. A pursuit has continued over water."

My heart split in two. At the same time that it was my deepest wish for Megan to be rescued and brought safely back, I also knew that I did not want Acksil to be captured or injured in that effort. Perhaps they were not travelling together.

"Go back into the town to search for Sir Radone," he said to the other Knight who had arrived with him. "Find any men that you can, to help you in locating him."

"Yes, Sir," replied the Knight, who turned back to the town.

The soldiers started to guide people to the river over the hill, and I realized how thirsty I was. It was surprising that I hadn't noticed how much my throat was burning from the smoke and ash I'd inhaled on my way through the town. Certainly, I'd known that I was not entirely comfortable, but it was now becoming nearly overwhelming.

"I'm just going to step over the hill for some water," I informed Sir Fhirell. The young woman and Kielen seemed to take that as the opportunity to come along with me, and the four of us made our way to the river's edge for a drink.

When we arrived, we all knelt down as though we were about to begin a prayer. Bowing over the river, we each gathered the quickly flowing water into our hands. I brought my own to my lips and the miracle of this precious liquid flowed into my mouth and instantly cooled my throat.

At first, I was unsure as to whether my thirst would ever be satisfied. I plunged my hands back into the water and drank deeply, passing my wet fingers over my face. Truly, the Goddess was great to me at that moment.

I was brought back to the present when I noticed that Sir Fhirell was kneeling down beside me, drinking the water from the river as the rest of us had been doing.

Kielen was splashing the water with his hands, playing on his own while the young woman watched over him. It was good to see him looking happy, but the knowledge that his home had likely burned to the ground left a cloud of gloom over the image of his mirth.

I stood to speak with Sir Fhirell, and Kielen dashed over to me from the water's edge, taking my hand with his little wet one. As a soldier approached Sir Fhirell, I changed my path and took Kielen a few steps away. This allowed me to stay with the child, but I was also able to listen to what the two men had to say to each other.

"Sir Fhirell, there was no sign of him. He might have been taken," said the soldier.

"The men will keep looking until we know for certain," Sir Fhirell replied.

Without knowing it, I brought my free hand to my mouth. They must have been speaking of Sir Radone. Why else would it have been reported to Sir Fhirell, a Knight from Lorammel, and not to a local authority?

Before I could process my concern any further, there was a sharp cry of a Skydasher bird, overhead. Sir Fhirell raised his gloved hand and extended his arm upward toward the bird, which landed surprisingly gracefully on his fingers. If it were not for the worry that weighted my heart over Megan and Sir Radone, I would have been lost in the awe I felt from the scene.

Quietly speaking with her and bringing up his free hand, Sir Fhirell stroked her belly feathers a few times before he withdrew a note that had been tucked into the small carrier that was attached to her leg. After reading the brief message on the paper, he looked at me with compassion.

"Our journey ends here. We will be leaving as soon as it is possible," he informed me. "My ship will be returning us to Lorammel."

"Will the other ships continue the pursuit?" I asked as I swallowed the tears that were rising from the loss I felt over the last moments of the part that I would play in Megan's rescue.

"Yes," he replied. "Sir Varda's ship and another still sail."

I nodded, relieved to hear that there would still be two more ships after Kavylak's Warriors and after Megan. "Thank you, Sir Fhirell," I replied quietly, not knowing what else to say.

I looked around at the growing group of townspeople. There were so many! I hoped and prayed that they would be going back to their homes today. I wondered if the news of the fate of this city would ever reach me.

They gathered together in little groups. Some of them cried together. Others were still in shock; the emotion had yet to set in. That was likely for the best. It was not a sensation that I would wish on anyone.

"Should I be doing something to help?" I asked pathetically.

Sir Fhirell looked at me as he gently patted the bird. She was on high alert but looked perfectly content under the man's touch. "The only thing that can be done right now is to wait for the last of the fires to be extinguished. I am awaiting word that we should leave for the ships."

Kielen chose this moment to speak up "Can I go with you?"

"No," I replied, making sure to take any harshness out of the word. "Your mother will be back soon, and she would miss you too much if you were to leave with me."

To that, he simply nodded, appearing to accept my response.

"I'm glad to have met you, Kielen. You're a very good boy," I assured him.

A soldier, covered in ash and soot, came over the hill and walked toward Sir Fhirell. After a brief exchange of words, the soldier turned toward the people who were gathered and started to provide them with information as to what was happening and what they should be doing, depending on their circumstance.

"Miss Godeleva, we're going to leave now," Sir Fhirell addressed me.

I nodded and turned to Kielen. "You will be staying here and everything will be sorted out for you. You'll be with your mother soon, and she'll tell you where you're going next," I informed him.

His face crumpled and he looked as though he was next to tears.

"Oh, now," I said, crouching to his level. "You're being a very brave boy. You have been, all along. Why don't you go sit with your friend and hold her hand? She'll tell you all the things you need to know until your mother arrives. This will be a lot of help to the soldiers."

Kielen listened to me with large eyes before he stepped away, without another word. He took the hand of the young woman, and she gave him a comforting smile as she listened to the instructions from the sooty soldier.

When I was certain that Kielen would not try to return to me, I collected my bag and stepped up beside Sir Fhirell, ready to face a journey home that I was struggling to view as anything other than a confirmation of my failure. Sir Fhirell set a pace that was easy for me to match as long as I made a concerted effort to ignore the protests of my feet. As we took our first steps, he raised his hand and Mikkhaw spread her powerful wings to take flight.

Despite my determination, my body was beginning to ache from exhaustion. It was a battle not to slouch and slump with each step. The smoky irritation in my throat forced me to cough and when I raised my hand to cover my mouth, my injured wrist throbbed in protest. The handle of my bag dug mercilessly into my palm.

Now that things were calming down, it was becoming ever-more clear that I was not meant to be on this rescue mission. I had been a fool to try to come along. I'd put myself and many others at risk. I may even have made Megan's situation worse.

The walk wasn't short but we didn't speak. It felt as though too much had happened to be able to carve out the words that had been embedded within it all. That would take more time. For now, I focused on keeping myself upright and moving.

The saving grace of our walk was that it was nearly all downhill. It was becoming increasingly evident that we were heading directly toward the docks. It wouldn't be long before I was standing on the deck of Sir Fhirell's ship, once again.

When we arrived, I stepped down into the boat and took a seat. Sir Fhirell did the same. A couple of sailors soon joined us and they took up the oars, rowing us back toward a ship that had never looked as welcome as this one did to me.

As we were rowed, I looked back over Fort Picogeal. Smoke was still rising from certain places, but it came as somewhat of a relief to know that the fires seemed to have been concentrated on two specific areas. From within the city, it had appeared as though every place was ablaze. Now that I was seeing it from more of a distance, it was clear that while there were several buildings that would be lost, it was not the entire town as I had previously feared.

I was drawn out of my thoughts as Sir Fhirell spoke to me for the first time since we had left the people in the woods.

"Sir Vorel has been injured," he told me in a tone that made it clear that he was warning me so that it would not come as a surprise when we arrived on the ship. "I don't know the severity of his wounds."

A deep frown creased my face. "That's terrible news. Was he able to find the missing child?" I hoped he would at least be able to claim a victory to soothe him from his pain.

"As far as I know, the child and mother are both fine."

I nodded, glad to hear that at the very least. Before I spoke again, I hesitated, but managed to push the words through my lips. "How was Sir Vorel injured?"

"He is burned." Sir Fhirell's tone was flat.

Even before my mind could fully understand Sir Fhirell's words, my hand rose to cover my mouth. It took a complete moment before I was able to take it in. It was as though my mind was attempting to refuse what I was hearing.

"I'm so very sorry to hear that, Sir Fhirell. I have medicine for pain, if you think it could be of help to him. I brought it with me as I was afraid that Miss Wynters might need it..."

"Thank you. I will be sure to request it from you if our ship's surgeon feels that it would be helpful."

I nodded and swallowed down the tears that I was determined not to shed. Glancing up at the sky, I saw Mikkhaw circling above. She seemed to be watching over us throughout our return. I allowed myself to wonder how long she had been our soaring guardian without my knowledge.

Returning my gaze to sea level, I watched the approach of the ship. It had seemed the more pleasant scene when compared to the smoke rising from the town, but my opinion on the matter changed quickly as the distance between ourselves and the vessel closed.

At first, when I had heard the sounds of a man crying out in agony, I thought that it was possible that I was mishearing the calls of the sailors on deck, who were preparing the ship to return to Lorammel. It was a matter of minutes before I knew, without a doubt, that this little fantasy could not be true.

Crossing my hands over my heart, I prayed for the man, whom my soul knew was Sir Vorel.

Great Goddess, I beg of you to have mercy on the man whose pain is calling out from the ship and travelling over the sea. Please give him strength and ease his suffering so that he may rest and heal to return to your service...

It had been my intention to continue, but my hands made their way from my heart to my ears to block out the sound as though without my consent or control.

A hand rested supportively on my forearm, and I opened my eyes to see that Sir Fhirell was watching me with concern. I gave him a nod of appreciation, but I could not bring myself to uncover my ears. It felt as though I were somehow at fault for the man's pain. Had I not stowed away on the ship, perhaps he would not have been in the town where the fires were burning. He may not have had to come ashore, at all.

As we reached the ship and prepared to board, the screams stopped. I hoped that my prayers had been answered and that the man had fallen unconscious, where the pain could not find him.

With that, I was finally able to withdraw my hands from my ears, and I rested them in my lap, feeling genuinely rattled. Sir Fhirell's hand gently travelled down my forearm to meet one of mine, holding it in a gentle form of sympathetic embrace.

"It will be alright," he assured me. His voice was steady and confident. I couldn't help but believe him.

Closing my fingers around his, I felt some of the strain ease from my body and, more importantly, from my conscience.

"May I stay with him for a while?" I asked. "Perhaps a little bit of company might bring him some comfort. I am the only one on this ship who is not needed for other tasks."

"I will permit it," he said after a moment of thought. "If you should find that it is too much for you, Miss Godeleva, no one would think any less of you if you were to admit this and return to the captain's cabin, where you will feel more calm."

"Thank you. I will try, at the very least."

After he nodded, we traveled the rest of the way to the ship in silence.

I was assisted onto the deck of the ship by a Knight who was unfamiliar to me. When Sir Fhirell stepped onto the deck and greeted him, I learned that his name was Sir Beal. He was neither tall nor short, with chin-length brown hair and brown eyes of nearly the identical shade to his hair.

"Where is Sir Vorel? Miss Godeleva would like to see him," he asked Sir Beal.

I felt my respect for Sir Fhirell grow as he made a priority of ensuring that I would receive my strange request to spend time with a Knight who had come to great harm. I could tell by the expression that Sir Beal gave to Sir Fhirell that he did not feel that this was necessarily a wise choice. However, Sir Beal set his judgment aside after the briefest twitch of Sir Fhirell's eyebrow. It was enough to tell him that Sir Fhirell had already made his decision, and he did not wish to repeat himself.

"Sir Vorel is in his cabin," replied Sir Beal.

"Do you know where that is, Miss Godeleva?" Sir Fhirell asked me.

"No, but I don't wish to be a nuisance. Which door is it? I will find my way and go there directly," I replied to Sir Fhirell before directing a nod of gratitude to Sir Beal.

"I will take you," Sir Beal offered.

"Thank you," I said to him and curtsied to Sir Fhirell. "Thank you for everything."

"I will be down soon," Sir Fhirell said with a deep nod in reply to my curtsy.

Following Sir Beal, I kept up the pace so he would not think that I was wasting his time in a task that he clearly felt was ill-advised. He was certainly not rushing, but his steps were quick and far more confident on the moving deck of the ship than were mine.

"Are you aware that Sir Vorel was injured, Miss Godeleva?"

"Yes. He was burned," I confirmed. "Thank you for your concern and your caution, Sir Beal."

We descended a steep ladder-like staircase that brought us to a lower deck. Though Sir Beal needed to duck his head just slightly, to travel down the narrow corridor, I was able to walk upright and just clear the beams overhead.

"Have you ever seen the victim of a fire?" he asked as we slowed to a stop in front of a door.

"No," I answered honestly. "But I am prepared to see a man who looks worse than anything I have ever seen or imagined. I must do this, Sir Beal."

"If the Goddess is merciful, he will not be conscious." As he spoke, his fingers quickly and knowingly made the sign of the Goddess.

My hand mirrored the gesture. "I will pray for this blessing."

With no more than a nod, he opened the door to Sir Vorel's room. It was not a large space. Next to the table hung a hammock, and on the floor was a large, lidded pitcher and basin.

My eyes fixed on the unconscious man who was lying on a long table that had been brought into the room and was affixed to the floor. He was stripped to the waist, and as his face was free of burns, my gaze wanted to remain trapped there and not travel down to the places I knew would be much more difficult to witness.

Swallowing hard, I let my eyes wander down over his body. The smell of singed hair and flesh hung heavily in the air. I forced myself to breathe it in; to demand that my senses become accustomed to it so that it would not be allowed to control me. Despite the fact that his face was untouched by the flames, his hair had been burned in sections. There were patches that were shorter, brittle, and crinkled.

The majority of the left side of his body, and most of his left arm, had been licked by the fires. The right side was not as badly burned, but it was still peppered with scorched and blistered skin. The medical supplies that were neatly resting nearby were a clear sign that his wounds had already been cleaned, but bandages had not been applied.

The shock I felt was a blessing. Instead of gagging or sobbing, the pain was pressed so densely within me that it hardened into stone.

Great Goddess, I beg of you to hold me up. Give me strength to help this man. Let me calm and soothe him. Allow me to make the choices that will ease his suffering, which must be profound. Please, Great Goddess, let me be his gift as you gave the friendship of Megan Wynters to be mine. Let me show him your greatness and your blessings as I have been shown them.

Steadying myself, I walked confidently but quietly to the tableside and looked him over in his entirety, familiarizing myself with every detail of the hurt and harm that he had endured. I needed to see it all with my mind and with my soul, and I needed to block out my heart and the sadness it would force me to feel.

Instinctively, I started to hold my breath but I deliberately released it, breathing normally as I reached out and gave Sir Vorel's hair a gentle stroke. My stomach flipped when pieces of charred hair broke away into my hand, but I let them slip to the floor as I made the decision to cut his hair for him before we reached Lorammel.

"The journey home should not be long, Miss Godeleva. We are all praying for good winds," Sir Beal said quietly.

"We are, indeed," I agreed just as softly, acknowledging that I would be among those who were praying. I set to work. Kneeling in front of the pitcher and basin, I scrubbed my hands and arms nearly to the elbows, and rinsed them with the cool water from the pitcher.

"Is there anything that I can bring you, Miss Godeleva?" The tone of his voice and the expression on his face had changed. I had passed some sort of test. Under other circumstances, my heart would have swelled with pride, but this time it could not. My heart was locked behind the solid barrier of my compacted emotions.

"I cannot think of anything. Should I need something later, I will ask."

"He will be wrapped in bandages later. The breath of the Goddess must wash him first."

"I will keep him as comfortable as I can until then."

"I must go above."

I nodded. "We will manage here. If we cannot, I will call for help."

After a slight bow, Sir Beal exited the room, and I was left alone with Sir Vorel. I dampened a cloth and gently wiped his face, hoping that this would help to ease him in his sleep. I folded the fabric and left it on his brow to remind his body that the fire was gone and that he was in a safe, cool place where he could rest and heal.

I wished that I could hold his hand, but I was afraid to touch him. Instead, I spent my time arranging my little medical kit on top of my bag so that it would be ready if I should need it. Carefully, I climbed into the hammock, finding that I was rather inept at it at first, but that as long as I remained still, I could be reasonably comfortable. I watched Sir Vorel the entire time, feeling the passing of every minute; of every second.

*   *   *   *   *

It was not unbearably long before the door opened with a soft knocking. It was Sir Fhirell. He looked slightly cleaner and neater than he had the last time I'd seen him, and it suddenly made me feel much dirtier than I had the moment before. But Sir Fhirell's attention was not on me. His solemn expression was directed toward Sir Vorel.

As gracefully as I could manage, I climbed out of the hammock. It was not the descent that I would have preferred, but I was still glad that I accomplished it without falling.

When Sir Fhirell finally looked at me, it was as though he were tearing his thoughts away from elsewhere.

"Would you like to freshen up, Miss Godeleva? I will remain here while you are gone."

"Thank you, but I have already washed up a little. I don't have much in terms of clean clothes. I packed very poorly for myself."

"We should be home by tomorrow night at the latest."

"I will manage," I said, though I didn't know how. I could change my stockings and under-things tomorrow, but I wouldn't be able to appear much cleaner than this until arriving home.

I don't mind, Great Goddess. I can endure these basic discomforts. I will place my focus on the comfort of Sir Vorel, not on my own. That is what is important now.

Sir Fhirell looked back at Sir Vorel. It was as though I could see his heart sinking. Though very little about him had changed, I could still see the turmoil that was spinning in his mind, and the ache that he felt from seeing his friend in such a state.

"He hasn't woken," I assured him, speaking softly. "I'm glad for that."

"He will need medical treatment that we cannot provide here. I'm glad that you are here for him, Miss Godeleva, and that you brought medicines with you. He will need as much help as we can give him. I will pray that he remains unconscious for the remainder of this journey."

I wrung my hands, wishing that there were something else that I could do or that I could offer.

"I will be sending Mikkhaw ahead of us to the Headquarters to alert them of our return and of Sir Vorel's condition. This will allow them to have a doctor ready, and it will let them notify his wife. Is there anything that should be said to Lord Godeleva in my message?"

"Only that I am safe and that I am looking forward to my arrival home. Thank you, Sir Fhirell."

Resting a hand on my shoulder, he gave it a gentle squeeze. "You have been very brave."

I looked into his blue-green eyes, momentarily taken off guard by his gesture. "It is kind of you to say, Sir Fhirell, but I'm not sure if my actions are as brave as they may seem. I feel as though I am merely numb, right now. It is as though I am incapable of feeling. It is easy to seem brave when one is not held back by emotions."

"You are likely in a great deal of shock. It is natural, and it will pass."

"That must be it."

"You are a strong woman, Miss Godeleva. You have not given up, regardless of the numbness you are feeling now. It isn't until we experience such challenges that our true strength has the chance to show itself."

"I will take your words to heart, Sir Fhirell," I said and decided to shift the conversation away from my own actions; a topic that was not entirely comfortable to me. "You must be looking forward to returning to your family."

"I will be glad to see them as, I'm sure, you will be happy to see your own."

"It would be easier to look forward to my return if I did not suspect that Lord Godeleva will be quite angry and profoundly disappointed in me."

"If you think it would help at all, I would be more than happy to speak to Lord Godeleva of all the good you have done here."

I was taken aback. "Good?" I asked foolishly. The only contribution that I could call to mind was in the form of detours, burdens, injury, and putting the captain of a ship out of his quarters.

"You have made the best of an awful situation. You helped to lead the townspeople to a safe place. You clearly soothed that little boy when his mother was missing. Now, you are doing what you can to help to bring comfort to Sir Vorel. You have achieved all of this while keeping yourself safe at the same time. You have done quite a bit of good, Miss Godeleva."

I was touched. Never could I have imagined that anyone would have seen my desperate efforts to assist as being genuinely helpful.

"I don't know how much sway such words would have on Lord Godeleva, once he has already formed his opinion on the matter...but if you should happen to mention that I was not entirely a burden, I would not object," I replied, shame-faced.

"You were never a burden, Miss Godeleva. You merely caused us to take the scenic route on our mission, instead of the direct one." He smiled in a way that allowed a gleam of playfulness to be expressed in his eyes.

I could not but return his smile, though mine was less playful and more hopeful.

"I must go above," he said. "I will have food brought to you."

"Thank you. I will watch over Sir Vorel, and I will call for help if he should need it."

I watched him glance at Sir Vorel one more time, before he left the room. My attention was then drawn to the injured Knight who lay silently on the table. Changing the cloth on his forehead, I watched him sleep, hoping that every passing moment was helping to heal his ghastly wounds.

When he did finally move, I started. I knew that there was a possibility that he could awaken, of course, but it surprised me nonetheless. A long moan escaped his lips; one that was the result of immense pain.

"Shhh, Sir Vorel. Gently," I spoke in as soothing a voice as I could produce through the rapid beating of my heart. "I will give you some medicine to ease you. Will you swallow it for me?"

His eyes opened only a little and they fixed on me. There was no sign of true recognition in his expression. "Yes," he replied through a haze of semi-consciousness. "Pain," he sputtered.

I worked quickly to open my bag and extracted some of the urac root powder from the medicines that I had taken with me from Lord Godeleva's collection. I mixed it with a small amount of water so that he would be able to drink it.

"I'm going to pour some medicine in your mouth. It will help to dull the pain. You must swallow it so that you don't cough, Sir Vorel," I instructed him.

As he opened his mouth, I slowly poured the liquid into it. I thanked the Goddess for making certain that he did not cough, which would have been agonizing to him.

By the time I was finished pouring the liquid into his mouth, I was sure it would already be starting to take effect. This was a powerful herb. It was one that had to be taken with great care and knowledge. Before me, I could see the Knight easing and relaxing. Certainly, he was still in considerable discomfort, but the pain was no longer causing every muscle to tighten.

"A letter has been sent by way of Sir Fhirell's Skydasher bird. It won't be long before your wife will be alerted that you will be arriving home by tomorrow night. She will find it to be a great comfort to know you'll be with her soon, I'm sure," I said, hoping to speak of subjects that he might find comforting. "I will stay with you until our arrival in Lorammel," I added, stroking a hand over his hair. "You were very heroic."

"Miss Godeleva?" he asked in a confused tone, appearing to focus on me for the first time. His voice was a raspy whisper.

"Yes, that's right. It seems that I'm to be your nurse today. You must tell me if there is anything you need."

"I feel a little better. Thank you for the medicine."

"I will give you more in a little while. Would you like a sip of water?"

His head moved in a small nod.

I stepped over to the pitcher, poured a splash of water into the cup, and brought it back to him. When he seemed ready, I started to dribble the cool liquid into his mouth, just as I had done with the medicine.

He looked up at me and I stopped the water, taking it as the signal that he'd had enough.

"Thank you," he croaked.

I smiled at him in a way that I hoped he would find comforting. I was trying to appear as though all was well and that I hadn't a care in the world other than helping him. I washed all worry from my expression and my tone. He had enough concerns. It wasn't up to me to add to them.

"I'm going to give you a bit of a haircut," I informed him, sounding positive about the experience. "There are a few little singed pieces in your hair. I'm sure that your wife will be very impressed with a shorter style. I've heard that cropped hair is becoming the fashion among men in Lorammel." I tried to punctuate the statement with a confident smile.

It didn't have the effect I had wanted. In retrospect, I couldn't imagine how I'd thought that anything as trivial as a fashionable haircut could matter at all to a man whose body had been badly burned.

"She will be devastated," he said sadly.

"She will be upset," I said caringly. I was not about to lie to this man and pretend that a woman would be pleased that her husband had sustained such injuries. "Any woman who loves her husband would be saddened to think that he was in pain. But she will not be devastated. She will help to care for you when the doctors have treated you, and she will enjoy having your company at home for a while as you heal. She will be grateful that the Goddess chose to send her husband home, when She could easily have opted to take him for Herself."

"I should never have gone in there. How stupid I was."

"Trying to decide whether or not you made the best choice will not change the way that things happened, Sir Vorel," I told him. "Your intentions were very good and you saved a child. The mother will never stop thanking the Goddess for you. You were very brave."

"Sometimes, it does not pay to be brave."

"I can see how it would feel like that, but both the child and the mother would disagree." I leaned down and kissed his cheek.

His head gave a slow shake. "I did not save the child, Miss Godeleva. He had already escaped the building. We didn't know that before I went in."

"I'm sorry."

What else can I say to him, Great Goddess? How do I bring comfort to a man who is as deeply wounded as this one, and who has discovered that it was all for nothing? Please, Great Goddess, show me the way to help to bring your light back into his eyes.

"I'm sorry, too, but I am glad the child was safe. No one deserves to suffer the fate of fire," he agreed.

"As am I," I replied and stroked his face with my fingers before running my hand over his hair, petting it as though I were comforting a sick boy. His pride was wounded. His body was in ruins. In the absence of his true mother, a motherly-type was sure to be welcome.

He shifted slightly on the table and winced, stiffening. I felt my own body freeze until he could relax again.

"I don't imagine this was how you envisioned your journey home." His words were followed by a wry smile.

"None of this is in any way as I had imagined it. I have discovered a great deal about the reality of things on this trip, Sir Vorel. I have failed in my grand effort to be a brave heroine, but I have not failed to learn the lesson that the Great Goddess has been kind enough to show me. So I will take care of you as much as I can and, until we reach Lorammel, we can be heroes to each other."

His understanding smile told me everything that words could not. We had a connection through our well-intended, selfless, and yet entirely ill-advised approaches to heroism.

"You should probably sleep. Would you like me to sing to you a little?"

"Yes. That is, unless your voice is more painful to hear than these burns are to feel," he teased. It lightened my heart to hear his faint little joke.

"If you feel that it is as terrible as all that, I will give you enough medicine that you won't be able to tell anymore," I promised jokingly.

"Agreed," he said simply and shut his eyes.

I couldn't help but laugh at how seriously he accepted my offer to save him from my potentially wretched voice. Taking his uninjured right hand in my own, I started to sing a soft lullaby that every child of Syliza had heard from his mother's own lips.

As I sang, he closed his fingers around my hand and released a sigh that seemed to discharge much of the tension he had still been holding in his muscles. How it warmed me to think that I was bringing him even the tiniest wisp of comfort. Instead of stopping after the first song, I allowed it to flow into a second that I hoped would be equally soothing and familiar to him.

By the time I'd finished the second song, he was fully asleep. His hand had slackened in mine and his face looked slightly calmer.

Thank you. You are truly merciful.

After a few moments, I gently released his hand, humming softly to myself. I stepped up to the hammock and climbed in, trying not to allow my mind to run through the memories of the day. I was determined to look only to the future.

Chapter 12

Megan

I didn't know how long I had been pacing in my small room, waiting for Sleaze Ball or someone else to return, but I was pretty sure my frantic pacing had worn a hole through the bottom of one of my socks.

After a while, I went over to the bed to check out the clothes that had been left there as I had intended to do, pre-Sleaze Ball. There was a long black dress that was identical to the one that I had been given to wear before I had become a slave. It was probably the same one. I decided that cleaner was better, and I changed into the dress, chucking my pants into the bathroom.

I sighed and sat on the bed, noticing for the first time that it had a pillow, a luxury that had been taken away from me when I had become Galnar's slave. I picked it up and hugged it to myself.

This was stupid. I was stupid. Once again, I was being tricked by Galnar. He didn't have Irys. He wanted me to think that he did, just to mess with my head and unnerve me. Mission accomplished.

Galnar's score: 2. Megan's score: 0.

No one was coming.

Hugging the pillow closer to me, I lay on my side and shut my eyes, convincing myself that Irys was fine.

My eyes sprang open with the abrupt sound of a sliding bolt. I scrambled to my feet, tossing the pillow just as the door to my room was thrown open.

Sleaze Ball entered, pushing a wheelbarrow-style contraption. On top of its flat surface lay a very beat-up Sir Radone. Sleaze Ball jerked up the handles, dumped the damaged Knight on the floor, backed up, and left the room, without so much as a glance in my direction.

I stared wide-eyed at the unconscious Knight, who lay in a rumpled heap on his side. My disbelief cemented me to the floor.

"Thank me for your friend."

Galnar stood in the doorway, watching me and waiting for a response.

My anger spiked.

"How could you do this?" I whispered, not hiding my contempt for him; or my disgust.

His expression darkened, and his eyes, that had returned to their muted grey shade, immediately flickered orangey-red. I felt certain he was about to work his fire mojo on me, but he didn't. Without taking his gaze from mine, he walked up to Sir Radone and kicked him hard in the back. The Knight exhaled sharply, and a small amount of blood sprayed from his mouth onto the floor in front of him.

"No! Stop it!" I coughed and rushed toward Sir Radone and dropped to my knees in front of him. I looked up at Galnar. "Thank you, Captain Galnar," I said quickly, hoping that this would be enough to appease the maniac.

He nodded and grinned, looking proud of himself. "I'm going to have food sent for you. I thought you would like dinner with your friend."

Oh geeze. He was gonna send us a bowl of eyeballs, or acid, or something worse.

"Thank you, Captain Galnar," I repeated like a good robot.

He nodded and left, slamming the door and turning the bolt. I felt better knowing there was a locked door between us.

I looked at Sir Radone, who seemed to be unconscious again. I hesitated to touch him. Tentatively reaching out a hand, I finally decided to gently stroke overtop his tangled brown hair. I was too afraid to touch his face. Even with his beard covering half of it, I could see that his skin was swollen and bruised. I didn't want to cause him any additional discomfort.

"Sir Radone," I whispered.

He moved, shifting slightly. His eyes opened slowly. One was puffy and didn't open well, but I could see recognition in his bright blue irises.

"You...Miss..?"

I nodded. "Megan," I said.

"Miss Megan. I'm sorry." He reached out and gave my knee a little pat.

"No, no," I shook my head. "You have nothing to be sorry for, Sir Radone. You fought bravely. I was the one who gave myself up. You didn't do that. I thought that they would have left you alone. I didn't know this would happen. I'm the one who is sorry."

I was sorry. Sorry that I ever let myself believe that Amarogq and his wolves wouldn't keep attacking this man. I took the hand that had patted my kneed and held it.

"They did stop. You were very honourable," he wheezed. "Captain Galnar still wanted to question me."

So, it wasn't Amarogq after all. It was Galnar.

"That man is a monster," I whispered, more to myself than to the Knight.

He gave a small nod but then looked slightly hopeful. "Miss Godeleva. Did you see her?"

I shook my head, frowning. "No. I was taken away. I never saw her."

He listened but his gaze softened as I spoke, and he gave my hand a small squeeze. "She may have escaped."

"I'm hoping that she has," I whispered. "She's very smart."

He nodded and coughed, spraying a few flecks of blood in front of him. My heart immediately pounded faster at the sight of him coughing up blood. Just how injured was he? Was the blood in only his mouth or was he bleeding internally?

"Sir Radone, can I help you in any way? Can I get you some water? Can I help you to the bed where it will be more comfortable for you?" I tried to sound calm but desperation was evident in my voice.

He shut his eyes for a moment but then opened them, shaking his head. "I'm fine here. I don't want to be moved," he said. "I may sleep a little," he added, closing his eyes.

"Okay," I whispered. "You sleep. I'll stay here with you."

Before I had finished my sentence, he was already drifting off. I watched his face for a few seconds but turned my attention to his chest, watching his upper body rise and fall with his breathing. I was terrified that he might die.

Was this really Galnar's plan? To beat a man nearly to death and then lock him in a room with me so I could watch him suffer through his last moments and die?

The door unlocked and opened with no warning. Determined to protect Sir Radone, I braced myself for anything.

Sleaze Ball strolled in, carrying a tray. He set it down on the floor, just out of arm's reach. He looked at me, licked his lips, and then left.

Okay. My appetite is officially gone.

I looked at the contents on the tray and was glad that my appetite had been ruined because eating any of the food that had been sent would have been tortuous with my raw throat. Galnar had sent dry toast, hard-boiled potatoes, and a couple of raw carrots. I take it back. I would have preferred a bowl of eyeballs. They, at least, would have been easy to swallow.

Galnar: 3. Megan: 0

Clenching a fist, I grumbled in frustration and debated whipping the tray of food at him the next time I saw him. It took everything in me not to launch it at the door.

"Eat, Miss Megan,"

The Knight startled me from my rage. I hadn't realized that he had awoken.

"I'm not hungry, Sir Radone."

He slowly reached out a blind hand and rested it on my lower thigh. "Tell your body to be hungry now," he encouraged gently. "It will help you to be strong and to think. You will need to think if you are ever to leave here."

I listened to his words. They made sense. I might not be a slave anymore, but I was still a prisoner. I couldn't take food for granted. Who knows how often I would be fed, and keeping my strength up would be important if I ever wanted to get out of here. Still, my body wasn't interested in being sensible at that moment.

"I won't waste the food but I don't think I can eat right now. Are you hungry?" I coughed.

He gave a tiny shake of his head. "No. Save the food for when you can eat it. Put water on it if it is too dry."

"I will," I promised.

He nodded and then gave a sharp cough. His eyes rolled back into his head and he passed out.

"Sir Radone!" I whispered, giving his shoulder a gentle-but-firm shake. He didn't respond, but I could see that he was still breathing, which helped to calm my racing heart.

I didn't know what to do for him, but I desperately wanted to help this man. What could I give him that would ease his pain? If he wouldn't eat, maybe he would drink water.

Swiftly, I removed Sir Radone's hand from my leg, gently laying it on the floor, and I stood, heading for the bathroom. I filled the mug with water and returned to his side, realizing that I'd probably have to wait until he was conscious before I could start giving it to him.

I placed the cup on the floor beside me and reached out, stroking the Knight's thick hair.

"Please get better," I begged him in a whisper. "Please."

I hated this. I had no idea what to do. I wished Keavren were there to give me some advice.

He didn't come. No one did. Sir Radone remained unconscious, and I never left his side.

It felt like hours had passed before I finally heard the door unlock. I turned my head toward the door. It opened only a fraction of the way, and Aésha poked her head inside.

"May I come in?" she whispered.

"Yes," I nodded. I would have welcome almost anyone's company.

She slipped inside the room, shutting the door, and smiled.

"I do love to play nurse," she winked.

Three things immediately stood out to me about Aésha. The first was that the bruise and swelling that once marked her face were entirely gone. Her skin looked as flawless as ever, making me think that either she had access to some sort of healing magic, or she had the best makeup in the world. The second thing that caught my eye, was that while she was still wearing a black jumpsuit-like military outfit, with tall boots, she had traded in her pants for shorts. Finally, a silver metal box was hanging from a brown strap on her shoulder. Based on her "nurse" comment, I assumed or – at least hoped – it might be a first-aid kit.

I didn't smile back at her playfulness. I wasn't in a laughing mood.

"Is he going to be alright, Aésha?"

Her smile faded when she took in my expression, and she knelt beside me, looking at Sir Radone.

"I don't know, Baby. I didn't actually know he was here with you."

If she was lying, I couldn't tell. She sounded genuine.

"Galnar did this," I whispered.

"Then he should be alright. Captain Galnar wouldn't put a body in here with you," she confidently assured me.

I sighed relief. Knowing Sir Radone would survive eased some of my tension.

She opened the metal box and extracted a little square package. She unwrapped it, revealing what honestly looked like a red sugar cube. Plucking it from the package, she held it between her fingers and brought it up to my mouth.

"Hold this under your tongue and let it dissolve, Baby," she instructed.

"What is that?" I coughed.

"It will heal your throat."

Yeah, right. Why do I feel like she's trying to give me hardcore drugs and not a throat lozenge?

"Would it help him at all?"

Meh, if it is a strong drug, Sir Radone could definitely use it more than I could, at the moment.

"I don't know what's wrong with him," she replied, glancing at the Knight again.

"I don't know, either. He's coughing up blood. Does that mean he's bleeding internally?"

Her brow furrowed slightly as she gave him a more thorough sweep with her eyes.

"Let's get you fixed up first. Then we'll look at him," she said, turning her attention back to me.

I looked at the cube and debated declining it, but I was tired of coughing and swallowing razorblades.

I took the small cube from her and held it under my tongue, allowing it to dissolve. It disintegrated quickly and transformed into a mildly sweet-flavoured viscous substance. I swallowed, and the liquid slid down my throat, coating and instantly soothing it.

I was amazed. My throat felt a million times better, and the urge to cough was gone.

Remind me to write a thank-you letter to Qarradune's god of medicine. I'm in love.

"Thank you," I said, not masking the awe in my voice.

I watched her carefully stroke Sir Radone's hair back, and my feelings toward her softened. She didn't need to be nice to him. She was choosing to be a comfort. I hadn't expected that.

"Are you alright?" I asked her. She had been whacked off a horse, after all.

Aésha grinned. "I'm with you, aren't I, Baby?" she said as if she couldn't be happier.

I gave a small smile and a nod.

She extracted a piece of cloth from her kit and dipped one end into the cup of water I had placed on the floor. She wiped down Sir Radone's face, cleaning the blood from his mouth.

"His lips are cracked. He needs water," Aésha told me without sounding concerned.

She fished an irrigation syringe out of her kit and sucked up a bit of the water from the cup. Gently opening the Knight's lips with her thumb, she dribbled a bit of the water into his mouth. He didn't wake up, but he licked his lips and swallowed the water.

"Give him a little at a time as much as you think you can, without making him cough," she instructed.

"I will. Thank you," I said appreciatively.

I was grateful to receive this advice. Without it, I probably would have done something stupid that would have had him choking on water.

"He's rough," she admitted as her eyes trailed over his body. "This isn't Amarogq's work."

I nodded. "Thanks for saying so. My guess is that it was Galnar." I was ready to blame that guy for everything.

She didn't confirm or deny my suspicions. She only looked at me with a caring expression and kissed my cheek.

"I can't stay, Baby. I'm not supposed to be here. I'll leave the syringe with you," she smiled.

She's not supposed to be here? Why would she bother to risk coming?

I might never know why, but it didn't matter. All that mattered was that she had, and she had brought me comfort when I needed it the most. I wouldn't forget that.

"Thanks, Aésha," I said with heart behind my words.

She nodded and said, "Keavren plans to break in later."

I smiled more, glad I'd be seeing Keavren.

"Take care of yourself, Baby. I'll leave you another sugar cube."

She handed me another cube of medicine which was still wrapped in paper. I took it from her and slipped it into the pocket of my dress, knowing darned well that thing was anything but a sugar cube.

"Thanks, again."

She grinned at me and waggled her brows. "I should come back with more things you can hide in your clothes."

I gave my head a small shake at her tease. She was seriously strange and unpredictable.

She chuckled softly at my response and stood, heading to the door. She stopped to blow me a kiss before she left and locked the door behind her.

I looked at Sir Radone. Nothing had changed. He was still out. I gave him a bit more water, using the syringe as Aésha had shown me. He swallowed it without coughing.

After a while, I drew up my knees, wrapped my arms around them, and rested the side of my head down, facing toward the Knight. I watched him with lazy eyes, wondering when Keavren would show up.

Chapter 13

Irys

It wasn't long before there was a soft knocking on the door, and Sir Fhirell entered with a tray in his hands and a folded blanket over one arm. As soon as he was inside, I extracted myself from the hammock.

In whispers, we discussed Sir Vorel's condition, and I told him about the urac root powder that I had administered to him to ease the pain from which he was suffering. I felt warmed by the smile he shared with me when I mentioned that I had sung Sir Vorel to sleep with a lullaby.

He handed me the tray as he spread his blanket over a clear spot on the floor. Smiling, I understood that we were to have a little picnic lunch, and I arranged the tray on the blanket, taking a seat as daintily as I could. There was soup, bread, and tea, and it all smelled delicious. The scent of the food flooded my senses. I wasn't certain whether the ship's cook was especially skilled or whether my senses were merely delighted as a result of my heightened hunger. Either way, it was taking all my strength to resist the temptation to tear into the bread and drink down that soup.

At the thought of drinking the soup directly from the bowl, I realized that Sir Fhirell had forgotten to bring spoons with him. I decided to wait and allow him to notice for himself so I would not appear ungrateful for the meal.

As though he had read my mind, he picked up a bowl with both hands. A playfully sly grin crawled across his lips before he drank from it, holding my gaze – which must have looked quite shocked – the entire time.

Was I being dared? Or worse, was I being tested? I was not about to show this Knight that I could not survive without a spoon. At first, I picked up my teacup and sipped it, attempting to warm up to the idea of drinking the soup in a similar way. I stared at the small, deep bowl for a brief moment and lifted it to my lips, attempting to remain as ladylike as I could. Though I had an entire collection of etiquette guides on the bookshelf in my sitting room, I was certain that there wasn't a single mention of drinking soup without a spoon.

Feeling rather proud of myself, I glanced up to see if Sir Fhirell looked at all impressed with my achievement. I attempted to mask my horror as I noticed that he had torn off a piece of his bread and was now dunking it into the liquid of the soup. Surely, he would not expect me to do the same!

I began eating my bread as quickly as I could, within reason, so that it would be entirely consumed before he could decide to test me on soup-dunking. Having finished the bread, I returned to drinking the soup and allowed myself to taste it for the first time. It was actually quite lovely. Simple, of course, but the recipe had a charm and richness that was rather unexpected.

Now, I could feel Sir Fhirell's eyes on me. He was not staring at me, per se, but he was certainly glancing in my direction every time I took another sip of the broth.

To distract myself from the awkwardness I was feeling, I decided that engaging him in conversation was the most appropriate strategy.

"Is your sister as fine a painter as they say she is?" The truth was that I hadn't actually heard very much about Miss Vivida Fhirell's skill as a painter, but she frequented the painter's supply shop that was situated directly next to one of my favourite bookstores, and it seemed safe to assume that if she was purchasing the pigments, canvas, and brushes with such frequency, she must have developed a certain level of skill.

"Yes, she is very talented. Many of her paintings have won ribbons. Lady Anglemore has recently commissioned a piece from her."

"It must be thrilling for her to have received such an important order from someone like Lady Anglemore." The Anglemores were a large and highly respected family whose great standing shielded them from any judgment that could be directed toward some of their more unusual choices. I'd heard, for instance, that they were inclined to adopt foreign children instead of having their own!

"I think it's good for her. It is a talent and it is one she enjoys. Do you have such a talent, Miss Godeleva?"

I shook my head even before I took the opportunity to think on the subject. There wasn't anything I could do that I would consider to be a gift.

"I'm not especially good at anything. I do like to read and I am fond of singing and playing the harp, but there are dozens of young ladies who could easily outshine me in any of those things."

"I think I would like to hear you sing and play your harp one day, so that I may decide for myself. I think that you are merely being modest," he said with a warm but slightly teasing grin.

I could feel roses blossoming on my cheeks. "I'm not being modest, I assure you, Sir Fhirell. I usually play only for myself and Lord Godeleva."

"Lorammel is filled with events that allow young ladies to share their musical gifts with society. I hope that you would be so kind as to alert me if you should ever choose to lend your voice to such an occasion."

I was genuinely flustered. "I'm sure that Lord Godeleva would never allow it," I said, feeling pathetic. "He knows that I am not fond of being the centre of attention or performing in front of an audience."

"You are nervous when performing in front of others?"

"Yes. I can't imagine that I would be good enough for people to listen to me. It would be better for someone else to share their skills. I'm not awful. Sir Vorel didn't cry out when I sang him a lullaby," I laughed nervously, "but I don't feel that I am talented enough for a group to hear me. Even if I were, I'm not very fond of having people watch me."

He considered my statement for a long moment before responding. I was starting to believe that I had said something inappropriate. Finally, he appeared to come to some kind of conclusion.

"This only demonstrates exactly how important Miss Wynters must be to you. You risked being the centre of attention in quite a significant way because your goal mattered enough to make it worthwhile."

"I thought it would be. I thought I would be of help in saving her," I agreed solemnly. "I didn't know it would be like this." I finished my soup and rested the bowl down.

We sat silently for a while, sipping our tea, lost in thought.

When we were both finished, we set all the dishes back onto the tray and stood. Sir Fhirell picked up the tray and looked over to Sir Vorel. "I'll have broth sent for him, in case he should wake and feel hungry."

"I will add a little urac root powder to it and will sing to him again, if he wakes," I assured him.

"He is fortunate. If you were not here, his caregiver would not be as sweet."

I couldn't help but disagree. To me, it didn't seem that Sir Vorel was fortunate at all, despite my presence. Were it not for me, he would not have been injured in the first place.

"I'm sure that whoever would have cared for him would have been very kind."

"Kind, yes. Sweet, no. There is a meaningful difference."

"Then I suppose Sir Vorel's fortune is for my sweetness as everything else I have done has been based on foolishness."

"How quick you are to belittle yourself. Are you always this way, or is it unique to this trip?"

"I spend a great deal of my time alone. A young lady must have someone to correct her foolish ways. In my case, I must rely on myself for it."

"Ah, but on this ship, there are no rules for young ladies. We've never had the need. While you're here, you needn't be so ready to chastise yourself for your choices."

"Young ladies must be proper no matter where they may be, even if rules have not yet been established for them," I replied, joining in with the little joke.

"I stand corrected. You are clearly the expert between us when it comes to the subject of young ladies."

I chuckled warmly and found myself hoping that he would stay a little longer.

"Do you plan to stay in Lorammel long before you leave for Gbat Rher?" I hoped the question hadn't seemed too out of place. I was genuinely interested, and it gave me the opportunity to continue our conversation.

"My intentions had been to go in a week or two, whenever our supplies could be prepared and the participants fully ready. Now I will also need to make some additional arrangements with the Knights as Sir Varda is away and I am second-in-command. My hope is to leave as soon as can be managed."

"Are you keen to arrive there?"

"I am. I know that the longer we wait, the longer the people of Gbat must wait." There was a pause before he added, "I think it's only right for you to know that Sir Radone is missing."

I felt my hope slipping. "Perhaps he and Miss Wynters are hiding from the fires in the city and will turn up when things start to settle." Could that have been it?

Great Goddess, are they safe? Would I know if Megan were in danger or worse..? Would I feel it in my soul if the world had lost such a person? Would you tell me if I had not proven myself worthy, and you had withdrawn your gift of her friendship with me?

"That is possible," Sir Fhirell replied before looking at me in a studying way. "Do you feel that you are to blame for this?" The question was direct and my answer would clearly define the way that he would proceed, in some way.

"I am to blame for this, Sir Fhirell," I replied firmly. "If I'd had the courage to say something at the Masque – just one word to one person – none of this would have happened. Miss Wynters would not have been kidnapped, a rescue would not have been needed, Sir Vorel would not have been injured, and Sir Radone would not be missing. I was a coward and everyone else is paying for my cowardice."

"Miss Godeleva, there is no way to know that this is the case. If you had said something to someone at the Masque, you may have stopped all this from happening. Equally, you may have been the signal that the Warriors were awaiting for an attack on your guests. Many people could have been hurt. You were not silent because you were a coward. You were silent because you did not take it upon yourself to place all your guests at risk. Things may have happened this way because you did not speak, but only the Goddess knows whether or not this was the better choice. Had something else happened, you would have blamed yourself for that, too."

"You're right. Yet, I still feel that I am to blame for all this. I cannot change my heart."

"I know that feeling all too well. But you must not allow it to dictate your fate. You may feel that you are responsible for the present, but you still have the chance to change your future."

"Yes. It is exactly that belief that drove me to this point. It is the reason that I have made the choices that I did; to come along on this rescue. I have been failing miserably at redeeming myself."

"Give yourself time to heal. You have not had time to think rationally on everything you have suffered. Your pain has been a deeply emotional one, but it has taken its toll on your body as well. You are exhausted and you have your own wounds to overcome." He placed a gentle hand on my bandaged arm, for a brief moment.

"You're right," I said softly as though I could barely find my voice. But where my voice was lacking, a spark of an idea fell into its place. "Would you allow me to beg a favour of you? I know that you have already done a great deal for me. In fact, I'm practically already in your debt..."

He looked curious and even somewhat amused at my stumbling words. "Please, make your request."

"Would you be so good as to play postman for me, if I were to give you a letter addressed to someone in Gbat Rher?"

"I would be honoured." His smile was warm enough that it could have brought the temperature up in the room. Suddenly, my body was not as heavy, and I was more at ease."

"Thank you very kindly. I have been hoping to send my best wishes to a friend who lives there and to let him know that I kept a promise that I had made to him. It will feel good to know that he may one day learn that his trust was not misplaced."

"If it is within my power, your friend will know that you have kept your promise."

"Thank you." What good that knowledge did to my heart! Thinking on Kolfi reminded me that despite the foolish decisions I had made of late, my intentions had been good. Occasionally, my actions had even managed to be helpful.

"As much as I would like to remain and continue this conversation," Sir Fhirell said after sipping his tea in silence for a few minutes, "I must return above deck."

"Of course," I replied, coming back to the present. I glanced over at Sir Vorel. "Is there any way for me to cover him? I'm afraid that he might become chilled as he is."

"I will send the ship's surgeon. He will know."

"Thank you. I will do what I can to be of assistance to him."

"Is there anything you need? A book, perhaps?"

"No, thank you. I intend to watch quietly over Sir Vorel and to try to sleep when I am not needed."

"Sleep is a good activity in such times."

"I hope for a little, but when I close my eyes, I don't like what I see."

Without replying, he gave me an understanding look. He set down the tray and took my hand, raising it to his lips so he could place a kiss just below the knuckles of my second and third fingers. He held my hand for a delayed instant, giving it the gentlest squeeze, which I returned before he relinquished it.

Instead of saying anything at all, we watched each other for another moment, until he exited with the lunch tray. How right the world felt, if only for that brief time. The door clicked shut and my body released a breath that had been held for too long. Reality reappeared before me.

Sir Vorel continued to sleep as his exquisitely ruined body granted him a temporary respite from the agony of consciousness. I bent down to kiss his forehead, but was interrupted by the sound of the door as it opened. I straightened and turned to see a middle-aged man with greying hair. He nodded to me and approached the table on which Sir Vorel lay, setting a cup of broth down upon it.

Leaning his hunched back forward to peer at Sir Vorel's burns, through small, thick spectacles, he ignored me rather thoroughly until his analysis was complete.

"I will give him the broth if he wakes," I offered. "He has had a dose of urac root powder and has been sleeping calmly."

"Mmm," he muttered as his only acknowledgement that I had spoken.

The man completed his observation of Sir Vorel, looked thoughtful for a moment, and left the room without another word. At first, I thought this might have been all the attention that Sir Vorel would be receiving, but the man – whom I could only assume was the ship's surgeon, sent by Sir Fhirell – returned with a few supplies.

He walked back up to the table and proceeded to construct a type of fabric tent over Sir Vorel, covering him without actually laying the blanket directly onto his skin.

"Make sure you don't move this. It's not to touch him. Make sure he doesn't move it, either," he said plainly. I jumped at his words, not because they were spoken loudly or fiercely, but because I was starting to believe that he had forgotten that I was present.

"I will," I promised, glad that some warmth was being provided to the poor injured man. "I will be certain to have you called if I notice anything out of place."

"If anything about him changes, I want to know right away," he said firmly. Without ceremony or waiting for me to reply, he left the room once more.

Stepping up to Sir Vorel, I made sure that he seemed to be as comfortable as possible and gave his forehead a little wipe and a kiss. This seemed important to me after having watched the ships surgeon's lack of bedside manner. I felt that somehow Sir Vorel would know.

Convinced that I had done all I could for the man, I looked over at the hammock. I was tired. Overtired. As much as I wanted to sleep, my mind was spinning with thoughts of every shape and size. Glancing down at my bag, it occurred to me that the smallest amount of urac root powder might be just the thing to pass the voyage more peacefully and to ensure that I would be more alert if I were needed upon waking.

I wouldn't give myself nearly the dose that Sir Vorel had received, of course, but just enough. With rapid movements, I extracted the medicine and added a dusting to some water, which I swallowed in a single unladylike gulp. Barely a moment had passed before I could feel the muscles in my face and body slackening. How lovely it seemed to be forced to release all those tensions that had been knotting my shoulders.

Unaware of exactly how I arrived in my hammock, I found a comfortable position nearly right away and may have been asleep before my eyes were fully shut.

*   *   *   *   *

It was a moan that woke me. Upon opening my eyes, it took a delayed moment before I recognized my surroundings and the source of the sound. Still, when the realization that the moan belonged to Sir

Vorel struck me, it woke me as though a pail of ice water had been upended over me.

"I'm coming," I assured him in a voice that clearly had not woken as rapidly as the rest of me. It was by only the grace of the Goddess that I was able to extract myself from the hammock without falling. Immediately afterward, I was by his side.

Taking his hand, I spoke softly to him. "I'm here, Sir Vorel. Do you need more medicine?"

His eyes were anything but calm as he held my hand in return. "Yes," he said through gritted teeth.

"I will fetch it for you," I said and released his hand so that I could prepare the urac root powder for him as quickly as possible. My fingers trembled as I tried to take the greatest care to measure out the powder and mix it with the water.

He took the liquid gratefully, to the point that I found it difficult not to administer it more quickly than the slow dribble we had used the previous time. When he had taken the dose, I stroked his hair so that we could wait for the effects to ease him.

I felt as though I were breathing for the first time when I finally saw the relief cross his face. I asked him if he would like some of the broth that had been brought for him, but he refused. He would not even take more water than what had been mixed with his medicine.

"If Lord Godeleva will permit it, would you allow me to visit you while you heal, Sir Vorel?" I asked, realizing that I had no idea how long we had sailed while I was asleep and that we could be nearing Lorammel. Once we arrived, there would no longer be any reason for me to stay by his side.

"Perhaps," he replied, making me feel as though I may have overstepped my bounds.

I felt driven to try to do something else to comfort him and this brought to mind an idea that I'd had during an earlier conversation with him.

"Would you allow me to cut your hair? Just a trim of the parts that have been singed. Perhaps it will even feel a little nicer for you."

"Yes," he agreed simply but without enthusiasm.

Extracting my mending kit from my bag, I brought the scissors over to Sir Vorel. They were small but very sharp sewing scissors. With meticulous care, I snipped away as much of the crispy curled pieces as I could, while maintaining an even style to his hair. Never having cut hair before, I took away only a little bit with each clip. I didn't feel that either of us were in much of a hurry, and it wouldn't hurt if I took my time.

"You can cut whatever needs to be removed. I don't mind if it's short. I trust your judgment," he said after a while, smiling to me a little as he spoke.

I released a breath I hadn't realized I was holding. "I will leave as much behind as I can. Right now, I'm trying to keep it even."

"Will you speak to me or sing to me as you work? You have a lovely voice. I like listening to you."

"Thank you." I was touched. "I wasn't sure that you would remember that I sang to you. Did you want another lullaby? I don't mind if you sleep while I finish your hair."

"I do remember. I'm nearly sorry that I fell asleep. I would have liked to have heard more."

"Don't be sorry for sleeping. I'm glad when you rest. I can always sing to you when you wake. I will sing for you but in the hopes that it will bring you sleep, darling Knight."

He smiled up at me for as long as he could keep his eyes open, but they drifted shut as I started to sing. I gently combed through his hair with my fingers and trimmed away the burnt pieces. I sang every lullaby I knew, following them with a few softer songs that weren't lullabies but that were equally soothing. I continued for as long as I worked on his hair, unsure as to whether he was sleeping or simply resting with his eyes closed.

When I was satisfied with my work, I put the scissors away and seated myself in the hammock, finishing my song and hoping that Sir Vorel was resting well. As soon as the tune was done, the door slowly opened, startling me.

"I'm sorry to have surprised you," Sir Fhirell whispered. "I waited until you stopped singing. Is he asleep?"

"Yes…I gave him a little lullaby to help him to rest. He asked me to. I didn't realize that I had been singing as loudly as I was."

He entered, smiling to me, and shut the door as he crossed the room to look at Sir Vorel. Turning his attention back to me, he said, "You did a good job removing the damaged parts of his hair."

"Thank you. I thought it might be more comfortable for him," I replied and then confessed, "I also thought it might be easier on his wife. I know it didn't help much, but at least there is one less piece of evidence that reminds her of what he has undergone."

"Every bit helps, Miss Godeleva. I'm sure you've done more than you realize." His tone brightened. "Speaking of Sir Vorel's reunion with his wife, we will be arriving in Lorammel soon. The winds have favoured us. We're nearly home."

"I'm glad. It will be good for Sir Vorel to be treated in a hospital."

"It will. Although, with the way you sing, I'm surprised his wounds have not already healed. I found your voice to be very soothing."

"You flatter, Sir Fhirell." I could feel the blush crawling up my face from the base of my neck.

"I merely extended a well-deserved compliment. I have heard few other voices that could compete with yours."

I was flustered and could think of nothing intelligent to say, so I fell back on being polite, instead. "Thank you, Sir Fhirell."

"You have brought Sir Vorel a great deal more comfort than I thought would be possible in his condition. I should be thanking you."

"I'm glad to have contributed in some way." Though my intention was to leave the statement at that, I felt suddenly driven to share my deeper thoughts with Sir Fhirell. He had been such an understanding and kind man, until now. I needed his reassurance. I wanted him to know me. "I have to admit that while half of me longs to return home and put this behind me, the other half is afraid of what I will find there," I confessed.

"If you would allow it, I would like to see how you are doing once you settle in again, Miss Godeleva."

This took me by surprise. How caring he was. "Of course. I would like that very much and I'm sure Lord Godeleva will be honoured by the interest you have taken in the wellbeing of his family."

The way he smiled in response to what I said led me to believe that there was a great deal he was thinking, without speaking nearly as openly as I had done.

"I must return above," he said with regret in his tone. "I hope you will be able to rest a little before we arrive. I'll return again once we have docked."

"Thank you. I will alert someone if Sir Vorel's condition should change."

He smiled and held my gaze for an extended moment before he bowed to me, to which I curtsied before he left. It saddened me a little that we would be unable to speak further. I could sense that, in my heart of hearts, I was hoping he would live up to his word and would call at the estate to visit me.

After giving a final check on Sir Vorel, I decided that Sir Fhirell was right. This was a good opportunity to rest a little. I hadn't anything better to do, and I expected that I would need to be at my very best when it came time to face Lord Imery.

I chose to use a small amount of the urac root to help to ease my anxiety and to rest. Despite the fact that I'd used less this time than the last time, it felt as though it was having an even more powerful effect. Perhaps I was more tired this time but, for the moment, I didn't have the mental capacity to think it through. In fact, I was barely able to make it to my hammock and climb in.

Once I was settled, I sang softly to myself, choosing a lullaby that I had already sung for Sir Vorel. If I had finished the song before falling asleep, I did not remember doing so.

Chapter 14

Megan

"Rani?"

I opened my eyes, startled by his voice. I must have drifted off.

"Sir Radone," I answered softly. "It's alright. It's me, Megan."

He shifted, and a series of coughs burst forth from his lungs. I moved to my knees, alarmed by his coughing.

"I thought you'd left, Rani." He coughed a lot more but then smiled as if he couldn't be happier.

Um? Maybe he forgot my name...

"It's alright, Sir Radone. I'm here," I told him, reaching out to take his hand to try to comfort him.

Still coughing, he smiled more and nodded to me.

"Look in on Naida. She's in the garden," he said blissfully.

Oh, no. He's hallucinating! He must think I'm this Rani- person. What do I do? Should I play along?

No. I couldn't pretend to be someone I wasn't. It didn't seem right, no matter how much I wanted to know who Rani and Naida were. What I could do was cut out the formalities to make our exchange more personal.

"Rral," I said, addressing him by his given name, remembering that he had told it to me when we had first met. "It's alright. Would you like some more water?"

Another series of coughs racked his body. He brought up his hand to his mouth in response. When the worst of the coughing was over, he brought his hand down and there was blood on it and on his lips.

Any calm I had left, diminished at the sight of the blood. I fought back the urge to cry, and I stroked his hair instead, in an effort to try to calm us both.

"You're alright," I told him, but I knew my words were more for my benefit than his. "Just rest now. Save your strength."

"Always worrying," he smiled in a loving way, coughing again. "It will be fine, Rani."

Although he was looking directly at me, it was like he was looking through me. His eyes were glazed over like he was in a daydream.

"It will be fine," I agreed quietly. "Sleep now," I urged, not wanting him to talk anymore, to save him from another coughing fit.

He nodded, but then said, "First, give this to Oradalf."

He pulled a thick silver ring off his middle finger and held it out toward me but dropped it before I had time to accept it. The ring clattered to the floor, but he didn't notice. Clearly, the Rani in his mind had accepted it.

I picked up the ring up and held it in my hand.

"Alright," I told him. Naturally, I had no idea who Oradalf was, but I decided I'd hold on to the ring until Rral was better. Then I could give it back to him, so he could give it to the intended owner.

He smiled in a blissful way and coughed a little.

"I love you, Rani."

I instantly welled up and a tear slipped from my eye. I assumed that Rani was his wife.

"I'm sure she loves you, too, Rral," I whispered. "You'll see her again soon," I promised.

A small, peaceful smile graced his lips. "Yes," he whispered, shutting his eyes.

He didn't speak again. I could tell that he was already drifting off to sleep. I clutched his ring tightly in one hand and stroked his hair with the other, letting my tears flow freely down my face.

I didn't know how it would be possible, but I vowed to myself, at that moment, that Rral would see Rani again, and he would give his ring to Oradalf. He was going to be okay, and I was going to be okay.

When Rral seemed to be in a deep sleep, I gave him a little more water, and he swallowed the tiny amount of liquid as he had before. Satisfied, I decided it was time to take Rral's advice and get some food into my system. I would need my strength but first, most importantly, I had to blow my nose in the worst way.

Slipping Rral's ring into my pocket, I got up and went to the bathroom to deal with my crying-induced snot factory. When I could breathe again, I splashed a bit of cool water on my face and took a nice drink of it as well.

Feeling much better, I returned to Rral. Kneeling down, I picked up the syringe and gave him more water.

He didn't react.

I tried again with no success.

I looked at him more closely and knew that something was wrong. He looked too still and too relaxed.

"Rral?" I queried in a loud voice.

He gave no response.

Dropping the syringe I shook him firmly with both hands. His body sagged and flopped under my grip; all the tension in his muscles were gone.

"Rral!" I yelled, terror and panic seizing me. "Someone! Help! Please, come quick! Rral!" I screamed, shaking him.

Oh, God! He's not breathing!

Using all my strength, I pushed Rral over onto his back and continued to scream for help. Since he wasn't breathing, I knew I had to give him CPR. I took a class once, years ago, but I was pretty sure I still remembered the gist of it.

Positioning myself over Rral, I started to pump my hands in a rhythm on his chest.

The door to the room was suddenly thrown open. I looked up to see Galnar bursting in.

"Galnar! Help! Please! Rral's not breathing! He needs help!"

At first, he stared at me like I had completely lost my mind, but then a look of utter surprise flooded Galnar's face as his gaze shifted from me to Rral. It was like he couldn't believe what I had just said, or he couldn't process what he was witnessing. His grey eyes looked back to me, and his surprise melted into solid stone.

"You will be dealt with," he said without emotion, turning and leaving the room.

"Wait! Where are you going?" I yelled at him, but he didn't return.

I didn't waste any more time. Rral needed my help. I continued my attempt at CPR.

I kept up my efforts until I felt a hand touch my shoulder.

"Megan...come on. We'll go somewhere else now, alright? Someone will come for him," Keavren said quietly.

I paused my motions and looked at Keavren like he was nuts.

"What are you talking about, Keavren? We can't just leave him! We have to help him!"

Keavren drew me away from Rral and, to my relief, began to inspect him. He reached out a hand and placed it on his chest and then placed his fingers at the side of his throat. He then leaned down and listened at his mouth. I watched him intently, waiting for him to tell me what the next step would be to help Rral.

"I'm really sorry, Megan."

That threw me. I wasn't expecting an apology. I looked at him and was about to ask him what he meant, but then it all made horrible sense. The sympathetic look he was giving me; the compassion in his voice. He wasn't apologizing. He was expressing his condolences.

"No," I whispered.

The sympathy in his eyes grew deeper.

"No," I told him, my voice rising with my firm decree. "He's not dead. He can't be. Aésha said Galnar wouldn't do that. She said he wouldn't leave me with a body," I protested.

"I don't think he meant to, Megan," Keavren spoke softly. "Aésha didn't mean to mislead you."

I looked at Rral and allowed myself to realize what I'd known the moment I had touched his limp form: there was no life in his body. He was dead.

Keavren placed a hand on my shoulder. "Can I please bring you somewhere else?"

I continued to stare at Rral's body. I was so overwhelmed with shock, I felt numb.

"What about him? What are they going to do with him? Who's going to tell..." I trailed off. My short-lived numbness had been overrun by unbelievable sadness.

Who would tell Rani? How would Oradalf get his ring?

The tears spilled out of my eyes.

Keavren slid his arm around me and drew me in close.

"I will come back and take care of him, myself," he whispered.

I looked at Keavren and nodded, not knowing what else to say. Reaching out my hand, I gave Rral's hair one final stroke.

"I'm so sorry."

"Do you want me to carry you?" Keavren asked.

I shook my head and he stood, holding his hand out to me. Taking it, I climbed to my feet and held Keavren's arm, when it was offered. I was so lightheaded from shock and crying that when I started to walk, I almost felt like I was floating.

We exited the room and Keavren shut the door in a quiet way as if Rral were only sleeping and he didn't want to disturb him. We walked down the hall at a slow pace and headed up a flight of stairs. I wasn't paying attention to where we were going. I probably should have, but I couldn't bring myself to care. All I could think about was that Rral was dead.

We must have arrived at our intended destination because Keavren opened a door to a room and gestured for me to enter. I did, looking around. We were in someone else's room. It was much larger than the one I had been given, with three times the space. The bed in this room was also larger and could easily accommodate two people. The layout reminded me of Galnar's room, except this definitely wasn't his room.

Not only was the décor different, but the bed was decked out in black and bright pink bedding, and a sheer pink curtain surrounded it. There was also a desk and a dresser with little personal knick-knacks scattered here and there. There were two closed doors, which indicated that there were an additional two rooms.

I didn't know who owned this room, and I didn't care. It held about as much interest for me as a dark cave. I just wanted everything to go away; to close my eyes and hibernate until I could wake up on my own world.

Hearing someone enter the room, I turned and saw Sleaze Ball. He didn't look at me or Keavren. Keeping his head down, he brought a cot into the room and set it up quickly against a wall, without a word. I looked away from him and stared down at my hands. He was one of the last people I wanted to see.

"Want me to make up your bed?" Keavren's quiet voice touched my ears.

"No. I can do it."

"I'm going to go and keep my promise now."

I looked up from my hands and nodded. "Thank you," I whispered.

"Aésha will be back soon," he assured me.

He didn't hide the worry in his eyes as he saw the lack of emotion on my face.

"I'm really sorry, Megan."

"Me too, Keavren."

He nodded and watched me with an expression that made it obvious to me that he wished there were something he could say that would help the situation or make me feel better, but we both knew that wish was futile.

Finally he left, allowing me to embrace the miserable peace of aloneness that I far preferred to the company of anyone aboard this ship. I ached for Irys. I ached for Thayn. I ached for home.

I made up the cot with the fresh sheets and blanket that had been provided, trying to focus on the task to prevent my mind from thinking about Rral. It didn't work.

I flopped down on the cot when I was finished and felt something hard dig into my outer thigh. Fishing a hand into my dress pocket, I pulled out Rral's silver ring. My vision blurred with tears.

Rani, I'm so sorry.

The door opened, and I immediately closed my hand around the ring, hiding it from view. I wouldn't let any of them see it. I wouldn't let them take this away from Rral, too. I would find a way to get this ring to his family. He was a Knight. When I saw Thayn again, I'd tell him about what happened, and I'd ask him to help me find Rral's family.

The cot sank as Aésha sat beside me.

"I just heard," she said softly.

I looked at her and nodded, quietly adding without emotion, "I just want to be alone."

"This is my room. We're going to be sharing for a while," she explained, keeping her voice gentle. "So I'll be here, but I won't bother you."

"Thank you."

"If you want anything, you just say. If you don't want to sleep on your own, you can slip in with me. Just do what you have to do, Baby."

I nodded.

She gave my knee a rub, got up and exited into one of the two other rooms. Based on the sounds and the smells that followed soon after, I guessed the room was a kitchen.

While she was gone, I slipped Rral's ring back into my pocket, and I lay down on the cot, curling up on my side. I shut my eyes.

After a while, I could hear Aésha moving around the room. She walked up to my cot. When her shadow fell over my face, I opened my eyes to look up at her.

"There is soup in the kitchen. It's still hot, if you want some."

"Thanks, maybe I'll have some a little later, if that's alright." I had fully intended to keep my promise to Rral, but I just couldn't stomach the thought of food.

She nodded kindly. "Of course," she said and reached out to give my shoulder a stroke.

A soft knocking at the door drew her attention from me. She sighed and walked over to it. I didn't turn to see who it was. I could hear her talking quietly to someone, and then she shut the door and returned to my side.

She sat on the edge of the cot in front of my hip and slipped something soft into my hand.

"That's for you," she said softly. "This was sent to you as proof, to show that she's alright, and she's going home."

I looked at her, confused, and opened my hand to reveal a small folded piece of white fabric. I unfolded it, to examine it more closely and saw the purple monogram. It was a handkerchief I'd seen before, at the Godeleva estate. It belonged to Irys.

I looked at Aésha with a twinge of hope, searching her face for any sign of play or deception. There was only understanding and something close to sadness.

"You mean it? She's safe? She's not here?" I wanted to hear her say the words.

"She's not here, Baby. We weren't after her."

I clutched the handkerchief tightly and drew it up against my chest like a stuffed toy.

"Thank you," I whispered to her.

"You're welcome, Baby. Keavren brought it. I'd be willing to bet that he got it from Acksil."

I nodded, wondering how Acksil managed to get it. Had he seen Irys?

"This is our little secret, alright?"

"I won't say anything," I agreed.

Nodding at my words, she leaned down and placed a light kiss on my forehead.

Drawing away, she said, "I'm going to go to bed in a while, but you can wake me if you want to talk or if you just don't want to be alone."

"Thanks."

She gently stroked my face in a motherly kind of way, before getting up and heading into the kitchen.

As she moved around the rooms, I brought Irys' handkerchief to my lips and kissed it.

I'll find a way back to you, my friend.

The light to the room shut off, flooding the room in darkness. I heard Aésha climb into her bed and then there was nothing but blackness and silence. Drawing my legs up, I curled into a tighter ball, desperate to feel secure, yearning to feel safe.

Slipping my hand into my pocket to hold the ring, I held Irys' handkerchief tighter and found no comfort. These cold and lifeless objects were only reminders of what I had lost. Unbearable loneliness engulfed me, and I felt that if I stayed lying on the cot for one second longer, I'd either die or go mad.

Getting up, I made my way over to Aésha's bed and stood at the edge. I hesitated for only a second before I climbed in beside her. I needed to be close to someone who was warm, with a beating heart – even if that person was my enemy.

Aésha turned her head to look at me and then turned fully onto her side, bringing an arm over me and drawing me in close. I slipped my arms around her, in response, and broke down.

The tears flowed freely, and she just let me sob, rubbing my back and stroking my hair.

When the worst of it was over, she drew back a little and quietly looked at me in the darkness, lifting a hand and dabbing my face lightly with her own handkerchief.

"I…" I started to say, but stopped, having no idea how to express my jumbled thoughts into words.

She merely nodded with understanding. "I know, Baby. I really do," she whispered.

I believed her.

"I…I don't want to be alone," I confessed.

I'd thought it was what I wanted, but it wasn't.

"You're not alone, Baby."

She kissed my forehead and I hugged her. It was strange. Even though I no longer felt so alone, I didn't feel any safer. Yet, somehow, I felt less afraid.

Chapter 15

Irys

"Miss Godeleva," spoke a soft, male voice.

Opening my eyes was a strikingly challenging effort. I still hadn't managed to do so, when I realized that a hand was lightly shaking my shoulder. Until that moment, I hadn't felt the motions at all.

"Sir Fhirell?" I asked as I realized whose voice I was hearing. At my own words, it dawned on me that I had managed to sleep through the sounds of someone entering the room and, if that were the case, I could have slept through Sir Vorel's cries for help. I awoke much more fully and looked with wide eyes at the man who had woken me. "Sir Fhirell! Is anything wrong?" My voice croaked as I battled to become alert.

His calm smile reassured me ahead of his words. "No. Nothing is wrong. The ship is beginning to dock. I promised to tell you when we were approaching the city."

"Yes. Of course. I seem to have fallen into quite the deep sleep. I'm entirely disoriented. I shall rise."

"Whenever you are ready. Sir Frayne is outside the door and will come in to take care of Sir Vorel, if you'd like to come up on deck."

Hauling myself from the hammock without a hint of grace, I nodded to Sir Fhirell. "I will be but a minute."

My fingers combed through the loose parts of my hair as I stepped up to Sir Vorel, who was still asleep. I was glad. It meant that it would allow him more of an opportunity to heal, while sheltering him from his pain. It also meant that I wouldn't be able to say goodbye to him. Leaning down, I kissed him on the forehead.

I nodded to Sir Fhirell, who picked up my bag, and we stepped out the door. I squinted into the bright sunlight as I curtsied to Sir Frayne. He had been waiting immediately outside, in the narrow corridor.

He bowed to me in return. "Safe travels home, Miss Godeleva. You've done a very kind thing for Sir Vorel."

"It was a privilege to help him. I hope his healing is a quick one."

"We all hope for that," he said warmly as he entered the room to watch over Sir Vorel."

Carefully, I climbed the steep steps from below deck to above. The crew was working hard to prepare for disembarking. The harbour master was already aboard, and a tug was drawing us toward the docks. Beyond that, was Lorammel.

How beautiful and alive, the city looked. The pale stone and wooden buildings stood proudly along the shore. The rooftops of other structures behind them, peeked up to show that the city was a vast one and this was not merely a fishing village. Plumes of smoke puffed from the chimneys of houses, shops, and factories, keeping time with the pulse of this vast city, while maintaining its life for yet another day.

"Do you have everything?" asked Sir Fhirell, breaking me out of my reverie. I was leaning against the rail, attempting to stay as far out of the way of the busy sailors as I could.

"Yes. The only thing missing is my courage, but I don't believe I have that, here."

I was given an understanding smile. "I think you still have a great deal of it, Miss Godeleva. Just because you feel anxious, it doesn't mean that you aren't also courageous."

"I can only pray that I will have enough to face Lord Godeleva."

Please, Great Goddess, give me the courage to face Lord Imery.

"Lord Godeleva will be happy to see you safe and home again. Remind yourself of that." He smiled. "I will return to escort you when the time comes."

"I will do my best to stay out from underfoot, until then."

With a light chuckle, he walked away and I turned back to watch our slow approach to Lorammel and whatever future it held for me.

The docking process felt as though it took longer than the entire journey but as I watched the lowering of the gangplank, it still felt as though we had arrived too soon. I wasn't ready.

I took Sir Fhirell's arm as it was offered and wondered if I would survive on my own when the time came to let it go. He carried my bag in his other hand.

Making every effort to look dignified as I stepped down the gangplank, I imagined that Sir Fhirell couldn't have failed to detect how heavily I was leaning on him. It was as though I was unable to control my legs.

"Honour and glory," he said to a pair of Knights who stood at the bottom of the gangplank to welcome us. They replied in kind and all three men placed their fists over the gold Knights' medallions that were affixed over their hearts. Sir Fhirell had paused to set down my bag in order to complete the gesture.

"Miss Godeleva!" A man's voice called my name from aboard the ship. I looked up to see the entire crew lining the nearest rail, facing me. In unison, every man bowed to me. "For Sir Vorel!" the same man called out. From where I was standing, I couldn't tell which one of them was the one who was speaking.

Glancing at Sir Fhirell, I could see the pride in his eyes.

My heart pounded in my chest, and I released Sir Fhirell's arm, sinking into a deep curtsy to show my respect for every one of the men who had risked themselves to rescue Megan and to keep me safe; despite how foolish I had been.

When I rose, the peace of the moment was broken by their sudden shouts, all speaking at once. At first, I was afraid that I had somehow offended them and that they were angry with me. The noise was overwhelming. However, as I picked out some of the words from above the others, I realized that this was not at all the case.

"Thank you for caring for him!"

"You're the best nurse a Knight could ever have!"

"You're beautiful!"

"Sing for us again!"

"Marry me!"

I couldn't help but laugh. I waved to them and managed to find the nerve to blow a kiss at the man whom I believed was behind the proposal.

The noise eventually died down, and the men returned to their duties but their gift to me was a powerful one. I was now able to stand on my own feet. My pride had returned. I was ready to face Lord Imery.

The docks were bustling with life. It felt as though half the population of Lorammel must have been there at the waterfront, completing one task or another. If it weren't for the crowds, I would have spotted the coach much more quickly. It was decorated in the cream and gold Godeleva colours and with the crest mounted on its door. It was drawn by a team of two gorgeous horses.

As we approached, a footman stepped down and bowed to us. "Miss Godeleva, welcome back. I'm pleased to see that you have returned safely."

"Thank you. It is good to be home," I replied to him, slightly less formally than I should have. I was eager and nervous to see Lord Imery and found it very difficult to concentrate on anything else.

"Lord Godeleva extends his gratitude to you, Sir Fhirell," continued the footman. That drew my attention as did his following words. "Unfortunately, he was unable to be here in person as he had business to which he was required to attend."

My heart sank. I shouldn't have been surprised that he was not here to meet me. There was no way for him to know exactly when the ship would be arriving. He would not have been able to afford to lose hours of his busy day in order to sit here and wait for me. Still, it hurt to think that he would not be sitting in the coach to greet me when the door was opened.

"I understand. Please tell Lord Godeleva that it was an honour," replied Sir Fhirell.

I looked up at him, feeling the pang of our parting suddenly striking me. "Thank you again, Sir Fhirell. I do look forward to the next occasion to see you."

"As do I. Would you like me to escort you back home, Miss Godeleva?"

"I'm grateful for the offer, but I couldn't possibly ask another favour of you. You have your own home and family to whom you must long to return. After all we have been through, I'm certain that I can survive a brief coach ride, unscathed."

He kissed my hand, and I smiled softly in return. "I will speak with you again soon and will let you know how Sir Vorel is healing."

"I'd like that very much. I hope you will have good news for me."

"I hope for the same." With that, he stepped back from me and handed my bag to the footman.

I took the footman's assistance to climb into the carriage and started when I found myself looking at Desda. I had expected to be alone.

"Hello Desda," I said, speaking quietly. For a reason that I could not identify, the occasion seemed to warrant hushed voices. Glancing out the window, I saw that Sir Fhirell was still standing there, and I gave him a small wave.

A smile warmed his face, and he waved back to me, just as the carriage started to move.

"Are you alright, Miss Godeleva?" asked Desda, respecting my choice to speak softly. Her expression was deeply concerned.

"Yes. I'm longing for a bath and I am in rather low spirits, but I am quite unharmed," I said, speaking frankly with her. She was sweet and caring and yet she would never be what Lasilla had been for me. I would try to speak honestly with her, but it was impossible to believe that she could truly understand why I felt the way I did. Lasilla would have understood.

"How is Lord Godeleva?" I asked, unsure that I wanted to know. "Please tell me truthfully and do not try to shield my feelings."

I could tell that I would not like the answer when Desda looked away from me and appeared to reply to her hands, which were clasped in her lap. "He is quite unhappy."

Though this was not what I wished to hear, I appreciated her candor.

"Unhappy in that he is saddened or that he is angry?"

"Both, I believe, Miss Godeleva."

"Is there anything that you could tell me to prepare me for when I must face him?"

"I'm not sure. I'm certain he will be happy to see you. I would say that he is more sad than angry."

That candor for which I had been thankful only moments ago, appeared to be fading. Her natural inclination to shelter me from what I did not want to hear was working its way into her words.

"Do you think he will be at home when we arrive?"

She shook her head. "He is at the Palace."

"That is probably for the best. It will give me a moment to freshen up, before he sees me." I mirrored her effort to express a positivity I did not feel.

"I will have a bath prepared for you, straight away."

"Thank you."

Silence filled the carriage for the remainder of our journey, which was blessedly not a long one. As we drew up the front drive, what struck me the most was how much everything appeared the same. It was foolish to think that the estate would have altered in any way because I had not been in it, but the sheer ordinariness of the scene through my window was grating to me.

When the door was opened, I stepped down and prepared to go back to what remained of my everyday life.

Chapter 16

Megan

I woke to a familiar sound and tensed. A sliding bolt indicated that a door had been locked or unlocked. Keeping my eyes closed, I waited for someone to enter. No one did. There was only silence.

Sighing a bit of relief, my body sank into the soft mattress.

Wait a minute...a soft mattress?

My eyes flew open and I sat up looking around my dimly lit surroundings. It took me only seconds to remember where I was.

Aésha's room.

A frown pulled down my face as I remembered the reason why I was there. Rral was dead.

I looked to the side of the bed where Aésha had slept and found that it was empty, except for a note that lay on her pillow.

I picked it up and read it:

> *Baby,*
>
> *Had to go out. What can I say? The boys can't get through the day without me. Be back in a couple of hours.*
>
> *There's coffee made in the kitchen. It's in the silver thing with the black lid.*
>
> *You look hot when you sleep.*
>
> *Bet you're dreaming of me.*
>
> *Aésha*

That woman was a relentless tease. That said, a cup of coffee sounded really good to me right now.

I slipped out of bed, discovered the bathroom, and used the facilities. It felt refreshing to splash a bit of water on my face after all the crying I had done, last night.

I walked into the small kitchenie-space and saw a mug beside an insulated metal pot on the counter, which I assumed contained the coffee. I picked it up and poured the contents into the mug. I was right. Usually, I'd take sugar and cream, but I didn't feel like looking for them and felt that the strong taste of black coffee would better suit my dark and bitter mood. I also wasn't in the mood to search for food. I would eat today but, for now, I'd start with the coffee and would work my way up to solids.

Turning my attention to the coffee, I inhaled the aroma of the hot, dark liquid, letting its steam invade my nose. Leaning against the small counter, I took a long and slow sip, shutting my eyes. I let its rich flavour and smell flood my senses, pretending for a single moment that I was in my kitchen back home. I smiled, half expecting to hear Aunt Vera wishing me a good morning.

Sighing, I left the kitchen. My intended destination had been the cot, but a glow of light coming from the wall caught my attention.

Oh my gosh! Is that a window?

I walked directly up to the wall-with-light and, sure enough, it had a window. I hadn't noticed it yesterday because it had been covered by a metal shutter that was now only partly blocking the thick glass. I set the mug on the floor and pushed the shutter to see if it would slide up further. It did, allowing me to delight in the full view of the outside world that the window offered.

This wasn't some lame circular ship porthole. It was a surprisingly large rectangular window that was about a foot and a half tall and about four or five feet wide. It was high enough that I could easily raise my arms and rest them on the bar that served as a thin ledge, and rest my chin down on my arms while standing.

Aside from the ultra-comfy bed and coffee, this was definitely another perk of Aésha's room. I picked up my mug and stepped right up to the window. I wasn't expecting to see anything more than a vast expanse of water and was surprised to find that my assumption was wrong.

The ship wasn't moving. Not only could I see land in the distance, but four of the ship's rowboats were currently bobbing gently in the water, several meters away. There were two people per boat and, from what I could see, based on their uniforms, all eight of them were Warriors. Pressing my face up to the thick window pane, I spotted Galnar first. His white hair practically gleamed in the sunlight. My hand tightened around my coffee cup with anger. I looked away from him and focused on the other guy in his boat. He was blond and didn't look familiar. I checked out the other boats. I spotted Keavren and Acksil in one, Aésha and Arik in another, and Amarogq was with a silver-haired Warrior I also didn't recognize, in the remaining boat.

A bunch of other smaller-but-longer rowboats were approaching the Warriors from the coast. I had no idea what was going on. The men and women from the land seemed to be just ordinary people. They weren't dressed in uniforms, but in an array of brightly coloured clothes. Some of the boats carried children. Did these people not realize that they were rowing toward a group of soldiers with scary powers? It took everything in me not to pound on the window to try to warn them somehow. If the window could be opened, I might have yelled out a warning. As it was, all I could do was watch.

As they drew closer to the Warriors, I noticed that the boats were filled with lots of different stuff. Some were filled with what I guessed was a variety of fresh, colorful vegetables and fruits. Other boats contained what I assumed were clothes, and others were filled with various items made from what I imagined was wood, metal, ceramic, or other materials. From where I was watching, it was too hard to make out anything ultra-specific, but it became obvious as the people neared the boats and began to hold up various items toward the Warriors, that they were selling goods.

Is this some sort of water bazaar?

I watched, wondering what would happen. The sellers either didn't care about this large sea vessel in front of them, or they were entirely oblivious to it. My eyes darted nervously to each of the Warriors' boats when they were an arm's length from the sellers. I was ready for something bad to go down.

A woman held up what looked like a yellow sundress to Aésha, but Aésha shook her head and the woman held up a pink one instead. Aésha nodded her approval and reached out for the dress. She took it from the woman who had offered it to her, and smiled.

At first, I thought Aésha had bewitched the woman into giving her the dress for free but, to my surprise, the woman held out her hand, and Aésha put her own hand over the woman's. I couldn't see what she gave her, but it had to have been payment of some kind because the woman look satisfied and put whatever Aésha had given her into her pocket. In fact, I noticed that all the Warriors were actually paying for the items that they were purchasing – even Galnar.

I watched Galnar for a moment, wondering what a man like him would buy from these friendly-looking people.

Ha! Probably a knife that he can use to stab them with...

He appeared to be arguing about something with one of the sellers, who was holding up a variety of different items, for Galnar's inspection. Finally, the man held up a small, brown cube-shaped box. Galnar nodded his approval, took it, and paid for it. My brows lifted in curiosity.

What the heck did he just buy? It can't be anything good. I bet it's a bomb.

Taking sips of my coffee, I watched the trade until the Warriors were done making their purchases. When they were finished, they rowed back to the ship, and the sellers made their way back to the shore. I wondered if the Warriors did this sort of thing often.

While most of them had purchased clothing or some other item, the majority of what had been bought was fresh produce. It suddenly occurred to me that this must be how they had managed to serve fruits and vegetables on the ship. I found that interesting because, until that moment, it had never once crossed my mind to question where the food I was given had come from. It's not that I thought that they had a greenhouse aboard the ship, or something. It was simply that I didn't think about it at all. I just ate what was put in front of me. I wondered if the Sylizan sailors did something similar. If so, that might explain why I ate so well when I had been rescued by Thayn.

Thayn...

Slipping my hand into my pocket I slid my thumb back and forth over the smooth ridges of Rral's ring. I would keep my promise to him. I would eat, I would get stronger, and I would find my way back to Thayn.

I left the window and deposited my empty coffee mug into the kitchen sink. With nothing else better to do, I decided that as I waited for Aésha to return, I'd lie down on the cot.

However, when I made my way to the cot, I was pleased to discover that, at some point while I had been asleep, the bag Aésha had given me after my recapture had been delivered to her room. It was currently propped up against the cot. I opened it and saw the remainder of my clean clothes, the toiletries bag, and the book Keavren had re-lent me. I smiled a little.

Thank you, Keavren.

A book was exactly what I needed, right now. Having an idle brain would only lead me to think about Rral's death all the more. I was having a hard enough time keeping the image of his dead body out of my mind.

Grabbing the book, I lay down on the cot and flipped through the pages until I found where I had last left off in the story of "The Soldier and the Dangerous Dragon." The book was about as good as its title, but it was fun enough to keep my interest.

Not much time had passed before I heard the lock slide over. Setting the book aside, I sat up, facing the door.

Aésha entered, carrying a large bag and a box. She shut the door with her foot and grinned at me.

"Good morning, Baby," she beamed. "I brought you breakfast."

"Thanks."

"Gift for you," she said, placing the box she was holding onto the cot.

I raised a brow. "A gift?"

She nodded and said, "For breakfast I've got bread, rehydrated eggs, and what I think was once some kind of meat," she laughed. "I could also heat up the soup from last night," she offered, heading into the kitchen.

"Anything's good," I called after her, wondering what the heck rehydrated eggs would taste like.

I turned my attention to the brown cube-shaped box that she had said was a "gift." Picking it up, I read the words "Do Not Shake", which were stamped on the top of the box.

What is this?

The box had a good weight, but wasn't heavy, and there were several small holes in it. I examined it, perplexed, partly because I didn't understand why anyone would want to give me a gift and party because the box looked oddly familiar.

I paled as the memory of Galnar accepting a box that looked identical to this one flashed through my head. I almost dropped it.

Oh my God! He sent me a bomb.

Gently, I set the box back on the cot and stood up.

"Um...Aésha? Who's the gift from?"

She briefly poked her head out of the kitchen to say, "It's from your secret admirer."

She had to be kidding. I laughed nervously.

"Yeah, right," I said.

She didn't elaborate further, and I was too afraid to ask if it was from Galnar, on the off chance that she would say "yes." I stared at the box in deep concentration and had to fight the urge to disobey the warning and shake the box. I decided that it couldn't possibly be a bomb, poison gas, venomous snakes, or something dangerous along those lines because I seriously doubted Aésha was going to be cool with bringing something into her room that could harm her, too.

I heard the sound of dishes being placed on a table and looked over. I saw that Aésha had decided to serve the leftover soup and had poured me a bowl and a glass of water.

"Thanks," I said, for the soup, and then added, "Do you mind if I open the box now?" Curiosity was getting to me.

She nodded, "Sure, open it whenever you want. I'm going to get some bread to go with the soup." She smiled and headed back into the kitchen.

I opened the box and looked in disbelief at its contents. A small black kitten lay motionless in the bottom.

I swear, if this is a dead kitten, I'm going to hunt Galnar down and kill him.

I reached in and sighed relief when I felt that the kitten was both warm and breathing. I gently took it out of the box and held it close to me. It didn't stir in its sleep. The cat was entirely black, except for its underbelly, which was white. Stroking its soft fur, I cradled it and stood up, heading over to the small table Aésha had set up for dining.

She had already returned with the bread and was watching me with a small smile.

"Did you know it was a kitten?" I asked quietly.

"Yes. I have a little business-box for it and some food."

"Did you get the kitten from the people you bought the dress from this morning?"

"I didn't," she looked amused, "It's not a gift from me. The business-box is, though. Those things are gross," she nodded towards the kitten.

"So...it's from Keavren, then?" I ventured. I could see Keavren getting me a kitten. He seemed like a kitten-giving kind of guy.

"It's a secret," she winked.

I rolled my eyes. "Does it really have to be a secret?"

"Yes, because it's more fun for me that way."

I sighed. "Do you at least know if the kitten is a girl or a boy?"

She looked thoughtful. "I thought it said what it was on the box."

"Oh," I said. I hadn't even thought of checking that.

I returned to the box and, keeping the kitten securely cradled in one arm, I lifted the box, turning it around. Finally, when I looked on the bottom, I saw a sticker that read "CHG15478245V Feline. Fairwilde. Female"

Whoa! That is one intense identification code.

"It's a girl," I informed Aésha, happily.

"That sounds right for these quarters," she nodded. "Come eat your soup, Baby."

Nodding, I smiled a bit and sat at the table, resting the kitten in my lap while I ate the soup and ate some bread. The meal was actually pretty tasty and slightly comforting. Once I was finished, I drank the water, which felt refreshing after the salty taste of the soup. I set the glass down and fixed my eyes on Aésha, who was sitting across from me and was slowly nursing her own beverage.

"Why would someone get me a cat?" I hoped she'd be a bit less secretive about that.

She shrugged. "I guess that's a secret, too."

I looked at her for a long moment. "You like a lot of secrets."

"Only when I know them," she grinned.

I stroked the kitten, noting that she was doing her best impression of an unconscious rag doll.

"Has she been tranquilized?"

"Yes. She'll wake up drunk, so keep an eye on her. Put her in her business-box a lot, in case she needs to use it. We'll put water out for her somewhere, too. She'll be fine, "Aésha said, not going to any length to hide the fact that she wasn't thrilled with having a kitten in her room.

So, why would she bother? Is she doing it because she was ordered to? She couldn't possibly be doing it for my benefit, alone.

Could she? Or was she just like Galnar, playing games with my mind?

I wondered if I would ever get the truth from her.

I thought for a moment, and then said, "You told me that Galnar wouldn't leave me with a body, but he did anyway. Why would he do that, Aésha? Does he really hate me so much? Does he really want to see me suffer that badly?"

"Baby, stop thinking so hard. You're giving me wrinkles. The giant wasn't supposed to die. You were given your friend. When that turned sour, you were given me."

I looked at her, trying to figure out what she meant by that. Were Aésha and the kitten Galnar's subtle way of showing regret? His "sorry your friend died, that wasn't part of my plan, but here's a new friend and a bonus kitten" demented apology? If it was, I didn't care. Rral was dead because of him.

A slight movement in my lap immediately distracted me from my thoughts. Dropping my gaze to the kitten, I saw that she was coming to life. She opened one groggy eye at a time, revealing bright blue eyes.

"Aw, she's waking up and she has blue eyes," I whispered in an excited gush.

"Wonderful," Aésha said dryly, but she was smiling at me and the cat.

"Miew," the kitten squeaked.

"Hi," I whispered back, carefully stroking her head.

She yawned, opening her jaws wide, exposing very needley teeth. She stretched out her full length before retracting to her normal kitten-size, and then re-curled into a ball and went back to sleep.

Aésha got up from the table and stepped up behind me, massaging my shoulders.

"I need to go back to work for a while. Will you be alright here for a few hours?"

"I'll be alright," I nodded.

"I also brought you some fresh clothes. They're in the bag," she indicated a bag near her dresser.

"Thanks," I said to her, "And thanks for the soup."

"Anything for you, Baby."

"I'll make sure the kitten doesn't wreck any of your stuff."

She smiled. "Thank you. Then we'll all survive this," she teased and then kissed my temple before heading out the door and locking me in.

I picked up the kitten, who was still sound asleep, and kissed her tiny head between her ears. A blue eye peeked open. She was adorable, and I was in love.

Abandoning the table, I carried my little ball of fur over to the cot. I sat down, placing her in my lap. She yawned and stretched before attempting to stand on shaky legs.

"Hi there, Trembles," I cooed at her.

She turned to look at me, fully noticing my existence for the first time. She put a paw on my belly and looked up at me.

"Miew."

Smiling at her, I leaned down and gave her head a bit of a nuzzle before I picked her up and held her close to my face.

"Hi precious."

In response, she reached out with a paw and placed it smack against my cheek.

Okay, mental note: delicate, she ain't.

Laughing, I set her down on the floor to see what she'd do. Looking uncertain, at first, she took a few wobbly steps to the right and fell. The sedative she'd been given was taking its time wearing off. That being said, she was persistent. She got back up and took a few more steps, then immediately stopped. Something had caught her attention.

It took me a moment to realize that all her focus was targeting a small fluff. She was looking at that fluff with the intensity of a lioness. Without a doubt, I knew that fluff was going down.

Blam! Without warning, she pounced on it and then tipped over. It didn't matter, that fluff was good and dead.

"I think you got it," I informed her.

Lying on her side, she looked at her paw and noticed that the fluff was stuck to it. She licked her foot and ate the white substance.

Um...I hope that wasn't a toxic fluff...

She got up and, though she was still unsteady on her feet, she started to explore. I followed her, to keep her out of trouble and because it was fun. I'd always wanted a cat or a dog, growing up, but we could never have one because Aunt Vera was allergic. I was going to savour every minute of this experience.

She explored for a while until, without warning, she flopped on her side. Her tail tapped the floor a few times and she looked up at me before putting her head down.

Okay, I guess we're done exploring.

Since she seemed content for the moment, I decided to take this opportunity to change from the dress I was wearing into some of the fresh clothes Aésha had brought for me. I felt so much better wearing pants and a t-shirt again. I remembered to transfer Rral's ring and Irys' handkerchief to my new pocket. I never wanted to be without them. They were my lifelines.

Scooping up the kitten, I took her to my cot and set her on my lap as I rifled through my bag to find my brush. I swept it through my hair a few times and chucked it into the bag.

With the kitten still in my lap, I lay on my back. She crawled up to my neck and snuggled right in. Smiling, I stroked her body with one hand and picked up Keavren's book to read.

I must have dozed off at some point, because the sound of knocking startled me awake.

I looked at the door, wondering who was knocking. Should I tell them Aésha wasn't here?

"Miss Megan Wynters?" queried a smooth male voice that was unfamiliar to me. "I'm Mez Basarovka. May I come in?"

Chapter 17

Irys

After I was washed and dressed, I sent Desda away. I wanted to be alone. Though I'd expected to want to rest, I was agitated and could not settle. I was inclined to visit the rooms that had been Megan's as though I might feel the presence of my friend there, but I remained within my own suite.

My sitting room, though entirely restored to its prior flawlessness, was stained in my memory with the vision of Lasilla's lifeless body and Captain Galnar's attempt on my life.

I cringed at the remembered sensation of the blade as it was slowly drawn up the inside of my forearm, and I shrank away from the sitting room, dropping into the chair in front of my vanity. I hoped I might hide from my thoughts by occupying myself with familiar tasks, such as brushing my hair.

A knock at the door gave me the escape I needed from the unwelcome recollections.

"Irys, it's me." It was Lord Imery's voice.

Taking a moment to glance at my reflection in the vanity mirror, I watched myself as though I could will something in my appearance to change. Something important. Something beyond the surface. Nothing changed. I stood and faced the door.

"Come in." I could hear the hesitation in my own voice. The cowardice.

The familiarity of the sight of Lord Imery, stepping into the room, surprised me. It could have been any normal day. He looked as he usually did when he would come to speak with me after having discovered a new and fascinating fragment of information from some rare volume that had made its way into his study.

He was dressed impeccably, and yet still somewhat mischievous, with his wavy brown hair tied back out of his way. His round spectacles sat low on his nose as though he expected to have to read upon entering my suite. On another man, the slight stubble that was growing in on his face might have suggested a carelessness with his grooming. This was not the case with Lord Imery. Somehow, he made it clear that this was a deliberate part of his appearance.

I curtsied deeply before him. This was not my typical greeting for him, but I felt that he deserved an additional expression of respect today. At the same time, I hoped that he would be merciful with me after seeing how seriously I was taking the situation.

In utter silence, he watched me sink into the curtsy and rise again. I kept my head tilted down, softly looking up at him through my lashes, for the purpose of easing the stern – nearly angry – gaze he was directing at me. For a moment, I thought that he would begin to shout at me but, all at once, he rushed forward and embraced me. My response was instantaneous, and I held him tightly in return.

"Don't ever do that to me again," he said in a voice laced with such a spectrum of emotion that I could hear just as much relief and happiness as I could anger and hurt.

"I'm sorry, Lord Imery." I was. I wasn't sorry for everything I'd done, but I was immeasurably sorry for having caused him such distress.

"Were you hurt?" he asked as he drew out of the embrace.

"No." I shook my head to emphasize the point. "I'm tired and sore, but I'm not injured."

"Were you safe the entire time?"

"Yes. As much as was possible."

"Good." He sighed and walked away from me as though he were about to start pacing. It was a behaviour I rarely saw in him, and I knew it meant that the difficult questions were not long off. "Why did you do it, Irys?" he asked, turning to look into my eyes. His own expression was deeply disappointed.

Indicating the sitting room, I crossed into the adjacent space, from which I had previously cowered, but that was now the least of my concerns. I took a seat on one end of a settee, neatly arranging my skirt before I rested my hands in my lap. If I couldn't feel calm, I wished to look composed at the very least.

"I didn't feel as though I had the choice," I responded when I could find the words. "I know that it must have been the result of some form of madness. Thinking back, I cannot see the reason in it but, at the time, it was as though my very soul depended on it. I know that if I were to repeat the circumstance, I would have done the very same thing."

He looked as though he was trying to understand me, but I couldn't decide whether or not he felt that he was able to comprehend my response.

"And now? What do you think of your choices?"

It hurt me to think of the truth, but he deserved to hear it. "I think I made a grave mistake and that I placed myself, and many others, in unnecessary danger."

"Is there a risk that this 'madness' of yours could return?"

My heart sank in my chest. "I would like to say 'no'. If I were to answer you with all honesty, I would say that I would no longer choose such a path. But, if it were a madness that caused it in the first place, then how could I possibly tell you for certain, Lord Imery? Please understand that at that time, I had been attacked by Captain Galnar, I had lost Lasilla, and Megan Wynters was kidnapped. I felt as though it was entirely my fault. How could I have made a clear-headed decision? I chose to do what I felt was right and what I felt was good."

"You didn't do as I had directed. That is what you should have done. You should not have done what you felt. You should have done as you were told." I couldn't recall ever having heard his voice sounding more stern. "I know how much Miss Wynters means to you, and I know you lost Lasilla. I am also well aware of the fact that you were personally attacked. Still, how could you have believed that you could contribute, in any way, to a mission being conducted by the Knights?"

When the tears spilled over onto my cheeks, I felt frustrated with my own weakness. I tried desperately to cling to my composed appearance but it was very unlikely that this would be possible with wet cheeks. I forced my voice to break through the tears. "I have nothing to say but that I am sorry to have disappointed you, Lord Imery."

"You have disappointed me, Irys." The words cut into me more deeply than Galnar's blade. "Your actions have also hurt my trust in you."

With a shaking hand, I dabbed my eyes with a handkerchief. "Yes, Lord Imery." They were the only words I could manage between gasps of air. It was all I could do to stop myself from sobbing. At the same time, it wasn't what he wanted to hear.

My response seemed to stiffen his resolve where he might otherwise have shown some empathy.

"I don't think you understand the true impact of your actions, Irys. You may not have entirely damaged your reputation but that is only due to the great lengths to which I have gone to manage this catastrophe. If you ever again do something this foolish, you could be ruined. Do you understand that? You were only just formally introduced to society. You were a success. All of Syliza saw you dance with the emperor at the Masque. But only hours later, you did this…" He paused as though he had to catch his breath. "You can't do anything like that ever again. Do you understand?"

"Yes, Lord Imery." My voice broke midway through speaking the words, and I was forced to repeat them.

He stepped closer to where I was seated, and I braced myself for another character-lashing but, instead, his eyes softened, and he sat down next to me, drawing me closer to him with an arm around me.

"Have you no kind thing to say to me, Lord Imery?"

"I'm glad you're home, Irys. I was devastated when I discovered you had left. I nearly followed you on a later ship, but Commander Varda talked me out of it. All I have been able to do, since that moment, is to worry about you and your safety. You're the only family I have left, Clever One." He kissed my forehead at my hairline.

"From the moment I left, I longed to return home, yet I've been terrified of having to face you." My confession shook in my throat. "I wish I could do more than to repeat that I am sorry for having hurt you and worried you, but I can think of nothing else."

"There is no need to be scared," he said as his second arm came around me to complete the embrace that his other had started. "You're home; where you belong. Things will settle down again. Sir Varda will return with Miss Wynters, and you will move past this. We all will."

"I will pray for it."

He nodded and gave my hair a stroke. "I would have liked to have been home when you arrived. I had an audience with the Imperial Couple today. It is what delayed my return."

"Were they informed of my actions?"

He shook his head. "They believe that you have been unwell."

"Thank you."

"The only people who know what truly happened are the Knights who were on the mission with you, the crew aboard Sir Fhirell's ship, and Lady Brensforth. I did what I could to protect your name and mine."

"Thank you, Lord Imery." It came as a relief to hear that Lord Imery had contained the rumours to such a limited group. I hoped that the word would spread no further. Still, it irked me to think that Lady Brensforth – who still somehow managed to keep Lord Imery's interest in their courtship, after several weeks – knew of what I had done.

Drawing away from me, he looked me over as though for the first time since my arrival.

"You look exhausted, Clever One. I don't imagine you were able to sleep much on the ship?"

"I managed a few hours, here and there. On the way home, I volunteered to care for Sir Vorel. He was badly burned, and I was able to keep him company and soothe him throughout our return."

"That was very kind of you. How did Sir Vorel suffer such an injury?"

"There was a fire at Fort Picogeal. Sir Vorel helped a woman who said her child was trapped in a burning building. He went into the fire to try to find him."

"He is a brave man. Did he save the child?"

"He is. Everyone survived," I said in a carefully worded reply. I didn't have the heart to tell Lord Imery that the child had already escaped and that Sir Vorel's burns were for nothing. I wanted him to be seen as the hero he was and not as someone to be pitied.

"That is good news, at least. I pray that he will heal quickly so that he will be able to enjoy the pride in his heroism."

"I hope for the same. I have never seen such pain in a person, before. Only urac root powder could make it bearable. I sang him lullabies until the medicine could put him to sleep. He would hold my hand until he drifted off. He was combating the fear of having his wife see him in such a condition."

"That was very compassionate of you," he said as he gave my hair a gentle stroke. "But here I am talking to you again when I have only just observed how fatigued you must be. I will leave you to rest and will check on you in a few hours. Perhaps you will want to join me for dinner, by then."

"I'm sure I will."

Nodding and rising from the settee, he strode out of the room, shutting the door behind him.

I watched him leave and stared at the closed door for a long moment. I knew he was right about my need to rest, but I was feeling anything but restful. Pacing about the room only deepened the sensation of restlessness. I found myself avoiding my reflection in the mirror. Somehow, it seemed wrong to see myself looking washed and neat when Sir Vorel was suffering torturous pain. Even worse were the thoughts of Megan. I didn't want to imagine what she might be facing.

Dropping to my knees, I crossed my hands over my heart and shut my eyes.

Great merciful Goddess, I beg you to hear my prayer. Please, show me what I must do to be of use to those who would do good in your name. Help me to see what you would want me to do so that I may walk in your light.

What do I do now? I'm lost, once again. I am trying to be good and to do as you would wish me to, but I feel powerless and directionless. Great Goddess, every time I try to expand my reach from beyond these walls, I am forced to hurt someone else who does not deserve such pain. How do I make a difference and remain good at the same time? Please, have mercy and teach me the way. Light your path before me so that I may follow it.

My fingers made the shapes of the sign of the Goddess before I re-opened my eyes. Nothing in the room had changed, though one thing did stand out from the typical décor of the space: the bag I'd brought with me on the journey to rescue Megan.

I felt drawn to it: this final connection to my most recent failed attempt to do something profoundly good and meaningful. Climbing to my feet, I crossed the room and opened the bag. Sitting near the top, was the envelope of urac root powder I had been dispensing to Sir Vorel.

It was as though I had stumbled on a new way to do as I was told. Lord Imery wanted me to sleep. That was precisely what this herb could provide, while taking my own suffering with it; just as it had done for Sir Vorel and to a lesser extent for me, while on the ship.

Tapping a small amount of it into my palm, I placed the envelope back into the bag, which I tucked out of sight. I mixed the powder with a glass of water and drank the liquid until the glass was empty. In a matter of seconds, I could feel everything slowing down. Even my blinking was delayed.

I stepped out of my shoes and shuffled toward my bed, which looked very close but took a surprising number of steps in order to reach it. My body sank heavily into the soft bed, and I pulled the blanket over myself from the side, instead of having to try to climb underneath it from the top; a feat that seemed to require far too much effort, at that moment.

Sleep quickly grabbed hold of me.

Chapter 18

Megan

Mez Basa-whata? Who the heck is that, and why does he want to see me?

"Miss Wynters?"

"Uh, yes." I sat up, remembering the kitten at the last second, and catching her before she slid off me. "You can come in."

Holding the kitten, I stood to face the stranger who opened the door. I was not prepared for the man who stepped inside. It wasn't his Warrior uniform that stood out to me, it was his overall appearance.

He was easily a head taller than I was and had long silver hair that flowed freely down his back. I don't mean like old man silver hair, either. I mean silver like the colour of the actual metal. I had sterling silver rings the same colour as that guy's locks! His silver hair and piercing icy blue eyes were the perfect match to his fair complexion. If it weren't for the fact that a warm smile caressed his face, he could easily have looked super-intense.

Although he didn't have pointy ears, this man was the first person I'd ever seen, in real life, who could pass as an elf from modern fantasy fiction. That being said, he didn't possess that stereotypical willowy "pretty boy" elf look. While he did have nicely chiseled features, he had a strong jaw and broad shoulders. Tall, "silver," and handsome he was; "pretty" he was not.

Like all the Warriors I'd previously encountered, he looked physically fit, but he definitely wasn't burly like Keavren. His uniform jacket was unbuttoned and hung open, almost rebelliously, revealing a black shirt underneath. Yet it didn't seem like he was showing off. Somehow, he managed to look simultaneously casual and oddly majestic. It was like he was military and non-military at the same time. This guy was a conundrum to my eyes.

"Megan Wynters?" he confirmed more than asked, "I'm Mez Basarovka. I need to ask you a few questions, if you don't mind. Would you rather that we talk here or in my office?"

I didn't know what struck me as more strange: the fact that he was polite, the fact that he seemed considerate, or the fact that he was giving me a choice.

"I'm Megan Wynters. You can ask me questions here."

Considerate or not, I didn't feel like going anywhere with this Mez-guy. If he was a Warrior, that meant he likely had some kind of freaky skill. I knew it didn't actually matter if we stayed here or went to his office. It's not like I was any safer from him or any other Warrior in Aésha's room than I was anywhere else on this ship. Still, I wanted to stay in the surroundings that I currently knew best.

He nodded to me with a smile that should have been warm enough to melt his ice-blue eyes.

"Sure," he said easily. "I just thought you might like a change of scenery."

"I'm alright here," I stated firmly, holding the kitten closer to me.

He nodded. "Mind if I sit down?"

There he goes again, being polite and respectful. Okay, if that's his skill, he's officially my favourite Warrior.

"Go ahead."

"Thank you."

I watched him pull out one of the chairs from the table and take a seat. I mentally cringed when I realized that I hadn't cleared the table of my dishes. Oh well, it's not like this guy's opinion of me mattered.

"Mind if you sit down?" he chuckled with amusement.

In response, I took a seat on the cot, resting the kitten in my lap. She curled into her signature sleeping ball.

When he noticed where I'd chosen to sit, he repositioned his chair so it was angled in my direction, but he didn't move closer. He respected my space. I liked that.

"I swear I'm not here to hurt you. I just have a few questions to ask you. I'll make it all sound very nice," he promised.

He seemed genuine, and he appeared friendly, but I knew all too well with these Warriors that appearances were deceiving. I'd cooperate because it was the smart thing to do, but I wouldn't let my guard down around this guy. Warriors couldn't be trusted.

"Okay."

His brow rose. "Sorry?"

What? Oh, yeah. Stop saying "okay," Megan.

"I mean, yes. Ask away," I reworded, making a sweeping gesture with my hand to further punctuate the point that he could start the twenty questions game.

He nodded and took out a pencil and a small pocket-sized notepad, flipping it open.

"Alright, so for this official record," he tapped his notebook, "you're Megan Wynters. You're not from Kavylak, but you speak our language fluently?"

I nodded.

Is he a reporter, or something?

"You're eighteen cycles?"

"Yes."

"Unmarried?"

"Yes."

"Ever married?

Seriously?

"No..." I didn't hide it in my tone that I thought his question was silly.

He raised his brow again, obviously wondering what was up with my attitude.

"Do you have some kind of aversion to marriage, or is there some other reason that you answered that way?"

"Oh, I don't have anything against marriage, but I'm only eighteen," I stated, like that in itself made it obvious that I wouldn't ever have been married.

He nodded. "So it's a cultural difference, I'm assuming."

"I guess so," I shrugged, not elaborating and having no interest in questioning him about Kavylak customs at the moment, in case he wanted to know more about my own culture. The less he knew about me, the better.

"Well, I wouldn't assume that our cultures would be the same, since you don't really think you're from anywhere around here."

I nodded.

"What was the last thing that you remembered doing before you came here?"

"I don't know. I just remember waking up here," I answered, easily feeding him that practiced lie.

He nodded and shut his book, tucking it and the pencil away into his pocket.

Guess the interview's over...

"What was it like where you used to live?"

...or not

"I'm sorry, but I really don't remember." I did my best to sound genuine and decided to focus on the kitten, stroking her fur, hoping he'd realize that he'd hit a dead end with me and would move on to other questions – or just go away.

"None of it? You don't remember the place where you lived? Earth?"

My head snapped up in shock when he mentioned Earth. How did he know about that? Then, I realized that it had to have been Xandon who had told him.

"No," I said more solidly, trying to keep my cool.

"Did that happen recently? Your having forgotten, I mean?" he asked caringly.

"Why does it matter?" I asked, holding his gaze, which was surprisingly challenging because that dude's eyes were intense.

"Because it's a part of you. An important part. Forgetting it must be a painful loss, especially as you are still learning how to live here. I would find it very unsettling if I couldn't remember the one life that seemed familiar to me."

I couldn't figure this guy out, and I didn't know what he was up to, but I was done with his game of questions. It was time to be blunt.

"Why are you asking me these questions? Why are you really here?" I asked flatly.

He nodded calmly in a "fair enough" way. "I'm asking you these questions because I have been sent to help to decide what type of life you will be living once we arrive in Kavylak. You have been released from your slavery, but you'll still need to have some kind of job. You will be a denizen and will have the chance to earn your citizenship. For now, the preference is to keep you close to the Warriors so that we can keep an eye on you...and your kitten," he tacked on with a smile to the cat.

If it were possible, both of my brows would have floated above my hairline. Again, he surprised me by being the first Warrior I had encountered who gave me direct answers to my questions. Mind you, they could be a pack of lies but, if they were, to his credit, at least he didn't tell me "it's a secret," or "I can't tell you."

Well, it's nice to know that I won't be a slave or a prisoner, anymore, when we arrive in Kavylak. I'll be a denizen, whatever that is. I guess it means I'd be some kind of half-citizen, or something? Like a demi-zen? Meh, it doesn't matter. Hopefully, I'll be rescued by then. Besides, I have no interest in becoming a Kavylak citizen. If I can't find my way back home, I'll definitely want to be Sylizan.

"Um, so let me get this straight. You're here to assess me? To find out where I'll fit in, in Kavylak?"

"Yes. And, to find out where you stand emotionally. You've just been through a lot," he said compassionately, adding, "...that's an understatement, in fact."

Okay, I was wrong. He's not a reporter. Apparently, he's the ship's counsellor. Do I tell the counsellor that as soon as I get the chance, I'm getting the hell out of here and heading back to Syliza? No. Probably not a good idea. I need to keep remembering Rral's advice. Be smart, Megan. Don't put yourself in any unnecessary danger. Be nice to the crazy people from Kavylak.

"Yes," I agreed that I had been through a lot. "Thank you for telling me the truth."

He nodded. "I'm not here to trick you. Maybe, by the end of this sluggish ship ride, you'll come to believe that. I don't really have any way of proving that to you, quite yet."

I didn't say anything in response. There was nothing to say without lying or being unfriendly. He knew I didn't trust him, and I didn't believe I ever would, no matter how much time passed.

By this point, I was pretty sure he was going to leave, but he only took off his jacket and hung it on the back of the chair, getting more comfortable in his seat, like he was about to have a chat with an old chum. I almost felt inclined to offer him a beverage.

He shifted slightly, and my eyes trailed over his black t-shirt-clad torso, of which I now had a better view. Yeah, he was definitely fit. He had a nice bod...

"Do you remember your parents?"

"Huh? Parents?" I flushed, snapping out of my self-induced trance, feeling stupid and hoping that he hadn't noticed that I'd unintentionally checked him out.

"Yes. I was trying to think of someone specific from your life before coming here, to help you remember."

Bless the man. If he had noticed, he didn't let on.

"I don't think you can help me remember," I told him, really hoping that he'd just accept that and drop the subject.

"Because you're choosing not to tell me," he said with a nod as though he was fine with that. "I thought that if I pestered you enough, you might just give up and tell me, just so I'd shut up about it." He smiled.

I flushed again, this time because I was such a bad liar, and we both knew it. I sighed and fixed my best "I mean business" stare on him.

"Look, if I told you what I remembered, you'd think I'm crazy, which won't be good for my job interview."

He shrugged. "On the contrary, it might mean you get something easier." He grinned playfully at me. "They don't give the complicated jobs to the crazies."

My lip twitched and I almost smiled at his comment. Under other circumstance, I would have laughed.

"Alright," I said. He wanted me to level with him. Fine. "I'm not from Qarradune. I'm from another planet, another world known as Earth, and I'm from a country called Canada. I lived there, my whole life, with my Aunt Vera who raised me for as long as I can remember. I went to take a nap one day, and when I woke up, I was here."

He listened without interruption, looking calm and interested. Finally he nodded.

"Did you wake up in a bed here?" he asked.

"Yes, in a depressing black dress."

He scrunched his nose slightly. "Alright, bad first impression. I can see why you don't want to tell me anything," he said understandingly as if the reason I wanted to keep my past to myself was because of the horrible dress.

I smiled that time. I couldn't help it. I really did hate that dress, and this guy had a sense of humour.

"Were things similar in your world to the things you see here?"

I tilted my head from side to side. "Yes and no," I said, finding the answer to that question difficult to put into words. "Some things are similar, but nothing is really the same. I think the only way you'd ever be able to truly understand what I mean, is if you were to go to Earth and see what it's like, compared to here."

He nodded. "Do you have cats?

"Yes."

"So some things like that are the same," he reasoned.

"Yes. Horses, birds and, I suppose, other animals that I haven't yet seen – like dogs, I guess, if you have those, too."

"Yes. In fact, I used to have one," he nodded and then added with a grin, "I'm glad your Earth has dogs, and it's not all cats."

"I take it you're not a cat person," I smiled, stroking the kitten's head. To my delight, she purred softly.

"No. I tried to be, once."

"What happened?"

"We decided to go our separate ways," he said as if he had broken up with his past-cat in a friendly divorce.

I couldn't imagine him with a cat, a dog, or any kind of pet, for that matter. It was weird to think of him, or any of the Warriors as having something normal and wholesome, like a pet. They were just so...bizarre. Thayn, on the other hand, I could easily imagine having a big, sweet dog, like a Golden Retriever. Awww.

I stopped myself from slipping into a full-on Thayntasy and focused my attention back on the Warrior. Since I had told him a bit about me, I wanted to know a bit about him, including what his skill was, for starters.

"So, um...Mr...Warrior, do you have a skill?"

Shoot! That might have come out better if I could remember his last name. Smooth, Megan.

He smiled. "Just call me Mez."

"Mez," I nodded.

He nodded and then said, "I do have a skill. My skill is like a form of brainwashing. But that's not at all why I was sent to talk to you, and I have absolutely no intention of using that skill on you. Before I became a Warrior, I was trained as a psychiatrist. I was sent to talk to you because I'm a good person to talk to, even if it is for an interview."

I smirked at his response. Mez really did have a nutty sense of humour.

He, on the other hand, wasn't smiling. He sat in front of me, calm and relaxed like an open book, waiting for me to digest the meaning of his words. He was the perfect picture of patience and understanding.

No. Please tell me he's kidding. Please tell me I'm not sitting a few feet from a guy who can somehow brainwash me.

I tensed as the memory of Aésha charming me at the Masque flooded my mind. She made me feel things for her that I never would have felt of my own volition. If she could do that, was it really so hard to believe that he could also warp my mind?

"Seriously? You brainwash people?"

"If I have to," he nodded, easily. "But, as I said, that's not why I'm here. I do find that it works against me to tell people my skill before I try to use it."

"Yeah. I can see why that might be a bit counterproductive," I laughed nervously.

Paranoia surged through me when I suddenly realized that he could have been brainwashing me the whole time, but the feeling left me, just as fast. There was no way he was brainwashing me. I didn't feel any different. Nothing had changed.

"I'm not doing it now," he smiled, obviously reading the panic on my face.

I laughed again. "I know you're not because, if you are, you're terrible at it."

"Exactly," he agreed. "If I'm doing it now, then I'm really not getting very much information out of you. I'm not even getting a laugh from tricking you into thinking you're an especially vocal barnyard animal."

I laughed outright at his words, imagining Aésha coming back to her room to find me mooing like a cow or braying like a donkey.

"If I'm really nice to you, will you brainwash me into thinking I'm not here?" I was only half-teasing.

For a moment, he looked like he was contemplating my request but was clearly being a goof. He smiled and shook his head. "No. I'd rather use our fun-filled time together to convince you that you like it here. And I'd like to do it the normal way. Brainwashing gets so boring, after a while."

I shook my head at him unable to suppress my smile. What a nutcase.

"Do they have your favourite foods here?" he asked curiously. "Other than on this ship, I mean. I'm the only one with the good food on this ship."

I shrugged. "I don't know. Do you have pasta? I really like lasagna."

He paused for a bit before he asked, "Was that a word?"

I smiled with a nod, answering, "Yes, it's an Italian dish. But I doubt you know that word, either."

His second long pause told me I was right.

"No. No, I don't. But I'm glad you're saying it, at least," he smiled. "Alright, so let's start from the beginning. What is...laniania?"

I burst out laughing at how he'd mispronounced lasagna. The kitten stirred at the sound of my laughter and looked at me like "Shh! Keep it down! Sleeping!"

I stroked her head and said, once I had control over my voice, "It's..." Another round of laughing took me over when I replayed "laniania" in my head again. "Sorry," I apologized as I worked on getting control again.

He chuckled and looked amused. "No apologies. I like thinking that I'm that funny."

I grinned and explained, "Lasagna is made out of flat noodles, tomato sauce, and cheese. Other things can go in it, too, like vegetables and meat, but I like it best with lots of noodles, sauce, and cheese."

"Do you know how to make..." he paused and looked a little wicked for a moment before saying, "laniania noodles."

I laughed again. "No. I don't, Mr. Baska," I said on purpose, because we both knew that I didn't remember his last name, and I felt like being silly.

He looked playfully horrified when I purposely butchered his last name.

"I thought we agreed on 'Mez!'"

I nodded and laughed.

Finally, when the worst of the laugh-attack was over, I answered his question about the noodles. "I've never made them, but I think they're made from flour and a few other ingredients."

"If you know what the ingredients are, maybe I can get them the next time we stop at a port, and you can see if you can get noodles out of them," he suggested.

I looked at him curiously. "You want me to make noodles? Why?"

"Because you don't even want to walk around the ship, see my office, or the top deck. If you can't at least leave this room, then you can butcher your favourite food in a tiny kitchen, maybe even with a friendly new person: Mr. Baska..."

I snorted laughter. "And what makes you think I want to be friendly with Mr. Baska?"

"I'm your key to laniania," he said, straight-faced as if it couldn't have been any more obvious.

"Okay. You've got me there," I laughed.

"When you say 'okay' is that the 'yes' word from earlier?" he asked.

"Yes."

"In that case, okay."

Aw, he okay-ed me. Unlike Keavren, Mez sounded like he'd been using the phrase his whole life.

"I hope you'll be willing to speak with me again. I didn't get most of my interview questions done, but I think I like talking to you this way a lot more anyway," he said.

"Sure. I wouldn't mind talking to you again. Next time, I may even leave the room. The thought of seeing your office has me intrigued." It honestly did. I was trying to imagine what his office would look like. My guess is that it had to be interesting. I couldn't picture this guy in some stuffy grey room.

"I can even bring you to the open deck above, if you want some air."

I smiled at the thought of fresh air. "I'd like that."

He nodded. "There's only one rule. It's not mine, but it has to be followed while we're travelling from one place to the next."

"What's that?" I asked suspiciously.

He reached behind the chair and slipped his hand into his jacket pocket. He pulled out what looked like a piece of black leather that was looped at either end. The loops were close together, and one loop had a buckle that I guessed was used to adjust the straps.

They might not have been metal, but I knew what they were, all the same: handcuffs.

"We need to wear this 'friendship bracelet' while we travel. We don't have to wear it in my office, but if you get the sudden insatiable urge to swim while we're on the top deck, I could get into some serious trouble."

I nodded. "I get it. Rules are rules."

He put the "friendship bracelet" back into his jacket pocket before picking up the coat and standing. He pulled the jacket on, sweeping his silver mane out from under the fabric. His hair was easily as long as Thayn's, if not slightly longer. I'd never seen so many men with hair that length before. I wondered if it was a fashion on Qarradune.

"When would be a good time to speak with you again?"

I shrugged. "Whenever you're free, I guess. My schedule is wide open."

"How about after dinner, but not late."

That surprised me. He wanted to see me again, today?

"Um, sure. This evening is fine." Cause seriously, it's not like I had anything better to do and, strange or not, this guy was interesting.

He nodded. "I'll come back after dinner."

"Okay."

"Okay," he repeated with a smile and headed to the door to leave.

"Hey, wait," I called after him, before he left.

He turned to face me.

"How do you say your last name?" I really wanted to know.

"Basarovka."

This time I paid attention when he said it. "Basarovka," I repeated. Wow, sounds kinda Russian-ish.

He smiled when I said his name and then left, locking the door.

See you later, Mez Basarovka.

Chapter 19

Irys

It took me a moment to realize that the knocking I was hearing was not in my dream. It was coming from my bedroom door and, from its urgency, it was apparent that it must have been happening for a while.

"Irys?" asked Lord Imery's voice in a concerned tone.

"Yes? Yes, I'm sorry. Please come in," I croaked, sitting up and rubbing my eyes.

Great Goddess, is it morning or night time?

"Were you still asleep?" he asked, looking rather surprised.

How much time had passed since I'd gone for my nap?

"Yes. I'm sorry. I didn't mean to oversleep. I must have been more tired than I had realized."

"Are you alright now? You still look exhausted."

"Yes. I barely slept on the ship, on the way home. I was caring for Sir Vorel, and the room had only a hammock. Is it dinnertime?"

"It is. A hammock must be dreadful for sleep. I'm glad you can rest properly, now that you're home. We can have a little meal in my study if you would be more comfortable there than in the dining room."

"That sounds nice, Lord Imery. It will be good to spend some time together."

"I will have it arranged." He gave my foot a pat through the blanket. "You may join me after you have had the chance to freshen up."

"I will."

With a nod, he turned and left the room. As much as I was still struggling to wake, I found myself looking forward to having a meal in Lord Imery's study, like old times. I rose and washed my face, fixed my hair and did what I could to shake the wrinkles from my skirt. I wouldn't typically leave my suite with my dress in such a condition, but I couldn't find the energy to call Desda to change it. This would have to do.

* * * * *

I knocked lightly on the study door and was barely required to wait before his voice welcomed me.

"Come in, Clever One."

I smiled to myself upon hearing the familiar greeting and the use of my nickname, and I entered the room.

The study was a room lined in books on dark wood shelves. Opposite the door was a window that stretched from the floor to the ceiling for a stunning view of the side gardens. Before it, was Lord Imery's desk, a piece that was always covered in the latest books that had caught his interest as well as the piles of notes he had taken. A few of the artifacts he had recently collected would also often make their way to the surface of the desk, particularly when they were to be the subject of his note-taking.

Somehow, despite the disorder of the desk's surface, he managed to make it look as though it were a deliberate part of the room's décor.

Following a brief curtsy, I crossed the room to sit in my usual chair across from where he was comfortably ensconced, still reading his book. As I arranged my skirt, I had the sudden feeling that everything was back to the way it used to be. I could nearly fool myself into believing that nothing had happened; that when I'd gone out into the gardens to read that day, I had not been kidnapped by Kavylak's Warriors. I had not been Captain Galnar's slave, and I had not been attacked at the Masque. Instead, I'd enjoyed my book and had returned in time to discuss it with Lord Imery over a fine dinner.

As comforting as that was, in a way it was also oddly unsettling. How could everything feel right and normal when it had gone so terribly wrong? Perhaps these doubts were a fog that was left behind by the urac root powder I had used to help me to sleep. My mind certainly felt a grogginess that should not have been there. I hoped I didn't look as drowsy as I felt.

I waited patiently for Lord Imery to finish his page and, when he did, he set the book aside and smiled at me.

"It's nice to see you up and about," he said as he looked me over. "After dinner, I think you should return to your room to rest. You look as though you haven't slept in days."

"I was thinking of doing a bit of reading before I try to sleep again," I said, but I had to agree with him. "It has been an exhausting few days. I'm sure a solid night of rest is all I need."

"I'm surprised that Sir Fhirell didn't give you the Captain's Cabin, at the very least. A shared room with a hammock is hardly an appropriate accommodation for a young lady."

"I had the Captain's Cabin on the trip away from Lorammel. On the way home, I was caring for Sir Vorel. I was offered better quarters, but I chose to stay by his side. He was waking at irregular times and needed to be medicated. I didn't have the heart to leave him alone, and I knew that I was the only one on the ship who didn't have any other purpose for being there."

His brief nod told me that Sir Fhirell was forgiven for whatever offense he had previously been blamed, in the opinion of Lord Imery.

"I did appreciate that he kept me abreast of your wellbeing among the letters to the Knights, carried by his Skydasher bird."

"Sir Fhirell was very good to me. He is a very understanding and patient man. I appreciate that he allowed me to feel as though I were contributing by bringing comfort to Sir Vorel."

A soft knock interrupted our conversation before a large tray covered by a cloche was delivered. The scents that escaped the silver cover hinted at the delicious flavours that were contained within it.

As the dome was removed from the tray, I was pleased to see that I was right. A number of light-but-comforting dishes had been selected from among those that Lord Imery and the staff knew were my favourites. This one little symbol was a warm welcome home, despite the lectures and comments about my appearance that I had received so far.

"Would you like a bit of wine?" Lord Imery asked as he indicated the two stemmed glasses of amethyst liquid on the tray.

"Yes. Thank you. A small sip sounds lovely."

I lay my napkin in my lap and smiled to myself as the coziness of our casual little meal started to sink into my entire body. This was just the setting to ease my anxieties.

We ate quietly for a while, savouring the tastes and the silence. Finally, when the moment felt right for the return of discussion, I took the opportunity to speak.

"What will I do tomorrow, Lord Imery?"

He appeared to be surprised by my question. "You may help me with my research," he said decidedly. "A new artifact from Pomoro has recently come into my possession. This is the perfect thing to distract you from the excitement of the last few days."

"How lovely," I said. I knew that it should have been an honest reply. I hoped that it would be if I let the idea settle in my mind for a while. After a sip of the wine, I smiled. "I look forward to it. I haven't studied Pomoro in any great depth."

Perhaps my enthusiasm would have been greater if the artifact had been from Gbat Rher. How disconnected I felt from our research. This had never bothered me before. Now, I found myself wishing we were investigating something to which I could feel a personal connection.

"I have a few books about other similar artifacts that you can read to prepare for your examination of this piece," he reassured me, though I felt anything but reassured. I felt trapped. It must have been the haze around my thoughts that was holding back my interest.

"Perhaps I will start one of them tonight. That way, I will be more prepared for the day, tomorrow."

"Only if you are ready. There is no need to push yourself tonight, Clever One."

"I haven't anything else to do, aside from reading and sleeping."

Lord Imery looked thoughtfully at me. "Miss Wynters' possessions have been kept in her bedroom for her return. I wanted you to know that I have not given up on her, either. She will be back again, and all her things will be waiting for her."

It was his way of telling me that he understood the pain of waiting. He had lost me and had worried about me. Now, he wished to show me that he understood my suffering in losing Megan and my worry over her safety.

"Thank you, Lord Imery. It is a comfort to return home to familiar things. It was a comfort to me and it will be to her."

With only the slightest nod, he returned to his meal, suggesting that the topic was now closed.

I granted us another silent moment before I started a new subject of discussion. "Will you need me for the entire day, tomorrow?"

"No. I will be heading out for part of the afternoon."

"I was thinking of sending a note to Miss Vivida Fhirell. She paints and is quite skilled, I hear. I thought it might be nice to be friends with her."

"Certainly. I have seen one of her paintings. She has talent. I assume that you spoke of her with Sir Fhirell?"

"Yes. Only very briefly, but the thought of having a lady friend with whom to discuss art and other such things sounded very appealing. I hoped you might approve."

"You are welcome to invite Miss Fhirell here for tea."

"Thank you, Lord Imery. I may do just that. I hope she will want to visit me again and will bring some of her artwork for me to see one day."

"I'm sure she will if you become friends and you ask her to."

I smiled to myself. "What do you think of the Fhirells?"

"They are a good family. Lady Onoria Fhirell is a strong and handsome matriarch. They have been through a great deal, over the cycles, and have even managed to overcome a considerable scandal. It takes quite a family to rise above such things."

"A scandal? Because of whom?"

"Lord Fhirell. Sir Fhirell's late father."

"I didn't realize Sir Fhirell's father was a Lord. Why has Sir Fhirell kept his Knight's title, if that is the case?"

"I'm not entirely sure. Personally, I think it is foolish of him to ignore his true title. Perhaps he is trying to distance himself from any connection with his father."

"What happened to cause such a scandal?"

"Lord Fhirell was a gambler and had a reputation for being somewhat of a scoundrel. He was also known to over-imbibe."

"How awful for them." Scandal had always frightened me. As though it weren't enough to draw disgrace upon yourself, one would have to suffer the knowledge of having brought it upon the entire family as well.

"Many people believed the family to have been ruined. Even Mother thought the Fhirells would need to leave Lorammel and return north to Arlienn to stay with Lady Fhirell's family, or even head all the way south to Azurosola to live with Lord Fhirell's family."

"I'm glad they have recovered. Sir Fhirell is a fine Knight."

"They have done what many other families would not have been able to achieve when faced with the same circumstances. Lady Fhirell is a smart woman and has many powerful friends to support her."

To that, I smiled, and we continued our meal in silence. I pondered over many things; the Fhirells and Miss Wynters, in particular, but also Sir Vorel. After a few sips of my wine, I felt bolder than I usually would.

"Would it be alright if I were to inquire into how Sir Vorel is healing?" I asked before my confidence could have the chance to wane.

"Of course. Would you like to make this inquiry yourself or would you like me to do it for you?"

"Oh, I'm not trying to make you any more busy than you already are. I don't mind sending a little note to the Headquarters. I'm sure the Knights will reply." I found myself secretly wondering if I should specifically address the note to Sir Fhirell. I wanted to ask him, over the others as I felt nearly certain that he would respond to my request for news and that his response would be honest.

"Depending on the reply you receive, we may pay Sir Vorel a brief visit," he suggested. I could tell that he was trying to show support for something that was meaningful to me, and it touched me that he would take the time out of his busy day to visit a man whom he barely knew.

"I'd like that, very much. I will understand if he is not yet receiving guests. He is in quite a terrible condition, Lord Imery."

"If he is not up for receiving guests, perhaps Lady Vorel would be interested in receiving you. I'm sure she would like to know that you care about his wellbeing."

"You're right. I will make a point to write to her as well, once I hear from the Knights."

"Indeed. It wouldn't hurt you to expand your social circle. Lady Vorel will be a good woman for you to know. She will help you to keep your mind off matters that are troubling you at the moment."

Suddenly, his gesture to permit me to visit Sir and Lady Vorel didn't seem quite as supportive in the way I had assumed. Indeed, he had intended it as an opportunity to do something important for me, but the gesture was not meaningful in the way that I had been hoping, for myself. It was as though he were arranging for me to meet another little girl with whom to play. I felt suddenly drained of energy. "Yes, Lord Imery. Thank you for thinking of me."

Nodding to my comment, he looked at me for a moment, studying me as he leaned forward in his chair.

"Irys, what's wrong?"

"I'm merely tired. I think the wine has been too much for me. It is bringing on a fatigue."

Though he didn't look fully convinced, he did not pursue the subject. "I know you're still very upset over everything that has happened. Rest is what you need most right now."

"Thank you for understanding, Lord Imery." I rose to my feet, choosing to take his advice.

Though I would have expected him simply to return to his reading, and possibly to ring for a servant to have the dishes cleared away, he stood and stepped up to me, drawing me into a warm embrace.

"It will all be well again, Irys." He ran his hand down the length of my hair, and I gave myself to the comfort of the motion.

"Perhaps I will be able to believe that when Miss Wynters has returned."

"She will return. Sir Varda rescued her once. He will do it again."

"I pray that he will do it, soon. It saddens me to think that things will never be as they once were."

Drawing out of the embrace, he looked at me with tenderness in his gaze, and he stroked my cheek with the crook of his warm finger. "It saddens me, too. This week, we can do our best to cling to the things that are most familiar to us. You may devote as much time as you'd like to help me with my research."

The gesture did bring me some consolation. While it was not necessarily ideal, it was familiar and warm. "Thank you. It will be good to have purpose."

With a kiss to my forehead, he nodded to me. "You will feel better. I promise. Should you ever need me at all, Clever One, you can always come to me. Even if it is late."

"I always need you, Lord Imery," I replied, looking into his eyes and realizing that my words were genuine.

"I need you, too, Clever One. We're the only family we have."

Standing up onto my toes, I kissed his cheek. "We are. I'll go to bed now, Lord Imery. Is there anything I should start to read, tonight?"

He brightened and crossed the room to a table that held several stacks of books. Selecting one of them, he returned and offered it to me. It was an old leather-bound volume about a period of time in Pomoro's history. I could only assume it would be relevant to Lord Imery's investigation into the latest artifact he had added to his collection.

"Goodnight and sleep well," he said.

"Thank you. Goodnight, Lord Imery."

When I left the study, I had every intention of returning to my suite so that I could write my notes to Miss Fhirell and to Sir Fhirell, at the Headquarters of the Knights of Freyss. However, instead of stopping at my own door, I passed it and continued until I reached the guest suite that had belonged to Megan.

I took a breath and held it as I rested my hand on the knob. It was difficult to think that I didn't need to knock before entering and that, no matter how much I prayed for it, my friend was not on the other side of this barrier.

I have prayed for it, have I not, Great Goddess? Have I not spent enough time in sending my thoughts to you and in worship of you? Have I not been pleading with you at every moment that I have not been actively trying to follow your Light? If I have displeased you, please send me a sign. I will do as you wish, if you would only tell me what it is you want from me.

The perfume of at least a dozen bouquets of flowers was the first thing to greet me as I opened the door. While my first thought was that of pride, believing that Megan had been such a tremendous success at the Masque that many new friends or prospective suitors had sent her these arrangements, it didn't take long to spot the signature blue orchids of Emperor Gevalen that made up the three largest floral displays in the room.

An uncomfortable feeling slithered over my body as I approached the first of the three and extracted the card that was tucked among the stems.

"Get well soon, my exotic bird.
"G."

I jammed the card back into the arrangement as though it had stung me. Taking a breath, I withdrew the second and third cards from their respective arrangements and read them.

"Looking forward to our next dance.
"G."

"When you feel better, you will join me for tea at the Palace.
"G."

I put the cards back, staring at them in revulsion. This didn't feel right at all. Certainly, it wasn't the typical behaviour of a married emperor to send flowers – particularly so many – to a young lady he had met during only the briefest encounters. Why had Lord Imery not told me of these gifts?

Glancing at one of the bouquets that did not contain any orchids, I read the card.

"Feel better soon, Miss Godeleva.
"Sir & Lady Skyleck"

I read every card on every bouquet. They were all from families with whom Lord Imery typically associated, and who had – like the Imperial Couple – been informed that I was ill in order to disguise the fact that I had run away aboard one of the Knights' ships.

So many lies. So many well-wishes from people who barely knew me, and who were likely using my apparent illness to draw favour from Lord Imery.

Desperate to escape the flowers and everything they represented, I rushed into the bedroom, which was blessedly free of any hint of petal or stem. Even the bedside vase was empty, at the moment.

Pacing like a madwoman, I finally came to rest on the bed, curling up with one of the pillows and attempting to imagine a time when all would be right again; when Megan would be safely returned. How my mind begged for it to be true. How it reached out for Megan and pleaded with the Goddess to bring her back to this very space. As my thoughts drifted to prayer, my hand brushed against a soft piece of leather.

Withdrawing the treasure, I brought the object out from under the pillow. It was a book. I opened the cover, thrilled to have made some connection with Megan through the last book she had been reading when she was here.

Easing open the cover, I read the hand-written words: *"For Megan, so that her words can be as free as she is."*

A journal! A gift to my very soul. This was not just any book, but was rather a window into the mind and thoughts of my dear absent friend. I hugged the book to myself as though embracing Megan, herself.

Quickly, I shut the book and set it on top of the one Lord Imery had given me. I would save these sweet pages so that I could savour them later. I would not waste them while I was still surrounded by the nauseating scents of the flowers from the adjacent room.

Steeling myself, I arose and walked quickly from the bedroom into the corridor, and jumped when I saw that there was a male servant standing outside my suite as though stationed there as a guard. I nodded to him as I approached my door, and he merely nodded in return without addressing me or impeding my progress.

In my room, I placed Lord Imery's book on the table next to the settee in which I intended to sit while I read it. I tucked Megan's journal under my own pillow. It seemed only right to provide her book with the same degree of privacy that she had chosen to give it.

With the books in their proper places, I left my suite once more, exiting through the bedroom door, which I shut behind myself. The servant remained at the door to my sitting room. My initial instinct had been right. He was placed there as some form of guard.

I walked back to Lord Imery's study and knocked.

"Come," he said simply.

I entered, curtsying before I approached his desk.

"Is everything alright, Irys?" he asked with concern. Certainly, he was not expecting to see me as soon as this.

"I'm not sure, Lord Imery," I replied honestly. "I visited Miss Wynters' room."

It took a moment before the realization showed in his eyes. "The flowers. I'm sorry, Irys. I completely forgot about them. They have been arriving since you left. I had Desda place them in the guest suite."

"There were so many from the emperor. His cards..." Struggling to express myself, I realized that I hadn't yet identified what it was that I was feeling. Were there words for such a thing?

"Yes. I know," he sighed. "He does appear to have a growing interest in you, but don't worry, Clever One. Nothing will come of it. He does this from time to time. He has an eye for pretty things."

"How could he think such things? He's married."

"He is. As I said, you needn't worry about anything. The emperor is not a threat to you and, even if he were, you must know that I will always protect you."

"I know you will," I agreed. "One of his cards said that I must have tea with him at the Palace when I'm well. What shall I do?"

"We can honour his request. I will go with you. I won't leave you to visit the emperor on your own, Clever One."

"Should I dress very plainly when we go? I would rather not draw any more of his attention."

He shook his head. "Dress as you would dress if you were going to have an audience with the emperor who had not sent you the flowers. He is not going to try to pursue you. You amuse him, and you are pretty. He will have tea with you and enjoy your company, nothing more."

He was right. At least, I hoped he was. "Thank you. I feel better now. I was merely surprised by his enthusiasm. I should return to my room to rest now. My imagination seems to be running away with me."

He smiled kindly at me. "It is entirely understandable. Rest well, Clever One."

With a curtsy, I turned to leave, but paused before opening the door as I remembered the servant who was positioned outside my suite.

"Is the estate guarded now?" I asked, looking back over my shoulder at him.

"There are a few guards," he replied.

"Inside?"

"On the grounds, mostly. I take it you've seen Toslen outside your rooms?"

"Yes."

"He is there for your protection."

"I thought as much. Thank you, Lord Imery. Goodnight."

"Goodnight, Irys."

I exited the study and returned to my suite, nodding to the man I now knew as Toslen.

"Goodnight, Toslen," I said as I entered my sitting room.

He smiled to me in a pleasant way and before I shut the door behind me, I heard him reply. "Goodnight, Miss Godeleva."

For reasons I could not understand, the guard placed outside my door did not give me a sense of security. Instead, he served as a reminder that there was something against which Lord Imery felt I must be guarded. I considered locking my door but left it as it was and went to my bedroom to prepare for bed.

The bed was turned down and my night clothes were laid out. Desda had anticipated that I would choose to make this an early night.

"Desda?" I asked, more to let her know that I was in my suite than to request anything of her.

After a brief moment, she stepped out of the bathroom, carrying a little vase of flowers that she placed on my bedside table, after a quick curtsy. Blessedly, there wasn't a blue orchid among the blooms.

"I didn't hear you return," she said pleasantly.

"I've only just stepped in. I'd like to get ready for bed now."

She helped me to change into my nightclothes, and I tried to find comfort in having my hair brushed out, but Desda's presence felt like a reflection of Lasilla's absence. It wasn't fair to Desda, who was doing a perfectly lovely job in serving me. Still, I could not seem to shake the feeling.

"Goodnight, Miss Godeleva. Sleep well," she said when her tasks were complete.

"Thank you. You as well, Desda."

Once I was alone in my room, the exhaustion pressed down on me with an astounding weight and, yet as I lay in my bed, it felt as though I were as far from sleep as I had ever been in my life. After a short while, it became unbearable, and I dragged my heavy body from my bed to prepare a touch of urac root powder for myself.

By the time I had returned to bed, I could barely keep my eyes open. I curled up with my pillow and smiled to myself as my fingers brushed the leather spine of the book that I'd tucked beneath it. Holding onto the precious volume, I gave in to the darkness.

Chapter 20

Megan

"I think you got it that time, Pounce," I informed my kitten, who had successfully attacked her fifth floor fluff since she'd been up and moving around. I had named her Pounce after I saw her pounce on her third fluff. The name really seemed to suit her overall pep, movement, and playfulness.

It had been a couple of hours since I'd met Mez. At least, I guessed it had been that long. There was no way to know for certain. I didn't have a watch and as far as I could tell, Aésha didn't own a clock. In that time, I'd finished Keavren's book, named my cat, fed her, had cleaned up the dirty dishes, and investigated the kitchen to find out where everything was stored. I had also showered and found a ribbon, so I could tie my hair back in a low ponytail. It felt good to get it out of my face.

Now I was following Pounce around and was pleased that it appeared that the sedative which had been used on her had worn off. She wasn't wobbly anymore.

The door unlocked, and I turned toward it at the same time Aésha entered. She shut the door and smiled, walking over to me like a wild cat stalking its prey. She draped her arms around my shoulders and, for a second, I thought she might kiss me. She didn't.

"Hi..." I said uncertainly.

"Hi," she smiled. "Would you like dinner?"

I nodded, feeling less awkward with her question. "Yes. I guess I should eat something, soon. Mez is coming back this evening to talk to me again. I met him today."

"Oh, did you now?" She looked both amused and pleased. "What did you think?"

He's a nutty elf without pointy ears.

"He's..."

"Hot," she subbed for me.

"Interesting," I finished.

"But hot," she grinned.

I decided to sidestep the disaster that would have resulted if I made a comment about her statement and asked, "Who is he? I know he's a Warrior, but he says he's here to interview me. Is that true?"

"He's my brother and he's hot," she shrugged," I didn't know he was coming to see you. I'm just here to sleep with you," she teased. I laughed because, for once, I got the joke.

"Wow, I didn't realize I needed so much attention. You're here to sleep with me, and he's here to talk to me. Don't I feel so special," I teased back.

"Maybe, if you talk to him right, he'll sleep with you, too."

"Uh..." and just like that, my ability to tease is gone and now she'd given me a mental image that was going to make it awkward to see Mez again.

Thanks for that, Aésha.

She laughed, fully enjoying my reaction. "I'll see what I can find for dinner."

She kissed my forehead and sauntered into the tiny kitchen. I hadn't even realized I'd been staring after her like a star-struck idiot until she was out of my sight. Honestly, I was starting to wonder if I had a gay side I didn't know was there.

A ripping sound drew me from my thoughts.

Crap! I'd forgotten about Pounce!

Whipping my head around, toward the noise, I spotted her. She was by Aésha's bed and was using one of the hot pink bed curtains as a scratching post.

"Pounce! No!" I whispered sharply, dashing toward her. She stopped immediately and looked at me with big, round, sweet eyes when I scooped her up. "Look what you did," I scolded softly, pointing to the shredded curtain.

She purred and nuzzled into me. I swear she knew that by acting cute, it would get her off the hook. She was right. I wasn't mad at her, and we both knew it. She was too cute to be mad at. That said, Aésha was likely going to kill me.

"Suckup," I told her.

She quit purring and licked her front paw. I brought her over to the cot and rested her down. She instantly hopped down and began to make her way over to Aésha's bed, again.

"Pounce," I warned her.

"Good name," Aésha complimented, coming out of the kitchen with two plates that she set on the table.

"Thanks," I said, swiping up Pounce again and heading over to the table to eat.

Taking a seat, I looked at what she'd served. I knew it wasn't French toast but that's what it most closely resembled. There was also a piece of fruit cut up on the side of the plate. It gave me an apple vibe. I pierced a piece of the fruit with my fork and took a bite. Yup. Definitely apple-ish.

Aésha pushed a container that looked like a creamer in my direction. My eyes lit up as I realized it could be syrup. Picking it up, I poured the contents on the fried bread and grinned from ear to ear when warm melted chocolate drizzled over my food.

"Chocolate!" I declared happily. "This is great."

"Compliments of Keavren," Aésha smiled.

Aw, he's the best! I need to send him a "Thank You" note.

"That was very nice of him – of both of you, actually. You're both so..." I paused thinking of the word Keavren had used and then remembered, "crisp."

"You'll find that most of what I do is crisp," Aésha told me, biting into her fruit with a solid crunch.

"Oh? Is that another skill of yours?"

"No. That's just who I am."

I chuckled. "I'm glad I'm sleeping with someone crisp," I said as if that's always been a dream of mine.

"Never settle, Baby," she laughed, amused.

I smiled, and we finished our dinner in a comfortable silence. I glanced at Pounce on my lap and saw that she was staring across the room at nothing. I didn't know what was going on in that kitty brain of hers but, whatever had captured her interest, must have been catnip-level awesome.

Aésha stood to pick up the plates and take them into the kitchen. I stood as well, letting Pounce jump down to the floor.

"Did you want me to wash up the dishes for you?"

She shook her head, "We can do it together."

Giving me a playful look, she hip-swayed into the kitchen. With the way that she said that, and by her movements, you'd swear we would be doing something other than washing dishes. What freaked me out was that a small part of me felt disappointed that we would just be doing dishes. Honest to goodness, what was up with my thoughts when I was around her? I needed to think about something else to set my mind straight.

Heading into the kitchen, I asked, "Mez said he might take me up to the top deck when he comes by to talk to me tonight. Is it cold up there? Will I be warm enough in my shirt?"

She paused scrubbing the metal plate with a rag and grinned at me.

"Don't put on anything else. Then you'll get him to take his jacket off, to give it to you."

I laughed until I realized she wasn't kidding.

"Aésha, you can't be serious."

She raised a brow. "Do you or do you not want him to take off his jacket?"

I could feel my face flushing, mostly because I was remembering when he'd taken his jacket off earlier, and I'd caught myself checking him out.

"No. I mean, I wouldn't be adverse to it, but he won't have to if I'm properly dressed," I babbled.

"Are you saying that you don't think that my brother is hot?"

"No."

"Then don't wear anything other than what you have on so that he can give you his jacket," she said like I was a really slow learner.

I sighed. "I'm not interested in your brother, in that way, Aésha."

"Well one of us has to be, and I've already been turned down," she said, playfully placing her hands on her hips before turning back to finish washing the plate.

Wait a minute...did she have the hots for Mez? I thought she liked Arik.

"Um, well, if it makes you feel any better, I highly doubt I'm his type," I informed her, snagging the towel on the counter to dry the washed plate.

"You're right. He really doesn't like women who are too attractive. No wonder he turned me down." She shrugged.

"Maybe he's just flustered around you because you're so attractive and confident," I offered.

She laughed. "I'm sorry. I thought we were talking about Mez."

"We are. Why? He never gets flustered?"

"He never gets flustered." She nodded handing me the second washed plate to dry.

I found that hard to believe, because everyone gets flustered from something. Even Thayn, the most confident man I'd ever met, got flustered from women's nightgowns and women's shoes. He'd probably collapse if he saw Aésha's current skin-tight uniform.

"He's just one of those strong silent types but that doesn't mean he can't get flustered."

She nodded and looked at me like she was struck with a bright idea. "You're right. I think you should try to fluster him."

I sighed again and shook my head. She was impossible. A knock at the door saved me from having to continue the conversation.

"I wonder if Arik is here to join us in bed." She laughed, tossing the dish rag in the sink and leaving the kitchen to answer the door.

Oh, man, please let it be Mez and not Arik. I stayed where I was, still holding the second plate and listened when I heard the door open.

"You know, I've always liked that jacket," Aésha purred in greeting.

"...it's the uniform. You have one too," Mez chuckled.

Relieved to hear that it *was* Mez and not Arik, I quickly stacked the plates, depositing them in the proper cupboard and hung the dishtowel on a wall hook to dry.

I exited the kitchen and made my way to the door, grabbing my boots, along the way, and pulling them on my feet. When Mez spotted me over Aésha's shoulder, he smiled.

"Good evening, Megan. Are you all set?"

"Hello again, Mez. Yes. I'm ready to go," I said, joining them at the door. I turned to Aésha and asked, "Will you watch Pounce for me?"

Mez smiled at the name, and Aésha nodded, "We'll get into all sorts of mischief together."

"Perfect."

"Be good you two," she grinned at us. "Don't do anything I wouldn't do."

Mez laughed and whipped out the "friendship bracelet". "I have all sorts of plans," he joked, clearly for Aésha's benefit.

I stepped up to Mez and held out my right arm to him. He secured the half-inch-wide leather strap around my wrist before securing the opposite end to his own. He pulled the strap tighter around his wrist, buckling it and locking it into place. This immediately tightened the one around mine since the two straps were linked. It didn't hurt, but I officially couldn't slip out of the leather cuff. He gestured with a slight forward-tilt of his head that we could go, and he started walking. I followed.

I gave a brief "see ya later" smile to Aésha, who looked like she was playing the role of my proud college roommate, watching me head out on a blind date that she'd set up for my benefit.

I turned to watch where I was going as she shut the door. There were a few soldiers in the hall but, other than that, it was pretty quiet. It never ceased to amaze me how very metal and boring this ship was. All the halls and doors looked the same: grey, dull, lifeless. It really gave you the impression of what it might be like to be a sardine in a tin can.

Mez walked at a comfortable pace, and we climbed up several flights of stairs. I noticed that while he was wearing his Warrior's uniform, he wasn't wearing his military boots. Instead, he wore snappy black and white oxfords that reminded me of gangster shoes. I liked them.

"I like your....," I started to say to Mez, but the rest of the words died on my lips. We had reached the top deck, and I was instantly greeted with a welcome blast of cool air and a gorgeous sunset. The sky was a cascade of blood reds, rich oranges, and a deep purple. The marigold-coloured sun was sinking below the darkening, yet glistening, water which was sparkling in the light of the fading sun's rays. I was in awe. I couldn't recall ever having seen a prettier sunset.

"You like my?" Mez asked.

"Huh?" I turned to look at him, having forgotten he was even with me. "Oh!" I declared with a laugh, flushing a little when I understood his question. I had never finished my earlier statement. "I like your shoes."

He chuckled and smiled genuinely at my compliment. "Thank you."

"They're really cool. I haven't seen anything like them since being here. They kind-of remind me of shoes from back home," I told him.

He wore a look of confusion, for a moment, and I knew it was because of something I'd said.

"Sorry. I meant they're, uh, crisp." That expression wasn't coming naturally to me.

"Cool?" he queried with both amusement and interest.

I nodded with a growing smile. "'Cool' is my equivalent to your 'crisp'. I'm a cool-sayer."

"Okay," he replied. "I can have cool shoes," he said looking rather proud of himself, in a way that I found endearing.

Unlike my inability to naturally work Qarradune expressions into my vocabulary, Mez was a pro at Earth slang. I resisted the urge to high-five him.

"Speaking of 'cool,' are you cold?"

This was it, my chance to potentially score his jacket, just like Aésha wanted. My decision was easy. I wasn't going to be a stupid flirt with him or listen to Aésha. I'd do what I want and be myself.

I shook my head. "I'm fine," I told him because that was the truth. It was very windy and cool, but the air didn't have a bite to it.

He nodded. "Let me know if you do get cold. We can go in," he said easily.

"I will." I smiled at his words and was glad that he hadn't offered his jacket. I did understand that offering it to me would be slightly problematic, with us being tethered to one another, but the fact that he didn't even suggest it made me feel that he was respecting my space to his utmost ability, given the circumstance. Gotta give him points for that.

"Mind if we go to the rail?" I asked him.

He shook his head, and we walked to it. The deck was buzzing with soldiers and crew. Some were running around doing various tasks, some were having a discussion, and others stood watch. A few of the men cast curious glances in our direction but, mostly, they just ignored us. No one approached us.

I rested my free hand on the rail and turned my attention back to the sunset. Both the water and the sky seemed to go on forever. I was glad I had put my hair in a ponytail, earlier. The wind was blowing my hair and the ribbon that held it, over my shoulder. Every so often, a few red strands would reach up and tickle my face. I had no idea how Mez managed not to freak out, with his long hair blowing freely. I glanced in his direction. He was staring out over the water, looking calm. To my surprise, his hair didn't appear to be in a thousand knots. It just fluttered in the strong breeze, rising and falling like floating silk around us.

I watched as the silver threads of his hair occasionally reached up to touch the skin of my arm. I swear his hair felt as soft as it looked. Wow. I wished my hair was half as nice as his. I never thought I'd be jealous of a guy's hair. I bet if his imaginary sister didn't have hair as nice as him, she'd be mad about that!

Hmm. I wonder if he actually has a sister. He said he had a dog, once. Does this mean he has family, somewhere?

"Let me know when you're ready for some serious-talk."

Blinking back to the moment, I looked at Mez. "You really know how to kill a sunset," I teased as if I'd been starring at its magnificence and not contemplating his hair and making up potentially imaginary siblings for him.

"It's one of my special skills," he chuckled. "That one doesn't get as much praise as the other one."

I shook my head at his silliness. "Alright, go ahead. Let's get 'serious,'" I emphasized serious in the most non-serious voice I could muster.

He nodded and waited a moment before asking, "Was the first time you met Rral Radone, the Knight, when he came into the house where you were hiding with Aésha and Keavren?"

Any play I had in me fled with the sound of Rral's name. Pretty sunsets and silky silver hair lost all their charm and appeal.

"Yes, that was the first time. I had never seen or known of him before then." The previous pep in my voice had died.

"Do you know why he was with Irys Godeleva?"

"No," I answered solidly. "I hadn't expected to see her, and I don't know why she was with him."

"Did you talk to him while you were running from the Warriors?"

I nodded uneasily, not wanting to relive the time when Rral and I were being chased down in the woods by Amarogq's wolves. "We didn't talk about much of anything."

Mez nodded. "Did he mention ships?"

"Ships? No." I felt my heart lift a little.

Ships? Could that mean that Thayn was still coming for me?

"Did he know who you were?"

"No. I don't think he knew anything about me. I guess it's possible he did, if he was with Irys for a while but, if he did, he never said. We really didn't talk much. We were too busy running away from you guys."

"Did he talk to you much while you were aboard the ship?"

"He did a little but, mostly, he just slept and encouraged me to eat food. He was hurt really bad, he hallucinated, and thought I was someone called Rani," I blurted, not having meant to tell him that.

Mez listened respectfully and nodded with understanding. "Did he tell you anything about being 'rescued' or people coming for you? Did he reassure you that Syliza was on its way?"

"No," I said honestly and secretly wished that he had.

"Do you read Gbat?"

I raised my brow. "Probably. I can understand it and speak it."

He nodded, without questioning the strange way I'd answered his question. "Did you read his journal?"

"He had a journal?" That was news to me.

"Yes. The handwritten book he kept. You didn't read it?"

I shook my head. "I didn't even know it existed."

He nodded and paused as if he were making a decision, before he reached into his coat and extracted a little brown beat-up leather book, from an inside pocket. He held it out to me.

Hesitantly reaching out, I took the book from him. I looked at it and then at him. "Is this it?" It was more of a statement than a question.

"Yes. There is nothing in it about people coming to rescue you. We have a language specialist on board and he read every word. It is mostly just a few notes about how his days went."

I nodded to him. "I get that. That's the kind of stuff I write in my own journal," I said, remembering my journal for the first time, since my kidnapping.

"You have a journal, too?" Mez asked curiously.

"Yes. Well, I mean, I did. I don't have it now."

He nodded. "Where is it?"

I shrugged. "I guess it might still be back in Syliza." If it was where I had last left it, it was hidden under the pillow of my bed at the Godeleva estate. I hoped whoever found it wouldn't read it. I should have figured out a way to put a lock on it. Oh well, on the bright side, I was glad that it was there, instead of here. If I had it with me, it likely would have been confiscated. Who knows who would have read it, and what kind of trouble it would have caused?

"If we stop by my office, I'll give you a new one. Otherwise, I'll bring you one, tomorrow," Mez said.

At first, I was surprised but that quickly faded into suspicion. "Are there any rules associated with this journal you're offering me? Can I write anything or am I going to get thrown in jail if I say something too free-thinking?"

"I'm not giving you something so that other people will read what you've written. But, if you want to be exceptionally safe, don't write anything about Captain Galnar."

I knew he wasn't joking, but I didn't have a problem with his suggestion. Galnar was the last person I wanted to write about, and he certainly wasn't worth a hand cramp. I nodded to Mez and then looked out over the water as the last dwindling hints of the sun's light touched the rapidly darkening sky.

"Have you been thinking about the time before you came here, at all?" Mez asked.

"You mean Earth?" I clarified, glancing at him.

"Yes and what brought you here."

I really didn't want to talk about home, again. I didn't get why he'd care, which made me suspicious of his intentions for wanting to know. What would he do with the information? Who would he tell?

"You know...I have really good bribery snacks," he tempted with a crooked smile, no doubt picking up on my hesitation.

"Oh, ya?"

He nodded. "Really good. You can see for yourself, whenever you're done with the sunset."

"I'm done with the sunset," I told him, curious to see what sort of snacks he did have.

He gave my wrist a brief, friendly little tug, by pulling the hand that was strapped to mine, to let me know that we were heading back inside. I took a final look at the sky and inhaled a deep breath of fresh air, following Mez below deck. We walked down only one deck and then headed toward the back of the ship. We stopped at a door, which he opened. He turned on the wall lights, revealing what was definitely the best room I'd seen on this ship, so far.

We stepped in, and I let my eyes rove over his office. It had several large windows, facing the stern of the ship. None of the windows were covered, and they provided what would otherwise likely have been a stunning view, if the sky wasn't so dark and if the light from the room hadn't been reflecting parts of the office, in the glass.

The other most notable feature of the room, was that it had a wall lined with bookshelves. Each shelf had a thin band across it, which was obviously meant to keep the books from falling, in the event that there were any kind of motion. I noticed, earlier, when I had been familiarizing myself with Aésha's kitchen, that a similar kind of band was also used in the cupboard to provide the same kind of security. However, as was the case the first time I had been aboard this vessel, I still hadn't felt the ship move to indicate that we were sailing on water.

Hearing the door shut behind me, I turned to look at Mez, who had already begun working on unlocking our "friendship bracelet." When he was finished, he walked to a large, dark reddish-brown wood desk that was bolted to the floor in the middle of the room. He set the strap on top of its surface. I, on the other hand, walked right up to the window, to look out.

"You have the best view," I told him, pleased to see that stars were beginning to make an appearance.

"I love my office. It's almost as good as my snacks."

I smiled and looked at him over my shoulder. Mez had settled into a seat at his desk and had propped his feet up, crossed at the ankles, on top of the desk. He had ditched his jacket and looked entirely comfortable. I turned from the window and walked toward him, taking a seat in one of the two chairs facing his desk. I set Rral's journal gently down on the vacant chair.

"So, about those good snacks..."

He laughed and opened a top drawer. "Sweet? Salty? Sour?"

"Sweet." I didn't need to consider my options.

Mez nodded and began investigating and moving items I couldn't see, from what I assumed was his stash of "good snacks".

"Hmm, I have two kinds of cookies. I have these weird chewy things that I thought were something else and I bought a lot of them," he said, shifting more contents. "I have a chocolate bar..."

"I think I'll try one of those weird chewy things you mentioned. It sounds so strange I think I have to try one."

He laughed and took out a jam-style jar that was filled with plump, dark red spheres. He unscrewed the lid and gave the jar a gentle push in my direction. "They're all yours," he told me with a grin, definitely not hiding the fact that they weren't his favourites.

I reached for the jar, drawing it closer to me but left it on the desk. I plucked out one of the hard candy spheres and looked it over, briefly, before popping it into my mouth. I sucked, a bit, on the candy on the outside and found it to be sweet. When I finally decided to chew it, I discovered that it had a gummy center that was slightly sour, giving the candy a sort-of sour cherry taste. It was a fun treat. I liked it.

Mez had been watching my reactions to the candy, with interest. I smiled at him. "It reminds me of candies I've had on Earth," I told him. "Thanks."

He smiled, looking pleased by my response. He picked up a pen and wrote my name on the jar lid.

Waddaya know? An ink well-free pen!

"I'll keep them here for bribery," he teased.

I laughed at that.

"So, have you thought about how you came to be here?" he asked, pushing the jar even closer to me, with a smile.

I smirked at him and took another candy. Before I ate it, I asked, "Why does it matter to you? Is it because you want to know or because Xandon wants to know?" I honestly had a hard time believing that he genuinely cared about my past or how I got here.

"I want to know, and I am supposed to have a better understanding of you before we arrive in Kavylak. I'd say the means that brought you here would likely be an important thing to know."

I thought about that as I finished the candy. The truth was, I really had no idea how I had gotten here. I was still hoping I'd be enlightened, but it hadn't happened yet. I wanted to know, more than anything, because I was pretty sure that knowing how I got here was my key to getting back home.

"I have no idea how I got here," I leveled with him. "I've thought about it every single day since I've been here, and I still have no clue as to what happened. I'm still hoping I'll wake up from this nightmare."

He nodded. "Would you allow me to try something to help you to remember?"

"Try what?" I asked suspiciously.

"A memory technique, of sorts. I promise that it won't hurt, and you don't need to leave this office to do it. In fact, if you want it to stop, all you need to do is tell me."

I stared at him oddly, having no idea what sort of technique he was going to use or how he would employ it. That said, I had a sneaking suspicion his skill would play a role. I was tempted to tell him I wasn't interested, but my desire to give it a try won out. I was willing to try just about anything if it would help me to remember.

"Okay."

"Okay," he agreed with a small smile to me and walked around the desk. He picked up Rral's journal from the free chair and set it on the surface of the desk, before taking a seat.

"Ready?" he asked.

I nodded, my heart beating faster.

"Shut your eyes and picture blackness," he said calmly.

I was surprised. For some reason, I thought he was going to whip out a pocket watch on a long chain and swing it in front of my face, or something. Taking a deep breath, I complied, shutting my eyes and picturing blackness.

"Alright. I'm going to ask you to open your eyes in your mind, not your physical eyes, and look around you. I want you to see the place where you were before you came here. Your last memory there," he explained. "I'm going to make you feel more relaxed and focused so that you can concentrate on what you're doing," he added.

I focused on his voice, listening to his instructions; trying not to feel tense. I concentrated on my breathing and thought about my bedroom, where I had last been before Qarradune. The more I thought about my room, the more I slipped into my comfort zone and relaxed. When I felt ready, I opened my eyes in my mind and was stunned at how vivid my imagination was. Everything I could see in my room was exactly as I last remembered it. It looked so real; more real than any memory or daydream I'd ever had. My lips curved up into a smile, and I could feel my eyes watering under my closed lids as I was overcome by the emotion of it all.

"Where are you?" Mez queried in a smooth, gentle tone.

"I'm in my room," I responded. My voice sounded far away, to me.

"How does it look?"

"Exactly as I remember it. My bed isn't made, there's a stack of books on my desk..." I trailed off as I looked around my room and imagined I was wandering around in it. My soft, grass-green blanket was bunched up at the foot of my bed. My teal duvet with the yellow suns was haphazardly hanging off one side. All the novels that I had promised myself I would read, that summer, were piled on my desk, along with magazines and a few university brochures.

"Any good snacks?"

I smiled. "No. Aunt Vera would kill me if I had food in my room."

"She sounds smart. You don't want bugs."

"Nope," I agreed.

"Is your favourite childhood toy there?"

"Yes."

"Tell it I said 'hi,'" Mez said.

I smiled. "Mez says 'hi'," I told Mr. Inquisitive, my brown teddy bear that was resting against my pillow, where I typically left him. He'd been my favourite, ever since I was four and had received him as a birthday gift from Marina, one of my aunt's good friends. His once shiny and soft fur had become dull and worn from being well-loved, over the years, but he was still perfect in my eyes. I picked him up, in my imagination, and wished I could somehow pull him beyond the boundaries of pretend.

"Spend as much time in your room as you want but then go about the motions of what you last remember."

Still holding Mr. Inquisitive, I walked around my room, imagining that I could feel my feet sinking into the soft beige carpet. I looked at the cat calendar on my wall and saw that it was displaying the month of July as it had when I'd last seen it, in person. I wondered how much time had actually passed since I'd left.

Not wanting to think on that, I decided it was time to re-enact everything I'd done prior to my "arrival" on Qarradune. I lay on my bed and settled Mr. Inquisitive back into his spot. I picked up the book on my nightstand and opened it to the page I'd bookmarked.

"Okay, I'm in my bed, reading."

"Okay. Is it a good book?" Mez asked.

"No. Not really."

Mez chuckled softly. "Then you should probably put it down and have a nap."

"Okay," I agreed, putting the book down and mentally shutting my eyes as if I were getting ready for a nap. Once again, I pictured only blackness and wondered what Mez was going to ask me to do next.

Chapter 21

Irys

The mirror was shattered, but the whiteness of the light it reflected remained as pure as it had ever been. The ancient brilliance was beyond the confines of the glass shards that littered the stark floor.

Only moments ago, she had seen him; lost in the heat of his icy gaze. How she longed to meet those aquamarine eyes, once more. How her heart stung with the fresh pain of this long-suffered loss.

With every step, her bare toes evaded the jagged razors of the shards as she searched for a piece that could still contain him.

A crystal tear slipped from the pale skin of her cheek and smashed into prisms on the largest remains of the broken portal. Behind the droplets, he was there. Xandon.

Grasping this final crystalline slice, she clutched it in her fingers and gasped as the remaining pieces cracked around her, ground into deadly dust.

Xandon remained, watching her from within this single reflective window; love pooled deeply in his eyes. She leaned toward him as he reached his strong hand out to her, and brought her own fingers to meet his. As she touched the glass, he was gone. In the mirror, only Irys remained.

*　　*　　*　　*　　*

Light screamed into my eyes when I awoke, driving me to bury my face in my pillow. The pain it caused me was nearly as powerful as the anguish that lingered deeply in my heart from the images of the dream. As the fog of the nightmare and the image of Xandon lifted, so did the agony it had left behind, allowing my heart to slow its frightened gallop.

My mouth was dry enough that when I coughed, dust would have been puffing from my mouth if it were possible. I needed water. If only Desda had placed a glass of it at my bedside the night before.

Squinting one eye open, I checked to see if, by some miracle, a glass of water had somehow made its way to my nightstand, overnight. It hadn't, of course. Groaning and feeling as though Chaos, itself, was sinking into my stomach, I crawled off my bed, dragging many of the bedclothes along with me.

Still tangled, I blindly pulled my way forward along the floor, desperate to reach the bathroom where I could drink as much water as I wanted. My head felt as though it were splitting, and I struggled to find my way with my eyes slammed shut.

I hadn't travelled very far before my hand came upon a smooth lump on the floor. Moving my fingers over the object, I couldn't seem to figure out what it was. Peeking an eye open, I discovered that it was a large brown boot.

Before I had the opportunity to try to decide why such a boot would be located in the middle of my bedroom floor, large warm hands took hold of me to lift me to my feet.

"Irys, can you hear me?" asked a man's voice. No, not just any man; it was Lord Imery's voice.

I froze.

"Oh, Goddess...Lord Imery?" I forced my eyes open and peered up at him through the blindingly bright light.

"Yes," he replied, looking concerned. "Desda couldn't wake you."

"I just need some water," I said. I could barely think of anything else. Even the humiliation of having been caught crawling across my bedroom floor was something I would need to wait to suffer. For now, I had to have something to wet my mouth.

"Desda will bring you water. Let's have you sit on your bed, for now." He eased me back toward my bed, untangling me from my sheets as he did.

"Thank you. I'm alright. I had a bad dream, and I have a headache," I said pathetically.

We sat together, and he brought his arm around me to steady me. When Desda returned with the glass of water, I drank the entire thing without pausing for a breath. My thirst had taken over, and I hadn't any choice as to how much water I would consume.

Lord Imery asked Desda to have a light meal prepared for me, and she left the room.

"I'm sorry I worried you," I said when I was finally able to speak again.

"Did you want to talk about your dream?"

"It wasn't entirely clear. I don't remember very much, anymore, aside from the way I felt. I only know that it wasn't a good dream. Is it time for me to get up?"

"It was time for you to rise about three hours ago."

"I'm very sorry, Lord Imery, but I can't remember what we had planned for the day. What is it that we are meant to be doing?" Everything was a blur. My mind was as hazy as my vision.

"You were going to help me with my research. A little food and some tea will help you to clear your mind, Clever One." Although his words sounded confident, his expression still hinted at concern. I could tell that he was worried in a way that he was attempting to hide.

"What is it, Lord Imery? Did I scream when I had the nightmare as I did the last time?"

"No, you didn't scream, but I'm growing more concerned about you, Irys. Your recent behaviour and your nightmares are very worrying."

"I'm fine. I've only just returned, and I'm finding my way again. I'll work on your research and soon I'll have Miss Fhirell to tea. Once Miss Wynters returns, all will be well again, I'm sure. Please don't worry."

He smoothed his hand over my hair, in a comforting way. "I will give you time to heal and will return to my study. You can join me there when you are ready for the day."

All I wanted was to go back to sleep, but I was certain that this would only cause him greater concern. "Thank you. I'm sure that a few moments to wake up will be all I'll need," I assured him.

With a kiss to my head, he stood and left the room. I shut my eyes to try to capture even the briefest moment of rest before Desda would return with my breakfast. It felt as though my eyelids had barely had the chance to shut when Desda gently shook my shoulder.

"Miss Godeleva?" she asked with barely-hidden alarm.

"I'm awake, Desda. Thank you." I pried my eyes open to see her worried face and furrowed brow.

"I've drawn a bath for you and your breakfast is ready."

I was surprised that I had been asleep long enough for her to be able to do as much as she had. Perhaps I had slept, after all.

"That sounds lovely," I said in words I didn't mean. "I'll take my bath and dress before I eat." The last thing I wanted was to have to face a meal. I hoped my appetite would decide to return once I was dressed and ready.

Unfortunately, that was not the case. After stumbling into the bathroom and nodding off more than once in the embrace of the warm and gently-perfumed water, I was scarcely able to keep my eyes open, even as Desda helped me to dress. Finally seated, with my meal in front of me, I sent the maid away so that I wouldn't have an audience as I struggled to eat the contents of this small but seemingly insurmountable dish.

I ate as much of the plate as I could and pushed the rest around with my fork until it could be styled to appear as insignificant as possible. In case someone reported my leftovers to Lord Imery, I didn't want it to seem as though I'd left much behind.

Standing, I needed to hold onto the table to steady myself. This wouldn't do at all. I scuffed over to my bag and looked through its contents until I came across the envelope of ptimyus. It was a sticky, compressed powder that was known for its properties for easing a flustered spirit.

Bringing it with me, I took up the spoon from my breakfast tray and carried them to the nearest candle, which I lit with some difficulty from my failing coordination. I tapped a lump of the powder into the bowl of the spoon and closed the envelope. Holding the spoon over the flame, I watched it melt into a syrupy liquid that smelled far less than appealing. As soon as it had liquefied, I blew on it to cool it a little before drinking the contents of the spoon, all at once.

The flavour was unlike anything I had ever tasted or ever wanted to taste again. My eyes slammed shut, and my breath caught in my throat but before I could utter one sound of complaint, I felt my body relax and my mind loosen. A smile reclined across my lips as I was strengthened but equally unwound.

Returning the spoon to the tray and the envelope to my bag, I suddenly felt much more prepared to face the day. At the same time, even if I wasn't prepared, that was alright, too.

As I walked by the mirror at my vanity, I rolled my eyes at the smiling girl who looked back at me. How ridiculous she looked; styled to appeal to Lord Imery's tastes and not her own. It was no wonder she was covering up her true thoughts. I chuckled to myself and stepped out into the hallway.

Toslen was still there, guarding my room. I wondered if he had been there since the night before or if he had gone to bed and had already returned for duty. The thought struck me that he might just sleep right there, standing up, and it nearly made me burst out with laughter. I smiled brightly to the man.

"Good morning, Toslen," I declared as I passed.

One of his eyebrows raised in surprise and that nearly caused me to want to laugh again.

"Good morning, Miss Godeleva," he said. "You're looking exceptionally lovely today." He walked behind me as I made my way down the hall.

"Thank you," I said as the idea planted itself in my mind that he might actually be following me. Of course, he could merely have been travelling the same way, out of sheer coincidence, so I stopped in my tracks to see what he would do.

Glancing over my shoulder, I saw that Toslen had stopped as well. I turned quickly to face forward, so he wouldn't be able to see the wide grin that had spread its way across my face. Once again, I started walking, and I heard his steps begin as well.

"Are you testing to see if I'm following you, Miss Godeleva?" he asked in a voice that was riddled with amusement.

"Yes," I replied through laughter. "I have determined that you are."

"I am," he said with his own chuckle.

"Are you going to visit Lord Godeleva in his study, too?"

"No, but I'm going to make sure you make it there safely. You never know what can happen when travelling the length of a hallway," he joked.

I paused in front of Lord Imery's study door and looked back to Toslen. "It seems you've done your job well. I've arrived at my destination. Good morning, Toslen."

Raising my hand, I knocked on the door, but I nodded to him when he bowed to me, in a respectful way.

"Come," said Lord Imery's voice. I took a moment to place a more serious expression on my face. It needed a couple of tries, but I managed to make the appearance stick. When it did, I entered the study, shutting the door behind me.

Lord Imery's expression brightened as he took the chance to look me over. I smiled to him in return.

"How are you feeling?" he asked hopefully.

"Much better. A bath and a breakfast was all I needed." I felt as though he needed the lie. It was better for us both.

I walked up to my usual chair, observing the odd sensation of nearly floating in my steps. Smiling at the sensation, I took my seat and arranged my skirt around myself. It took a great deal of effort not to giggle, though there wasn't anything specific that had tickled my sense of humour.

"I'm very glad to hear it, Clever One. You look as though you have been recreated." He handed me a book. "The page is marked," he said and took a moment to look content before going back to his own research.

Opening the book, I turned to the first marked page. It took me several tries to be able to focus on the words in front of me. At first, they danced around the page, and I started to wish that it were possible for me to dance about the room in a similar way.

How funny that would be!

Of course, I decided against it. I was determined to prove to Lord Imery that we could return to normal and that he should not feel the need to worry over me. I poured all my focus into the pages and the words they contained. My eyes forced the dancing letters to stand in their designated rows and to behave themselves.

After a certain time had passed, Lord Imery looked up from his work. "What do you think, so far?"

It was only then that I realized I'd barely read anything, at all. Usually, I would become entirely engrossed in a book, losing myself to it. Today, I felt as though I were trying to force a key into a hole that was far too small.

"Quite unexpected," I replied vaguely, hoping this would be enough to satisfy him for the moment and to give me time to read more of the book before he wished to discuss any of it.

He nodded. "I don't think I've ever seen you as focused on your research."

"It is quite the subject," I said, feeling guilty that I was only barely aware of what the topic actually was. "Oh! Before I allow myself to become lost in the book, once again, I have meant to ask you if you have heard any news of Gbat Rher."

Although it was true that I was deeply curious about Gbat Rher and its current situation, I knew that I was inquiring only to steer the discussion away from the book that I was greatly struggling to understand.

"It's funny that you should bring it up. I was thinking of having you write another article, Clever One. I was quite impressed with the first one you wrote and so was the emperor. In fact, there will now be a group, led by the Knights, which will be making its way there to help to assess the damage and to determine what materials and supplies are needed in the rebuilding process."

"Yes, I've heard of this mission! It will be Sir Fhirell who will be leading it, if I am not mistaken. I had no idea that my article had anything to do with that decision."

"It played an important role in showing His Majesty the heart of the issue while turning his attention to the genuine need in our newest province."

"How thrilling!" I exclaimed with pride. "May I speak with some of the people who intend to go on the mission so that I may quote them in my article? Then, perhaps they would be willing to speak with me again, on their return, so that I may update the situation with the latest news in a third article."

He chuckled, looking entertained by my enthusiasm. "I'm sure that can be arranged. If writing articles is something that interests you, perhaps you would like to start writing about our studies as well."

I couldn't honestly say that this appealed to me nearly as much as the situation in Gbat Rher, but I nodded all the same. "Perhaps. I suppose we will need to see how well my other articles are received before I will be accepted in more academic circles. Thank you for your belief in me."

He smiled and we settled back into our reading. I wondered if I would be able to focus on my studies more effectively than I had before; particularly now that I was feeling giddy over the potential for another article or two about Gbat Rher. A knock at the door saved me from having to try, quite yet.

I chuckled at the sound, and Lord Imery raised a brow at my reaction, but a servant drew his attention away from me by entering the study.

"Lord Godeleva, Lady Brensforth is here to see you."

I smiled at the servant who respectfully inclined his head to me. It didn't bother me nearly as much as it normally would that Lady Brensforth was here to visit Lord Godeleva. Somehow, I felt perfectly comfortable with her presence.

"Thank you. Please tell her I will be down presently," Lord Imery replied, reading a final paragraph to his book before he marked the page and shut the volume.

The servant bowed and left, and I turned my attention to Lord Imery. "What about our research? I thought we were to spend the day together."

He made no effort to disguise his surprise over my reaction, but he chuckled warmly to me. "It will still be here when I get back. You may continue to read, if you wish to keep up our efforts without me."

I felt as though I might cry. It's not as though he were going away. In fact, reading about the history of Lord Imery's new artifacts was the last thing I felt like doing. Still, I didn't want him to go. I nodded so that I wouldn't need to risk hearing my voice break.

"I shouldn't be long, Clever One," he assured me.

Swallowing hard to steady my voice, I smiled to him. "Please give my best to Lady Brensforth."

He rose and gave my hand a little squeeze before leaving his study.

Though I tried to read a little, I didn't try very hard. My heart wasn't in it. Instead, I stood and brought the book with me, with the intention of returning to my room.

As I left the study, I smiled a little to Toslen, who was waiting for me. This time, it wasn't nearly as amusing to see him as it had been earlier. Perhaps it was the effects of the ptimyus, earlier, that had made things appear differently than they were now as the effects were starting to fade.

I walked swiftly toward my rooms, hoping to avoid any discussions with anyone. The thought of being sociable was greatly unappealing to me.

"Everything alright, Miss Godeleva?"

"Yes," I quickly replied to him. "I just want to read in my room."

"May I ask what you're reading?"

I held the book out so that he could read the title, not wanting to admit that I couldn't remember what it was. His expression changed from one of curiosity to disapproval.

"Are you being punished?" he asked with a smirk.

He deserved a stern look for having spoken to me in such a way, but a smile forced itself to my lips. "No. It is important research."

"Ah," he replied, still looking playful. "I suppose smart people, such as yourself and Lord Godeleva, would see such a book as important, not just boring."

"It is important to the advancement of knowledge," I replied, attempting and failing to say the words with any degree of seriousness. I paused outside my door in order to be able to face him.

"Well, I hope you're enjoying the advancement of your knowledge. If you need anything, I'll be right out here."

"Thank you, Toslen," I replied. I no longer felt the urgent need to return to my rooms. In fact, my preference was suddenly to be able to stay out in the hall and speak with my new guard. However, that would be entirely inappropriate. I turned and entered my room, shutting the door behind me.

I walked briskly to my desk and opened the book.

Goddess, please help me to steady the words. They are jumping around on the page, and I cannot hold them still enough to read them.

After what felt like an eternity of struggle, I'd barely finished a page of reading and my notes consisted of a single line. In sheer frustration, I picked up the book and hurled it across the room. It struck the wall, spine-first and fell to the floor. A couple of pages fell loose and lay there next to the tome from which they had been amputated. This was possibly the most destructive act of my life and, yet, I felt no remorse.

I hated that book. It was boring and holding me back from who I truly was. It was stopping me from doing anything important. I wanted to rescue Megan. I wanted to help in Gbat Rher. Instead of doing something real, I was sitting at home, reading about an artifact that perhaps a dozen people in the country would ever find interesting.

Rising, I paced my rooms. It didn't help. I couldn't bear to stay still any longer. As I turned to leave my bedroom, I caught my reflection in the mirror. It was mocking me. It was rubbing it in.

"Shut up!" I bellowed at that spoiled little girl.

I jerked around as a knock came from the door. "Miss Godeleva? Is everything alright?" It was Toslen's voice.

"Everything is fine!" I replied in a chipper voice, hoping he would believe he'd misheard me, earlier.

"Sorry to bother you," he answered and said nothing more.

Breathing a sigh of relief, I tiptoed up to the sitting room door and locked it before doing the same with the bedroom door. When I turned to face the room, I spotted my reflection in the vanity mirror, once again.

Goddess, why must that girl be such an irritant? Look at her! So prissy and spoiled. Such a coward!

I glared at the image, and my reflection glared back at me. How I hated her. It dawned on me that I should do something to give her a dose of reality. I would teach her that a real person cannot remain a precious little girl forever.

Snatching the scissors from my embroidery bag, I grabbed my hair into my fist and watched the girl in the reflection yank it straight up into the air. I was surprised at how threatening the expression was on her face, but I wouldn't let her stop me. I wouldn't let such a brat intimidate me.

I raised the scissors and hacked through the hair, cutting its length in half. The perfect waterfall of ringlets that once tickled the small of her back now reached only as far as her shoulder blades.

Her response wasn't what I had expected. She looked shocked. Horrified. I wanted to taunt her about it as she had ridiculed me, but the confidence had left me.

A knock at the door nearly caused my heart to stop. "Clever One? May I come in?"

Goddess, please save me!

Looking down, I saw scissors in one hand and half the former length of my hair in the other. I stuffed the scissors into my vanity drawer and raced to the window to throw the hair out.

"Of course," I said, trying to sound calm. "Oh yes, it's locked. I'm coming," I added as though I had forgotten that I'd turned the key in the door, only moments beforehand.

I gave myself an extra second to try to catch my breath before I unlocked the door, twisting my hair up into a bun that I held in my hand. I opened the door and tried to smile as naturally as I could.

"Why was the door locked?" he asked with a furrowed brow. "Why are you holding your hair like that?"

"I felt safer with my door locked as I didn't know if you and Lady Brensforth would be going out," I lied. "I was just in the middle of pinning up my hair when you knocked. I'll just finish it now." It felt as though I would never again have another honest thing to say.

"I wouldn't have gone out with Lady Brensforth without telling you first."

I nodded to him as I rushed over to the vanity and began jamming pins into my hair to try to hold the bun in place. "Of course. It was silly."

It was increasingly clear that I was doing a terrible job at fooling him. His expression was growing ever more perplexed. After studying me for a moment, he approached me.

"Irys, what has happened to your hair?"

"I...styled it," I answered, pathetically.

"Styled it? Let it down."

For a brief moment, I considered refusing, but my hands wouldn't listen to me. I was already pulling the mess of pins out, and the badly lacerated purple strands fell unevenly, not even reaching the midpoint of my back.

He looked at me as though viewing something disturbing. "Why did you do this?"

"I..." my voice broke. Suddenly, I realized that this was all the result of an argument I'd been having with my reflection. "I don't know."

His face shifted to concern.

"Please don't be upset," I begged after a silence that was becoming painful.

"I'm beyond upset, Irys. I don't even recognize you, anymore."

"I'm still myself, Lord Imery. I just changed my hair a little. I shouldn't have done it. It was a mistake. It will grow back. I'll have Desda fix it, for now." My words were tripping out of my mouth, and my eyes filled with tears.

"Come sit with me, Clever One," he said, his voice softening dramatically. His hand settled at the base of my back, in a steadying way, and he led me to the sofa in my sitting room.

Great Goddess, please distract him from the book on the floor. I will do my best to repair it, so his feelings won't be hurt. My tantrums aren't his fault.

I took a seat, arranging my skirt in a dismal attempt to appear neat and proper. He settled in next to me and took my hands in his.

"I need you to tell me what's wrong," he began. "Whatever would possess you to mutilate yourself in such a way?"

"I'm sorry," I responded, holding his hands in return. "I came back to my room to read, but I found myself feeling desperately alone. I couldn't focus on my reading. I had such dreadful thoughts filling my mind: my worries about Miss Wynters, my foolish attempt to take part in her rescue, the flowers from the emperor..." I had to pause to regain control of my voice, which was trembling terribly. "Lasilla used to be here when I needed someone. I miss her, dreadfully."

I withdrew one of my hands from his so that I could extract a handkerchief from my sleeve and dab at my eyes. It was a meagre attempt to manage the tears that were now falling freely.

My hand was shaking, even as I clutched at the soft square of fabric. As I lowered it, I was drawn into a protective embrace.

"I know you miss her," he said quietly as he brought his arms fully around me. I let myself sink in against him and sobbed as I hadn't done all this time. It was agonizing at the same time as it came as a profound relief.

I didn't try to control the tears. Finally, I was able to let them out, and I did so for several minutes. Lord Imery didn't try to settle me.

He merely held me to remind me that he was there. It was precisely what I needed.

As I regained control over myself, I took a few longer breaths. "I'm very alone, right now, Lord Imery. Please forgive me as I find my way again."

"I'll help you in whatever way I can, Irys."

"Please don't be too upset when I make mistakes. I'm trying very hard."

"I know you are." He stroked my hair, and I tried not to allow myself to be lost in another round of tears when I felt his hand touch my back where the length of my hair used to be.

"I think I will send that note to Miss Fhirell and see if she'd like to take a walk in the public gardens." It was not my intention to remain this broken, sobbing fraction of a person. I hoped that he would see that I did intend to help myself to recover from my despair and that I was trying to do the things that a proper lady should.

"That sounds like a very good idea, but I would prefer it if she were to come and visit you here. You can walk around our own gardens. You've always loved them, at this time of the cycle."

"You don't want me going out?"

"No," he confirmed.

It was as though he had placed me inside a cage. I was trapped in my own home.

Seeing my displeasure, he gave my hand a squeeze. "I understand that you need time, and I will be patient with you. You must also understand that I need time. You haven't been yourself, and I want to be sure you're safe."

"Yes, Lord Imery. When I'm ready to meet Miss Fhirell, I will ask her to visit us here," I said obediently. I could feel myself slipping into our old ways, but my heart and my soul were no longer a part of our exchange. Certainly, I wanted him to be pleased with me, but I realized that it was no longer for altruistic reasons. My words and actions were now a means to assuage his concerns so that he would allow me greater freedoms.

"I know it is difficult, Irys, but I'm not keeping you here as a punishment."

"I understand, Lord Imery. I haven't given you any reason to trust me. Staying in our beautiful home is not a punishment. I have always been happy here. Most people would beg for such an imprisonment."

"I'm glad you can see my position in this."

I nodded. "I will have Desda fix my hair. There is no reason for me to wait before starting to put things right again."

This pleased him and his expression warmed. "To start things off on the right foot, I will tell you that I had come to see you with good tidings. Lady Brensforth brought news of Sir Vorel. I'd mentioned that you had been caring for him and it seems that she already knew of your kind work. She is a good friend of Lady Vorel."

My spirit lifted, a little. "How has he been healing?"

Great Goddess, please may this news be of the easing of Sir Vorel's pain. You are all that is great and wise. You know that Sir Vorel is a good man whose injuries were sustained through a noble and selfless act. Please relieve his suffering, and mine, by having healed his wounds.

"He continues to heal, and the doctors are optimistic that he will escape infection."

"That is very good news. Thank you, Lord Imery." *Thank you, Great Goddess.* "It could not have come at a better time. I needed to hear of something promising. Please thank Lady Brensforth, on my behalf."

"I certainly will," he said as he rose and rang for Desda. Turning, he strode over to the book and carefully picked it up, tucking the dislodged pages back inside.

"I'm very sorry. I will read it tonight," I assured him. My shame was genuine.

"Would you rather not work on our research for a while, Irys?"

"I wouldn't know what to do with myself without our work."

He studied me for a long moment before nodding and resting the book down on the table, next to where I was seated.

"I won't work when I am not able. I won't let it come to this again, Lord Imery," I assured him.

"Good. I hope you will talk to me if you should ever think that you are approaching this point."

"I hope it is all over now. I will make friends and am looking forward to beginning the new articles about Gbat Rher."

"I hope for the same. I will see you at dinner, Clever One." It was more than clear that I had not convinced him that my return to normalcy would be quite that easy.

On his way out the door, he paused without facing me. "Please don't lock your room door again, Irys." Though it was phrased as a request, it was more than clear that this was not a matter that was up for discussion. If I were to disobey, there would be consequences.

"I won't. Not if I know you're home. I understand that you won't go out without telling me."

For a moment, it was as though he was going to say something else, but he simply proceeded to exit my room, closing the door behind himself.

Barely a breath had passed before Desda silently entered the room. Though she hid her surprise well upon noticing my hair, I did catch the flash of shock that made its way into her eyes before she was able to correct it.

"I know," I said, acknowledging the unspoken matter. "Will you please cut my hair to make it neater, Desda?"

Though I walked over to my vanity, I never once looked at my reflection in the mirror. Instead, I sat very still and watched the items on the surface of the piece.

"Yes, Miss Godeleva," she replied, walking quickly to fetch the scissors and everything else she would require to recover my look. Carefully, she dampened the ends of my hair and trimmed them, shaping layers to make the style appear to be deliberate. I could tell that she was doing her best to remove all the jagged pieces while still shortening it by as little as possible.

When she was finished, I thanked her and rose from the seat so that I would no longer risk facing the reflection in front of me. I dismissed her, and she stepped up to the door as quietly as she had entered, promising to fetch me when dinner was ready. Instead of leaving, she paused there, looking at me.

"I know I'm not Lasilla, and I doubt I will ever fill her shoes, but I hope you know that I'm here for you, no matter what you need."

My tension rose as Desda spoke. Her words were sweet and heartfelt, and it was very understanding of her to say what she did, but they also served to remind me that Lasilla was gone and would never return to me. It also showed me that I was far more transparent to her than I was to Lord Imery. I would need to be careful in front of Desda's eyes, if there were ever anything I wished to keep to myself.

"Thank you, Desda. I do expect us to become closer, with time," I assured her. To me, my words sounded genuine.

Desda nodded to me and curtsied before leaving the room. She was smarter than I had guessed. Now, she left me in peace.

How I wished that I could lock the door. The thought of Lord Imery's suspicions, Desda's surprising understanding of me, and even Toslen, immediately outside the door, made me feel vulnerable. It was as though I couldn't breathe. I was surrounded by eyes that were watching my every move.

Rummaging through my bag, I looked for something that would ease my mind. The words on the labels seemed to blur before my eyes, so I allowed my fingers to simply select something on their own. Once I had chosen an envelope, I brought it close to my face and studied it until the letters stood still. "Ringaor," it read.

I'd read about ringaor. It was a type of sap that dried into a solid that could be ground into a powder. It was once given to people who would be undergoing surgery in order to allow them to escape from the pain. That was exactly what I wanted: an escape from this pain and to be able to feel as though I were breathing again.

Upending the envelope over my mouth, I watched as the fresh silvery-white powder slid from the opening. I fought the inclination to spit it back out, again. After only the smallest amount, I could feel an acidic burning slithering from my tongue down the back of my throat. Dropping the envelope into my bag, I coughed until, quite suddenly, the burning subsided.

I looked up and found that I was no longer in my room but was, instead, standing on a concert stage, with a sizeable audience cheering for me. I waved to them and stepped onto centre stage. Taking a deep breath, I opened my mouth and allowed the smooth current of a favourite melody flow from my lips. The crowd hushed as I began. They were awed and stared, wide-eyed, at me as the colours of the tune flew around them. As I held the final note, they shot to their feet, applauding with tears in their eyes.

They called my name, and I curtsied humbly. Over and over I heard my name repeated until it began to fade, becoming a single lingering voice.

"Miss Godeleva?" it repeated, and I wondered why it had been spoken so questioningly. I shut my eyes in the hopes of figuring the answer but, when I opened them, I discovered that I was back in my room and there was a frantic knocking on my door.

"Hmm?" I inquired, still swaying slightly to the rhythm of the song I'd only just finished singing.

The door opened sharply and Desda stepped inside. "Miss Godeleva?" she repeated.

"Desda?" I asked, not entirely sure if she was entering my room or crossing my concert stage.

Her face was riddled with concern, and I giggled when she realized that she had forgotten to curtsy to me. "Dinner is ready, Miss Godeleva," she said with hesitation in her tone. I had to laugh again. How amusing Desda was!

"Of course," I replied through the laughter. From my vanity, I picked up my beautiful butterfly comb, wondered at it for a moment and tucked it into my hair. Desda must have left as she didn't appear to be in my room any longer. I didn't mind. It was dinnertime!

Into the hallway I strolled, feeling the lightness of life as one would feel an embrace from a loved one.

"You have quite the voice, Miss Godeleva," said Toslen, causing me to laugh, once more. I'd forgotten all about him!

"Thank you, Toslen," I replied and smiled to him. How very comical he was! "You needn't follow. I'm merely going to dinner with Lord Godeleva."

"I know when I'm not wanted," he chuckled. "I'm glad you're in a better mood, now. Perhaps I should start reading more boring books!"

I laughed merrily and shook my head to his comment about the books.

He seemed pleased with my response, so I proceeded down the stairs. Never had they seemed as challenging as they were, today. It was as though each step were floating on water. I carefully took each stair, holding onto the banister to keep me from falling or floating away. I wasn't dressed to swim in the water under these steps, after all.

Reaching the bottom, I was struck with laughter as I heard the click of my shoes on the marble. Why had I never noticed how funny that sounded? I was still giddy when I reached the door to the dining room, but I swallowed my giggles and curtsied to Lord Imery who rose from his seat, upon seeing me.

He smiled at me, looking entertained. Perhaps he'd realized how funny the sound of shoes were on the marble, too.

"Good evening, Lord Imery," I greeted him, taking my seat as my chair was pushed in by a servant whose name I could not remember, for the moment.

"Good evening, Clever One. You seem to be in better spirits."

"I've been singing, and I'm very happy with the improvements Desda has made to my look."

"That's good to hear."

We continued our light discussion, for a while, until dinner was served. How shiny everything looked. This must have been the glossiest meal we'd ever had! I would have wondered at it longer, but my thoughts were distracted when another footman entered the room.

"My apologies for interrupting, Lord Godeleva. Sir Skyleck is here to see you."

"Oh, yes," Lord Imery replied, shaking his head. "I will be with him shortly." After the servant left, Lord Imery turned his attention to me. "I'm sorry, Clever One. I completely forgot that I had invited Sir Skyleck here to talk, this evening."

"That's alright. I'll finish my meal and see if I can catch up on my reading. I should make it an early night, again."

"I'll come and say goodnight to you before I retire for the evening." As he walked by me, to exit the room, he gave my shoulder a quick press with his hand.

I smiled up at him and then picked at my shiny meal until I was no longer hungry. With a bounce to my step, I returned up the stairs in the direction of my rooms.

Toslen was still outside my doors, upon my return. "Did you have a good dinner, Miss Godeleva?"

I playfully saluted him and giggled, "Yes. Now I'm ready to return to my concert."

"May I join you?"

"I don't think you have a ticket."

"Do you think you could make an exception for me?"

"It's not up to me. I'm merely the performer."

"To whom must I speak, if not you?"

I paused and furrowed my brow, feeling genuinely stumped. "I don't rightly know."

"If that's the case, I'm sure they won't mind if I sneak in for a listen."

"That's very flattering, Toslen, but I'm afraid it simply cannot be managed." I chuckled and entered my room, walking directly to my reading chair.

When I turned and sat onto the powdery-blue seat, I was startled to see that Toslen had entered my sitting room, behind me, had shut the door, and was presently smiling at me.

"What are you doing here?" The play was gone from my tone.

"I told you. I want to attend your concert," he replied, the grin never leaving his lips.

"I'm not ready to sing, yet."

"I don't care about your singing, Miss Godeleva. I want some of whatever it was that made you sing at that 'concert' in the first place."

"My singing was a choice. I was only joking about the concert," I insisted, trying to sound firm. I stood, hoping to appear more collected.

"Look, I'm not going to do anything to you. I just want some of what we both know you're taking. We also both know that you don't want Lord Godeleva to know about this. This doesn't need to be difficult."

Every pore on my body was perspiring. "If I give it to you, will you leave me alone?"

"Of course."

"You can't come back for more. I don't have much. I won't have more to give you."

"Sure. Fine."

"You must promise. Give me your word that you will never bother me again."

"Yes. Fine. I promise."

I could feel his eyes on me as I walked away from him and into my bedroom where I'd hidden my bag. He followed me into the room, and I cringed at the mere thought of his presence in such a private space. Withdrawing the second and only remaining envelope with ringaor in it, I held it out to him. He reached out for it, but I kept it just out of his grasp.

"You promised," I reminded him. "This is all I have."

"I did promise," he agreed, his gaze fixed on the envelope. His arm remained outstretched, waiting for me to relinquish it to him.

I wished that I could meet his stare, but I was too much of a coward. "Take it and go."

Instead of leaving, he opened the flap and turned the envelope over, pouring much of its contents into his mouth, just as I had done earlier. I watched as any tension he'd had in his face slid away. Calmly, astonishingly calmly, he smiled at me and offered the remainder of the ringaor.

"Your turn," he slurred.

I glanced away from him and met the gaze of the girl in the vanity mirror. The judgment in her eyes stung me profoundly. I knew I shouldn't take it from him, but I also knew there wasn't much left and that it would help me to be able to forget the strain that was nearly overwhelming me.

Snatching the envelope from him, I left the bedroom, hoping he would follow. I dropped into my settee and, from there, I finished off what was left in the envelope.

He stumbled back into my sitting room. "You've got a really nice room," he mumbled.

I didn't care what he was saying. The world was becoming easier. Everything was slower. It was simpler. I leaned back against the settee and let it cradle me.

"I picked it," I finally replied, not knowing how much time had passed since he'd made the comment. I'd meant to tell him that I'd chosen my own décor, but the words failed to serve me.

He laughed, nearly giggling.

I giggled with him. I giggled until I couldn't remember why I was doing it. Shutting my eyes, I gave a long sigh and relaxed for what felt like only a brief moment.

Chapter 22

Megan

The mirror was shattered, but the whiteness of the light it reflected remained as pure as it had ever been. The ancient brilliance was beyond the confines of the glass shards that littered the stark floor.

Only moments ago, she had seen her; lost in the heat of his icy gaze. How she loathed to meet those aquamarine eyes, once more. How her heart hardened with the fresh pain of this long-suffered loss.

With every step, her bare feet crushed the jagged razors of the shards as she searched for a piece that could still contain him.

Blood smeared onto the largest remains of the broken portal. Behind the red stain, he was there. Xandon.

Bringing her foot down, hard, on the final crystalline slice, she tried to smash it but succeeded only in cracking the remaining pieces around her, grinding them into deadly dust.

Xandon remained, watching her from within this single reflective window; triumph burning deeply in his eyes. She had failed. He had seen her. She fell to her knees before the indissoluble glass. He reached his cold metal hand toward her and grasped her shoulder.

Megan shut her eyes and screamed.

*   *   *   *   *

I gasped, and my eyes sprang open. I rapidly blinked to make sense of my surroundings and realized that I was in Mez' office. He was kneeling in front of me with one hand on my shoulder and the other stroking my face. He looked worried.

"Megan, can you hear me?" The concern in his voice made me think that this hadn't been the first time he'd asked me that question.

My heart was racing, thundering in my ears, and my temperature was through the roof. I felt as though I had just awoken from a terrible nightmare. Like the last time I had an experience like this one, all I could remember from it was Xandon. I felt panicked. What had happened to me? I looked at Mez with wild eyes.

"It's alright," he said reassuringly. "You fainted. How do you feel?"

"I...I don't know," I stammered. "What happened?"

"I was trying to help you to remember. I was using my skill to help you feel comfortable as I told you. You were just sitting with your eyes closed, remembering, and then you seemed to lose consciousness," he recounted. "Would you like a bit of juice? I don't have any water here, right now."

I listened to him, slowly nodding as I remembered everything that he was saying. I remembered feeling comfortable and happy when I conjured up that vivid memory of my room, and I remembered taking a "nap." Everything else that happened, afterward, was a blur, except for Xandon. I couldn't shake the look of his haunting eyes. It was as if he were looking into my soul. I shivered and shook my head, trying to rid my mind of the image. Standing abruptly, I walked to the window and wrapped my arms around myself.

"Do you remember anything?" Mez asked.

"No." I really didn't want to get into it.

"Your temperature shot straight up. You were very warm. Has that happened before?"

"Yes. Once," I said, eyeing his approaching reflection in the glass.

"Do you remember what happened, that time?"

I turned to face him. "No," I lied. "I'm tired. I should probably go back to Aésha's room now." I wanted out of there.

He observed me for a second. "Okay," he nodded and went over to his desk, opened a drawer, and withdrew a small book with a blank, brown cardstock cover. He approached me and held it out.

"Here," he said, "If you can't tell me, tell this. I won't read it, but you need to tell someone what you're bottling up. Look what it's doing to you." He held me in a friendly gaze that showed his care and concern.

It should have brought me comfort, but it only made me all the more tense and frustrated. I took the notebook from him and held it in a shaking hand. I quickly dropped my hand to my side to hide the shaking, even though I knew he'd seen it.

Mez reached out and surprised me by taking my free hand and holding it gently between his steady and warm ones.

"It's alright," he assured me.

I slowly shook my head. "No, it's not," I whispered. "Nothing is alright."

"Why do you say that?"

I stared incredulously at him. How could he ask such a preposterous question when he knew I was far, far away from home? My temper flared.

"I'm not supposed to be here," I seethed. "I'm supposed to be in another world, having fun with my friends in the summer, before I head off to university. I'm supposed to be applying for jobs. I'm supposed to be agonizing over whether or not that guy I met a month ago wants to ask me out on another date. I'm not supposed to be here, in this nightmare, where you make people slaves, and you hurt them, and you hurt the people they care about, and you hurt me!" I shouted, my voice growing louder with each syllable. "I hate it here, and I hate you!" I spat, pulling my hand free from his and taking a step back.

Mez didn't look upset, angry, or even surprised by my outburst. He simply listened without interruption.

"I understand," he said with compassion. "I'm sorry that this has happened to you," he added sincerely, "but thank you for being honest with me."

I gave a tiny nod but remained silent. I wanted to stay angry, but I couldn't. I was mad at this situation, but I wasn't actually mad at Mez. None of this was technically his fault. If anything, he'd always been decent to me. I did want to rage at someone, but he wasn't the one who deserved it. Unable to keep up my anger, I felt sadness creep in, threatening to swallow me whole. My eyes clouded with tears but crying was the last thing I wanted to do, right now, especially in front of him.

I turned toward the window and stepped as close to it as I could, without actually touching it, so that I could get a clearer view of the sky. In the reflection, I saw Mez move toward the door, and the lights in the room suddenly went out. I snapped my head around, to look at him, wondering what he was doing. He approached but only nodded his head in the direction of the window.

I turned and understood why he'd done it. It was a crystal clear night, and all the stars and the pearlescent moon were out. I focused on the glittering constellations that were truly breathtaking. As I browsed the heavens, I noticed that one of the stars looked bigger than the others, and it was notably blue.

"Is that a star?" I asked. "That blue one?"

"Yes," Mez said, stepping up beside me, "The Blue Star."

"It's pretty." It really was. I'd never seen a star like it.

"It's special. It moves across the sky in a path completely different from all the other stars."

"Really?" I asked, glancing over my shoulder at him. I didn't realize that stars even moved. Suddenly, I wished I'd paid more attention during my astronomy lessons.

He nodded. "Where I grew up, it was very cold for parts of the cycle; far colder than you will see in the capital city. If you were to go out at night during the coldest season and look up, the star would be so blue, you'd feel as though it must be getting closer to you. It was just that clear."

Listening to him, I continued marveling at the celestial landscape. It was beautiful. The bright-blue star looked like a twinkling sapphire among a sea of diamonds. I had never noticed it before, I guessed because all the night skies I'd seen had been cloud-covered.

Turning to face him I said, "Where I live in Canada, it gets really cold at certain times of the year, too. It gets cold enough that if you don't have shelter, you'll freeze to death."

"Are years like cycles?" he queried with interest.

"I'm not sure, but I think so."

He nodded. "It sounds like you grew up in a place not too different from where I did, weather-wise. Did you wear fur for half the cycle-year?"

I shook my head. "No, I only wore super-warm coats for about four months."

"How long is a month?"

"The average is thirty days. There are twelve months in one year," I explained further.

"There are six seasons in a cycle," he said, "Each season has fifty days. Perhaps there are two months to a season, if a year and a cycle are truly similar."

Hmm, that's interesting.

"What season is it now?" I asked.

"It's the Warm Season."

"Before I came here, it was the month called July, on Earth."

I watched him repeat "July", quietly to himself as if he were trying to cement it into his memory, or as if he found the word fascinating.

"We don't have blue stars on Earth, though," I told him, with a small smile. "We've got a lot of stars and some bright ones, but I've never seen one quite as pretty as that."

"We only have one blue star. It's unique...like you," he smiled.

I smiled a little more

Meh, at least he didn't call me "nuts." I'd settle for unique.

"Maybe that's where I'm from," I joked. "Do you think you could find a way to launch me up to that star?"

Mez smiled, looked at the star and then back at me. "I tell you what, if I ever do touch it, like I thought I could as a child, I will hold onto it long enough that you can climb back on."

Aww, that was so sweet!

"Thanks. I believe you," I said and knew that my words weren't empty.

I focused on the blue star, again, wondering if it could possibly be Earth. I doubted it, but it felt comforting to imagine that it could be. That, even if it was a gajillion miles away, I could still see it. I saw that star as a sign of hope, home, and freedom.

Freedom...that reminds me...

"Why am I no longer a slave?" I asked abruptly, turning my gaze on Mez.

"Short answer: it's classified. Long answer: you made the right impression with the right people," he responded without so much as flinching.

I knew he'd be direct. He didn't hesitate or squirm in the way I knew Keavren would have, if I'd asked him that same question. That said, his answer had me curious. The "classified", I had expected, but who the heck had I made the right impression with? Xandon? I doubted Galnar freed me from being his slave, out of the goodness of his black heart.

"What right people? Xandon?" I pressed.

"Again, I can give you two answers. Your choice: our usual short answer, or I can make up a spectacular lie," he grinned.

It didn't surprise me that this information was top secret, but I'd hate myself if I didn't ask in the off-chance he'd actually tell me or give me some kind of hint. I was amused to no end that he'd make up a lie. I wondered how good a storyteller he was.

"Okay. Let's hear your spectacular lie," I challenged.

His grin faded into a pleased expression. "Good choice. So, after your unscheduled departure from our ship, Captain Galnar was so upset that he came to cry on my shoulder. I could barely make out what he was saying through the sobs, so after I put him to bed, I consulted with Keavren," Mez told me straight-faced as if every word were true. "With Keavren's description of you and Acksil's affinity and skill for painting, I got to see what you look like. Naturally, I had to meet you." He flashed me a dashing smile. "So, I hijacked the ship, brainwashed everyone aboard, and the rest, you know," he finished, simply.

If I didn't know that his story was complete-and-utter bull, I could have easily believed that that's what went down. Mez was, indeed, a spectacular liar. I was beginning to think that Aésha was right. Nothing did fluster this guy.

I laughed and clapped, a couple of times. "That was quite the tale."

He nodded and headed to the door, turning the lights back on.

"Are you ready to go back to Aésha's room?" he asked me.

I nodded, with a yawn. I was exhausted and all talked-out.

He nodded his head like "no problem" and took his jacket off, set it on the back of his chair, and extracted the cuffs from the pocket.

"Don't forget Rral Radone's journal," he reminded me, making a slight gesture with his hand, toward the book on his desk.

"Oh yeah, thanks," I said.

Approaching the book, I was about to take it but stopped when I saw that there was a small black strip of leather with a buckle and a rectangular metal tag, resting on top of the journal. I picked it up to examine it more closely. It looked like a collar; a collar the perfect size for a cat. My eyes moved to Mez, in surprise.

"You got Pounce a collar?"

"Yes," he confirmed.

I smiled. "Aw, that was really cool of you, thanks."

I looked back at the collar and noticed there was something written on the tag. I examined it more closely and read: "To Megan, From Mez."

At first, I thought it was kind-of weird that he had this inscribed on the tag, but then its meaning sank in. Galnar hadn't gotten me a kitten, after all.

"You? It was you?" I looked at him with a bit of awe.

A warm smile lifted his face, and he gave a modest nod. "You needed someone."

"Thank you, Mez. I really love her," I told him, getting a bit misty-eyed.

"You're welcome, Megan."

Smiling, I stacked the journal I'd been holding on top of Rral's, secured them in the nook of my left arm, and carried the collar in my right hand. I stepped up to Mez and held my right arm out to him, so he could cuff it, which he did. Locking the cuffs and slipping the key into his pants pocket, he opened the door, and we stepped out.

"You're a pretty cool guy, Mez." I told him as he shut the door.

"As cool as my shoes?" he asked and did a side-to-side tap with the toe of his shoe.

I laughed. "Better."

"Wow. I'm very cool," he said as if the idea of out-cooling his shoes was a serious victory.

I grinned and nodded, walking with him as he lead the way back to Aésha's quarters.

"You should give Aésha a hug when you see her," he said as we descended a flight of stairs. "She likes you a lot, and she gives good hugs. You need it, after what I've put you through."

I considered his recommendation and finally nodded. "I will. I've tried to shut everyone out, but it's very hard. Plus, she is pretty, uh, crisp."

"She certainly is," he laughed. "And she uses her crisp-self to try to get you to think things you usually wouldn't and do things that you might not otherwise do. It's all in play, but you're never the same after talking to her," he said, amused.

We wound our way through the ship, taking stairs and walking along halls until Mez finally stopped us at a door. I tried to pay attention to the route he took, but I knew there was no way I'd be able to re-find his office, without help. The ship was too maze-like – and much larger – than I had initially realized.

When he extracted the small key from his pocket to unlock our cuffs, I said, "I'm sorry about freaking out at you, earlier. It's not really you I'm mad at."

He smiled and gave his head a little shake. "I know. It was just something that needed to come out," he said with understanding and unlocked the leather cuffs.

I nodded. Yup, it definitely needed to come out.

"Will I see you tomorrow?" I asked.

He shook his head. "No. Tomorrow, you'll need to find your own snacks."

I raised a brow, wondering if he was kidding.

"Kiss her!" came Aésha's playful order from behind the door.

I jumped, startled, looking at the door as if it had struck me. Mez only sighed and smiled, unlatching it for me.

"Goodnight, Megan."

"Goodnight, Mez," I said with a smile and walked into the room.

I watched him shut the door, and I turned to see Aésha lying in bed with Pounce on her belly. She was filing her nails and Pounce was watching the nail file like it was a mouse. It was a funny sight.

Setting the journals down on the cot, I pulled off my boots and walked over to the bed, carrying the collar.

"I've got something for you, Pounce," I informed her, scooping her off Aésha.

Sitting on the bed, I slipped the leather collar around her neck and buckled it in place. She squirmed, a bit, but didn't put up too much of a fuss. Aésha continued to work on her nails but was watching us out of the corner of her eye.

"There. Look how pretty you are!" I declared. Pounce didn't look impressed. I had to laugh at her sour expression. I let her go, and she hopped off the bed.

I turned to look at Aésha. "I have to give you something, too," I informed her.

She nodded. "Just let me prepare." She set the nail file aside and licked her lips, pressing them together. "I'm all yours."

I chuckled. "I need you to sit up."

She sat up and then I hugged her. It was a loose hug, at first, but then I held her more tightly. She brought her arms around me, warmly and protectively.

"I know, Baby," she whispered and rubbed my back with one hand, holding me tightly with her other arm.

I nodded against her shoulder and whispered, "I really hope you're my friend, Aésha. I want to believe that you are."

She drew back slightly, so she could look me right in the eyes. "I'm your friend, Baby. We all do what we have to do, but I'm your friend," she told me, solidly.

I looked back at her and took her words to heart.

"Go get ready for bed, Baby," Aésha said, reaching up and stroking my face. "You look like you could sleep, sitting up."

I nodded and kissed her cheek, withdrawing from her and heading to the bathroom. As I got ready for bed, I pondered the words she'd said to me. In a lot of ways, it made sense. I knew, without a doubt, that if given the opportunity, I would leave her and everyone here behind, in a heartbeat. That didn't mean I couldn't be her friend, then and there, if the circumstances permitted it. Equally, she could be a friend to me as long as she was able to, but could also turn on me if she was ordered to do so.

It was a weird friendship. Neither one of us wished each other any ill will, but we both knew that we could end up on opposite sides at any time.

I slid my hand into my pants pocket and tightly clutched Rral's ring and Irys' handkerchief. Just like Aésha, I would do what I had to do.

Chapter 23

Irys

"I said what's going on here?" bellowed an angry male voice.

Prying my eyelids away from each other, I discovered that Lord Imery was standing over me, irate. What was more surprising, was that he was roughly pulling an equally startled Toslen off the settee, beside me.

"Lord Imery?" I asked, attempting to stand, but I twisted oddly and fell to my hands and knees.

"Lord Godeleva," Toslen sputtered, being held up by his shirt.

"Did you touch her?" Lord Imery demanded. "Irys, are you hurt?"

"I...I don't think so. What happened?" I stammered, trying to climb to my feet. My gown insisted on wrapping itself around my legs, forcing me to remain on the floor.

Lord Imery directed his shouts back to Toslen. "Why are you in here and what happened? Why were you with her?"

"The concert..." Toslen's reply was weak and confused. He was looking around the room with a complete lack of recognition.

Lord Imery shoved him toward a number of our male servants, whose presence I'd only just noticed, at that moment.

"Take him downstairs. I will deal with him later."

I was already considering falling asleep in my twisted gown on the floor when he knelt in front of me and stroked my hair. "Irys, stay with me. Are you hurt? Did he give you something to eat or drink?"

"I don't know," I replied. I hadn't any recollection of how I'd come to be there. "Wasn't I reading?"

He didn't reply. Sliding his arms beneath me, he picked me up and carried me into my bedroom, laying me gently onto the bed. I sighed as I sank into the soft blankets, which seemed to embrace me.

"This bed is soft. I love this bed," I said as every muscle relaxed.

My face was stroked, and I realized that I'd closed my eyes, again. Lord Imery was standing over me with deep concern on his face. "Remain here. You're safe now. I will return in the briefest moment."

I nodded and turned to wrap my arms around my pillow, closing my eyes again. I could feel Megan's journal under my hand. It was nearly impossible to stay awake.

Suddenly, Lord Imery was there again. Time must have passed. He was holding the empty ringaor envelope.

"Irys, did Toslen give you any of this? Is this what you took?"

"He gave it back," I said, rubbing my eyes. "It was the medicine from the rescue voyage on the ship."

He stared at me for a long time. "I see," he said finally.

"You do?" I asked because I certainly hadn't any idea what was happening. "What is it?"

"I've been blind," he responded. "You should rest now. You're safe, but you need your sleep."

"I'm very tired," I agreed. "Would you like to sleep, too? This bed is very soft."

"I'm not tired." He slipped my shoes off my feet, and I giggled as I moved my toes.

"I will have Desda come to help you into some night clothes."

"Thank you. Goodnight, Lord Imery."

If he replied, I was no longer awake to hear it.

*   *   *   *   *

My curtains were thrown open, and the shockingly bright light of the early morning came screeching in on me. I recoiled and turned my back to the light.

"Desda," I called her name as a scold. "I'm still sleeping."

"It is morning, Irys," spoke Lord Imery's voice. I peeked at him through the slit of one eyelid, which was shaded by my hand as much as I could manage. "It is time to wash and dress. You will eat your breakfast, now."

I sat up but slid back down to my pillows, exhausted. What was it that had helped me to rise, yesterday? How could I fetch it without Lord Imery noticing?

"Come now, Irys. Get up. Desda, help her, please." His voice was kind, but it was clear that there would be no opportunity to argue with him.

"Your bath has been drawn, Miss Godeleva. I'll help you," Desda spoke softly and assisted me to the point that she was likely the only one between us keeping me upright. "We'll just have a quick bath, to freshen you up, so your breakfast won't be cold."

I didn't care. The thought of food was turning my stomach. With Desda's help, I walked into the bathroom and was bathed as I shifted between waking and sleeping. Afterward, I sat shivering in my robe as she dried me. She dressed me in a simple gown and braided my hair as though I were a little girl.

"It will be well again, Miss Godeleva. Lord Godeleva is doing everything he can to strengthen you." It was clear that she was attempting to soothe me but all I wanted was to rest.

We walked back into my bedroom together but, instead of allowing me to return to my bed, Desda continued to guide me into the sitting room where Lord Imery was already seated at a little table, reading. A domed dish on the table covered what I could only assume was my breakfast.

I sat into the chair and nodded my gratitude to Desda before directing my attention to Lord Imery.

"I appreciate that you've had breakfast arranged for me, but I'm not hungry, quite yet."

"Nonsense," he replied with a pleasant smile. "It's a light and lovely meal that I selected especially for you. We'll share the time together, and I am going to watch you eat every bite."

I winced as he raised the dome. I stared in disgust at the food. There was a scrambled egg, a slice of buttered toast, and a dish of melon. It didn't matter what they were. They repelled me.

Lord Imery set his book aside and smiled to me. I began to protest, once more, but he picked up a piece of the toast and placed the corner of it into my mouth, silencing me. Taking it from him, I bit the corner from the bread and chewed it, gagging as I swallowed. This did not deter him. He did exactly what he'd said he would do. He sat there, watching me choke down every morsel from the plate.

He chattered on to me, throughout the entire trial, telling me of the news he'd read in the morning's paper and of the things he planned to accomplish that day. My ears could barely distinguish one word from the next. I was aching for something to help me stay awake or something to force me to sleep. It didn't matter what it was. This was intolerable.

Upon the close of the longest meal of my life, he picked up the tray of empty dishes, instead of calling for a servant, and he walked to the door of my room.

"I'll be back to see you, shortly, Clever One," he said simply, then was gone. I heard the lock turn in the door, and I burst into sobs.

Dropping from my chair to my hands and knees, on the floor, I cried until I was certain that I would be sick. I crawled into my bedroom, to where I'd hidden the bag with the medicines, but it wasn't there. Desperately, I felt around the area on the floor, searching for something that may have fallen out. There was nothing. I cried out in frustration and curled up on my side.

I must have slept there, because my face was dry when I opened my eyes, again. I rose and scuffed to the bedroom door and placed my hand on the knob, in case Lord Imery had locked only the sitting room door. The knob wouldn't turn. I pounded on the door, shrieking to vent my fury.

Hysteria was taking me over, and I let it. My head was throbbing, and my muscles howled. My stomach was threatening to empty itself at any moment. Breaking into a cold sweat, I slid down the door to the floor, weeping loudly, though no tears were falling. My eyes were dry.

I tried to settle there; to fall asleep. Anything, to make it all disappear. Try as I may, I could not remain still. I pulled at my hair and pounded on the door with my fists. Using the doorknob, I pulled myself back to my feet, with the intention of kicking at the door, when I caught a glimpse of motion, out of the corner of my eye.

It was *her*. The girl in my reflection had been watching me the entire time. I tore at the sleeves of her ridiculous dress and yanked at her purple hair, but she wasn't afraid of me. I shouted at her and flew at her, driving my shoulder into hers. She shattered before me and glass scattered over the surface of the vanity and onto the floor. Picking up one of the larger pieces of the glass in my left hand as I steadied myself with my right, I was shocked to see that she was looking back at me from this jagged, broken shard.

I roared at her, but it was for nothing. She was stronger than me. Blood dripped onto the floor, but it was not hers. I threw her away and fell backward in the process. After a few breaths, I lay back, staring at the ceiling.

There I remained, unmoving and unfeeling, until there was a soft knocking at my door. I hadn't any idea of how long I'd lain there, nor did I care. The door opened, but I couldn't make myself look at the intruder. It didn't matter. I knew who it was.

"Good morning again, Clever One," Lord Imery spoke calmly as friendly as he had been at breakfast. Desda followed him in and withdrew a hand broom and dustpan from a low cupboard in the wall. I could hear the tinkling of the broken glass as it was moved from the floor into the dustpan.

At the same time, Lord Imery had brought a small basin of water and a cloth to me and had set it down on the floor next to where I continued to lie. I turned my head to watch his movements as he wet the fabric and carefully cleaned the small cuts in my hand before rinsing the cloth and repeating the action.

I felt nothing. A fresh, dry bandage was tied to the hand and the extremity was returned to the floor beside me.

"Have you been keeping busy this morning?" He asked as though it were a normal day. "I'm going to help you up now," he said, crouching next to me as he gently took me by the shoulders and guided me to a sitting position. My eyes slammed shut, and I groaned in protest. Everything was spinning.

He must have seen that I was not necessarily lying on the floor because it was where I wished to be. Taking mercy on me, he picked me up. It took only a brief moment to reveal that his mercy was limited. He did not bring me to my bed. Instead, he placed me down in my reading chair and spread a blanket over my lap before he sat across from me.

"'The Rise and Fall of the Geometric Period in Pomoro Pottery'," he said as he opened the book to which that noxious title belonged.

I whimpered, slumping down in the chair, but he was not deterred. He read to me for hours, breaking only when he stood to ring for a meal. After lunch – a proceeding that was not unlike that of breakfast – he returned to our history lesson, which was equally as abominable as it had been before we had stopped to eat. For my part,

I remained in the chair, miserable, cold, and sick, until the day ran itself out.

Shutting the completed book and setting it onto the end table, Lord Imery rose and picked me up, installing me onto my bed.

"Please," I begged in a voice that crackled from lack of use. "Would you let me take something to put me to sleep? I need help."

"I am helping you, Clever One," he responded in a caring tone.

I cried for more than an hour. He held me the entire time, hushing me and holding my hand, despite my alternating rounds of pleading pathetically and raging viciously at him. Whenever it was that I fell asleep, he was still there.

Chapter 24

Megan

Mez hadn't been kidding. He didn't return the next day or any of the days that followed, which genuinely surprised me because I was under the impression that I'd be seeing a lot more of him. When I asked Aésha about him, she never gave me a straight answer and only teased me about it, so I stopped asking.

I couldn't figure out why he never came back, and my paranoia grew. I had all but convinced myself that I had somehow revealed something to him during our talks that would eventually lead to trouble for me – or worse – someone I cared about. I imagined him laughing at my expense with Galnar and Xandon, but then I would look at my kitten. I'd pick her up, cuddle her, and read the tag on the collar that he had given me, reminding myself that no matter what Mez might be doing and no matter the reasons for him not returning, he had given me the only joy I had on this ship. He had given me Pounce.

At first, I thought it was strange that I'd spent so much time wondering why Mez hadn't returned until I finally realized that the reason I thought about it so much, was that I liked him. I didn't like him in the same way that I liked Thayn, but he was an interesting guy and, in another life, Mez could have been an awesome friend.

Time dragged on and I was glad to have both a kitten and a new journal to keep me occupied. I played a lot with Pounce, and she must have killed at least a thousand fluffs. When I wrote in my journal, I was careful not to write anything about my time in Syliza or about Irys or Thayn. I stuck to writing about what I had learned about Qarradune, in general, and my life back on Earth. In the off-chance someone read my journal, I didn't want them knowing my thoughts on people they could actually hurt.

I also didn't write about Rral. I knew it probably would have been good for me to vent about my feelings regarding his death, but I didn't want anyone reading about that, either. It bothered me to no end that they had already taken his journal from him and had read it. I refused to let them take any more of Rral than they already had. I'd keep his memory and his ring safe from his enemies.

His enemies…

It turned out Rral had more enemies than just Kavylak. When I had finally worked up the nerve to read his journal, I discovered that Syliza wasn't the pretty lily-white country I had dreamed it to be. According to Rral, Syliza hadn't just taken over his country, Gbat Rher, they had ravaged it, consumed it until there was almost nothing left. In the takeover, Rral had lost his wife, Rani, his daughter, Naida, and his son, Oradalf. There was no family to mourn his death. He had been the last.

It saddened me that I couldn't pass his ring on to anyone in his family, but it brought me some comfort to believe that he had been reunited with his family in death and had found peace. I decided that until I found someone else who knew Rral and would cherish his ring, I would keep it and never let myself forget the man who had died to protect me.

Keavren had visited me a few times as well. We had some nice, uneventful chats, and he brought me more of his adventure books. I noticed that each book had the word "dragon" in the title. The one I was reading now was called "The Dragon's Maiden," and was a total trash-read, but it kept me from boredom.

I was curled on my side on the cot, reading, and Pounce was fast asleep in the cove of my belly. It was just after lunch, a meal which I shared with Aésha, every day. She always managed to bring me something sweet. This particular lunch had featured a chocolate cookie for dessert.

Another thing she'd brought me that was sweet, was more fresh clothes and a pair of black flats like the ones I'd had pre-slavery. I was grateful to have shoes to wear, other than my boots.

It took reading the same line in the book three times before I clued into the fact that I hadn't been reading for a while. My eyes were growing heavy. Seeing no reason to fight sleep, I shut them and rested the book down.

A minute had barely passed when, without warning, Pounce gave a big "meow" and sprang off the cot. My eyes flew open, and I saw her bolt from the room and into the kitchen.

What the...

"Pounce?" I called, sitting up. "What's wrong..." I didn't need to finish my sentence. I saw what had spooked her. A grey wolf appeared, lying next to my cot. He panted and looked up at me with the bright eyes of a happy dog.

Amarogq.

A quiet knock sounded at the door.

"Is that you Amarogq?" It wasn't a question. I knew it was.

"Yes. Is it you Megs?"

"It was, the last time I checked."

Um, did he just call me Megs?

"That's good. Am I welcome to come in?"

"Yes."

Amarogq unlocked the door and entered, looking like his usual Warrior self. He shut the door behind himself and walked up to me.

"You look good," he complimented me.

"Thanks," I said, but I didn't see how I looked any different than I had the last time we'd met other than, maybe, my hair looked less messy. I was wearing my typical black pants, t-shirt, and socks, and my hair was in a ponytail.

"May I?" he asked, indicating a space on the cot, near to where I was sitting.

I nodded, and he took a seat. I glanced at the wolf who appeared to be sleeping at my feet and then toward the kitchen where Pounce had fled. Not hearing any worrisome sounds from the kitchen, I decided I'd fetch her later, when the room was wolf-free.

"I just wanted to make sure everything was crisp between us."

I looked at Amarogq and nodded. "I know you weren't the one who gave Rral fatal injuries," I told him, plainly.

"I wasn't," he agreed with more seriousness.

"Is that why you came here? To tell me that?"

He nodded. "That and to share a bit of a treat to eat, if you're interested," he said playfully with a crooked grin.

My brow lifted. "What sort of treat?" I asked carefully.

Instead of answering my question with words, he took a folded piece of leather from his jacket pocket and opened it up, revealing dried up pieces of meat.

Um?

"I made them myself," Amarogq said proudly.

I looked at the brown dried meat, and I gotta say, it definitely wasn't exciting me like Keavren's chocolate treats.

"When I get a bit of time at home," Amarogq explained, "I hunt game and dry some of it for trips like this."

"So...this is dried up meat from some animal you hunted?" I clarified.

"Yes," he smiled. "Try one," he added, enthusiastically.

He picked up a piece of the meat, ate it, and gave the piece of leather he was holding a gentle shake, toward me, to encourage me to take my own piece.

Meh, what the heck! Aunt Vera always said that I'd never know if I liked something unless I tried it, first.

I took a piece and examined it for a moment, before putting it in my mouth. The flavor wasn't bad, but it definitely wasn't anything I'd write home about. What surprised me more, was the chewing effort that was required. When I finally got it down, I had formulated my opinion. I wouldn't refuse it if I was really hungry or starving, but it definitely wasn't my new favourite snack. Unlike Mez, Amarogq didn't have the good snacks.

"That was...chewy," I said to him.

He nodded with a smile and asked, "More?"

"No, thanks. I'm good."

He nodded again and tucked the leather strip containing the meat back into his pocket.

"My fiancée says I can't cook." He chuckled.

I stared at him astonished. I wasn't excepting him to say that.

He has a fiancée? Is it bad that I find him pulling dried meat out of his pocket less weird than discovering he's engaged?

"You have a fiancée?"

"Of course I do." He grinned, unfazed by my poorly-hidden shock. "I'm a good looking guy! I'm smart, too. And humble. Very humble," he added.

"Oh, yes. Very humble." I laughed, but my humour was short-lived. I was still bewildered. Honestly, who would want to marry a Warrior? As friendly as they could seem, they were first-rate bad guys! His fiancée must be a total psycho or a serious ditz...or he's lying.

"Her name is Amorette. Unlike the wolves, it's sheer coincidence that her name sounds like mine."

Okay, he has *to be lying. One: Amorette is a very bizarre name for a psycho. Two: Amarogq and Amorette? That was too funny. It couldn't be real!*

"Wow, that's some coincidence," I said, playing along.

He nodded and said, "Mez calls us the 'Ams'." He laughed and rolled his eyes.

"That sounds about right," I said because, if it turned out he wasn't kidding, I had to give Mez points for that nickname.

"So, she lives in Kavylak?" I guessed.

"Yes, because otherwise, it would be hard to know her." He chuckled but then added, more soberly, "Hopefully, you'll be able to meet her and tell her how great you think the dried meat is."

"Is she a soldier, too?" I asked because maybe military types stick together.

"No." He shook his head. "I'm not even sure if she knows which side of a knife is the sharp one." He laughed but then stopped and said, "do me a favour and don't tell her I said that."

I smiled and nodded. I was starting to warm to the idea of his potentially fake-fiancée.

"Are other Warriors in relationships, too?" I questioned.

"Most of them aren't," he said but then grinned. "Just the best ones."

"What about Mez? Not that I'm asking because I'm interested or anything," I clarified. "It just seems that he's the kind of person who would have someone," I babbled.

"No. Mez is alone," he said simply.

That genuinely surprised me. This seemed stupid, considering I had already thought that the idea of Warriors in relationships was hard to swallow, but I would classify Mez as one of the "best ones" and, if there was anyone capable of a relationship, it would be him.

I nodded and changed the subject, asking: "Are we close to our destination?"

"A few days. Not long at all. But we'll be stopping at a small port town, today, to stock up on fresh food and supplies. Warriors don't like to eat rations," he winked.

I nodded and hoped I'd be able to watch them make trades from the window, like I did the last time.

"I should probably go," Amarogq said, standing. "Aésha will be back any moment and if she sees me here with you, she'll be very jealous. She wants me, you know," he joked.

I snorted and replied, "Yup, she tells me that all the time."

"Mmhmm, I knew it." He nodded over-dramatically and then looked at the wolf. "Come on, Two," he said.

I watched the wolf lift his head, climb to his feet, and stretch. He then stuck his head in my lap and looked at me like, "pet me!"

I gave his head a few strokes, still wondering how it was possible for the wolf to be so alive and a ghost, at the same time. As if he could read my thoughts, Two turned and bounded out of the room, right through the closed door.

Yeesh! I'm never gonna get used to that.

Amarogq laughed and shook his head like, "that crazy wolf," and walked to the door, opening it.

"See you soon, Megs. I'll be sure to send Amorette by when we get home," he said.

"Sure. See you later," I said with a nod, and he exited the room, locking the door behind him.

I got up and went straight to the kitchen.

"Pounce?" I called. "It's alright, little one. They're gone, now."

I found her, almost instantly. She was curled up in a tight ball, looking frightened. I scooped her right up and sheltered her in my arms. She made a bunch of pathetic "miew" sounds, and I calmly stroked her for several minutes until she relaxed.

I walked out of the kitchen but before I could sit on the cot with her, I heard the door unlock, and Aésha stepped in.

"Hey, Baby," she greeted me.

"Hi," I said, noticing that she looked happier than normal.

"Want to come out and play with me?" she asked.

I looked at her, inquisitively, feeling a little hopeful and asked, "Do you mean to the town?"

She nodded and held up the leather cuffs, "It's going to be kinky."

I smiled and fought the urge to jump up and down. I was eager to get out of this room.

"Should I put on long sleeves?" I asked as I set Pounce down on the cot and hauled my boots on.

"Probably not. We're still in the South, but we're about to head North again, so you'll likely need it if we stop again or when we get home," she said and then added, "I'll keep you warm if you feel chilly." She waggled her brows at me.

I laughed. After spending days in her room, I had become accustomed to Aésha's sense of humor. I stepped up to her, extending my right arm, so my wrist could be cuffed to hers. She locked us in and looked disapprovingly at the cuffs.

"Too bad these don't come in different colours," she said as if it offended her that they didn't.

I smirked and looked at Pounce. She was sleeping like a little angel on the pillow, but I had a sneaking suspicion that it was all an act. As soon as we left, she'd be getting into mischief.

I walked out the door with Aésha. After shutting it, she led me down to the interior bay of the ship where the rowboats and other Warriors were waiting.

Chapter 25

Irys

Morning came, then a night. Then another morning and another night. They were long and painful. I had been ill physically, mentally, and spiritually, but I lived.

When morning arrived a third time, I opened clearer eyes to the world. I looked around the room as a fresh spectator who was ready to face her life. For the first time in days, a turned stomach was not the opening sensation to draw my attention. I rolled over onto my side, to take a sip of water from the glass on my nightstand, when I spied Lord Imery through the door to my sitting room.

Sound asleep, he was seated in a chair, his chin resting down onto his chest, and his feet up on a matching ottoman. It was a peaceful sight, and it warmed my heart.

Tiptoeing out of my bed, I crept into my ensuite where I washed up and replaced the bandage on my hand with a clean one. The laceration wasn't a bad one. I was fortunate. I slipped into a cream silk dressing gown that I particularly liked for its perfect weight and delicate lace cuffs.

On the way past my bed, I picked up the extra blanket that was folded at its foot and brought it into the sitting room, opening it and carefully laying it over Lord Imery's legs. Though he didn't open his eyes, a smile curled his lips.

I giggled; a girlish sound that brought about a sense of nostalgia as though the song of my own laughter had been absent since my childhood.

"I thought you were asleep," I whispered, not wanting to disturb the calmness of the moment.

He brought his hands to his face as though to massage it into wakefulness. How youthful he appeared, without his glasses. I could nearly imagine Lady Godeleva knocking on the door and scolding us for being late for breakfast before she would give us a naughty grin and promise to allow us honey on our toast.

"No. I never sleep. You were imagining it," he said with a smiling yawn.

"Ah," I playfully accepted his response. "Well, I'm feeling much better today. If you'd like to rest in your own room for a while, it might help you to face your day."

He opened his eyes and examined me, critically. "You do look much better," he agreed.

"Once I'm dressed for the day, you might even recognize me, again, just as I will recognize you once you put your glasses on." I chuckled, and he laughed in return.

"I think I will go without wearing them, today. I wonder how many people will fail to know who I am."

"Will you be staying in my room, again, today?"

"No." He shook his head. "I must make a visit to the Knights' Headquarters. Would you join me, if I were to extend the invitation?"

"That sounds lovely." *Goddess, how good it will feel to go outside after so many days in these rooms.* "Perhaps we can inquire about Sir Vorel. I might also see if I may speak with Sir Fhirell about his trip to Gbat Rher."

He simply nodded and brought his feet to the floor. "Are you anywhere near as hungry as I am this morning?"

"I don't think I am ever as hungry as you are."

"No, I suppose not. Allow me to rephrase: shall we take our breakfast?"

"I'll dress," I agreed with a nod and rang for Desda.

He rose, turning back to me, on his way out the door. "We'll leave after breakfast as long as you're still feeling as well as you do now."

I nodded and smiled to him, surprised at how easily the expression made itself available to me.

Though I'd assumed he was going to leave, he quite suddenly crossed the space between us and enveloped me in a protective embrace, to which I immediately responded.

"Thank you," I whispered to him.

"I love you, Clever One."

"I love you, too, Lord Imery."

As he withdrew from the hug, he gave my face a gentle stroke. It was clear that he'd needed me to hold him as much as I'd needed it from him. With a smile, but without another word, he left. For the first time in as long as I could remember, I was alone but was not lonely.

Before I could test the endurance of the feeling, Desda arrived with a bright smile on her face. "Good morning, Miss Godeleva. Don't you look well today!"

"Thank you. I feel much better," I said and took her hand. "Thank you for everything, Desda."

"You're welcome, Miss. We were all very worried about you."

"You needn't worry anymore," I assured her. "Now, I must be made up for breakfast and to be proper for a visit to the Knights' Headquarters."

"Oh, the Headquarters!" she smiled, conspiratorially. "We'll need to make you especially pretty for such a trip."

I chuckled and opened my wardrobe to choose my gown for the day. It was true that I did want to wear something attractive, but secretly, I was hoping to wear colours that would be appealing to Sir Fhirell. I wanted him to be willing to speak openly to me. I wanted to know about Sir Vorel as well as Sir Fhirell's mission to Gbat Rher. Perhaps he would feel inclined to tell me more than he would to a typical reporter, if I were distracting enough in my attire.

The Fhirell family colour was a rich dark bluish-purple that reminded me of the night sky that would follow a gorgeous sunset. I selected a light-weight silk brocade gown in a softer shade, but one that was very similar to his. It was a dress that Lord Imery had ordered for me for the season but that I had yet to wear for the first time. It had a long draped bodice and a simple bustle that poured the ripples of fabric down the back of the skirt from a silk rosette fastened on the rear waist.

It was tailored very smartly, to hug the curve of one's figure in a contemporary style, without crossing the line into anything too suggestive or revealing. It was one of F's designs, of course, and I knew my body would thank him for the minimal boning he had incorporated into its corset.

It was the finer details that I loved the most about it. Immaculate white lace cuffs were, after all, always to my taste. Down the front, there were no fewer than 20 embossed silver buttons that fastened the gown in a crisp line reminiscent of a regimental inspection.

According to my magazines, this was the very height of fashion, and it thrilled me that it just so happened to be in the perfect colour for today's occasion.

Once I'd made my selection, Desda helped me into it as she chattered away about some of the latest gossip from the city as well as from the house. Before catching herself, she revealed that Toslen had been dismissed the night he was discovered, and that the staff was saying that he had been sent to prison.

Toslen's dismissal came as a relief, though not a surprise. I thought about how much easier it would be to return to moving about the house without the feeling of having every step watched by someone hired to guard me. My mind travelled down the hall to the rooms that had been Megan's; the rooms that contained the flowers.

"Desda, have there been any more flowers from the emperor?" I asked.

"Yes, Miss," Desda replied after a moment of hesitation.

I frowned, wishing that Lord Imery had told me but understanding why he had chosen not to.

"I'm very frightened of him," I confessed to her.

"Are you afraid he will do something to you, Miss?"

"I'm not entirely certain," I admitted. "Lord Godeleva has said that he will keep me safe but, even as he assures me, his expression is always a grim one. I don't want to be an interest of the emperor. How could a woman want the attentions of a married man when he is not her husband?"

"I..." Desda began and then glanced to the door before proceeding much more quietly. "I probably shouldn't tell you this, Miss, but there are many whispers in the city about his Majesty and his preference for young women."

My stomach turned. "Then, it is not uncommon for him to focus his attentions on women other than the Empress?"

Desda glanced at the door again before she nodded.

"Thank you for telling me. I need to know such things. I'm far too sheltered. It has made me entirely unprepared to guard myself."

"You are safer than the others, Miss Godeleva. Lord Godeleva is powerful, too. He will make sure nothing happens to you."

"What did the emperor do to the others?"

"The rumours say that he...ruins the reputations of good women," she replied, awkwardly.

I nodded. It was all I needed to know. "I'm sure Lord Godeleva will keep me safe. He would never let anything like that happen to me."

"No, indeed, Miss."

"Let us think of lighter things," I said, giving her hand a squeeze. "Lord Godeleva and I will be headed to Lorammel Square this morning. Is there anything you would like from there?"

A girlish smile brightened her face. "I do like the little cookies with nuts on top, from that patisserie."

"Then you shall have them." I smiled. "Soon, I will learn what to bring you as a treat without first having to ask you what it should be."

"Thank you, Miss." She looked very pleased.

"Do I look like a young lady who could hold her own in an interview with the second-in-command of the Knights?"

"If you don't mind my saying so, Miss, you look as though you could do much more than that. You could capture his heart."

I chuckled. "Stop trying to make me blush so early in the day," I scolded playfully.

To that, she chuckled and curtsied before leaving the room.

I took a brief moment to observe myself in my hand mirror. The vanity mirror had not yet been replaced, but I didn't miss it. Before heading to breakfast, I tucked my little butterfly comb into my hair. It had been a gift from Lord Imery, and I wanted his strength with me today. Finally, as was my habit, I used my fingertip to slip the ring from my necklace under the front of my dress.

After an uneventful breakfast that felt surprisingly normal, I put on my cloak – into which I'd tucked a pad of paper and pencil – and pinned a matching hat into place. Soon after, I joined Lord Imery to leave.

"There will be no need to rush your interview," he said as we settled into the coach, and he knocked on the ceiling with his walking stick to signal to the driver to depart. "While I don't plan to spend all day at the Headquarters, I do have a few things to discuss with Sir Skyleck, and he can be rather longwinded when he wants to be."

"I hope to be efficient about it, but I hope to find out as much as I can," I replied after a chuckle to his comment at Sir Skyleck's expense. The laughter soon died on my lips as the thought of Emperor Gevalen passed across my mind, like a dark specter. "Am I still safe from the emperor, Lord Imery?"

My question was clearly unexpected. "Yes, of course. What would make you think otherwise?"

"The flowers. They haven't stopped."

"They haven't," he agreed. "But I have a feeling that his interest in you is waning. The flowers aren't arriving as frequently. Certainly, there has been enough time since he last saw you that his attention will have turned elsewhere."

"I shall do my best not to draw any attention to myself. I'd hate to think that I would remind him of my existence."

He smiled and took my hand as we continued the rest of the drive in silence.

Chapter 26

Megan

We climbed into a waiting boat with a Warrior I'd never seen before. He was buff with tanned skin and had light blue eyes and short, unruly sandy-blond hair, highlighted with sun-bleached blond streaks. He looked more like he should have been wearing showy swim trunks and holding a surfboard under his arm than wearing the harsh black uniform that he sported.

When he saw me, he flashed a gorgeous smile at me, revealing perfect white teeth. I swear, I almost heard a triangle chime. If this beach-Warrior were on Earth, he'd be on the cover of every teen magazine. Frig, I'd probably have a pinup of him on my wall. This guy had "male swimsuit model" written all over him.

"Hey, I'm Taye," he introduced himself.

"Hi, I'm Megan," I said, instantly liking how informal this guy was. I had known of his existence for less than a minute, and it already felt like we were chums.

"Isn't Arik coming?" Aésha asked Taye.

Taye shook his head and said, "Nah, he's got a new mission."

Aésha sighed and shook her head like she was disappointed in Taye and yet not surprised at the same time.

"Fighters," she muttered under her breath.

I looked at her, curiously, but didn't bother asking what that was all about. She wouldn't tell me, anyway. I wondered if Mez had gone on a mission, too, and that's why I hadn't seen him.

We sat down on the bench, and Taye rowed us out of the ship's opening. The sky was overcast but, even without the sun and a blue sky, it was still a pleasant day. The temperature was warm, without much of a breeze, and the water was calm.

Taye was rowing us toward a massive wide dock-structure with a market set up on it. As we got closer, I could see that there were rows upon rows of sellers, and boats were tied all around the docks, like a floating parking lot.

I recognized Keavren in one of the "parked" boats. He finished tying it and stepped out and onto the deck, joining Acksil. My eyes moved past them, and I saw Amarogq chatting and walking with Mez as they headed toward one of the sellers.

Nope. Guess he's not on a mission.

It occurred to me then as I watched the Warriors casually strolling through the marketplace, that no one was bothered by their presence. I had no idea where we were, geographically speaking, but I was pretty sure we were in Kavylak territory.

"Are you looking for anything in particular?" Aésha asked, startling me from my observations.

"Um, not really," I replied honestly. I hadn't given it much thought. I was just glad to be out of her room and in the fresh air. Besides, I had no idea what I could possibly want, on this planet, other than a one-way ticket to Earth.

"I want you to get anything you want," Aésha said. "Anything…" she emphasized with a tease as if she were implying lingerie or something.

I laughed and gave a little nod.

"We'll find you something good," she said, toning down her playfulness. "You'll be all set when we get home."

You mean when you *get home,* I thought but didn't share.

Taye slowed the boat to dock it and then stepped out onto the water to tie it, before hopping onto the deck and jogging directly over to a seller who was clearly selling something he wanted.

I stared, in disbelief, at the water and then at Aésha.

"Did I just see Taye walk on water?" I asked.

She only smiled at me and stood, giving my tethered wrist a little tug.

"Come on, Baby. Let's see what we can find for a little bit of fun."

Yup, I'd definitely just seen a guy walk on water. Well, at least Taye wasn't big on secrets. That may come in handy.

I stood and stepped onto the dock with her and looked around. Now that we were standing on the wood planks, I could see that we were on a massive raft-like surface composed of interlinked floating docks. As we walked, the dry wood beneath my feet bobbed slightly with our movements, but I didn't feel unsteady. It was just obvious that we weren't on solid ground.

When we entered the winding hub of sellers, we were surrounded by a cacophony of chatter, laughter, music, clangs, bangs, and the typical orchestra of noise you'd associate with a huge merchants' marketplace. There was also a diverse range of smells, from sweet floral scents and spicy aromas to the heavy stink of fish and sweat.

Aésha sauntered along, pausing at each booth, showing particular interest in one that sold decorative scarves and a variety of colorful bags. Some were made from woven wool, reeds, and other materials. She picked up a bright-pink silk scarf, to examine it closer. While I might have cared about these items if I were back home, I wasn't in a fashion-shopping mood. In spite of being grateful to have the opportunity to tag along, being handcuffed to a Warrior was a constant reminder of my situation, so this wasn't exactly a carefree shopping experience for me.

It surprised me, at first, that no one seemed to notice or care that I was cuffed to Aésha but then I remembered that, if we were in Kavylak, that meant that we were in slave country, so I guessed this wouldn't be weird to them.

My eyes wandered from the seller's items and caught sight of Mez. He was several feet away from us and was crouched down, talking to a little boy, who was wearing shorts and a shirt that had seen better days, and a little girl, who was in a worn sundress. Whatever he was saying to them was making them giggle. He reached into a bag that he was carrying and took out what appeared to be two wrapped lollipops. He gave one to each of the children, and they looked super-delighted and ran off, full of excitement. I felt my lips curve into a smile. That was seriously sweet.

He stood with a warm smile on his face and looked in my direction, noticing me for the first time. His smile grew, and he nodded to me before continuing on his way.

I watched him until he was swallowed up by the crowd and then I turned to Aésha, who was now carrying a woven tote-like bag on her shoulder.

"Is there anything that Mez particularly likes?" I asked her, deciding then that there was something I wanted to get after all: something nice for Mez.

"Mez, huh?" Aésha grinned, raising a brow. "Are you thinking of a present or are you hoping to look crazy so that he can re-evaluate you?" She teased.

I sighed and said, "Just a gift. He's done some thoughtful things for me. I'd like to return the favour."

She thought, for a moment, and chuckled saying, "He likes having the best snacks."

Oh yeah! His good snacks. Duh, Megan!

"Okay. Do you know what kind of snacks he likes?" I asked, realizing that I knew pretty much nothing about Mez and what he liked.

"He likes a lot of things," she said. "I think he'd like to have something he can watch a hot redhead eat." She grinned and then added, "Oh, wait...that's me."

I huffed playfully and shook my head. She wasn't going to be any help.

"He'll already have everything that he knows he likes," she said, pulling me to walk with her. "You'll need to get him something that you like, but that he'd never think to try, or something very odd but surprisingly good," she suggested, stopping us at a food seller.

I thought about what she said. It was good advice but, considering that I found lots of the food I ate here to be odd and surprisingly good, that could present a challenge. Then, I remembered a conversation I'd had with Mez when I'd told him about how much I liked lasagna. I wondered if they sold pasta here or something that resembled it.

Browsing the seller's goods, I saw fresh vegetables, fresh fruits, dried fruits, nuts, shellfish, fresh fish, odd looking baked things, but no pasta or anything else noodley, for that matter. Oh well, let's just keep it simple and pick something for Mez that I'd want to try.

Considering the options, I decided the nuts looked the most interesting. They would be crunchy, they looked tasty, and they should have a pretty good shelf-life, which is good for a ship. Plus, Mez likely thinks I'm nuts so, all in all, it was kind-of the perfect gift.

"I think I'll get him nuts. An assortment of them," I told Aésha, decidedly.

She nodded, looking amused, and told the seller what I wanted. The seller was all-too happy to serve her and practically drooled when Aésha smiled at him. He scooped the various nuts into a woven burlap-style bag and tied it, handing it over to Aésha who dropped it in her tote before paying him with a coin.

"Thanks, Aésha," I said to her.

"My pleasure," she purred, in her Aésha way.

Feeling content and satisfied with my gift for Mez, I strolled along with Aésha, allowing my eyes to drift over all the goods and the people who were bustling about.

"Beautiful lady!" called a man's voice. I turned my head at the sound, to see a scruffy man who appeared to be in his early forties looking at me. He was holding up a pair of seashell earrings that looked like the cheap stuff you'd find at any beach tourist trap.

"You must have this!" he declared to me.

I looked from him to Aésha who had stopped walking. She grinned at me like she was up to no good and walked us over to the seller. I thought she was going to talk to him, but it rapidly became clear to me that both she and the seller were waiting for me to respond.

"Oh, uh, they're very pretty," I said awkwardly.

My eyes shifted from the seller to the items he was selling and that's when I spotted a young man, sitting behind the seller, on the floor. The young man's long mouse-coloured brown hair was tied back in a knotted ponytail, and he wore a dull brown strip of cloth around his head that covered one of his eyes, making me think that he had an eye injury. The rest of his clothes were ratty looking and the same colour as the band around his head as if they were cut from the same cloth. He was working very hard at weaving grass. My heart sank a little at the sight of him, and I frowned. I had a bad feeling he was a slave.

"You like woven work!" The seller suddenly exclaimed, startling me.

I shifted my gaze to him.

"We have so many beautiful pieces. Please, look!" He encouraged, enthusiastically, gesturing to an assortment of necklaces and bangle-style bracelets that were laid out on the table.

The man on the floor turned toward me and got onto his knees, holding out a newly finished bangle-like braided grass bracelet in the palms of his mostly-clean hands, to display it to me.

"They're all very lovely," I said, "That one is very nice, too," I told the man, feeling very not in my happy place.

"Try it on!" insisted the seller, meaning the bracelet the young man was holding.

I looked at Aésha for help, but she was busy looking over the seller's jewelry with an unimpressed expression on her face.

"Uh...alright," I said and reached for the bracelet from the kneeling man who relinquished it to me. He never once met my gaze, but it felt like he was still watching me with his one good eye, through his peripheral vision.

I examined the bracelet. It was mostly beige with green and teal woven threw it. It was simple but pretty.

Raising my cuffed hand and dragging Aésha's arm with me (she didn't seem to care), I slipped the bracelet onto my right hand.

"There! You see? It suits you! He's very skilled at details," the seller said. Although the praise should have been meant for the actual bracelet maker, it sounded more like the seller was praising himself.

The seller reached out and took the bracelet off my wrist and said, "Have a look. You can even see the detail of the band underneath."

I humoured him and looked on the band's inside and saw an inscription had been woven into it. It read: "*Don't give up.*"

I looked at the seller, hiding my shock at what I'd read. He didn't seem to notice and continued to prattle on, taking the bracelet from my hand and slipping it back onto my wrist.

"He works with different materials, but he has a specialty with that," he told me.

"You're very gifted," I said to the younger man, looking at him and then nearly gasping at what I saw. He was holding what looked like a boutonniere of wheat tops in his palm. It instantly reminded me of the one Thayn wore as part of his masquerade costume. He looked up at me with one blue eye.

"Thank you," he said quietly, speaking cautiously as if he was only allowed to respond to me because I had talked to him first.

I looked at him more closely. At first glance, this man did not look like Thayn. He had brown hair, for one, and his posture and mannerisms were entirely different. That being said, if I looked beyond the dirt, the shabby clothes, and the hair colour, he did have a somewhat Thayn-esque appearance, and his hair was the right length, and his eyes were the right colour.

Oh my gosh! Could this actually be Thayn in disguise? No. That would be too much to hope for. I was seeing what I wanted to see.

"Hmm, I see you like more than just pretty jewelry." The seller grinned at me. "He is for sale as well, if you name a good enough price," he offered.

I blinked back to reality at his words. "What?" I asked and looked from the seller to Aésha, trying to figure out what had just happened.

"Did you want him?" Aésha asked me, doubtfully, thumbing to the kneeling man.

I was sure my brows raised higher than my hairline when her meaning sunk in.

Is she crazy? She thinks I would be interested in buying a person! On the other hand, what if that actually is Thayn? What if he has been in disguise and somehow wound up as a slave? Yes, that sounds absolutely ludicrous, but I also happened to see a guy walk on water today. This could be an opportunity for me to help Thayn or maybe someone else.

I stared at Aésha, unable to form speech as my mind swirled with indecision. Finally, I went with my gut and nodded.

"Ah, you see, I knew I could tell your taste," the seller said, rubbing his hands together.

Aésha gave a shrug as if to say "whatever" and turned to the seller and said flatly, "We won't pay full price for him. He's got one eye and you haven't even washed him. Just having to bathe him should save us a gold coin!"

She sounded like she was disgusted with the fact that she was buying a piece of furniture of such low quality, but she was doing it for her crazy friend who wanted it, so darn it, she was going to get a fair price.

The seller shook his head and argued, "He has enough vision for two eyes and look at his skill!"

"Any child can braid grass," Aésha scoffed, "and if that eye gets infected, we'll have lost everything we've paid."

They continued to haggle back-and-forth, rather aggressively, and I felt like shrinking into a corner. I looked at the young man, out of the corner of my eye. He remained kneeling, and had now bowed his head. The fact that they were arguing over the purchase of him as if he were a piece of furniture and not a person, and the fact that I had been the cause of it, made me feel nauseated.

I couldn't take it anymore. I had to stop this. I opened my mouth to tell Aésha to forget it, but it was too late. She had handed over the coins. The deal was done.

What have I done?

"Do you want him tied?" Aésha asked like she got me a new pet.

"No!" I declared sharply and shook my head, but then realized I was being too dramatic, under the circumstances. I was the one who was the weirdo, here. I cleared my throat and said, "No, thank you. That's alright."

She nodded and looked at the seller, expectantly. He, in turn, barked a few sharp words at the younger man, who quickly rose to unsteady, bare feet. The younger man's shoulders were slumped down, and he kept his gaze directed at the ground.

"Come on, you filthy thing," Aésha said to the young man as she walked us away from the seller. He followed behind.

"Anything else?" she asked me with a laugh, looking at me like she seriously couldn't believe that I'd just bought a slave.

I had to agree with her look. I couldn't believe it, either.

"No, I think I'm good," I said to her, in a state of disbelief.

"Good," she said and then laughed. "Looks like you got a bracelet, too," she added.

"What?" I looked down at my arm and noticed that I was still wearing the bracelet the seller had put on my wrist. I had forgotten about it. I blanched, shocked. I'd unintentionally shoplifted a bracelet.

Oh my God! I went to a marketplace and bought a bag of nuts and a slave, and stole a bracelet. What the hell is wrong with me?

We walked back to our boat. Taye was already sitting in it with his own bags, waiting for us. We stepped in and took a seat. The young man followed us, stepping into the boat with poor coordination on shaky feet. He grabbed the side of the boat to steady himself and then rapidly sat down on the floor, at my feet.

Taye looked at the man, then at us with mild curiosity and asked, "A new passenger?"

"Megan has surprising tastes." Aésha laughed. "I got a bag and a scarf. She got a one-eyed bracelet maker."

"Hehe." Taye laughed in a dumb-jock kind of way, then untied our boat and started to row us back to the ship.

I could feel my face flush with both shame and embarrassment. This was terrible, and I couldn't even logically be angry at them for laughing. I was the one who got myself into this mess.

The man at my feet was looking rougher by the second. He appeared entirely unsettled with the rocking of the boat and sat, braced, with his hands on the floor. He was even starting to look a little green.

"If you're going to be sick, do it over the side." Aésha instructed him but wasn't harsh about it.

He nodded and held onto the side with his chin on the edge as if he were prepared to be sick at any moment.

I felt awful for him and really doubted my Thayn-slave theory, now. Unless Thayn happened to be an amazing actor, there was no way this could be him. I'd seen Thayn on a ship. He was a man of the sea. Boats didn't bother him. It didn't matter. Even if this wasn't Thayn, I'd protect this man until I could safely set him free.

He's your slave, Megan, I reminded myself, *no one can hurt him as long as he's yours.*

I forced myself to believe that and focused on the bracelet on my arm, reminding myself of its inscription.

Don't give up.

We arrived at the ship, and the young man couldn't hide his shock when it suddenly came into view. Taye rowed us in and brought the boat to its initial resting spot where it had been docked before we left. He tied the boat, picked up his shopping bags, and stepped out onto the water, walking across it to hop up onto the edge of the deck.

I was glad to see that I wasn't the only one who was bug-eyed over his skill. The young man's one good eye was wide-open at

Taye's ability to walk on water. Taye walked on water as though he were stepping in shallow puddles on land.

"See ya," Taye said to us and headed off, not waiting for our response. That guy was so casual it was almost scary.

Aésha stood, and I did, too, climbing out of the boat with her. We waited for the man to follow us. He stood on shaky legs and stumbled forward but caught himself before he fell, scrambling quickly out of the boat.

"Please, follow us," I said as kindly as I could. "It's not a far walk."

He gave me a short nod and followed us with his head bowed, keeping exactly three paces behind. I took a calm and steady breath, trying not to hate myself for putting this guy in the same situation I had found so degrading when I was a slave.

When we reached Aésha's room, the man followed us in and kneeled. She shut the door and unlocked our cuffs.

Aésha stepped up to the man and said, "Get yourself washed. I mean *very* washed. You're going to be clean, from now on, or we'll sell you wherever we stop next," she informed him. "I'll get you some clean clothes. Behave, and you will be treated well here," she said, laying it all out to him.

He nodded rapidly.

Aésha sighed, turned to me, and smiled. She slipped her arms around me and said, "Maybe I'll think you're less crazy when he's clean." She winked.

I forced a smile.

"We'll be nice to him," she said and gave my ponytail a stroke. "Just keep him out of our way."

"I will," I promised.

She kissed my cheek and said, "I have to go talk to Mez about his nuts." She grinned wickedly.

"Thanks." I laughed. That struck me funny.

She nodded and left the room, locking the door.

I turned to look at the man who was kneeling before me. It was time for me to find out the truth about him.

Chapter 27

Irys

I peeked out through the curtains of the carriage window as we came to a halt in front of the Headquarters of the Knights of Freyss, and I smiled to myself. This would be the first time I would have the chance to enter this astounding building with an actual opportunity to appreciate it.

I'd been here only once before, but I was barely conscious at the time. Sir Breese had found me collapsed in Lorammel Square after the Warrior – Acksilivcs...Acksil – had brought me back from my capture by Captain Galnar. That was hardly the opportunity I needed to truly observe the building and its rooms. Aside from what appeared to be the medic's office, where I had been brought until Lord Imery could come to collect me, this would all be new to me.

The footman opened the door, and Lord Imery stepped out of the carriage, turning to offer me his hand so that I might step down as well. Together, we strode off the cobblestones of Lorammel Square and onto the clean ivory marble stairs that led to the main entrance of the building.

An apprentice, dressed in his brown squire's alternative to the green uniform of those who had achieved the full status of a Knight, opened the door for us. He nodded to Lord Imery with recognition and to me with respect as we entered a vestibule which was surprisingly dark in contrast to the bright exterior of the building.

I wondered if the original architect had included this moment in the shadows, deliberately as the entryway rapidly opened into the Grand Hall, a vast space into which sunlight seemed to rejoice as it poured through the vaulted skylight that made up the entire ceiling.

The Grand Hall was the heart of the building, from which its wings were spread. Down the adjoining corridors were offices and other rooms to which the public was not typically invited without a specific purpose. Here in this gloriously open space, the Knights and their apprentices would gather for discussions, would take their tea, or would welcome visitors who wished to speak with them as Lord Imery and I were doing today.

There was a wide, clear path straight down the middle of the Grand Hall, which was intercepted by several narrower ones that offered an uninterrupted route to the room's exits and the building's adjoining wings. Round tables dotted the floor, but the paths ensured easy navigation through the space for those who worked there. Though each of the tables was large enough for eight chairs, they were well spaced apart to provide easy passage from one place to the next and to give a certain level of privacy in conversations. The bulk of the hall was clearly a place for people to meet.

Alcoves were used as places where one could fetch a cup of tea, a little something to eat, or obtain the stationary needed to take down the details of a plan or to write a letter.

I wondered at it all as I watched dozens of people moving about and chatting at the tables; each with their own missions, for the moment.

Another apprentice approached us and bowed to Lord Imery. "Lord Godeleva, Sir Skyleck is expecting you and will be along shortly. Won't you please have a seat? There is tea, if you should want any."

"Thank you," Lord Imery replied. "Please tell Sir Fhirell that we'd like to speak with him as well, if he's here."

"Yes, Lord Godeleva."

A well dressed couple nodded to us on their way by, and I smiled to them as I walked to the table Lord Imery had chosen for us. I took the seat he withdrew for me.

"I'll have some tea brought for us," he said as he sat down in the chair next to mine. "Would you like anything to eat, Clever One?"

"Oh, no thank you. I'm all butterflies over my little interview."

He chuckled and then smiled over my shoulder as I heard footsteps approaching behind me.

"Ah, Sir Skyleck," he said, leaning back in his chair. "We were just talking about how lovely it would be to have some tea with our conversation."

Sir Skyleck directed a deep nod of his head toward us and smiled in a slithering expression. "Of course, Lord Godeleva, Miss Godeleva. I'll fetch it at once."

He turned and took several steps from the table before snapping his fingers in the air toward an apprentice. They spoke quietly, for the briefest moment, and the apprentice moved quickly toward the alcove with the refreshments. Sir Skyleck returned to us with his usual air of self-importance and seated himself to the other side of Lord Imery.

"Miss Godeleva, I'm glad to see that you're feeling better," Sir Skyleck said as his eyes appeared to stroll over the features of my face, taking in every detail of what he saw.

"Thank you. Yes, this is my first little trip out of the house since I have regained my strength. I'm still recovering, but I do hope to be my old self, soon enough," I said sweetly, hoping to downplay my wellness in case the next place Sir Skyleck would be scurrying was right to the emperor's ear.

"As do we all. Restoring your health is nothing to rush."

"Wise words," I replied and was relieved that this was all he needed to say in order to feel that he had done his duty in acknowledging me and could turn his attention to his discussion with Lord Imery.

The apprentice who had been sent for our tea approached with a tray onto which a service had been laid. He set it down on the table, bowed to us, and left without a word. I noticed that I was the only one to acknowledge him, and I set about pouring the tea for us.

The two men chatted about whatever business it was they had together while I sipped away at my tea and spent the remainder of the time sitting neatly with my hands clasped in my lap.

"Please excuse me for interrupting." My head snapped around as I heard Sir Fhirell's familiar voice, and I smiled to him. "I was told that you would like to speak with me." He bowed to us and took a seat next to me when Lord Imery indicated that he should do so.

"Thank you, Sir Fhirell. Good morning. I would indeed like the chance to speak with you if you have a free moment."

Lord Imery and Sir Skyleck returned to their conversation, not seeming to be at all interested in Sir Fhirell or anything that I might have to say to him.

"I always have a free moment for welcome company."

We turned our chairs slightly toward each other so that we might converse more comfortably without straining to hear each other over the other talkers at the table. I poured him a cup of tea.

"Thank you. I was hopeful that you might allow me to speak with you about your mission to Gbat Rher as I intend to write a follow-up article to my last one. It was very well received, and I wouldn't mind the chance to keep the topic in the public eye."

"Certainly," he said easily, sipping his tea.

I smiled and withdrew my notepad and silver pencil, twisting it to expose the core so it would be ready to use.

"Before we start, may I inquire into Sir Vorel's health?"

"Why, yes. He was sent home from the hospital, two days ago. His road to recovery will still be a long one, but he will heal. Lady Vorel is pleased to have him home again."

"I imagine she must be. Being home must also bring him some comfort. It is always much more tolerable to be unwell in familiar surroundings."

He nodded. "We are fortunate to be among those who can be healed at a hospital and who can also return home to great comforts."

"We are," I agreed. "Thank you for offering such a fine segue to the main reason for my visit." We shared a warm little laugh. "Would it be possible to arrange for an interview once you return home from Gbat Rher as well? I find myself feeling nearly desperate to learn more about the true situation in that province."

"I would not object to another chance to tell you about my experiences."

"Thank you. If only I could have been a Knight. I would have loved to go and see for myself; to help in such a meaningful way."

"You needn't be a Knight to go. There are many others who are travelling with us and who are not Knights."

"Oh? Are there any young ladies travelling with their maids?" I joked.

He chuckled, shaking his head. "No. Young ladies and their maids don't often accompany us on this type of mission. There are quite a few of us headed north, together. Several Robes are coming with us, along with a number of nurses, though most of the people who will be on the road with us are labourers."

"No reporters?" I giggled.

"No." He chuckled again. "That position has yet to be filled. You're welcome to it." He was teasing, of course, but it sent my mind wandering and the direction in which it was headed was to the north.

"Were it possible, Sir Fhirell, I would agree to your offer in a instant. Instead, I will content myself in speaking with you so that I may share all the details of your mission with others like me, who must wish Gbat Rher well from here in Lorammel. Still, I intend to hold you to your promise to deliver that letter for me."

"I know it is not at all conventional for a lady of your standing to participate in such a journey, Miss Godeleva, but if you are indeed as interested as you say, you are welcome. Know that, at least. What you would need to understand, though, is that you would be expected to take part in far more than simple reporting. We aren't entirely certain what we will be facing upon our arrival. You would likely not have the luxury of being the type of lady you were raised to be."

At first I'd smiled quite playfully at him, believing that he was joking. However, my grin rapidly faded as I realized that his invitation was a genuine one, despite the fact that he clearly didn't think I would ever accept it. How could I? Yet, I couldn't help but question him further.

"You would truly allow me to travel there with your group?"

"Yes." He spoke the word with such simple sincerity that I hadn't any choice but to believe him. "After hearing how you guided the frightened people when the city was burning and after seeing how you supported and cared for Sir Vorel, I have no doubt that you would have the strength for such a mission. At the same time, the decision is not entirely mine to make."

"I will speak with Lord Godeleva," I said before I could think. My heart was racing.

Great Goddess, could I truly go away on such a mission? What was pushing me to do this? What if Megan were to arrive home while I was gone?

So many questions flooded my mind. "Would I be able to bring my maid?" Certainly, that wasn't the most profound question I could have asked, but it remained an important one.

"As long as she has a strong heart, mind, and stomach, she would be welcome."

"I will think on this and will discuss it with Lord Godeleva. I will send word as soon as he has decided."

Great Goddess, I see it now. I can see that you are handing me yet another opportunity with which to prove myself to you. My mission to rescue Megan was not a test that I failed; it was another lesson. Please allow me to prove that I did learn from you. I see that I can help people. Thank you for sending Sir Fhirell to show me that I am strong in your service. I will not let you down.

"We leave the day after tomorrow. I do understand that this is not a great deal of time in which to decide or to prepare. Please tell Lord Godeleva that I will be more than willing to answer any questions or concerns he may have about your safety or abilities," he offered.

"Thank you, Sir Fhirell. Between the two of us, I hope we will, at least, be able to convince him that I have not taken leave of my senses."

"Should you decide not to travel, or if Lord Godeleva should choose not to allow it, I will still promise you that interview," he said with a grin.

If I'd wanted to stop the smile from crossing my lips, I would not have been able. I watched his eyes for a delayed moment, sharing a wordless expression of my gratitude. He seemed to have understood me well enough until now, perhaps he would know how much I appreciated his invitation as well, even without my having to say it out loud.

His eyes smiled. Yes. He had understood.

"I suppose I should start the interview," I said with a chuckle, realizing that I'd written next to nothing on my notepad. Scanning over the page, I discovered that I'd jotted down a few items I wanted to bring with me on the journey north. That was hardly worthy of the article I wished to write.

Sir Fhirell chuckled but before I could ask him anything, Lord Imery turned toward me and spoke. "Shall we be off, Clever One? My business is done here."

I brought my hand over the page of my notebook to cover the nonsense I'd written there. "Before we go, Lord Imery, I'd like to ask a question. It's that I have been invited to join in the relief mission to Gbat Rher, and I find myself wanting to accept...very much. I would be able to make a difference and to report on everything that is happening, first hand. Would you allow it...or at least consider it?"

Any lightness he'd had in his expression faded. "You're serious, Clever One?" he asked as though he was having trouble believing that I was not playing a joke on him.

"I am. I am driving myself to madness as I wait for Miss Wynters' return. All I can do is worry about her. I'm finding it nearly impossible to concentrate on reading. I am useless to your studies this way. If I go north, I can make a difference. Instead of worrying, I will be helping."

Lord Imery listened to every word, but he looked on me sternly. "We will discuss this at home."

I nodded. "Yes, Lord Imery. Sir Fhirell has offered to answer any questions you might have about the mission."

"I am aware of what the mission entails. I funded part of it," he replied and looked to Sir Fhirell. "Thank you for the time you took to help Miss Godeleva with her article. I'm sorry that we cannot stay any longer. I have another engagement for which I cannot be late."

Sir Fhirell stood and bowed. "Of course. I was happy to have helped. Good day, Lord Godeleva. Good day, Miss Godeleva."

"Good day, Sir Fhirell," I replied apologetically, curtsying to him before taking Lord Imery's arm and walking away with him.

"Am I to make my own way home, Lord Imery?"

"No. I will take you home before my next appointment."

"I promised Desda that I would bring her some cookies."

I could see that Lord Imery was making a conscious effort to remain patient. "We can't have you breaking a promise. We will stop at the patisserie before we go."

We walked in silence until we stepped out of the building. As soon as the door closed behind us, I looked up at him.

"Please don't be cross with me," I said quietly but very sincerely.

"I'm not cross with you, Clever One," he replied and indeed, he did not sound cross. "I know how much it means to you to help the people in Gbat Rher. It's admirable. However, I don't feel that this is the right time or opportunity for you. You are still healing from your illness and there is no way of knowing what kind of danger could await you there."

"Sir Fhirell said I could bring Desda with me. He believes in my ability to help after having seen me assisting Sir Vorel and the people of Fort Picogeal."

"I'm certain that your efforts were commendable, but it is not merely a matter of wanting to help and being able to bring comfort to an injured man. You will be facing people whose lives have been deeply upset and who may not be interested in sparing the feelings of a Sylizan lady. You will need to live in circumstances that are far beneath your experience and your station. Writing your articles will make a difference. You can play your part from Lorammel."

We crossed the square at a rapid pace. It was evident that Lord Imery wanted to finish our shopping so he could return me home.

"I understand why you would be concerned about those things. I assure you that I am equally concerned. It means a lot to me to make a difference, but I feel that I have more to offer than my articles. At the same time, it will make it even more certain that the flowers will stop being delivered to the house."

"I know you are not happy at home right now. This is a very difficult time for you and if there were any way for me to repair it for you, I would do it. I have made every effort to contribute to Miss Wynters' rescue, and I have been making sure that the people who should know about the plight of Gbat Rher are seeing your article and are receiving the resources that are needed in order to do something about it. Still, sending you away to a province in complete disarray is not the method I would choose to occupy your mind and to distract the attention of the sender of your flowers."

He opened the door to the patisserie for me, and I stepped inside before he followed me in. I was pleased to see that the cookies Desda had requested were there, and I quickly purchased them so that I would not frustrate Lord Imery any further by creating too much of a delay.

When we stepped into the Square once more, I gasped and clutched tightly to Lord Imery's arm as I spotted the emperor and his guards exiting the Temple.

Lord Imery's expression remained unconcerned. I tried to keep myself somehow hidden behind him, but I knew this was ridiculous. Though I was too afraid to look to see if we had been detected, I could tell when Lord Imery slowed our pace to a stop that we were about to turn to face Emperor Gevalen.

"Look who is well enough to be out and enjoying the beautiful sunshine," Emperor Gevalen said with a wide grin.

Lord Imery bowed, and I curtsied deeply, praying for the strength to rise to my feet once again. I held onto Lord Imery for dear life, afraid not that I would swoon but that I might die right there on the spot.

"Your Majesty," Lord Imery greeted the emperor without any sign of discomfort.

"Good morning, Your Majesty," I said softly.

The emperor's eyes refused to leave me. With amusement, he directed his words to Lord Imery, without ever bothering to look at him.

"If I didn't know better, Lord Godeleva, I would think you were hiding my little exotic bird from me."

"I have been very unwell, Your Majesty. I'm sorry," I begged, hearing the tremble in my own voice.

Please, Great Goddess, take his gaze from me.

"This is the first day that she has been well enough to leave the house," Lord Imery added.

The emperor must have heard him, but he didn't acknowledge the statement.

"Did you receive my flowers?" he asked me.

"Yes, Your Majesty. So very many of them. Thank you. I'm not deserving of such an abundance of fine gifts."

The emperor laughed. "Oh, you're deserving of them and more. Now that you are better, you must come and join me for tea. You will see how you are deserving of many more fine things than arrangements of flowers." There was a promise in his voice.

To this, Lord Imery came to my rescue. "Unfortunately, Miss Godeleva must postpone her acceptance of your invitation, Your Majesty. She will be taking part in the mission to Gbat Rher and as it leaves the day after tomorrow, she requires every moment to prepare before she departs. This illness used every spare moment she had for readying herself."

My entire world turned on its head. Was Lord Imery truly agreeing to allow me to travel to Gbat Rher? The realization of why he would do this landed quite heavily in my stomach. If he felt that the best choice for me was to go on the mission to the north, this meant that Lord Imery suddenly felt that the mission was safer than remaining here while the emperor was interested in me. He couldn't keep me safe here, after all.

I fought every instinct to run away from this man, whose eyes had yet to leave me.

"Why ever would you send such a beautiful young woman to that Chaos of a place?" Emperor Gevalen asked with distaste. He sounded as though he was asking if Lord Imery had fallen into madness.

"It is a cause that is very close to Miss Godeleva's heart. She has been preparing for it for some time, Your Majesty. Her article was a part of her research into her upcoming journey. She feels it is a great honour to serve her emperor and her country by giving her assistance to our fellow Sylizans who are in such dire need."

I nodded demurely, allowing Lord Imery to speak for me, particularly as Emperor Gevalen watched every move I made. It would take very little for me to spoil the effort Lord Imery was trying to make on my behalf.

"Is this how you truly feel, Miss Godeleva?" The emperor asked, still looking slightly perplexed.

"It is, Your Majesty."

"Had I known that you wanted to go on this mission, I would never have given my approval," he said with a chuckle that was meant to suggest that he was joking, but I suspected that he might have been serious.

"It was precisely because of your approval that I knew I must be a part of it," I responded sweetly, following Lord Imery's lead and using every possible moment to provide the emperor with praise.

The emperor's expression changed from dissatisfaction to amusement. I had given the right reply.

"My approval matters to you this much?" he asked, rolling the words slowly from his tongue.

"Your approval matters to all Sylizans, Your Majesty." I caught the motion of Lord Imery's nod of agreement out of the corner of my eye.

"I still do not think such a place is appropriate for a lady but, if this is what you truly want, Miss Godeleva, I will not stand in the way of it," he said magnanimously.

"Thank you, Your Majesty. You are great in all things."

"When you return, you will come to see me in the Palace and will tell me all about your experience."

"Thank you, Your Majesty. The thought of it will be with me for the entire journey." I was quite certain that this statement was entirely true, though it upset me to know it.

"As thoughts of you will be with me," he answered.

Crystals of ice formed in my veins. A blush crossed my face. Surely, the emperor believed that it was because I was touched and overwhelmed by his words. That was not at all the case. What I was feeling was nothing like what I was pretending to portray. The roses on my cheeks were the only evidence I could not hide my horror and fear of this powerful, disgusting man.

How pleased he looked with himself. Every hidden reserve of strength was needed to stop myself from recoiling when he took my hand in his own and kissed it, looking deeply into my eyes.

"Something else for you to think about," he said, finally relinquishing my fingers to me.

"Yes, Your Majesty," I whispered, looking down. Though the expression likely appeared shy and bashful, the truth was that I could no longer force myself to look at him. I wanted to wash my hand. If only I'd worn gloves today.

Only after he had turned and walked away from us, which he did without another word, could I lift my gaze again.

My fingers were nearly clawing into Lord Imery's arm, which I continued to hold with the hand the emperor had not soiled. When I noticed, I relaxed them, nearly expecting to see four finger-sized holes in his sleeve where I had been clutching him.

Lord Imery didn't speak. He merely turned us and walked us quickly toward our carriage. The pace was faster than was comfortable for me, but I was glad for it. If I had felt comfortable walking, then we weren't moving rapidly enough.

I was helped into the carriage and as soon as he was in and the door was closed, I brought my arms around him. He knocked on the roof at the same time that he brought his other arm around me.

"It's going to be alright, Clever One. While you are away, I will sort this out with the emperor. It won't be like this when you return."

"I believe you, Lord Imery." I looked up at him. "I'm threatened by him now, aren't I? Why else would you have allowed me to go to Gbat Rher?"

He nodded.

"I will be safe in Gbat Rher. I promise. I will go in order to be of help, but my first priority will be to return safely to you."

"You must be safe. You're the only family I have."

"If at any point, I feel that I will not be able to manage it, Desda and I will stop at the nearest inn and will send word to you to send men to come and collect us."

"If you reach that point, I will come to fetch you, myself. From there, we will travel to our nearest property and remain there, in hiding, until we are certain that we know how to keep you away from the emperor."

"I will not stop unless the worst has happened. I want to do this. I feel that I need to."

"I doubt very much that you will stop, Clever One. I'm glad that you have a plan in case things should go awry, but I would never have agreed to this if I did not feel that you would be able to conduct yourself properly and that Sir Fhirell would keep a careful watch over you. I may not have wanted you to go, but I do believe in you."

"Thank you. Thank you for all of this."

"Just be safe. That is thanks enough."

The carriage had stopped, but I did not step out, straight away. I kissed his cheek and remained there, sitting next to him with his arm around me.

"I will have the right clothing and supplies gathered for you. You should spend your time preparing. Eat and rest up. If you are not fully healed and strong enough, I will need to come up with some other way to send you off from Lorammel for a while."

"I will be ready."

"I must go to my appointment, but I will be back in time for dinner. I will see you then."

"I look forward to it," I said and kissed his cheek again before opening the door. The footman who was waiting on the outside helped me down, and I turned to wave to Lord Imery as the carriage pulled away and drove back to the road.

Chapter 28

Megan

Before I could speak, the young man looked up at me, straightened his shoulders, and rose to his feet.

"Are you alright?" he asked in the clear voice that I recognized as Thayn's.

Overcome with emotion, I couldn't answer him. I threw my arms around him and held him tightly, bursting into tears.

I felt his arms surround me and hold me securely.

"It's alright," he spoke softly. "We're coming. Wear the bracelet whenever you can. It will make you easier to identify by people who have only a description to find you. I'm just here to make sure you're safe until the rest can help us."

I listened to him and nodded against him, taking in his words and letting them calm me.

"Okay," I whispered and drew back a little to look at him, wiping the tears from my face.

He stroked a hand over the smooth part of my hair in front of my ponytail and asked, "You're not hurt? You're being treated well?"

"I'm not hurt. They're treating me fine," I said.

"Thank the Goddess," he said, sounding relieved. "You did wonderfully out there, Miss Wynters," he praised me.

"I'm so glad it's you, and I didn't guess wrong," I confessed and was actually happy to hear him call me "Miss Wynters," again. "But how did you get there? How was that even possible?" I asked with a slight shake of my head.

"We're far faster than your ship, but we couldn't see it. We had to sail ahead, stop at the town, and buy a place at the market where you were likely to stop next for water. We were fortunate that the weather has been this dry. Sir Kov was a convincing seller, I think," he grinned a little. "He's an accomplished sailor, too."

I looked at him, stunned and said, "The seller was another Knight? He was amazing!"

Thayn nodded, saying "We sold pieces for two days before you arrived. That is, this was our second day."

Wow, I feel special and lucky. Those guys are dedicated to their rescue missions!

"What about your hair?" I asked, lifting a piece of his brown locks.

"Dyed," he replied.

"And your eye? That's fake, right?" I asked.

He smiled and lifted the band with his fingers, revealing his other eye. It looked entirely fine, and he slid the band back into place.

"Are you going to stay here and pretend to be a slave?" I asked him.

"If I can." He nodded. "Or, I will sleep where the slaves do and come here and work for you during the day. I follow your commands. You own me, Miss Wynters. You tell me what to do. I will sleep where you say and do what you say, and I will do it gladly because it is a miracle to see you," he said and moved to stroke my face. He paused the action when he saw the dirt on his hands.

I honestly couldn't have cared less how dirty he was, at the moment.

"I must go wash, Miss Wynters," he said. "The Warrior warned me to."

He was right. Now that I knew it was Thayn, I wanted to draw as little suspicion to him as possible. I nodded and let him go.

He stepped back and looked at me for a moment, like he couldn't believe he was seeing me. I understood the feeling.

"You look beautiful," Thayn said with a softened smile.

I blushed at his compliment, feeling myself getting completely sucked in by him.

"I will see you when I have lost part of my weight in dirt," he smiled.

I smiled back and said, "Everything you need is in the bathroom."

He nodded and bowed to me like a Knight and headed into the bathroom, shutting the door behind him. The water started running moments later.

I couldn't help it. I did a quick and silent dance of joy on the spot as if someone just told me I'd won the lottery. He was here. Oh my gosh, he was here! I ran over to the cot, picked up the pillow, flopped on the mattress, and pressed the pillow over my face so I could muffle my excited squeal, which had been dying to get out since Thayn had revealed his identity. I kicked my feet a few times and finally pulled the pillow off my face. I lay on the cot like a starfish, keeping my eyes closed and releasing a calming breath.

"Oof!" I said when an unexpected weight landed on my stomach.

Opening my eyes, I wasn't surprised to see Pounce sitting on my belly. She was licking one of her front paws as if she had no idea I was underneath her.

I picked her up and kissed her head, resting her on my chest. She looked at me with her big blue eyes.

"This is so exciting, Pounce!" I whispered. "Things are going to get a lot better for us now. We're going to go to a better place," I informed her.

She stared at me for a moment, yawned, and then hopped onto the floor and strolled away.

Oh well, she'll be more excited when she finds out how awesome Thayn is.

The door opened, and I stood up. Aésha entered, carrying folded clothes and shoes. Based on the dingy grey colour, I knew they were slave clothes for Thayn.

"Has he been in there long?" she asked.

"No," I said. "I talked to him a bit, first."

She nodded, not looking surprised. "What's his name?" she asked curiously.

Oh crap...

"Um." I laughed nervously. "I didn't ask," I confessed. *Oops!*

She raised a brow and laughed and said, "Well, maybe you can ask him when you go check to make sure he's totally clean." She gently shoved the clothes and shoes she was carrying in my direction.

I took them from her and smiled. "I will," I agreed.

She nodded and looked back at me, wearing an expression like she was waiting for me to do something.

No...she can't possibly mean...

"You mean now?" I asked, surprised.

She laughed and said, "How are you going to know if he's clean if you wait a few days? Unless you want me to do it." She waggled her brows.

Oh, that would be so much worse.

"Alright, I'll do it," I said, trying to be as nonchalant about this as I could. Except, who was I kidding? There was absolutely nothing nonchalant about walking in on Thayn taking a bath!

"Good," she said. "Look for dirt, rashes, boils, or bugs." She curled her nose. "I don't want any of that in here. Goddess only knows where he was living."

I nodded and was confident Thayn didn't have any of that. Without delaying any longer, I walked up to the bathroom door and knocked.

"I have some clean clothes for you. I'm going to come in, alright?"

"Yes ma'am," he responded. His voice was quiet-but-audible and sounded different from his normal tone; just slightly scratchier and higher.

"You don't need to ask him," Aésha said, amused.

No, I really, really do.

I waited two extra seconds and opened the door, heading in quickly and shutting it behind me. I knew he was in the bath, so I kept my back to him as much as possible, to try to be as respectful of his privacy as I could. I set his clothes and shoes on the counter.

"Your clothes are on the counter," I said quietly.

"Thank you, ma'am," he said.

"What's your name?" I asked him.

"Balo," he said.

I repeated it out loud and then a few times in my head to remember it.

"Remember to give yourself a really good scrub," I said, for Aésha's benefit, in case she was listening at the door.

"Yes, ma'am," he responded obediently, and the water sloshed in the tub. I had no idea if he was actually engaging in a new round of scrubbing or if he was just splashing around.

"Good," I said to him and quickly exited the bathroom, closing the door.

Aésha was lounging on her bed with Pounce. They both looked like royalty, waiting to be served.

"His name is Balo," I said, walking over to them.

"It suits him," she said and clearly didn't mean that in a kind way, more like an "it's as boring and flawed as he is" way.

I sat on the bed and she shifted and rested her head in my lap.

"You made my dear brother smile," she said, looking rather pleased.

I didn't know to what she was referring, at first, but then I remembered the nuts.

I smiled and said, "Aw, I'm glad I did. He deserved something nice."

"Could it be that my brother is more your type than that dirty thing we dragged home and threw into my bathroom?" she asked, grinning.

Nope.

I shook my head at her. "Mez does seem to be a great guy, but he's not the one for me."

"Perfect." She beamed. "Then I'll keep you all to myself," she teased, kissing her fingertips and placing them on my lips.

"Wonderful! Then it's settled." I laughed and poked her in the side.

She laughed and said passionately, "Ohhh, do it again."

I did, poking her in the same place as the last time. I was happy to play along because I was in a fabulous mood.

She made an erotic groan and, exactly at that moment, the door to the bathroom opened and "Balo" stepped out and knelt. He looked way cleaner than before and was dressed in the standard male slave garb, complete with the foot-crushing shoes. He had tidied up his brown hair as best he could without using a comb, and I noticed the band covering his eye was a shade darker than it had been. I guessed that he had washed it, and it was damp.

I suddenly felt very awkward goofing around with Aésha, with Thayn in the room.

"Should we make him watch us?" she asked, implying that a lot more had been going on between us than a poke to the ribcage.

"No, not this time," I said, hoping she'd drop it.

"Where are you going to put him?" she asked curiously.

"You make him sound like a plant and not a person," I said but was glad she had changed the subject.

"He's a person who needs to stay somewhere. Are you going to want me to arrange for him to sleep with the other slaves on the floor? On the cot? Where will he go?" she asked.

I pondered the options. Part of me wanted to have Thayn go somewhere else so that it wouldn't be so difficult to keep up the ruse with Aésha around. The other part of me didn't like the idea of having him leave my sight. If I couldn't see him, I wouldn't know what was happening to him. The fear of losing him won out over my fear of Aésha discovering us. I'd just have to be ultra-careful and smart.

"He can stay here, on the cot." I decided.

Aésha nodded but then said, "Actually, it's Pounce's cot. Shouldn't you ask her?"

I nodded and looked at Pounce. "You're giving Balo your cot," I informed her.

Pounce raised her head from the bed and looked at me like, "Whatever. Shush!" She rested her head back down.

"All settled," I said to Aésha, and she laughed.

"Why don't you tell him that he can lie down on his cot for a while? That is, unless you want him to do something else. It's creeping me out to have him kneeling outside the bathroom," she said.

Yeah. Good idea.

"You can go to the cot and lie down, Balo," I told him.

"Yes, Ma'am," he said and quickly rose to his feet, walked to the cot, and lay down on it. He curled on his side with his back to the room. His body language made him appear frightened.

Seriously, Thayn should take up acting.

"Will you be alright alone, for a while?" Aésha asked, sitting up and looking at me.

"Yeah, I'll be fine," I said, and it felt good knowing that I would be.

"I won't be too long. Dinner is soon enough," she said. "And you know I can't go too long without touching you," she added with a passionate sigh.

I looked at her oddly, because even that line was a little much for Aésha, but her sly smile told me she'd made the comment on purpose, to freak out Balo.

Oh, boy. This is going to be an interesting couple of days.

She kissed my cheek and whispered in my ear: "I know why you bought him." She spoke knowingly.

I tensed.

Oh, no! Had she already figured it out?

"You can't rescue them all, Baby," she said, drawing back to look at me. "And if you somehow pay for a dozen slaves when we get to Kavylak, you'll never fit them all in your quarters." She chuckled.

"Well, I can try," I laughed nervously, swallowing my heart back down.

I realized then what Aésha thought were my reasons for wanting to buy Balo, the slave. She believed I'd done it because I wanted to save him from a rotten fate. She didn't know that the truth was that I'd done it only because I had believed it possible that the slave I'd bought might have been Thayn. I also realized what Aésha had done for me. She obviously wasn't wild about having a slave in her quarters, but she bought him on my behalf, because she understood how much I loathed slavery. She gave me the power to give him a better life; the power to set him free. Just as Mez had given me a kitten when I had needed comfort the most, Aésha had given me Balo when I needed to see that not everyone in Kavylak was bad.

She stroked my face, and I smiled softly at her. She left the room without another word. As soon as I heard the "snick" of the lock, I immediately got off the bed and went directly to the cot, kneeling down in front of it.

Having heard me, Thayn turned to face me and smiled at me, pushing himself to a seated position.

"Will you be alright if I'm here, all the time?" he whispered.

"Yes," I whispered back. "I think it might be safer."

He nodded. "Thank you. I'd rather stay here where I can know that you're safe," he agreed.

"I'm safe here. At least so far, I am. She's been really good to me," I told him, because she had. They all had, except for Galnar.

"You've done very well," he said, picking up my hand and holding it. "You have befriended them or at least let them think that you have. Doing as you are told, in this way, is the best thing that you could have done. You have very good instincts."

I nodded, feeling proud from his praise. It felt incredible to impress someone like Thayn.

"I was hoping that you, or someone else would come and find me, so I wanted to be ready to leave at any moment."

"I would always come for you, Megan," he vowed, dropping name formalities. "You can take that to heart."

"I will, Thayn. I do," I said and could feel my heart beating faster from his words as I climbed to my feet and sat next to him, never letting go of his hand.

"All I did was hope that you would come. It's all that kept me positive," I gushed.

"Nothing that they could do would have stopped me. There are two ships that have sailed on ahead. They will find a place to hide, and the men will make their way to the capital city where this ship is headed. It won't be long after our arrival that they will make their move to extract us," he told me.

I smiled from ear to ear, not even bothering to conceal the glee his words had erupted in me.

"I can't wait to go back to Syliza with you and to see Irys. Is she alright?" I asked, hoping he knew.

"I'm quite certain that she is. She was in Sir Fhirell's care the last I received word, days ago."

I nodded and felt some of the tension that I didn't even know I'd been carrying around, ease. I was glad she was safe.

"Sir Fhirell is my second," Thayn enlightened me. "He is also my closest friend. His mother has all but adopted me." He chuckled quietly. "He will make sure that Miss Godeleva is returned home very safely."

I nodded, glad to hear this, but my joy faded a bit when I realized that I had bad news to share with Thayn.

"I'm sorry to have to tell you this, but one of your Knights, Sir Rral Radone...he didn't make it."

Thayn sobered at my words and asked, "The Knight from Gbat Rher?"

"Yes. He was a very good man; honourable until the end. He kept me safe. He was brave and kind to me. He told me not to give up and to stay strong. I was with him when he died," I said, hearing the sadness in my voice. "I have his ring and his journal," I revealed, taking the ring from my pocket and showing it to him.

Thayn looked at the ring and then at me with great empathy.

"You honour his memory by keeping the ring with you. He would be glad to know that you're letting him remind you that safety is always nearby."

I nodded, released Thayn's hand, and hugged him. I couldn't help it. I really needed to be that close to someone who made me feel completely safe and whom I trusted implicitly.

He brought his arms around me and kept one arm steady, stroking my back in a soothing way with his other hand.

"You're safe as long as I am here, too," he said.

"Thank you," I whispered. "I'm sorry if I'm breaking a lot of Sylizan society rules by hugging you, but I really need to."

"I'd rather have the hug and a broken rule than do as we should and think that I am missing out on a way to bring you comfort," he said.

I smiled, drawing back a little to look at him. Wow, even with one eye and brown hair, he was handsome.

I laughed a little and whispered, "Can I tell you a secret?"

"Yes," he whispered back.

"I like you better blond."

"Good." He nodded. "My hope is that you'll never see me like this again."

I smiled, agreeing that this was a good deal.

"Can I tell you a secret?"

I smiled and nodded.

"The moment we return to Syliza, I'm going to ask to court you."

Woo! That sounds totally awesome, even though I have no idea what that means!

"I think I'd like that, but I have no idea what that means." I chuckled.

He laughed quietly and said, "It means that I'm going to put you on Chivalry with me, and we are going to ride out of the city to a place where we can hug without breaking rules. Then, I'm going to bring you home again, by a decent hour, before anyone knows the difference." He went on to add, "I just winked at you, but the band really ruined it." He indicated the cloth covering his eye.

I chuckled at his comment and thought about what he said, and I'm pretty sure he was essentially asking me to be his exclusive girlfriend. I just didn't know how serious a girlfriend he was implying.

"So, what you're saying is you want to be my boyfriend," I clarified.

He looked at me, confused for a moment. "Boyfriend" obviously wasn't a common word in his vocabulary.

"I want to see more of you so that I can know if I might one day like to make you my wife," he carefully explained, for further clarification.

Okay. Wow. Yup, I'm thinking he definitely means a serious girlfriend.

I smiled and nodded. "I understand, now. I'd like that. If you were to court me, I mean," I said and kissed his cheek, to further punctuate my statement.

He lit up at my words and my kiss. "Then it looks like I will be very happy when I tell you my secret on the day we arrive in Syliza," he said.

I was so excited. All I wanted to do was tell Irys who I would be dating...er...courting. There was no one else I could gush about it with, at the moment. Ah well, I guess Pounce was gonna get an earful.

I looked at Thayn with a bit of mischief as a thought came to my head. "So, does this mean I would have to wait until I was your wife to show you my shoes?" I razzed him.

He smirked. "I will discuss that when we're courting." He chuckled.

I had to laugh at first, but it faded out when I suddenly remembered where we were and who would be joining us sooner rather than later. I had to warn Thayn about Aésha.

"On a more serious note," I said, "when Aésha returns, she's probably going to say a bunch of stuff to tease me about you. It's a harmless tease, but I just wanted to warn you."

He smiled and said, "It's what she does. She's a Charmer. There are two of them. The other one is a man."

"Arik Atrix." I nodded.

"Yes," he said. "I won't cast judgment. We are all victims of their gazes."

I nodded and knew that while Thayn likely found Aésha super-attractive, I wondered if he had an attraction to Arik, too.

I decided that I should probably be completely honest with Thayn and warn him about my current sleeping situation, since he'd see that soon enough.

"At night, I sleep in Aésha's bed with her. We don't do anything but sleep there. She's been really supportive and, after seeing Rral die, I've had a hard time sleeping on my own," I confessed. "I don't know how I would have pulled through this without her."

Thayn listened respectfully and nodded. "I'm glad that you've found a way to feel secure here, Megan," he said with acceptance.

"Most of the Warriors I've met, with the exception of Galnar, really aren't so bad. I don't trust them like I trust you and the Knights, of course, but they've been kind and respectful to me."

"It's good that they're being kind to you, but you're right not to trust them. They each have their own somewhat magical skill. They are far more dangerous than they appear," he warned.

I nodded in agreement.

"Who else have you met?" he asked curiously.

"Keavren Fadeal. He's the first one I befriended and is likely the reason I'm still alive, in the first place," I told him, without revealing that Keavren assisted in my first rescue because I promised him I wouldn't. "I've also met Mez..."

"Mez Basarovka?" Thayn asked with greater seriousness, cutting me off.

"Yes," I said.

He nodded but didn't look happy to hear that. "He has powers over the mind. Be very careful what you believe from him, if you can."

"He told me the same thing," I agreed. "He didn't keep his skill a secret. I'm pretty sure he's never brainwashed me, though," I told Thayn, not sounding worried because I was entirely confident that Mez hadn't mind-warped me.

"If he had, I'm not sure that you would know about it," Thayn replied gently.

I thought about that, and Thayn did have a point. "I guess I wouldn't, but he talked to me when I was at my lowest, and I didn't feel any worse or better. In fact, I didn't feel different at all, so I don't think he did anything."

Thayn nodded. "I wouldn't worry about it too much but be cautious in the future."

"I don't think that's going to be a problem. I haven't seen him in days and soon we'll be leaving." I smiled. Deep down, I had to admit that I would have loved to have been there to see Mez receive my gift.

I thought of other Warriors I'd met and said, "I've also met Taye, whom you saw earlier. He's the guy who can walk on water."

Thayn nodded.

"There's also Amarogq. He's got ghost wolves or something. There's Acksil, but I don't really know what he can do," I confessed, still having no idea what Acksil's skill was.

"I know little of him," Thayn said about Acksil. "Only that he is a skilled fighter."

I nodded and was about to ask Thayn about the other Warrior I'd seen but had never met, the blond one who wore the circlet on his forehead, but Pounce suddenly came tearing across the floor, in front of us, from out of nowhere and pounced on what I assumed was a fluff. Oh, boy. Leave it to my cat to give a bad first impression.

"I think you got it, Pounce," I said dryly.

Thayn chuckled.

"Do you mind cats?" I asked him.

"Not at all." He shook his head. "I've had many. I can't think of a farm without them."

Oh, yeah! He grew up on a farm!

Releasing his hand and rising from the cot, I picked Pounce up and brought her over to the cot, sitting next to Thayn with the cat in my lap. She looked at me like I had really crossed a line but then got off my lap and went straight to his, rubbing her back against his chest. I laughed. I couldn't blame her for picking him over me.

"Hello, Pounce." Thayn smiled and stroked her, comfortably. She purred up a storm, sucking up all the attention he was giving her.

"She's very soft and very clean. She's never been in a barn." He grinned.

I chuckled and said, "She's a Fairwilde." I was proud of me for remembering that.

"Oh, you're a rare breed," Thayn said, obviously recognizing the name. "No wonder you've never been in a barn."

I grinned, liking that Pounce was a rare breed.

"One of the Warriors was really nice and gave her to me as a gift when I was really upset about Sir Radone," I explained, feeling it was best not to reveal who the actual gift-giver was.

He raised a brow. "That was an interesting gift; a good one to stave off loneliness."

"Yes," I nodded. "If it's possible to take her when we leave, I'd like that, but if we can't, I do understand."

I hated to admit it, but I'd always known that there was a possibility that if I were ever rescued and taking Pounce were to prove problematic, I would have to leave her behind. I loved her, didn't want to lose her, and would try my hardest to keep her but, at the same time, I wasn't going to sacrifice my life and future happiness for her.

"If we can manage her, we'll bring her," he promised.

I smiled at him. He was so freaking great. I was going to have the best boyfriend!

I rested my head against Thayn's shoulder, and he put his arm around me. Pounce curled up in his lap, and he continued to gently stroke her with his other hand.

This felt right, natural, and good to me. If I couldn't find my way back home, I was pretty sure I would find a way to live happily as Mrs. Thayn Varda.

Chapter 29

Irys

On the morning that Desda and I were to depart, she opened my curtains even before the sun had risen over the horizon. We had spent the entire previous day packing, unpacking, repacking, and making sure we had all the necessities for the journey, while still being able to fit it all into a very limited number of bags.

I was surprised that Desda had needed to wake me at all as I hadn't expected to sleep that night. Somehow, I managed to fall asleep and remain that way, throughout the night. When I rose, the two of us ate quickly and then worked industriously to wash and dress me.

My riding suit was to be quite different from the habits to which I was accustomed. The bodice of the deep green double-breasted jacket was fully boned, which meant that I wasn't required to wear a corset underneath. This was a feature I would certainly appreciate from very early on in our journey.

The jacket featured a roll collar with lapels and, while it had double points in the front, the short tails were squared at the back. What I loved most about it, was the double row of gold buttons down the front as each pair of buttons was linked with a small length of gold chain.

I wore a basic, soft white blouse underneath and packed several others just like it. The blouse had ruffles at the collar and cuffs, but nothing that would become a nuisance in the wind or that would interfere my grip on the reins of my horse.

The matching skirt of the suit was lightly draped in the front with a gentle bustling in the back. The draping at the front was the result of careful pleating starting on either side of the waist. The outcome was a very feminine sweep of the fabric that I found to be a very appealing feature for a dress as simple as this one.

The upper part of my hair was pinned into a simple roll, while the length of my hair was allowed to remain loose, over my shoulders. Though I would have liked to pin all my hair up, Desda and I agreed that it would be too much of a bother to try to maintain it throughout the ride and then to have to take it all down in the evening when we were certain to be very tired.

I chose a basic brimmed hat that was based on the latest fashion, only designed much more plainly. It was halfway between a touring hat and a riding hat, and we decided it would work nicely to keep my hair somewhat neat while it would also shade my face from the sun. I would have loved to have been able to wear a hat with lovely plumes jutting out from its band, but I was afraid that the first rain we faced would only ruin it. Instead, I selected an option with some playful ribbons that would flow behind me in the wind.

My boots were brown and practical. I disliked the look of them immensely, but I could not help but notice that they were possibly the most comfortable boots I'd ever worn.

I gave a final glance to the room and left it behind without looking back. I was afraid that if I'd turned, even once, I would lose my nerve and would lock myself inside until it was too late to go.

Descending the stairs, I spotted Lord Imery in the Great Hall, looking up at me. He was already dressed, but he looked tired. His night had been longer than mine.

We kissed each other's cheeks and held each other for a long moment. When I withdrew from his embrace, he spoke.

"We'll ride in the carriage to the Headquarters. I'd like to share a few minutes with you before you must leave," he said quietly. It was still too early in the morning to speak loudly, even if there wasn't anyone in the house who was still asleep.

"I'd like that."

Without delay, we walked outside. I saw my horse being ridden down the drive, with Desda's in tow. Our belongings were already packed in their saddlebags. Desda followed us out and climbed up with the driver of our carriage.

Her slim form was clothed in a sturdy brown skirt and jacket of exquisite wool that I insisted on purchasing for her, so she could wear it on our trip. It was very simply made but it would be cool enough in the early parts of our journey, warm enough in the later parts, and would dry quickly if it should rain.

Desda's tea-coloured hair was drawn into a neat bun, though it was hidden beneath her brown bonnet with a blue ribbon that matched her eyes precisely.

Lord Imery and I stepped up into the coach and, when I looked back out at the house, some of the staff had gathered on the stairs. I waved to them and several waved back. The gesture warmed me enough that it made me wonder if I was making the right choice in leaving this place: my home.

Without knowing it, Lord Imery came to my rescue. He spoke, taking my mind away from a path it should never have taken in the first place.

"I will watch for your letters every day. You must write to me and send them whenever you can," he said.

I gave his hand a squeeze. "I will," I promised. "I'm frightened," I confessed.

He gave me a sympathetic smile. "Good. If you are too comfortable, you won't be trying hard enough to be safe. Is there anything specific that is frightening you?"

"Only the unknown."

"A frightening thing, indeed."

"It is."

I wished I had prepared to say more to him. We had talked a great deal, the day before. Now, it felt as though there were important things to be said. The unfortunate thing was that I didn't know what they were.

The ride was far too short. When the coach came to a stop, I glanced at him and his eyes were asking me if I was certain that I wanted to go. The question was as clear as if it had been spoken in words.

"I'm ready. I will return with the first group to come back again," I told him.

"I will take care of everything here. When you return, there won't be any blue orchids waiting for you. We both have important missions ahead of us."

I wanted to say goodbye. I wanted to tell him I would be praying for him and that I would beg the Goddess to return me home as quickly as was possible. Instead, I could only hug him. Saying anything out loud would only have caused the tears to spill over.

We drew apart, and he opened the carriage door, exiting before turning to offer me a hand.

As I stepped down, I was looking at Lord Imery but, once my feet were on the cobblestone, I couldn't help but see the dozens of people and horses who had assembled and were ready to go to save the north.

Two Redrobes approached the group from the Temple, guiding their horses. When they arrived, they stood on their own in silence, possibly in prayer. The holy men in red would travel to some of the most troubled and dangerous places in the world to spread the Light of the Great Goddess. Their presence in this group was a clear statement as to just how risky this mission might be.

Great Goddess, am I the only one who feels this afraid? Could there possibly be any others in this group who wonder if they are making a grave mistake?

Glancing around me, I saw solid-looking workmen and uniformed soldiers saying goodbye to their loved ones or making final checks to ensure they hadn't forgotten anything. Here and there, women wearing armbands that identified them as nurses, were joining our group as well. They all appeared determined and ready.

Nervously, I withdrew my riding gloves from my pocket and pulled them onto my hands, which were nearly fully healed from having been cut by the mirror. Still, the soft, worn leather was comforting and familiar to wear. I was glad to have brought this pair and that I hadn't bought a new pair for the journey.

"I'm ready," I said to Lord Imery.

"You are," he agreed. We walked up to my horse, and he helped me on, handing me the reins.

Sir Fhirell walked up to us and bowed. I nodded my head to him in greeting.

"Good morning, Sir Fhirell," said Lord Imery. "The protection of the person dearest to my heart is in your hands. See that she is returned safely to me."

A smile graced Sir Fhirell's face. "On my honour as a Knight, it will be my mission above all else, Lord Godeleva."

As if by magic, the words of these two men filled me with confidence and with heart.

Thank you, Great Goddess. I know my path. I know what I should do. My way points to the north. There, I will do something powerful; something meaningful. I do this in your name.

"I will see you soon, Clever One," Lord Imery said as he reached up and gave my gloved hand a squeeze.

"You will, Lord Imery." I smiled at him, hoping my newly found certainty would shine through it.

Sir Fhirell nodded to me and walked over to his own horse. There were directions called out from the leaders of the traveling groups, and I tried to listen to as many instructions as I could hear.

Soon enough, the front of the line was moving. I turned to look at Lord Imery and reluctantly released his hand. He raised it to wave at me, following it by making the sign of the Goddess. I returned them both to him, and Desda rode up next to me, giving me a reassuring smile.

With a final glance to Lord Imery, I turned forward and, together with Desda, we followed our group on the road that would lead us out of the city. As subtly as I could, I withdrew a handkerchief and dabbed the moisture from my eyes.

*   *   *   *   *

The first stop, along our journey, was in a wooded area where a stream was running near to the road. The day had turned out to be quite beautiful. It was warm, but a breeze kept the air at a comfortable temperature.

I was very glad for the moment to rest. This was the farthest I had ever ridden and my body was aching. I was nearly certain that my legs were forming considerable bruises at every point that came in contact with the saddle.

Dismounting, I nearly fell to the ground, surprised at how wobbly my legs had become. I stumbled a little but regained my footing and walked my horse to the stream, so she could drink. Not far behind me, Desda was doing the same thing with her horse. From the way she was walking, I suspected that she was in a similar condition to my own.

"I don't think my legs have ever felt quite like this, Miss," she said with a wry smile.

"No, indeed. I would be very happy if they never felt this way again." I stroked my horse as we spoke and as the mare sucked down the offerings of the stream.

"How are you ladies holding up?" Sir Fhirell stepped up behind us. His confident smile and stride revealed that he didn't find the ride to be nearly as hard on his body as Desda and I were finding it on ours.

Glancing at Desda, I saw a little flush in her cheeks, and a shy smile touched her lips. She looked as though she was about to giggle.

"We're well enough, though very glad for the time to rest. Will we be riding for many more hours today?" I asked, hoping that I didn't sound as though the last thing I wanted to do was travel. I didn't want to appear ungrateful or as though I were complaining.

"We will ride for a few hours more. The weather is on our side, so we don't see any reason to cut things short."

"Lovely," I replied, wondering if there was any way for me to survive a few more hours on horseback.

Sir Fhirell gave us both a knowing smile. "You will find that a nice hot bath will help to soothe the aches. You will be spending the night at an inn. There are advantages to travelling as a Godeleva."

"In that case, I believe I will spend the entire night in the bath," I joked.

"Will we all be staying at the inn?" asked Desda.

"Only some of us. The rest of the group will be camped nearby. I will be at the inn as well. I promised Lord Godeleva that I would keep an eye on you, Miss Godeleva, but I fully intend to enjoy a bath of my own."

We all chuckled at that. Indeed, the idea of sinking into warm water would keep me going until we would arrive at that inn. How glad I was to be a Godeleva.

"Don't worry, Desda. You will share my room with me. I'm sure we'll manage to rest very well, there," I assured her.

Desda looked immensely relieved. Certainly, it would have been much more expected of me to have Desda join the rest of the travellers, but it wouldn't have felt right to enjoy the comforts of the inn while she lay on the ground under a tent, somewhere outside.

At that moment, the gentle breeze changed directions and, when it washed over us, it brought with it the scent of warm spices; cinnamon and cloves, among others. I inhaled it deeply and released my breath with a smile.

"Is there a bakery nearby?" I wondered, out loud.

"A bakery?" Sir Fhirell asked, chuckling. "No. Not for at least an hour."

"Perhaps there is a house somewhere off this road. Do you not smell the cinnamon and other spices?"

He took a breath but shook his head. "No. I smell nothing out of the ordinary."

"I do," Desda spoke up.

"It's only there when the breeze blows," I explained, and Desda nodded in agreement with me.

Sir Fhirell inhaled again, but it was clear that he wasn't detecting what we were. "I think you two are already road-weary and are dreaming of sweet treats."

"We haven't been travelling that long, yet." I chuckled and watched Desda extract a small cloth from a satchel she wore at her hip with the strap across her body. She unfolded it to reveal that it contained brightly coloured berries.

"Would you like some?" she offered, holding them out to Sir Fhirell and me.

Nodding my gratitude, I took several in my hand and started eating.

"Thank you," said Sir Fhirell. "Another benefit to travelling with a Godeleva."

I smiled and Desda laughed.

Another gust of the breeze brought the delicious scent back with it.

"Will we be here for a few more minutes?" I asked.

"Yes," he replied. "When we don't rush our resting times, we are able to travel longer before the next one."

"I think I might just see if I can prove you wrong by tracking down that bakery."

"Bring me back something tasty, would you?"

"I will but, after that, you can never tease me again about imagining things from having travelled too long."

"Agreed."

I looped my horse's reins around a tree branch and walked stiffly, inhaling the wind. My intention wasn't to walk very far but was simply to discover the source of the scent. If it was a kind of plant, I intended to sketch it so that I could send it in my first letter to Lord Imery.

Desda followed along behind me. "What do you think it is, Miss?"

"I'm not certain. Possibly a flower."

As I continued in one direction, the smell seemed to fade, so I changed my course and tracked it anew. When I felt as though I had reached the strongest point for the scent, I found myself standing at the base of a very large tree with very dense foliage.

Stepping up to it, I sniffed at the bark and then at a leaf. Neither smelled anything like the bakery spices. I looked up into the tree but saw nothing but leaves. I'd half expected to see a flower or moss, somewhere among its branches, but there wasn't anything visible. If I were to learn any more, I would have had to climb the tree. That said, I hadn't any intention of doing so. Quite suddenly, the scent faded away until it was only barely detectable.

"How very strange. I'd hoped to sketch the source of the scent. If it had been a flower or a leaf, I might have even dried one for Lord Imery. Whatever it is, it doesn't look as though we can reach it from here. I wonder if there are little tree critters up there, baking for a special occasion." I laughed, amused at the image.

Desda chuckled along with me.

"Shall we return to the group?" I asked.

"That would probably be best."

We returned to our group, which was slowly in the process of preparing to leave. Sir Fhirell was waiting for us near our horses.

"Did you find out what was making the fragrance?"

"It turns out that it was, indeed, a bakery," I playfully informed him. "Unfortunately, it was too high up in a tree for us to shop there."

"Oh, it was that kind of bakery. I didn't realize there were any of them this close to Lorammel," he teased in return.

"If we see another one along our journey, we shall have to send someone up to buy something. It smelled quite delicious."

"If it smells tempting enough, I will do the climbing, myself."

We mounted our horses and joined everyone as we returned to the road.

Chapter 30
Megan

"I think we're arriving somewhere populated," I said to Thayn as I looked out the window in Aésha's room.

It was the early afternoon of the third day since I had "purchased" Thayn, who was masquerading as the slave, Balo, from the seaside marketplace.

Thayn and I passed the time playing with Pounce, reading to each other the books Keavren had lent me, and chatting. Mostly, we stuck to small talk. It sucked because I had a million-and-one questions to ask him about his personal life, but it was too dangerous to engage in personal conversations because we never knew who might walk through the door or when. Thayn's safety was more important than my curiosity. Besides, when we were on our way back to Syliza, I'd have more than enough time then to ask him everything I wanted.

He did tell me a bit about Chivalry, which I was happy to hear because I really liked his horse, and I knew how much he meant to Thayn. We also came up with a pretty good sad-sob backstory for Balo, in case Aésha ever asked me, which she didn't. She also never inquired as to what I did with Balo when she wasn't there. She knew I talked to him and was likely friends with him, but she didn't suspect anything beyond that, and she didn't really care. Why would she?

Thayn walked up to the window and looked out with me and, after a moment, he said, "We're close to Capital City."

As we sailed by, I observed the green and rocky land, which became less filled with trees and grass and more populated with wooden houses. Eventually, the wooden houses became fewer. Grey stone and brown brick buildings took their place.

As we sailed closer to the capital, the buildings became denser. They were not what I would describe as pretty. Unlike Lorammel's buildings, that were designed with architectural features to give them style and character, these buildings were very block-like and uniform.

Aside from varying heights, they were virtual cookie-cutters of one another as if they were built to take up the least amount of space and materials.

The buildings here were also taller than those in Lorammel, where most of the buildings were rarely higher than three storeys. In Capital City, several of the buildings were five- or six-storeys in height. They were also dotted with stacks that occasionally puffed dark clouds of smoke.

Some of it was swept away by the wind, but it was obvious when the wind wasn't blowing. Instead of dispersing, the smoke would hang in the sky like some looming cartoon-dark storm cloud that just gave the city an overall grumpy feel. My lip curled.

Yuck!

"It's definitely not Syliza," I muttered.

"It's not Syliza," Thayn agreed.

The sound of the door unlocking drew us from the view. Thayn immediately sat down on the floor with his back to the wall as if he had been there, all along because that's what I'd told him to do.

Aésha walked in and flashed me her signature smile as she shut the door.

"Time to pack up," she said.

"I had a feeling we were close," I told her.

She nodded and, wasting no time, walked directly to her bed and hauled what looked like a hard-sided, large metal suitcase from under it. She flipped the lid open and started jamming what she intended to take with her, into the case. She pulled the sheer pink curtain down from her bed and added it to her stuff before moving in and out of rooms, to collect the other various items she wanted.

I walked to my cot and pulled my bag out from underneath it. I was about to start putting stuff into it but then realized I should probably have Thayn do that.

"Balo, could you please put the items I place on the cot into the bag?" I asked politely.

"Yes, Ma'am," Thayn said, in his Balo-voice, and got up from where he sat, beginning to pack the various items I wanted to take.

I grabbed all the clothes I'd been given and my flats as well as Keavren's books, and the two journals. I also grabbed Pounce's dishes and the remainder of her food. As soon as she saw me with the dishes and the food, she got all chatty and began winding around my legs.

"Thanks, Pounce, you really know how to help," I told her, putting the dishes and food down, so Thayn could pack it.

After pulling on my boots, I picked her up and looked in Aésha's direction and announced, "I'm ready."

"Good," she smiled at me. "Looks like you're ready to hit the city."

I nodded. I was. I was even wearing a long-sleeved fitted shirt (black, of course) because Aésha had said it would be slightly cooler in the capital city as it was farther north than where the small port town had been.

"Balo can come with me, right?" I asked to make doubly sure that there wasn't some rule for slaves when disembarking.

"He's yours," she responded. "You say where he goes."

"Okay," I confirmed.

Aésha finished packing and shoved her metal case over to the exit door. She stepped up to the window and looked out.

"We're nearly there," she informed us.

Suddenly, there was a very loud and drawn out "HONK" sound that echoed off the walls. I winced at the noise, and Pounce dug her nails into my arm. I almost dropped her but held on tight.

Ow!

"Hold on to something," Aésha warned and casually placed her hand on the wall, to brace herself.

Thayn sat, braced, on the cot.

I dropped to my bum on the floor, holding on to Pounce, ready for anything.

Moments later, the ship jarred to a halt as if someone had slammed on the brakes, and we'd hit a padded wall. A few dishes clinked and rattled in the kitchen, from the force of the jolt. Pounce squirmed and dug deeply into me and made a whole pile of miserable noises. I couldn't blame her.

Seriously, who was driving this thing?

"It's alright, Pounce," I said softly, to her to try to calm her, petting her head. "Do we still need to hold on?" I asked Aésha.

She shook her head and said with a smile, "Welcome home."

Thayn remained where he was, waiting for my order, so I gave him one. "Could you pick up my bag, please, Balo."

He nodded and stood as did I, walking up to Aésha who extracted a pair of the leather handcuffs. Knowing the drill, I shifted Pounce and extended my right arm to Aésha. To my surprise, she smiled, reached out, and attached the leather cuff to my left wrist, careful of Pounce.

I shifted Pounce back into my right arm, wondering what she was doing, until she led me over to Thayn and cuffed me to his right wrist, locking us together. She placed the key to the lock in my palm.

"You're the slave owner, now," she said. "I'll be taking you off the ship and onto the base, but then you'll need to follow the instruction you receive, from there."

The day before, Aésha had told me that I would be assigned quarters and employment, which had been chosen for me by Mez. In true Aésha fashion, she hadn't told me what my employment would be, no matter how much I hassled her about it. I just hoped I'd made a good-enough impression on him that I wouldn't be cleaning toilets.

"Okay. Thanks Aésha," I said, slipping the key into my pocket to join my two most prized possessions: Rral's ring and Irys' handkerchief. They were always tucked securely in my pants pocket so that they'd never be forgotten.

"Glad to have slept with you all these nights," she said with a wink and opened the door.

I was shocked to see that there were lots of people going by. I felt a light tug on the cuffs from Aésha and moved forward with Thayn. He was at my side, carrying my bag on his back. Pounce was tucked tightly under my right arm. Aésha walked ahead of us, leaving her own metal suitcase-trunk behind and her door open. It didn't surprise me that she would have someone else take care of that for her.

We followed closely behind her, joining the zombie walk heading up to the top deck. There were all different people around us: the ship's staff, crew, slaves, soldiers, and the occasional Warrior I didn't recognize, and those whom I did, like Amarogq. He wasn't too far ahead of us.

I knew the ship was huge, but how could there have possibly been this many people on board? Had we picked up a whole whack of people in the last town?

The air had a typical saltwater fishy aroma, but it was mixed with something else unpleasant that I couldn't quite place. We reached the large metal gangplank, and I was glad to discover that it had sturdy rails on either side as it wasn't a short bridge to the pier. We descended slowly. I was too focused on keeping Pounce secure and not losing Aésha, to really take in the city.

However, I did notice that the crowd of people moving about on land, began to move outward to create an empty space in the crowd as if they were avoiding an oncoming car. There was no car. It was something just as deadly: Galnar. As he marched forward toward a large central building that I assumed was the military base, people moved out of his way as if he had a radioactive ring around him. I felt a little better about the people of Kavylak, knowing that they, too, felt the desire to avoid him like the plague. I was starting to think that Kavylak wasn't necessarily bad. It was *Galnar* who was bad.

Hearing someone grunt and swear, in close proximity, I turned my attention to the sound and saw that Amarogq had pushed an annoyed-looking soldier out of his way and was running down the pier. I watched him reach the land and throw his arms around the cutest-looking young woman I'd ever seen, who was wearing the most enormous smile on her face. She had dark hair and was decked out in a white blouse, a short salmon-colored jacket, and an A-line skirt the same colour as her jacket, which went halfway down her shins. To complete her darling 1950s-esque look, she sported little, white, ruffled socks and what looked like black Mary Jane shoes. Amarogq kissed her like he hadn't seen her in a very long time.

Okay, I guess he wasn't kidding about having a fiancée. That must be Amorette.

When we finally reached land, I got my first real look and smell of the city. I was stunned. While Syliza had been kind-of like stepping into renaissance France, Kavylak was kind-of like stepping into the industrial revolution.

Like Syliza, there were no cars or motor vehicles of any kind. However, while there were horses and a few carriages, the capital also had lots of person-pulled rickshaw-style wagons that were carrying all sorts of luggage and goods, making trips from the ship to the base. I didn't recall anything like that in Syliza.

The streets were made of large, five foot by five foot, stone blocks that were black tarred on their surface; definitely not the pretty cobblestones of Lorammel. I assumed the tar might have been used to protect the feet of the horses and to provide traction.

Along the main roads was one factory after the next, producing materials in an industrial fashion. As we neared the military base, there were several shops built into the strip of buildings, above which there were a couple of storeys where I imagined the shop owners, or their tenants, lived.

The non-stop hum of the city was unrelenting. It was made up of the sounds of people yelling, carts being pulled down streets, machines running in factories, and other noise, all happening at once.

The smell was as overwhelming as the noise. My nose was assaulted by the heavy smoke in the air, the stink of factory production, horses, food, and even a sharp chemical cleaning odor. I could already feel a headache brewing.

Aésha walked us up to the tall, dark metal gate in front of the base. She showed a piece of paper to an angry-looking guard. I smiled pleasantly at him. He looked at the paper, then glared at me, glared at Thayn, and nodded to Aésha.

Sheesh! I'd hate to see the look he'd give someone who wasn't permitted entry into the base!

Aésha entered the military complex, and we followed her along the concrete path. I took in our surroundings. The military base was composed of several rows of housing that resembled something like one or two storey townhouses. There were other non-residential buildings mixed in as well, and at the core of the base, stood one massive grey stone building.

The immense structure had a commanding presence but lacked both warmth and character. Aside from its size, nothing in particular was remarkable about it. All its windows and doors were plain and the front of the building gave the impression that it was a giant, flat cube. However, as I was able to get a better view of the building, I discovered that it wasn't actually flat all the way around. The side of it I could see had sharper edges and angles. The architecture was still boring but, at least, it seemed to have been designed with a touch more imagination.

Aésha stopped walking, turned to me, and said, "Go to building 305A. It's just down there." She pointed. "You're in the second door." She handed me the folded paper she had shown the guard.

"Thanks, Aésha," I said genuinely.

"I'll see you around," she said, smiling. "Hopefully very soon." She winked.

"See you," I said.

She blew me a kiss and walked off, in another direction. I watched her stroll off toward the huge structure and wondered if that would be the last time I'd see her. I didn't contemplate the thought for long. Thayn and I had to get to 305A. I wanted to get out of the crowd. I didn't like being out in the open, in this strange land, surrounded by countless strangers. I felt small and exposed. I was so glad he was with me.

Glancing at Thayn, who was doing a good job of looking like a slave, I headed in the direction Aésha had indicated, keeping my eyes peeled for building 305A. Thankfully, it wasn't as hard to find as I'd thought it would be. As boring-looking as this place may have been, it was definitely functional, and everything was labeled sensibly and perfectly. Keavren hadn't been kidding when he had once told me that the capital was practical and that it functioned well.

It really is the land of filing cabinets!

We stopped in front of the building that had 305A painted on its side, in huge black letters. There were four doors to the building: two on one side and two on the other.

I didn't have a key, so I assumed one of the doors would be open. Shifting Pounce to my left arm, I tried the first door. It was locked. I tried the second, and it opened. Before stepping in, I poked my head in and called, "Hello?"

No one answered, so I entered. Thayn followed but left the door open. We were alone in what looked like an empty and very, very stark motel room. The natural light that poured in through the room's one small window, and its open entry door, revealed that there was a twin-sized bed with a pillow, fresh sheets, and a blanket folded on top of a bare mattress. In the corner was a box-shaped dresser and a desk with a chair. The desk would probably double as a small dining table for one to two people. There was also a floor lamp with a paddle-like switch. Aside from the entry door, there were two other doors in the room: one open and the other shut.

I looked at Thayn. "I guess this is home sweet home," I said sarcastically.

He nodded, looking about as unenthusiastic as I was. We entered, and he shut the door behind him, locking it. I set Pounce on the floor. She immediately froze on all fours as if she'd been set down on broken glass.

Pulling the key out of my pocket, I unfastened our cuffs, glad to get them off. I tossed the cuffs onto the table and put the key back in my pocket. Now that we were free, both Thayn and I began to thoroughly inspect the place as if we were looking for bugs or spy cameras. I looked through the open door and discovered a tiny bathroom with a toilet, pedestal sink, and shower stall. The faint smell of the potent cleaning chemical that had burned the skin of my hands while I was Galnar's slave, invaded my nose. Though fully healed, the tops of my hands prickled at the memory.

"Key," Thayn said.

I turned to look in his direction and saw that he had withdrawn an envelope with 305A-2 marked on it, from the nightstand drawer. It very obviously contained a key. I nodded, and he placed it on the nightstand.

Moving to the closed door, I pulled down on the lever, and it opened. I looked inside and saw a basic alley kitchen with another closed door at its end. I wandered in, went to the opposite door, and tried the handle. It was locked. I pressed my ear to the door to listen for sounds of someone on the other side, but there was only silence. Silence or not, I was pretty sure this door led to another person's quarters, and I shared this kitchen with them.

Oh, joy! A neighbour.

I quietly inspected the kitchen and found a small, cold cupboard that, I guessed, was kind-of like a fridge; a cupboard with a few simple dishes, most of which were metal; a cupboard with few basic food supplies; and a stovetop with no oven. There was also a small sink and tiny counterspace.

I left the kitchen and shut the door, locking it. I didn't want anyone walking in on us.

"I think we've got a neighbour," I whispered to Thayn, having no idea if these walls were paper-thin.

He looked up at me from where he was crouched, petting Pounce. He nodded, not looking surprised. Pounce, for her part, still looked unhappy with her new surroundings but at least she seemed more relaxed.

"Do you..."

Three solid raps on the entry door interrupted me.

Thayn kneeled on the floor but looked like he was ready to spring into action, if the need arose.

I walked up to the door but didn't open it.

"Yes?"

"Megan Wynters, open the door," commanded a woman's voice, making me jump.

I glanced at Thayn, nervously, because that wasn't Aésha.

Taking a quick breath, I unlocked the door and opened it. I was not prepared to come face-to-face with the blond bombshell who stood on the other side.

She was young, maybe my age or slightly older, and was the picture of military perfection. She stood, straight as an arrow. Her rich, blond hair was tucked back into the neatest bun imaginable. Her dark-grey soldier's uniform was flawlessly crisp as if she had ironed it after it was already on her body. She was holding a clip board with a few pages flipped over its back, in one hand.

She focused her large crystal-blue eyes on me, which I would have found pretty if I didn't feel like she was going to incinerate me with them.

"Megan Wynters?" she asked, in a voice that would have been sweet, if there hadn't been an authoritative edge to it.

"Yes, I'm Megan Wynters," I confirmed, quickly. I got the feeling that this woman wasn't a time-waster. She was all business.

She nodded and checked something off on a page, then held out a chain with a metal tag on it. It reminded me of military dog tags, except there was only one tag, and it was shaped like a square and was hanging from one of its corners. I took it from her.

"Put that on," she instructed in her no-nonsense tone. "It is your identification. People without identification are criminals," she told me, flatly.

Whoa. They don't mess around in Kavylak.

Immediately, I put the chain on over my head. I didn't want to be a criminal, least of all in this crazy place. I was a denizen, darn it!

The woman wrote something, then glanced at Thayn, and asked, "A slave?"

"Yes," I said.

"File appropriate paperwork before the end of tomorrow. I will make temporary note of his existence today," she stated and proceeded to make the note, without wasting a second.

Geeze, this woman is tightly wound up!

"You have been recommended for a position in basic written translation. Are you qualified for such tasks?" she asked. Although, with the way she aimed her big, angry, blue eyes at me, I felt it was more of a challenge than a question.

Seriously, did I tick this woman off, in another life?

"Yes," I said before I had time to absorb the meaning of her words. She probably could have asked me anything, and I would have responded right away, for fear that she'd stab me otherwise.

She nodded and wrote more. When she was finished, she took a medium-sized envelope out from under the sheet she was writing on, held it out to me, and said, "This is your assignment packet. Bring it with you."

I took it from her, and she turned the clipboard in my direction, holding out a pen. "Sign to acknowledge you have your identification, you will register your slave, and you have received employment," she commanded.

I nearly dropped the envelope when I rapidly switched it to my left hand, so I could sign with my right. After signing my name, she plucked the pen from my hand and turned the clipboard around, flipping the pages down. She marched off, without a word, toward another door and gave it two solid raps.

I shut the door to my quarters and locked it, looking wide-eyed at Thayn. I'd felt like I'd just failed the worst exam of my life, and I was pretty sure I had just agreed to work as a translator for the Kavylak military.

"She's intense," I whispered.

He nodded, stood, and asked, "Are you alright?"

"I think so," I said. I honestly had no idea.

He drew me into an embrace. I hugged him back, grateful for the contact and comfort.

"We can practice translating tonight, so you'll be ready," he offered.

I nodded, uncertainly.

I can't believe I've agreed to be a translator! I barely passed French in high school and, on Qarradune, everything looks and sounds like English to me. How will I tell one language from the next? What the heck was Mez thinking? Maybe he didn't like the nuts I gave him after all.

"You know lots of languages," Thayn continued, encouragingly. "You just need to figure out how to get them straight."

"You're right," I said, starting to calm down from my micro-freak-out. "I can do this. I'm going to do everything as best I can, and I'll find out how to register you tomorrow. I'll keep us safe," I said with determination as my rationality kicked back in. I would find a way to do what needed to be done until we could leave. I had to.

"It won't be long," Thayn promised. "They're already coming up the coast. Just keep your bracelet on and try to be where you should be, all the time. The odds are, it will happen at night when you're most likely to be home."

"I'll go wherever I need to, in the day, and come straight back here when I can. I'll keep a low profile. I don't want to draw any attention to myself," I told him. "Are you just going to stay here?" I asked hopefully.

He nodded. "Pounce and I will take care of the place. I'll cook, too," he offered.

"I'm glad one of us can cook," I said.

He laughed, and I smiled until I realized that we didn't have any food, at the moment.

"I'll figure out how to get food, tomorrow," I said. "I saw that there was a bit of stuff in the kitchen, but I don't know if we can take it or not, and I don't want to deal with a neighbour right now. Would you be alright with a protein shake for dinner? I think I still have a few that Keavren gave me, in my bag."

Thayn nodded, looking unconcerned. "We'll figure it out," he assured me.

"I'll go get us a couple of mugs from the kitchen. You look for the packets." I smiled and kissed his cheek, heading into the kitchen.

*   *   *   *   *

The rest of the evening was uneventful. We had our shakes and Thayn helped me with translation. We used Rral's journal and sentences Thayn had written in Sylizan and Kavylak, so I could compare them. It took some practice but, by the time my eyes were getting heavy with sleep, I felt confident that I had figured out how to tell one language from another. Or at least I'd figured out enough that I'd be able to get by, tomorrow.

Feeling thoroughly exhausted from the stress of the day's events, we turned in for the night. Thayn insisted that I take the bed and that he'd sleep on the floor. In return, I insisted that he take my blanket, which, to my relief, he finally accepted, after only a few refusals.

It was chilly in the room, so I remained in my clothes and curled up under the thin sheet. I felt miserable and couldn't wait to get out of there. The rescue ships couldn't come soon enough.

Chapter 31

Irys

As we travelled, the scent of rich spices came and went. I allowed myself to fixate on it in order to distract my mind from the length of the journey and from the aches of my body. I watched for types of flowers or trees that were unfamiliar to me and that might have been making the scent, but I could find none. I started to wonder if it might have been the smell of some form of tree creature that was native to this part of Syliza, but that never made its way into Lorammel.

Whatever the source, its importance died away, nearly entirely, when we rode up to a charming two-storey inn. It was delightfully ornamented with a corner turret with hipped dormers, enchanting curved glass, and a conical roof. Bay windows stepped out onto the verandah and added a warm draw to the building as did the quaintly designed chimney pots and a whimsical dentil eaves trim.

The sight couldn't have been more welcome. As I dismounted my horse, I clung to her saddle to make sure my legs would hold me. I'd learned from our previous stops that it was foolish to assume that I would be able to stand under my own power. To save my dignity, I took a moment to stroke the horse's face and neck and to tell her what a wonderful job she'd done throughout today's ride.

When I was fairly certain that I could walk normally, I handed the reins to a stable hand who was waiting for them. I turned and smiled tiredly to Desda. She looked fatigued but sturdier than I likely did. I led the way up the front walk and she followed, carrying our overnight bags.

Many of the others from our group were establishing themselves in a field across the road. Tents were being assembled and fires were being started.

Sir Fhirell walked up to us and looked as pleased to be at the inn as Desda and I were.

"Happy to be off your horse?" he asked jovially.

"Very much so. I think I shall be walking the rest of the way to the north."

He chuckled. "Stretch your legs and enjoy a good rest. Tomorrow will be a new day and you'll feel like a new person...mostly."

"I may take a little walk around the inn's property after I've had the chance to wash up a little."

"I wouldn't mind joining you," he offered, and I nodded my agreement.

"Lord Godeleva will be happy to hear that you've taken every precaution in protecting me against potential attacks from wildflowers in the inn's back garden," I said lightheartedly.

"Indeed," he replied with a laugh. Sir Fhirell's name was called, and he excused himself so that he could attend to the person who was summoning him. I watched him go, with the smile still on my lips. He was such a kind man, and I couldn't deny that he was also very handsome. When I turned back to Desda, I could see by her knowing and teasing smile, that she knew I had been observing Sir Fhirell slightly longer than I likely should have.

Instead of playfully scolding her, I reached over and took my bags from her so that she was only required to carry her own. Stepping inside the inn, I inhaled the rich scent of oiled wood and was greeted by a jolly-looking innkeeper who stroked his moustache to straighten it, in preparation for speaking. His hair was receding from his forehead but was neatly cropped for a very proper appearance.

"Welcome," he greeted us.

"Good evening," I responded. "Might you have a room suitable for a lady and her maid?" I wasn't exactly sure how I was meant to introduce myself to this man. Lord Imery had always handled the arrangements for our stays outside Lorammel and, even then, we usually stopped at Godeleva properties.

"We do, indeed." His eyes smiled until little sunshine-like creases in his face lit their outer corners.

"Lovely. It seems we will fit here, quite happily."

He chuckled, cheerfully. "Just for tonight? You're with the group across the road and the Knights?"

"Yes. Thank you." I gave him my name and made the necessary arrangements for our accommodations.

Extracting a key from a cabinet on the wall, the innkeeper turned toward an open doorway.

"Rimoth," he called. A young man of around twenty cycles appeared. He had hair the colour of polished pewter and bright blue eyes. Quite an uncommon look. In fact, I may ever have seen only one other person who looked quite like him. "Take Miss Godeleva and her maid to the big room on the second floor," he told Rimoth before looking at me. "Our best," he assured me.

I smiled sweetly to him and handed my bags to Rimoth before following him to the room. Rimoth glanced back at me, several times, with a look as though we should know each other. I was certain I'd never spoken to this man. Yet there was something somewhat familiar about him.

Once he had opened the door, he set my bags down into the room and handed me the key. The room was clean and sturdy looking. It smelled fresh but was absent of any finery or fancy décor. I was grateful for it. All I needed was a safe, clean place in which to rest my aching body. This provided exactly that.

Glancing at Rimoth, I noticed that he was still looking at me with familiarity.

"Were you recently a sailor, by any chance?" I asked, in case there was some way that he had been part of Sir Fhirell's crew, and that's why he seemed to know me.

He shook his head. "No ma'am."

"It is only that you look at me as though we should know each other. I was on a ship not too long ago, and I thought you might have been as well."

"I have seen you before," he confirmed. "We were never introduced. I was with the group of people from Fort Picogeal that you led into the woods to avoid the fire and smoke from the city."

"Oh!" I exclaimed before I could think of anything more clever to say. "Such a coincidence! I'm glad to see that you've found your way to a new place to live, after the disaster there."

"As am I. I left right after you must have. This is a good job, and it comes with a dry room of my own." He then shifted topics with what I would have assumed to be awkwardness in another man, though Rimoth appeared to be as confident as a Knight. "There's the main room here and that little door's to a water closet. There are extra towels and blankets in the cupboard and, if you're looking to take a bath, the bathing tub is two doors down the hall."

"This will do very nicely," I replied, hoping he would not detect my dismay at staying in a place with a shared bathtub.

"Should you need anything, merely ring at the desk," he said simply and left, shutting the door behind him and leaving Desda and me standing in the middle of this small but cozy space.

I took a deep breath and released it, preparing myself for these new circumstances and trying to find the best way to go about relaxing in them.

"We must get to the bathtub before any others arrive," I said with a wicked grin.

Desda laughed heartily. "I will draw the water and stand guard for you to be sure no one enters," she responded, quickly joining in my game to be sure that we would be the first to enjoy the bath.

"I will try not to be too long and then I will do the same for you," I agreed.

She giggled and moved quickly out the door. I heard her rapid footsteps as they went down the hall.

I took off my hat and laid it down along with my jacket, which I hoped Desda would shake outside, to remove some of the dust from the road. Gathering up my bag and the room key, I walked two doors down the hall where Desda was watching the water fill a gleaming white bathtub. I couldn't have been more grateful that this innkeeper was clearly determined to keep a spotless inn.

With the door shut, the two of us manoeuvred around the tiny room, to extract me from my clothes and boots. She washed my hair and then left me to soak, for a little while, in the very warm water while she did as she promised and stood like a sentinel outside the door.

The tub was at the wrong angle for relaxing and the room was stark, but the water warmed me so comfortingly that I could have fooled myself into thinking I was bathing at the Imperial Palace itself. I tried not to take too long, but I knew, in my heart, that I had spent too much time relaxing when there were others – including Desda – who were awaiting the same luxury.

I reluctantly stepped out of the tub and dried myself. Instead of calling Desda in, I dressed myself in fresh undergarments and a clean afternoon dress that I had brought for just this type of purpose, so that I would not be forced to wear my riding suit when we were not actually on the roads. How wonderful the soft fabric felt, and how lovely it smelled, compared to the scent of horses or that cinnamon-spice fragrance that had filled my senses since we'd left.

Before I stepped out, I used my bath towel to wipe down the inside of the tub, to return its initial gleam. It was my meager attempt at a bit of a gift for Desda who had been such a wonderful comfort and, on whom I knew I would be relying heavily for the remainder of our journey. I turned on the water to start to ready the bath for her, smiling to myself at how much fun it was to serve my maid.

"It is your turn, Desda," I said to her as I opened the door, feeling like a new person.

"Thank you, Miss!" Desda said excitedly as she noticed that her bath was already being drawn.

"Would you like me to stand at the door for you? The lock does appear to be a good one."

"Then I think I'll be alright, Miss Godeleva."

"In that case, I may just go for a little walk outside. I'll stay very near the building. I'm sure that Sir Fhirell will watch out for me if he's outside."

Desda's smile grew at the mention of Sir Fhirell's name. "He's a very handsome Knight."

"He is. Now stop teasing me and go take your bath," I scolded, playfully as though she were a naughty child.

Chuckling happily, she shook her head. "It's not a tease, Miss. I think he's sweet on you, too."

"Go on, before I lock you out of our room!"

She continued to giggle and stepped into the bathroom, shutting the door. I waited outside until I heard the lock turn over and then went back to the room to put my things away. Deciding to leave my hair down, to let it dry, I combed through it and walked out the door, locking it while keeping my promise to Lord Imery to be careful wherever I could.

It dawned on me that if I were to go out now, Desda would not be able to return to our room, so I walked back to the bathroom.

"I'm sliding our key under the door for you, Desda. Don't lock me out!"

"Yes, Miss." Her voice sounded calm as it echoed around the tiled room. "I won't lock you out."

I slid the key under the door and gave it a little push with my fingertips, then turned to go outside. My shoes thudded against the bare wooden stairs and then sank quietly into the runner of carpet at the bottom. I could already feel some of the tension returning to my muscles, making the softness of the carpeted floor a welcome sensation.

I decided to walk on the grass outside, instead of attempting to stick to walkways of cobblestone or gravel. Stepping out, I spotted Sir Fhirell, who was chatting with Sir Breese. I smiled. I hadn't realized that Sir Breese had also joined this mission. I bobbed a small curtsy to them as I passed, not having any intention of interrupting their discussion.

Both Knights bowed to me, touching their hats.

"You look much fresher," Sir Fhirell observed.

"I feel that way, too."

"Are you ready for that walk?"

"Yes. I don't mind strolling around alone if you aren't finished your conversation. I don't plan to go very far."

Sir Breese shook his head. "We were just finished. It is good to see you again, Miss Godeleva."

"It is good to see you, too, Sir Breese."

He bowed and walked away from us as Sir Fhirell approached and offered me his arm, which I took. Strolling slowly, we moved forward without any particular direction in mind.

Just as I was beginning to feel relaxed in the silence we were sharing, the smell of spices faintly returned.

"There is that scent again. It must be a flower," I remarked. "I wonder if anyone has ever tried to bottle it. It would be quite nice in a room."

"Ah, the imaginary bakery has returned, has it?"

"Yes, the bakery. You just can't smell it because you are still covered in a layer of road dust and horse," I joked.

He laughed quite merrily at that. "You don't think we should bottle that scent, too?"

"Not at all! My bath was the highlight of my day, Sir Fhirell."

"Then shall we see if we can find your imaginary bakery this time?"

I nodded. "I'd love to gather a sample of it, if I could. I would like to show it to Lord Godeleva. Perhaps he will know what it is."

Inhaling the air, I followed the scent as it became stronger, to the point that I felt that I had once again narrowed down its source to a tree. It wasn't the same type of tree as the last one, but this one was also densely leaved.

"You must be able to smell it now," I insisted. I could practically taste the aroma.

He inhaled deeply, and I could see the light come on behind his eyes as he detected it. "Ah, well now. That is odd, isn't it?"

"I find it calming and quite appealing. Desda said the same thing."

"It does appear to be coming from this tree, whatever it is. Shall I climb it to see if there is a flower up there?"

"Do you think it's safe?"

He chuckled. "I've been climbing trees since I could walk. I've chased my little brothers out of taller trees than this one," he insisted.

I removed my hand from his arm, and he jumped up, grabbing onto the lowest branch and pulling himself up onto it. He appeared to look around, to see if he could spot anything, and then continued to climb upward, looking completely comfortable in doing so.

"Nothing, so far," he called to me but then paused. "No, wait, there does appear to be something higher up."

"What kind of something?"

"I'm not quite sure. A dark lump."

"Be careful. If it's an animal, you could startle it, and it could drop on you."

"I will," he agreed and continued to climb for a short moment before there was a sharp hiss, and he gave a startled cry. There were three sharp sounds of something hitting branches, and I was certain that he was falling out of the tree.

Suddenly, some sort of rodent leapt out from the cover of the branches and ran as fast as it could down the trunk and across the grass before darting out of sight.

"I'm alright," Sir Fhirell called down to me before I could ask.

"Goddess," was all I could say. My heart was beating wildly in my chest.

It was only another short moment before Sir Fhirell was standing with his feet on the ground. I rushed to him and looked him over. "You're not hurt?"

"No. Only slightly more dirty than before. This isn't a trend I like," he said with a wry smile.

"What happened?"

"I'm not entirely certain. I thought I saw something moving but when I approached it, there was a loud hiss and some sort of rodent suddenly came hurtling down in my direction. I lost my balance."

"It didn't bite you or scratch you? You didn't hit your head?" I asked, filled with concern.

He smiled. "No. I managed to avoid it. I'm just glad I was able to catch myself before I fell."

I sighed relief and, when I inhaled again, I realized that the scent had nearly disappeared. "I wonder if that rodent was what was making the smell."

"I suppose it's possible. There didn't appear to be anything else unique about that tree.

"If it were the tree or something still in it, I'd assume we would still smell it."

"You're right. Honestly, I have no idea, Miss Godeleva."

By the time I tried inhaling again, the smell was entirely gone. "I wonder if the innkeeper knows what it is. It does seem to be rather common in this area. I think I shall go and ask him."

"Thank you for the very interesting and very confusing walk, Miss Godeleva. I look forward to finding out what you discover."

"It was quite the adventure, indeed, Sir Fhirell. I will be certain to let you know what I learn. See you soon."

"Alright, but next time, you're climbing the tree." He chuckled.

"We can send Sir Breese," I retorted, and we both laughed when he nodded.

We walked away from each other, and I paused at the door to the inn, watching him as he strolled to the field where the camp was now quite established. A gorgeous bird of prey gave its cry from overhead, and he whistled to it, raising his arm. I smiled at the glorious sight as the bird descended and gracefully landed on his offered forearm. I stared for an extra moment as he stroked Mikkhaw's head and neatly-tucked wings, then entered the inn.

At the desk, Rimoth was there instead of the innkeeper.

"Hello," I greeted him. "You wouldn't happen to know of a flower or some other type of plant in the area that smells like cinnamon and warm spices, would you? I've been smelling something like that and have been very curious about its source."

"A flower that smells like cinnamon? I can't say I have. Where did you smell it?"

"It's been all along the road for quite some distance as well as just outside, near one of the large trees on the other side of the inn. It is the strangest thing. As soon as we feel we've tracked it down, it fades away."

"Strange," he agreed with a shrug.

"Thank you, anyway. Have a pleasant evening."

"And you, Miss Godeleva."

Back up the wooden steps I went, pausing at the room door to knock before trying the knob. It wasn't locked, so I entered, announcing myself.

Desda was there and was combing through her hair. She smiled at me with a calm expression. Our underclothes from the day were hung about the room to dry. Desda must have washed them. It was a good idea as we couldn't be sure when we would next have such a chance. I wished the idea had been mine, but I was grateful that I was travelling with someone whose mind turned to such important tasks.

We chatted quietly until Desda fetched us a supper from downstairs. The food was simple but warm. It was everything I needed it to be. Setting the dishes outside the door, we washed up and agreed to an early night. I was glad that Desda was sharing a room with me. Under other circumstances, I would have wanted my privacy. Tonight, I was happy not to be alone.

Chapter 32

Megan

I woke to the sound of a loud ringing bell and sat straight up in bed disoriented, thinking a fire alarm was going off.

"They're here. Get dressed. Fast. We're leaving," Thayn said, whipping off his blanket and rapidly rising. He shoved his feet into his shoes and pushed the band that had been covering his eye up onto his forehead, giving him access to his full vision.

I didn't ask questions. I could hear people yelling outside. The rescue we had been waiting for had arrived. Scrambling out of bed, I jammed on my boots and was so glad I was still dressed. I didn't bother with my hair and left it down.

Thayn was waiting at the door with Pounce in his arms. He held her out to me when I joined them. I knew we'd be abandoning the rest of my stuff.

"If you have to, you need to drop her, Megan." He said it with sympathy, but he was serious.

I nodded and kissed Pounce's head, just in case, but held on to her tightly, having no intention of losing her. She looked rattled, and I felt bad for her, knowing that I'd be putting her through another upset. I wished I could tell her that things were going to be okay, and we were going to a happier life.

"Are you ready?" Thayn asked.

Before answering him, I took on my biggest nerve and kissed him on the mouth. My timing may have been inappropriate, but I had wanted to do that for so long, and I felt like I was in a now-or-never situation. My heart leapt when I felt him return the kiss before I drew away.

"I'm ready," I smiled at him. I'd been ready since I was swiped from the Masque.

Thayn smiled lightly and rested a hand on me, opening the door. It was dark and chilly outside. People were running with lanterns in every direction. Others were holding cones to their mouths to amplify their voices as they ordered people to head to bunkers. Those who didn't have lanterns seemed to be heading in the same direction.

Taking hold of my shoulder, Thayn stepped outside with me and gripped me tightly, without hurting me. He walked with me through the crush of people, keeping up with them and going in the same direction. He was looking around a lot, searching for a place to go that wouldn't take us to where the rest of these people were headed. At one point, he yanked me aside with him, squeezing us into a tight space between two house buildings.

My heart pounded loudly in my ears, but I remained focused and at the ready. I was prepared to do whatever had to be done; whatever Thayn needed me to do. I was determined not to be the reason we got caught.

"We need to try to find the Sylizans, get through the gate, or get over the wall," Thayn said quickly. "It would be best to find the Sylizans," he added.

I looked at him and nodded.

"We'll likely be headed toward fighting," he warned. "Stay with me and keep your eyes open."

"Okay," I said. "I'll do whatever you say," I promised.

He nodded, watched the people passing, and chose to keep us moving between the buildings. We squeezed our way through until we came out the other side. All the while, I was careful of Pounce. She had dug her claws into me so hard that she had pierced my flesh. I didn't care. The deeper she clawed in, the easier she'd be to hold onto.

Thayn took us down another turn, and we ended up along the edge of a wall, moving in the opposite direction of most of the people. The announcements, yelling, and ringing bell continued non-stop.

Finally, we reached an open space between the housing and other buildings. Thayn paused, listening and watching in the darkness. I followed his gaze but could see nothing. However, what my eyes could not see, my ears could hear: the distant sound of steel on steel. We were close to the fighting and were headed in the right direction.

I was thrilled and terrified, at the same time. I was delighted to be closer to the Sylizans, but I didn't want to see anymore fighting, let alone get caught up in it.

"I'm going to let go of you, but you have to stay with me," Thayn said, to my horror. "Do not lose me."

Ack! I really, really don't want to let go of him.

I swallowed hard, rose above my fear, and released him. As much as it was the last thing I wanted to do, now wasn't the time for me to panic, get clingy, or be stupid. I trusted him.

"If anything should happen to me, find any other Sylizan. Leave me. They'll help me. You help yourself," he told me, seriously.

I could feel my eyes brimming with tears at his words, but I nodded.

"You're doing fine. This will be over, soon," he said, looking deeply into my eyes and giving my face a soft stroke.

"Okay," I said softly.

"Do you see over there?" He pointed to our left, and I followed his direction, seeing two men sword-fighting. One was, very obviously, winning.

"There is a Sylizan soldier who is fighting with a Kavylak soldier, and the Sylizan soldier is winning," Thayn informed me. "We're going to run there because I'm going to take the sword from the Kavylak soldier when he falls."

"Alright," I said. I was glad Thayn was going to get a sword, but I still didn't like that someone had to die or get hurt, really badly, for it to happen.

"Then, we're going to try to leave with that soldier and get everyone out," he told me.

I nodded in agreement.

"Ready?"

"Let's go," I said because, if we didn't move soon, I was sure I'd throw up my protein shake.

Thayn nodded and looked at me, then looked out to where the soldiers were fighting and said, "Now!" exactly when the Kavylak guy dropped to his knees.

He took off, aiming directly for the fallen soldier, and I followed him in hot pursuit, with an iron grip on Pounce.

The Sylizan soldier braced himself, at first, when he saw us running in his direction but then relaxed when he recognized Thayn.

"Commander!" he exclaimed with relief.

Thayn nodded but immediately grabbed the sword he'd wanted. The Sylizan soldier raised his arm, signaled to someone else, and another soldier joined us. I moved to Thayn's side, panting from running and anxiety.

"We have to run," he said to me with urgency.

There was no explanation needed. I could see and hear the Kavylak soldiers who were bearing down on us.

We turned and ran but were almost immediately confronted by Kavylak soldiers. Thayn and the other Sylizans formed a barrier around me, doing their best to keep me in the middle as they battled our enemies.

I had to stop myself from closing my eyes and screaming, which was difficult to do. I forced myself to focus on everything around me to avoid getting hurt, to keep Pounce safe, and to be ready to follow Thayn's orders.

Everything was happening so fast, and it was hard to see. The only light came from torches and lanterns that were being raised. I would see flashes of steel and hear the sound of swords clanging and banging against each other, and the painful cries of the fallen. All I could do was hope that it would be over soon.

A maniacal cackle erupted from not too far away, and a chill shot straight down my spine, causing my entire body to shudder.

Oh, God! Please, no...

Not him...

Not now...

I looked in the direction from where the laughter had come and, sure enough, Galnar was there. He was still several feet away but was headed toward us wearing a sickeningly amused expression. His eyes were glowing as if his irises were on fire, an illusion likely created by the weird torch he was carrying. I focused harder on his torch-holding hand, and my eyes grew wider when I realized he wasn't carrying anything. In his open palm a whiteish-yellow flame burned, with red highlighting the very ends of the fire. It was unlike any fire I'd ever seen. He wasn't carrying a torch. He *was* the torch.

My God! Is the fire actually coming from his body? How is that even possible?

I watched in terrified fascination as he reached for the sword at his belt with his flaming hand, withdrew it from its sheath, and lit the entire blade on fire.

A loud boom resounded, pulling my attention from him, and a building not too far from where I stood, was hit by some sort of large projectile. I jumped at the sound and a shriek burst forth from my lips as a large chunk was taken out of the building, and splinters of wood and brick flew in every direction. On instinct, I turned my back to the flying debris I'd seen and sheltered Pounce. Neither one of us was hit.

"Run!" Thayn yelled.

I looked at him.

"Run for the gate!" he told me, speaking between breaths. "They're not far. They're the ones launching the attack."

I ran. He didn't have to tell me twice. My fight or flight mode had officially kicked in. I didn't want to be anywhere near Galnar or falling buildings. I had to trust that Thayn would make it out alright. He knew what he was doing. I was the liability.

I ran as hard and as fast as I could, ignoring the blasts and yells all around me, and avoiding people in my path. Finally, I saw the gate.

I was nearly there when a man's voice urgently shouted, "Megan!"

On instinct, from hearing my name, I turned my head and saw Mez running toward me. Before I could react, he pushed me, hard, sideways. My hands shot out in front of me, to protect myself as I fell to the ground.

Dazed, I looked up in shock to see Mez and wondered what was wrong with him, to cause him to push me like that. He stared back at me with wide eyes filled with pain, before coughing a spray of blood, dropping to a knee, and gasping.

It was then that I noticed the giant chunk of brick and mortar that lay broken behind him, realizing that he had likely just saved my life.

He pulled in a second breath of air, reached forward, and grabbed my wrist, holding it tightly. I gasped, unprepared for the strength of his iron grip.

"Get inside," he said. His voice was strained, and his teeth were rimmed with blood.

"No! Let me go!" I shouted at him, trying to pull away. He may have saved my life, but I wasn't going back inside. I was going out that gate.

"You'll be killed," he said, not letting go of me.

He stood and hauled me to my feet with a surprising amount of strength, considering that he'd just been hit by a ton of bricks, and began to pull me after him. I squirmed and tried to pry his hand off me with my free one and immediately stopped because I realized that I shouldn't have had a free hand.

Oh no! Pounce! I must have dropped her when I fell.

"Wait! Stop!" I pleaded frantically, digging my heels into the ground as I desperately looked around for my black kitten. "Pounce," I told him, "I lost her!" I couldn't see her anywhere. She was impossible to find in the darkness.

Mez didn't seem to care. He didn't stop or listen to my pleas. He continued to drag me along as I fought him, the whole way. Finally he stopped, wrenched me close to him, wrapping his arm around my back to secure me and banged on a metal hatch in the ground.

"It's Basarovka!" he yelled.

A bolt slid across and the door was pushed open. Mez wasted no time forcefully pushing me forward, making it clear to me that I had two choices: either go into the hatch of my own accord, or he'd make it happen for me.

"Hide. Please, Megan," he urged me.

I looked back at him with angry eyes, full of contempt, and turned away from him to enter the hatch. I didn't want to look at him. A familiar looking face appeared below me. I recognized Amarogq's fiancée, Amorette. She was wearing the same salmon-coloured skirt and jacket I'd seen on her, earlier. She extended her hand toward me, to help me down.

"It's alright. There's room," she assured me.

I took her hand but didn't say anything to her as I climbed down. She didn't realize how much I couldn't care less if there was room or not. I had failed Thayn and now I'd failed Pounce. My poor kitten was scared and probably hurt – or worse – and there was nothing I could do about it. I was trapped, again.

Amorette shut the latch and put an arm around me. I stiffened at her touch.

"I'm Amorette Racain," she said, introducing herself. "Are you injured?" she asked.

I shook my head and said quietly, "No, I'm fine."

I moved away from her and sat down on an unmade bunk, wrapping my arms around myself. Glancing around the dimly-lit, small rectangular-shaped room, I felt like I was in an underground metal shoebox. Everything, from the floors to the walls to the ceiling, was metal. There were two other bunkbeds, in addition to the one on which I sat, and a few lights on the walls illuminated the space.

Two young women were in the bomb shelter-style room with us. One had long black hair and was wearing a blue dress with thick tights and simple black shoes. The other was a brunette. Her hair was tied in a loose braid that hung down her back, and she wore a long white cloak-like dress. They were both silent and kneeling on the floor with their hands crossed over their hearts. They looked as though they were praying.

Amorette approached me, carrying a mug. "Would you like some water?" she asked, holding the mug out to me.

I nodded and took the mug from her, taking a long drink of the cool liquid that I hadn't realized my body so desperately needed. "Thank you," I said quietly.

She gave me a soft smile and sat next to me. I didn't stop her. "We might be here for a while," she told me and sighed. "I wish they kept things in here for music or something like that. It's almost worse that you can hear everything going on out there."

"Yeah," I agreed half-heartedly. She had a point. The sounds of all the fighting and commotion, though somewhat muffled, could definitely be heard. It almost sounded worse from in here than was in the midst of it.

I looked up toward the hatch and debated trying to leave. These women might try to stop me, but I could likely get away if I tried hard enough. I tightly gripped the mug as I thought about making a run for it, but my grip slackened as I let the ugly reality of my situation sink in. Even if I did get out, there was a much bigger chance that I'd be killed or maimed rather than escape. No. As much as I hated it, I would have to wait. I wanted my freedom, but I didn't have a death wish.

"That's Fiffine Wintheare and Whiterobe Ihleah," Amorette said, indicating the two kneeling women.

I nodded, but didn't inquire about them. At the moment, I didn't honestly care who they were. I just wanted to find my cat, find my soon-to-be boyfriend, and get out of here.

"So…you're Megan, huh?"

"Yes," I confirmed, figuring Amarogq told her who I was.

She smiled. "My fiancé calls you Megs."

Yup. Figured right.

"How long have you been seeing Mez?" she asked curiously.

What?

I blinked at her, a few times, not quite sure if I heard her right. "Pardon?"

"Mez Basarovka. Have you been seeing him long?"

"I'm not seeing him," I bluntly informed her.

Why would she even think that? What the heck has Amarogq said about me?

"Oh! Oops!" She chuckled. "I just thought because he brought you here that you were his girlfriend, or something."

I shook my head. "No. He just brought me here because he wanted me to get out of the action," I said and felt a little guilty now as I thought about Mez. I was still mad at him for leaving Pounce behind, but he'd saved my life, and I hoped he wasn't too badly injured.

"Well, I'm glad that he brought you here. Fiffine is Captain Aaro Wintheare's wife and Ihleah is practically Aésha's sister." She glanced over at the two women before looking back at me and said quietly, "But as you can see, they don't talk much at times like these, so it's nice to have you here, too. Even if you don't have the gossip I was hoping for." She smiled.

Great. If Captain Aaro Wintheare is another Warrior, I guess that meant I was in the bunker assigned to the Warriors' significant others. I wondered how she managed to stay so peppy and positive when the man she loved was fighting a war above her. I was sick with worry about Thayn and Pounce.

"What do you tell yourself to feel better when the man you really care about is out there fighting in all this?" I asked her.

"I tell myself that he loves me more than anything else in the world. So if there's anywhere he's going to go when this is all done, it's right back to me again," she said.

I nodded. It was a good way to think. I had to keep thinking that Thayn would come back to me, too.

"Is your boyfriend out there?" she asked.

I thought of Thayn, up there battling, and my heart sank further as I gave a little nod.

She took my hand in a comforting gesture. "What's he like?" she asked.

I felt my eyes well up. Between thinking about Thayn and her kindness, I could feel myself crumbling, but I wouldn't cave. I had to harden my heart. Now was not the time to fall apart. I wouldn't talk about him with her. I wanted out of this conversation.

I shook my head. "I don't mean to sound rude or ungrateful, and you seem really nice, Amorette, but I just don't feel like talking, right now," I levelled with her. She did honestly seem kind, but I had reached the point that the only people I wanted to talk to were Thayn and Irys.

To her credit, Amorette nodded with understanding. "It's going to be alright. It really will, Megan. They were crazy to try to attack us here with all the Warriors home." She patted my arm, rose from the bunk, and moved to another part of the room, leaving me in peace.

I sat there, brooding in silence, for what felt like hours as thoughts raged through my head. I was sick with worry about Thayn, about Pounce, and about my own fate. Exhaustion was overcoming me, and I began to ache for this whole world to go away.

Time stretched on, mercilessly.

Finally, the sounds of the fighting above us grew quieter until there was only silence. Shortly thereafter, two solid knocks sounded on the hatch.

"It is over. It's time to go home," said a man's gruff voice.

"Come on," Amorette said kindly to me, extending her hand to help me up.

I took it and rose to my feet, forcing a lame smile at her. She deserved better. I knew it. I just didn't have it in me. The hatch opened, and the two other women exited, first. I followed, next, and Amorette went last.

I noticed as I climbed out that the sun was starting to rise but, before I could process another thought, a hand slapped over my mouth. My eyes widened, and the Kavylak soldier holding me dragged me toward a carriage. I twisted and fought without any effect and could hear that Amorette was fighting her own battle behind me. I was shoved inside the carriage, landing on its floor.

"You can shut up and sit there, or I can knock you out. You have two seconds to make your choice," he spat, harshly, at me.

By the look in his eyes and the threat in his voice, I knew he wasn't kidding. I nodded, not wanting to be knocked out. He moved out of the way, and Amorette was shoved into the carriage with me, directly afterward. The door was slammed shut.

Amorette immediately tried the door, but it didn't budge. She sank to the floor and wrapped her arms around herself. I had no clue what was happening.

Were we just captured by renegade Kavylak soldiers, or are they Sylizans in disguise?

"What's going on?" I asked her.

"Rebels," she responded.

"What?" I asked, not comprehending the meaning behind her words.

Rebels? What rebels? No one ever warned me about rebels.

"Rebels," she repeated, looking at me with wide, terrified eyes. "We're being taken for ransom," she said, her voice breaking from her fear. "We're going to be gone for a long time."

I looked at her in disbelief, trying to process what she meant, but it was futile. I didn't understand. I had no idea what was happening, who these rebels were, or what they wanted. All I understood was that my sweet little Pounce was probably dead, and I was being taken even farther away from Thayn.

How will I ever find my way back to him now?

Chapter 33

Irys

Though Desda fell asleep very quickly, her back turned to me in the odd lumpy bed, I was not as fortunate. I allowed my mind to ramble through the day's events until I finally started to drift in and out of a light sleep.

Not much time passed before a soft sound scuffed from the far side of the room. I yawned and opened my eyes, listening with my breath held, to try to figure out if the sound was in reality or in some dream my mind had been attempting to weave. There was nothing but silence and the sound of Desda's slow breathing.

Carefully, I pushed the covers off myself and squinted through the darkness at any place in which something could have been hiding. I watched the floor for the movement of mice and prayed that any wildlife would choose to stay on the outside of the inn, for tonight.

As I was deciding that there was nothing in the room after all, and that I should try to go back to sleep, the familiar scent of spice filled my nose, and my eyes fell upon a dark shape bunched in the corner. I tried to decide what it could be, hoping it was my imagination and that it was merely a shadow from the hanging laundry.

The longer I stared at the shape, the more the smell intensified until a pair of glowing purple-blue cat-like eyes opened and shone toward me. A sharp hiss from the thing, caused my breath to catch in my throat.

"Shhh..." I tried to comfort whatever it was. Could a creature of that size really have mistakenly made its way into this room? I would have glanced at the window, but I couldn't take my eyes from the glowing pair that was fixed on me.

The creature didn't need to be comforted. Slowly, it rose to its full height, and I watched as the eyes continued to ascend in the darkness until they had reached the height of a man. This was no large rodent or cat. It was a person.

Rapidly, I placed my feet on the floor, next to the bed. I drew in a breath but, before I could make a sound, a low and quiet whisper of a voice spoke from where the eyes were glowing.

"Do not scream. If you do, I will kill that woman in your bed. Do you understand me?"

I nodded, covering my mouth. Somehow, I imagined that the glowing eyes could see me through the darkness. Apparently, I was right as this seemed to appease him.

"Where is Megan Wynters' journal?" he asked.

If there was anything at all that I could have expected him to ask, that question would never have made the list.

"Pardon?" I whispered apologetically, assuming I had misheard him.

"Megan Wynters had a journal. She left it at your estate. It was in her room. Where is it now?"

"It's in her room where she left it," I lied. "It's hers. I didn't bring it with me." That part was true.

He stepped forward, out of the darkest shadows of the room, allowing a bit of the moonlight from the window to shine upon him. His eyes didn't glow as intensely, this way, but I could see more of his features. He was tall and muscled. I couldn't tell the colour of his hair, but I knew that it was lighter than black and was styled in unruly spikes. His upper lip curled back as he looked upon me, exposing fangs that had been hidden beneath.

"You're lying. I can smell it on you."

Desda made a sound in her sleep, and both the intruder and I froze, staring at her as she rolled over a little but did not wake.

I backed away from the man as far as I could, until my heels touched the nightstand.

"I found the journal in her room and took it into my own," I confessed. "I missed her. She's my friend."

"Where is it now?"

"Is Megan Wynters safe? Have you seen her?" I hoped to learn at least that much before giving him the information he wanted.

"Tell me where the journal can be found, or I will kill the woman," he hissed, dangerously.

"Please stop saying that. You're frightening me, and you will make me accidentally make a noise and alert someone!" I whispered sharply.

"Then tell me what I want to know."

"It's still at the estate. It's in my room, on my bed, under the pillows. I'm telling the truth."

He studied me carefully, stepping slightly closer before inhaling. Finally, he seemed to be satisfied and nodded. "Yes," he said, accepting my words as being truthful. He turned toward the window with the clear intention of exiting that way.

"Stop," I whispered urgently. "Please. Is she alive?"

He stared at me and then gave a single nod. "She is."

"Are you a Warrior?"

He grinned a fanged grin before nodding and opening the window.

"Stop!" I whispered again. "Please don't put the people from my home in any danger. My bedroom is on the second floor in a suite with windows facing the front of the house, on the west side. That should be enough information for you to find a way to slip in and out without hurting anyone."

"If the journal is where you say it is and, if no one gets in my way, they won't die..." He stopped talking and quickly turned his head, to look out the window. A low growl escaped his throat.

"Shh. Please, you'll wake her," I begged.

Suddenly, Rimoth appeared in the middle of the room. He did not enter through the door, he simply appeared there where nothing had previously been.

"I thought I could smell your kind," he said with distaste to the Warrior.

I gasped and Rimoth looked confidently at me. "Don't worry, Miss Godeleva. He won't threaten you any longer," he said and then grabbed hold of the Warrior. They both disappeared. They were gone with no sign that they had ever been there.

I screamed and then covered my own mouth to muffle the sound. Desda sat up in bed.

"Miss Godeleva!" she exclaimed, scrambling to her feet. "What is it? What's the matter?" she asked as she looked around the room to see absolutely nothing out of the ordinary.

I walked right up to her and hugged her, shaking. "Nobody will believe me," I whispered, knowing that if I were to tell anyone what had happened, I would sound like a madwoman.

Desda returned the hug and rubbed my back. "Nobody will believe what, Miss Godeleva?"

There was a knock at the door before I could answer her. We both jumped at the sound but were relieved when Sir Fhirell identified himself.

"Miss Godeleva, I heard a scream. Are you and your maid alright?" he asked.

I grabbed my dressing gown from on top of the bed and put it on, tying the waist.

"Yes, Sir Fhirell. We're alright." I unlocked the door and opened it. "Please, come in. Something strange has happened."

Sir Fhirell was dressed, but it was clear that he'd thrown his clothes on, in a hurry. His shirt was not tucked in, and his hair was disheveled. He entered and shut the door behind himself, looking about. I wished the laundry weren't right there on display but decided my strength could be better used by focusing on the matter at hand.

Desda was dressed in her nightgown and robe and had returned to sitting on the bed.

"What happened?" he asked, looking us over, clearly still trying to discover the source of the commotion in this otherwise perfectly normal-looking room.

"Please do not think me mad. And please do not tell me that I was dreaming. I'm certain that everything I'm about to describe truly happened."

He nodded and, to his credit, he looked respectful and ready to listen.

"I awoke, not long ago, after hearing something in the room. At first, I could see nothing but, then I noticed that smell of spices had returned. When I tried to find out what it was, glowing eyes opened, in the corner of the room. It was a Warrior. He could see in the dark, and he had fangs. He was like the stories of the Sefaline."

The Sefaline were a reclusive, strong, cat-like people with fangs, claws, pupils in their eyes that were in the shape of vertical lines, and even had patterns on their skin such as stripes and spots. They were isolated to such a degree, that many people believed them to be mythical.

"The Warrior demanded the location of Megan Wynters' journal. He threatened to harm Desda if I called for help. I told him where the journal was, and he was just about to leave when..." I had to pause and take a breath before the next unbelievable part of my story could continue. "...Rimoth, the innkeeper's assistant from downstairs, simply appeared in the middle of the room; quite out of thin air. He didn't use the door. In fact, the door was still locked. I had to unlock it to let you in. He told me that he wouldn't let the Warrior harm me, then took hold of him, and they both disappeared at the same time. They simply vanished."

Desda looked at me as though I'd taken leave of every one of my senses, but Sir Fhirell simply appeared troubled as he considered everything I'd said.

"The Warrior must have been a Sefaline, and the innkeeper's assistant must be a Traveller," he said, sounding more like he was piecing things together for himself than trying to explain anything to me. "That is the only explanation that fits your story."

"A Sefaline...and a Traveller? Are Travellers not make-believe?"

"Some even believe the Sefaline to be myths but, from what you've seen today, it is clear that they exist. The same can be said for Travellers."

I shook my head in disbelief. Had I stepped into a fairytale world?

Sir Fhirell was not nearly as bewildered. "Why would the Warrior want Megan Wynters' journal to such an extent that he would be willing to track you down, this way? For that matter, why would the Traveller have revealed himself to you, to take the Warrior away?"

"I don't know. It was clear that the journal was his only concern. I think he believed that I might have brought it with me. I didn't read it, aside from the first page. It is at the Godeleva Estate. I can't imagine what Miss Wynters could have said in it that could be as valuable as that." I sighed from exhaustion. "I also couldn't guess as to why Rimoth would have done what he did for us."

At that moment, the Traveller reappeared in the room, still not bothering to use the door.

Desda gasped and grabbed hold of my hand. I was glad to be able to hold hers in return.

Sir Fhirell turned toward the Traveller and used himself as a barrier between us.

Rimoth smiled and spoke peacefully. "Please don't be alarmed. I have only returned in order to tell Miss Godeleva that the Sefaline is no longer a threat to anyone."

"Where did you take him?" I asked, unsure as to why that, of all things, was my first question.

"Why does it matter?" he asked me with amusement.

"He had intended to go to my family home. I want to be sure that he won't be reaching them, at any time soon."

"Very well. He is in Korth," he responded simply.

My eyes widened. As far as I knew, Korth was a country made up of barbarian clans that were continually raiding and warring with one another.

"Why did you come to help me as you did?" I asked him.

"Because you were brave and kind to us in Fort Picogeal and because I don't like the Sefaline."

"Thank you," I said with genuine gratitude.

"Where is it that you are headed, on this journey of yours?" he asked.

"Gbat Rher. We're going to help the people there who have lost everything. We want to help them to rebuild."

Rimoth smiled at me. "It is because of that kind heart of yours that I removed the Sefaline from here. Kind heartedness is a quality that is lacking in far too many people."

"Thank you. That is very nice of you to say," I said, releasing Desda's hand, to place mine over my heart.

"Would you like me to take you to Gbat Rher, right now?" he asked as though it would be a very simple task for him to complete, despite the fact that it was a distance that would still require days of travel on horseback.

"No. Thank you," Sir Fhirell said decidedly. "As much as we appreciate your offer, we will remain with our group and travel together as we have planned."

I nodded. "It was a very generous offer. Your assistance with the Sefaline was more than enough help."

Rimoth looked at Sir Fhirell and nodded but then he looked at me with a little tilt of his head. "You're sure?"

"I trust Sir Fhirell's decision."

"You say you trust his decision..." he started to say but then he disappeared and reappeared immediately next to me. "...I say trust your good heart," he concluded and put his arms around me.

I couldn't even scream. After a single blink, I was no longer standing in the room at the inn. I was in the middle of a very dark field. Rimoth released me, and I wrapped my arms around myself as my nightgown and dressing gown weren't quite enough to keep me warm against the chill of the night.

A field of stars shone down as pinpricks of light through black velvet cloth. It was enough to be beautiful but not nearly enough to illuminate the land around me.

The silence of this place was almost deafening. It seemed to magnify the sound of my own rapid breathing as I looked around for any sign of something familiar.

"Where are we?" I asked, shivering with cold and terror.

When Rimoth spoke, his voice sounded confident and pleased, teetering on amusement. "We're right where you wanted to be, of course. Welcome to Gbat Rher."

About the Authors

The Perspective book series was written by two authors: Amanda Giasson and Julie B. Campbell. After having met by chance in the lineup at their university bookstore on their first day of classes, Amanda and Julie became fast friends. They credit their survival of many of their 3-hour long lectures to their ability to escape to the world of Qarradune. The truth is that Megan and Irys were born of note-passing in the form of creative writing. While neither author condones this behavior in-class as it likely does nothing for a student's grades, it did happen to work out, in their case. It also helped to define the unique writing style shared by the authors in the creation of the story. The two authors have been steadily working on the Perspective book series, ever since.

Manufactured by Amazon.ca
Bolton, ON

24957990R00208